THE ARK

This Large Print Book carries the
Seal of Approval of N.A.V.H.

THE ARK

BOYD MORRISON

THORNDIKE PRESS
A part of Gale, Cengage Learning

GALE
CENGAGE Learning

Detroit • New York • San Francisco • New Haven, Conn • Waterville, Maine • London

GALE
CENGAGE Learning™

LIBRARY OF CONGRESS CATALOGING-IN-PUBLICATION DATA

Morrison, Boyd, 1967–
   The ark / by Boyd Morrison. — Large print ed.
     p. cm. — (Thorndike Press large print core)
   ISBN-13: 978-1-4104-2857-8
   ISBN-10: 1-4104-2857-5
    1. Archaeologists—Fiction. 2. Noah's ark—Fiction.
   3. Antiquities—Collection and preservation—Fiction.
   4. Turkey—Antiquities—Fiction. I. Title.
   PS3613.O7774A75 2010
   813'.6—dc22   2010021754

Published in 2010 by arrangement with Simon & Schuster, Inc.

Printed in the United States of America
1 2 3 4 5 6 7 14 13 12 11 10

To Randi, my love.
Thanks for believing in me.

PROLOGUE

Three Years Ago

Hasad Arvadi's legs wouldn't cooperate. He strained to pull himself to the wall so he could spend his final moments propped upright, but without the use of his legs, it was a hopeless task. The stone floor was too slick, and his arm strength was sapped. His head dropped to the floor. Breaths came in ragged gasps. He remained on his back, the life draining from him.

He was going to die. Nothing would change that now. This inky black chamber, a room hidden from the world for millennia, would become his tomb.

Fear over his own fate was long past. Instead, Arvadi wept in frustration. He had been so close to his life's goal — seeing Noah's Ark with his own eyes — but that opportunity had been snatched from him with three pulls of a trigger. The bullet in each knee made it impossible to move. The

7

one in his belly ensured that he wouldn't last another five minutes. Although the wounds were excruciating, they weren't as painful as falling short of reaching the Ark when it was within his grasp.

He couldn't bear the awful irony of the situation. He finally had proof that the Ark existed. Not only existed, *still* exists. Waiting to be found where it had lain for six thousand years. He had unearthed the last piece of the puzzle, revealed to him in ancient text written before Christ was born.

We've been wrong all this time, he had thought as he read. *Wrong for thousands of years. Wrong because the people who concealed the Ark wanted us to be wrong.*

The revelation had been such a triumphant event that Arvadi hadn't noticed the pistol aimed at his legs until it was too late. Then it had all happened so fast. The crack of gunshots. Shouted demands for information. His own pathetic pleas for mercy. Fading voices and dimming light as his killers stole away with their prize. Darkness.

Lying there awaiting his own death, thinking about what had been taken from him, Arvadi seethed with fury. He couldn't let them get away with it. Eventually someone would find his body. He had to record what had happened here, that the location of

Noah's Ark wasn't the only secret this chamber held.

Arvadi wiped his bloody hand on his sleeve and pulled a notebook from his vest pocket. His hands were shaking so violently that he dropped the notebook twice. With tremendous effort, he opened it to what he hoped was an empty page. The darkness was so total that he had to do everything by touch. He removed a pen from another pocket and flipped the cap off with his thumb. The silence in the chamber was broken by the sound of the plastic cap skittering across the floor.

With the notebook resting on his chest, Arvadi began to write.

The first line came easily, but he was rapidly becoming light-headed with shock. He didn't have much time. The second line was exponentially more difficult. The pen grew heavier as he wrote, as if it were being filled with lead. By the time he got to the third line, he couldn't remember what he'd already written. He got two more words out onto the paper, and then the pen dropped from his fingers. His arms would no longer move.

Tears streamed down his temples. As Arvadi felt oblivion closing in on him, three terrible thoughts echoed in his mind.

He would never again see his beloved daughter.

His killers were now walking the earth with a relic of unimaginable power.

And he would go to his grave without gazing on the greatest archaeological discovery in history.

■ ■ ■ ■

HAYDEN

■ ■ ■ ■

ONE

Present Day

Dilara Kenner wound her way through the international concourse of LAX, a well-worn canvas backpack her only luggage. It was a Thursday afternoon, and travelers crowded the vast terminal. Her plane from Peru had arrived at one-thirty, but it had taken her forty-five minutes to get through immigration and customs. The wait had seemed ten times that long. She was impatient to meet with Sam Watson, who had begged her to come back to the United States two days early.

Sam was an old friend of her father's and had become a surrogate uncle to her. Dilara had been surprised to get his call. She had stayed in touch with him in the years since her father had gone missing, but in the last six months she had spoken to him only once. When he had reached her on her cell phone in Peru, she had been in the Andes

13

supervising the excavation of an Incan ruin. Sam had sounded unnerved, even scared, but he wouldn't elaborate about what the trouble was no matter how much Dilara prodded him. He insisted that he had to meet with her in person as soon as possible. His urgent pleas finally convinced her to turn the dig over to a subordinate and return before the job had been completed.

Sam also made one more request that Dilara found puzzling. She had to promise him that she wouldn't tell anyone why she was leaving Peru.

Sam was so eager to meet with her that he had asked to rendezvous with her in the airport. Their planned meeting spot was the terminal's second-level food court. She got onto the escalator behind an obese vacationer wearing a Hawaiian shirt and a bad sunburn. He was trailing a roller carry-on and stood blocking her path. His eyes settled on her, then looked her up and down slowly.

Dilara was still in the shorts and tank top she wore at the dig, and she became intensely aware of his attention. She had raven hair down to her shoulders, an olive tan that she didn't have to work for, and an athletic, long-legged frame that caused less discreet men to ogle her inappropriately like this

14

creep was now.

She threw the sunburned guy a look that said *you've got to be kidding me,* then said, "Excuse me" and muscled her way past him. When she reached the top of the escalator, she scanned the massive food court until she spotted Sam sitting at a small table at the balcony railing.

The last time she had seen him, he was seventy-one. Now, a year later, he looked more like eighty-two than seventy-two. Frosty white tufts of hair still clung to his head, but the lines on his face seemed to be etched much more deeply, and he had a pallor that made him look like he hadn't slept in days.

When Sam saw Dilara, he stood and waved to her, a smile temporarily making his face look ten years younger. She returned his smile and made her way to him. Sam clasped her tightly to him.

"You don't know how glad I am to see you," Sam said. He held her at arm's length. "You're still the most beautiful woman I've ever met. Except perhaps for your mother."

Dilara fingered the locket around her neck, the one with the photo of her mother that her father had always carried. For a moment, her grin faltered and her eyes drifted away, lost in the memory of her parents. They quickly cleared and returned to Sam.

"You should see me caked with dirt and knee-deep in mud," Dilara said in her flat, midwestern cadence. "It might change your mind."

"A dusty jewel is still a jewel. How is the world of archaeology?"

They sat. Sam drank from a coffee cup. He had thoughtfully provided a cup for Dilara as well, and she took a sip before speaking.

"Busy as usual," she said. "I'm off to Mexico next. Some interesting disease vectors predating the European colonization."

"That sounds fascinating. Aztec?"

Dilara didn't answer. Her specialty was bio-archaeology, the study of the biological remains of ancient civilizations. Sam was a biochemist, so he had a passing interest in her field, but that wasn't why he was asking. He was stalling.

She leaned forward, took his hand, and gave it a comforting squeeze. "Come on, Sam. What's with the small talk? You didn't ask me to cut my trip short to talk about archaeology, did you?"

Sam glanced nervously at the people around him, his eyes flicking from one to the next, as if checking to see whether they

16

were paying undue attention to him.

She followed his gaze. A Japanese family smiled and laughed as they munched on hamburgers. A lone businesswoman to her right typed on a PDA between bites of a salad. Even though it was early October, the summer vacation season long over, a group of teenagers who were dressed in identical T-shirts that said TEENS 4 JESUS sat at a table behind her, texting on their cell phones.

"Actually," Sam said, "archaeology is precisely what I want to talk to you about."

"You do? When you called, I'd never heard you so upset."

"It's because I have something very important to tell you."

Then his deteriorated condition made sense. Cancer, the same disease that took her mother twenty years ago. A breath caught in her throat. "Oh my God! You're not dying, are you?"

"No, no, dear. I shouldn't have worried you. Except for a little bursitis, I've never been fitter." Dilara felt herself sigh with relief.

"No," Sam continued, "I called you here because you're the only one I can trust. I need your counsel."

The businesswoman next to Sam picked

17

up her salad plate and rose to leave, but the purse slipped off her lap to the floor near her feet, causing her to trip. She stumbled into Sam, who caught her.

"I'm sorry," the woman said with a light Slavic inflection while she retrieved her purse. "I'm so clumsy."

"I'm just glad you didn't take a bigger spill," Sam said.

She frowned when she looked down at Sam. "Oh no, I got salad dressing on your arm. Let me get that for you." She took a handkerchief from her purse, unfolded it, and dabbed his forearm. "At least you weren't wearing long sleeves."

"No harm done."

"Well, sorry again." She smiled at Sam and Dilara and headed for the trash can.

"You're as gallant as ever, Sam," Dilara said. "Now why do you need my counsel?"

Sam looked around again before speaking. He flexed his fingers, like he was working out a cramp. His eyes returned to Dilara. They were creased with worry. He hesitated before the words came out in a rush. "Three days ago, I made a startling discovery at work. It has to do with Hasad."

Dilara's heart jumped at the mention of her father, Hasad Arvadi, and she dug her fingers into her thighs to control the familiar surge of anxiety. He had been missing for three years, during which she had spent every spare moment in a fruitless attempt to find out what had happened to him. As far as she knew, he had never set foot in the pharmaceutical company where Sam worked.

"Sam, what are you talking about? You found something at your work about what happened to my father? I don't understand."

"I spent an entire day trying to decide whether to tell you about this. Whether to get you involved, I mean. I wanted to go to the police, but I don't have the proof yet. They might not believe me before it's too late. But I knew you would, and I need your advice. It's all starting next Friday."

"Eight days from now?"

Sam nodded and massaged his forehead.

"Headache?" she asked. "Do you want some aspirin?"

"I'll be okay. Dilara, what they're planning will kill millions, maybe billions."

"Kill billions?" she said, smiling. Sam was pulling her leg. "You're joking."

He shook his head solemnly. "I wish I were." Dilara searched his face for some hint of a prank, but all she could see was concern. After a moment, her smile vanished. He was serious.

"Okay," she said slowly. "You're not joking. But I'm confused. Proof of what? Who's 'they'? And what does this have to do with my father?"

"He found it, Dilara," Sam said in a lowered voice. "He actually found it."

She knew immediately what "it" was by the way Sam said it. Noah's Ark. The quest her father had dedicated his whole life to. She shook her head in disbelief.

"You mean, the actual boat that . . ." Dilara paused. The remaining color had drained from Sam's face. "Sam, are you sure you're all right? You look a little pale."

Sam clutched his chest, and his face twisted into a mask of agony. He doubled over in his seat and fell to the floor.

"My God! Sam!" Dilara threw her chair back and rushed over to him. She helped him lie flat and yelled at the teenagers with the cell phones. "Call 911!" After a paralyzed moment, one of them frantically dialed.

"Dilara, go!" Watson croaked.

"Sam, don't talk," she said, trying to keep her composure. "You're having a heart attack."

"Not heart attack . . . woman who dropped purse . . . handkerchief had contact poison . . ."

Poison? He was already delirious. "Sam —"

"No!" he yelled feebly. "You have to go . . . or they'll kill you, too. They murdered your father."

She stared at him in shock. Her deepest fear had always been that her father was dead, but she could never allow herself to give up hope. But now — *Sam knew. He knew what had happened to her father!* That's why he had called her here.

She started to speak, but Sam gripped her arm.

"Listen! Tyler Locke. Gordian Engineering. Get . . . his help. He knows . . . Coleman." He swallowed hard every few words. "Your father's research . . . started everything. You must . . . find the Ark." He started rambling. "Hayden . . . Project . . . Oasis . . . Genesis . . . Dawn . . ."

"Sam, please." This couldn't be happening. Not now. Not when she might finally get some answers.

"I'm sorry, Dilara."

"Who are 'they,' Sam?" She saw him fading and grasped his arms. "Who murdered my father?"

He mouthed words, but only air came out. He took one more breath, then went still.

She started CPR and continued the chest

compressions until the paramedics arrived and pushed her back. Dilara stood to the side, crying silently. They worked to revive Sam, but it was a futile effort. They pronounced him dead at the scene. She made the obligatory statement to the airport police, including his baffling allegations, but for such an obvious heart attack, they shrugged it off as incoherent babbling. Dilara collected her backpack and walked in a daze toward the shuttle that would drop her off at her car in the long-term parking lot. Sam had been like an uncle to her, the only family she had left, and now he was gone.

As she sat in the shuttle bus, his words continued to ring in her ears. Whether they were the ravings of a demented elderly man or a warning from a close friend, she couldn't be sure. But she could think of only one way to check whether Sam's story had any truth to it.

She had to find Tyler Locke.

Two

As his Hummer limo glided up to a bright blue jet parked at the ramp of Burbank's Bob Hope Airport's executive terminal, Rex Hayden took another swig of Bloody Mary in an attempt to take the edge off his pounding hangover. He'd been up all night partying after the Friday night premiere of his new movie. Now he was paying the price for two girls and three bottles of Cristal. Even with his shades, the morning sun made him wince. Thank God Burbank allowed celebrities like him to bypass all that crap at the security checkpoints.

Sydney would be the first stop on a grand tour of Asia to promote his latest action blockbuster. His customized Boeing Business Jet didn't have enough fuel to make it all the way to Australia in one shot, so they would have to go out of their way to refuel in Honolulu. But spending more time on the plane wasn't a hardship. He had purchased the modified 737 because it was the most luxurious thing with wings. A private bedroom, full galley, gold fixtures, enough room for his buddies to come along, and two smoking hot flight attendants that he'd selected himself. The plane was a flying hotel. It cost $50 million, but so what? He deserved it. At the age of thirty, he was already one of the biggest actors in the world. His last film had made more than a billion dollars worldwide.

Hayden tossed back the last of his drink and staggered out of the limo, his entourage following. Billy and J-man were on their cell phones, and Fitz handled the luggage. Three more cars pulled up behind, carrying the gaggle of people who managed his career: agent, manager, PR person, personal trainer, nutritionist, and a dozen others. Traveling with such a large group made the plane a necessity, and the best part was that his contract required the studio to reimburse him for the operating costs during the trip.

"Which bags do you want with you on the plane, Rex?" Fitz asked. "Or should they all go in the cargo hold?"

Hayden didn't need Fitz's stupid questions right now. His hangover threatened to make him sick. He couldn't do that out on the tarmac. Not in front of everyone. Man, he needed some caffeine.

"Dammit, Fitz, what do I have you around for?" he said. "Maybe my brother was right about you. I'm sick of making every little decision for you. Just get it all on board."

Fitz nodded quickly, and Hayden saw the fear in his face. Good. Maybe next time he'd grow a pair and do his job.

"Okay, you heard him," Fitz said to the driver. "And make sure they all get on. Miss one, and you couldn't get a job driving a hearse."

"Yes, sir," the driver said meekly and started handing suitcases to the airport's baggage handler.

Hayden climbed the stairs and ordered Mandy, one of the flight attendants, to pour him a coffee. Billy, J-man, and Fitz quietly sat around him while the rest of the passengers took seats in the front section. Hayden sank into one of the lambskin recliners and watched the limo pull away. He pushed the button linking him to the cockpit.

"George, let's go."

"Aloha, Mr. Hayden," the pilot said. "Looking forward to the islands?"

"I'm not getting off the plane in Honolulu," Hayden said, "so just cut that crap. Let's get the hell out of here."

"Yes, sir."

Mandy closed the door. The jet's engines spooled up, and the 737 began to taxi toward the runway.

The caffeine did the trick, and Hayden's headache began to ease. Now that he was feeling better, he let his eyes settle on Mandy. He knew how he was going to use his private bedroom over the next fifteen hours.

After exiting the executive terminal parking lot, Dan Cutter stopped the Hummer limo along the side of Sherman Way and threw the driver's hat onto the passenger seat. He got out and popped the hood to make it look like he had engine problems. Then he sat in the driver's seat and flipped on the radio scanner to listen to the control tower communicating with the taxiing 737.

Getting the bag onto the plane had been even easier than he thought it was going to be. Cutter knew that Crestwood Limos was Hayden's preferred company, so he had simply called to cancel the reservation and showed up himself.

He knew those celebrity types. They didn't pay any attention to the staff, never even asked for his name. They simply assumed he was their assigned driver and that all the bags would get on, so they didn't see him put an extra one on with the others. When that little chump named Fitz had threatened him, Cutter had momentarily entertained the notion of snapping the pissant's neck, just to show him how unimportant he really was. But then he remembered his mission. The Faithful Leader's vision. Everything they had worked for over the past three years. Getting the bag on the plane was far more important.

It had been Cutter's suggestion to test the device on Hayden's plane. A long-distance flight over water was exactly what they needed. The wreckage would be three miles deep, so the plane wouldn't be recovered even if it were found. Plus, it had the added bonus of Hayden. He had been a thorn in their sides for months, bringing undue attention to the cause. And the press would go into a feeding frenzy when the plane of one of the world's biggest stars crashed, providing the perfect distraction.

Bringing the device onto a commercial airliner for the test would have been much riskier. As checked baggage, it would have been out of his control for most of the time, during which too many things could go wrong. The device could be discovered, or it could simply be left off the plane for some reason and put onto another plane. Not to mention that whoever checked the bag would have to go with it; for security reasons, airlines regularly removed bags when the passenger was not on board. With Hayden's plane, Cutter had seen the bag go into the cargo hold himself, and now he could watch it take off, with him standing safely on the ground.

The tower gave permission for Hayden's 737 to taxi to the runway. Right on time, as Cutter knew it would be. If it hadn't, Hayden would have gone berserk. Guys like that thought the world revolved around them.

Now was the time. He opened his cell phone and navigated the address book until he found the entry he had programmed in: NEW WORLD. He pressed the green call button. After three rings, a click of the other phone answering. Then a series of three beeps told him the device in the belly of Hayden's jet was activated. He hung up the phone and replaced it in his pocket.

The 737 came to a stop at the end of the runway. On the scanner, Cutter listened for the tower to give permission to take off.

"Flight N-three-four-eight Zulu, this is Burbank tower. Hold short of the active and await further clearance."

"Acknowledged, tower. What's the problem?"

"We've got a fuel spill on the runway. Leaking truck."

"How long? My boss isn't going to like a long wait."

"I don't know yet."

"Should I head back to the ramp?"

"Not yet. I'll keep you informed."

"Gotcha."

Cutter stared at the idling 737 in horrified disbelief, kicking himself for activating the device before permission to take off was given. A lengthy delay could be a disaster. The weather was perfect, so he hadn't anticipated a delay. Now that the device was active, there was no way to turn it off. It was already working. If the plane returned to the ramp, he would have to get the device back somehow. That would be extremely problematic, not to mention dangerous. It was already too lethal to interact with. As the plane sat there, he was helpless. So he did the only thing he could. He prayed.

Cutter leaned on the wheel, his eyes shut tight, his hands clasped together, praying with all his heart that his mission would go on. God would not forsake him. His faith would overcome.

His entire life, Cutter knew he was destined to serve a greater purpose, and he was willing to lay down his life to attain it, as all his brethren were. It was only after he left the army, where he had gained the skills necessary to carry out God's plan, that he learned what that greater purpose was, and he had pledged himself to it without reservation. The acts he had committed to ensure a better future might be seen as barbaric to those who did not believe, but his soul was pure. The end goal was all that mattered.

Now that goal seemed to be in danger, but Cutter had no doubts. He was a fervent believer. His prayers would be answered.

After forty minutes of waiting, the miracle arrived. The radio squawked to life.

"Flight N-three-four-eight Zulu, this is the tower. The fuel spill has been cleaned up. You are cleared for takeoff."

"Thank you, tower. You just saved my job."

"No problem, George. Enjoy Sydney."

Within two minutes, the jet roared down the runway. As he watched the 737 soar over the mountains and turn westward, Cutter closed the hood and got back in the Hummer. For the first time that day, he smiled.

God was with him.

THREE

Wind whipped over the landing pad of the Scotia One oil platform, blowing the wind sock steadily toward the east. Located two hundred miles off the coast of Newfoundland, the Grand Banks were known for some of the world's nastiest weather, but the thirty-mile-per-hour winds and fifteen-foot seas hardly qualified as gale force. Just a typical day. Tyler Locke was curious to find out who was willing to brave the trip to meet with him.

He leaned against the railing, searching for the Sikorsky transport helicopter due to arrive any minute. No sign of it. Tyler zipped up his bomber jacket against the cold and inhaled the smell of salt spray and crude oil that permeated the rig.

He'd had almost no downtime since he arrived on the platform six days ago, so the brief moment staring out at the vast Atlantic Ocean was a welcome rest. A few minutes

were all he needed, and then he'd be re-
charged. He wasn't the type who could lie
in front of the TV all day watching movies.
He loved immersing himself in a project,
working nonstop until the problem was
solved. His need to stay busy was a product
of the work ethic his father had drilled into
him. It was the one thing his wife, Karen,
never could change about him. *Next year,*
he'd always told her. *Next year is the big
vacation.*

He was lost in thought, the old regret rear-
ing its ugly head, and he absently reached
to fiddle with his wedding ring. Only when
he felt bare skin did he glance down and
remember that it was no longer there. He
quickly pulled his hands apart and looked
back up to see one of the landing control
crewmen, a short, wiry man named Al
Dietz, walking toward him. At six feet two
inches tall and a solid build somewhere
north of two hundred pounds last time he
checked, Tyler towered over the diminutive
rig worker.

"Afternoon, Tyler," Dietz said over the
wind. "Come to see the chopper land?"

"Hi, Al," Tyler said. "I'm expecting someone. Do you know if Dilara Kenner is
aboard?"

Dietz shook his head. "Sorry. All I know

is that they have five passengers today. If you want, you can go wait inside, and I'll bring her down to you when they get here."

"That's okay. My last job was on a mine collapse in West Virginia. After a week of breathing coal dust, it could be forty below and I wouldn't mind being out here. Besides, she was kind enough to make the flight to see me, so I'm returning the favor by meeting her here."

"You should see them in a minute. You know, if she didn't make this flight, she's in for a delay. We're supposed to be socked in for at least twenty-four hours." Dietz waved as he left to make preparations for the landing.

Tyler had heard the weather forecast, so he knew what Dietz meant. In the next hour, the wind was expected to die down and fog would roll in, making a landing impossible until it cleared. He saw the cloud formation approaching from the west, and just beneath it about five miles away, a yacht slowly motored past. White, at least eighty feet long. A beauty. Probably a Lürssen or a Westport. Why it would be in the middle of the Grand Banks, Tyler couldn't guess, but it wasn't in any hurry.

He also had no idea why an archaeologist was so impatient to meet with him that she was willing to fly out here. She'd repeatedly called Gordian's headquarters over the last few days, and when Tyler took a break from his work on the platform, he'd returned her call. All he could get out of her was that she was a professor at UCLA, and she had to see him right away.

When he told her that he was going straight from Scotia One to a job in Norway, she'd insisted on seeing him before he left. The only way that would happen, he told her jokingly, would be if she took the two-hour flight out to the rig. To his surprise, she jumped at the chance and agreed to the trip, even willing to pay the exorbitant fee for the helicopter ride. When he asked why, all she would say over the phone was that it was a matter of life and death. She wouldn't take no for an answer. It was just the kind of mysterious distraction that could spice up an otherwise routine assignment, so he finally relented and arranged for the rig's manager to clear her for a visit.

To be sure Dilara wasn't yanking his chain, Tyler checked her credentials out on UCLA's Web site and found the picture of a beautiful ebony-haired woman in her midthirties. She had high cheekbones, striking brown eyes, and an easy smile. Her photo gave Tyler the impression of intel-

34

ligence and competence. He made the mistake of showing it to Grant Westfield, his best friend and his current project's electrical engineering expert. Grant had immediately made some less-than-gentlemanly suggestions as to why Tyler should meet with her. Tyler didn't reply, but he had to admit her looks added to the intrigue.

Dietz, who was now holding two flashlights equipped with glowing red traffic wands, moved to the edge of the landing pad near Tyler. He pointed into the sky above the other side of the pad.

"There it is," Dietz said. "Right on time."

Against the gray backdrop of clouds, Tyler saw a dot quickly growing in the distance. A moment later, he could hear the low throb of helicopter blades occasionally burst through the wind. The dot grew until it was recognizable as a nineteen-passenger Sikorsky, a workhorse of the Newfoundland oil fields.

He was sure Dilara Kenner was on board. She had made it clear in their phone conversation that there was no way she was missing the flight, and he believed her. Something about the certainty and toughness in her voice made her sound like a woman to be reckoned with.

Less than a mile away, the helicopter was

slowing to make its descent to the landing pad when a small puff of smoke billowed from the right turbine engine on the helicopter's roof.

Tyler's jaw dropped open, and he said, "What the hell?" Then he realized with horror what was about to happen. An electric shiver shot up his spine.

"Did you see that?" Dietz said, his voice ratcheting up an octave.

Before Tyler could reply, an explosion tore through the engine, causing chunks of metal to rip backward through the tail rotor.

"Holy shit!" Dietz yelled.

Tyler was already in motion. "They're going down!" he shouted. "Come on!"

He leaped onto the landing pad and dashed toward the opposite side. Dietz chased after him. Like a thunderclap after a distant lightning strike, the sound of the blast boomed seconds after the actual explosion. As he pounded across the center of the pad's huge H, Tyler watched the shocking destruction of the Sikorsky.

Two blades of the tail rotor were torn off, and the remaining blades beat themselves to death against the tail section of the helicopter. The powerful centrifugal force of the still-intact main rotor began to spin the helicopter in a tight spiral.

Tyler's brain was screaming at him to do something, but there was no way for him to help them. He skidded to a halt at the edge of the platform, where he had a full view of the helicopter. Dietz stopped next to him, panting with exertion.

The Sikorsky didn't immediately dive into the ocean. Instead, the tail swung around in a circle as the helicopter plunged downward. Only an expert pilot could control such a mortally crippled helicopter.

There was a flicker of hope. If the Sikorsky didn't hit too hard, the passengers might have a chance of getting out alive.

"Those guys are dead," Dietz said.

"No, they're going to make it," Tyler said, but he sounded less convinced than he wanted to.

By the time it had dropped several hundred feet, the helicopter's forward motion had stopped. Just before it splashed into the water, it tilted, and the main rotor blades churned the water like an eggbeater until they were ripped apart. The Sikorsky came to rest on the ocean surface starboard side up.

"They're trapped inside!" Dietz cried.

"Come on," Tyler said to himself, picturing Dilara Kenner's smiling face. His jaw was clenched so tightly, he thought his teeth might crack. "Come on! Get out of there!"

As if in reply, the door of the rapidly sinking helicopter slid open. Four people in bright yellow survival suits jumped out into the water. Only four.

Dietz pointed his flashlights at the floundering helicopter and asked, "Where are the rest of them?"

Tyler was shouting now. "Get out of there!"

The nose of the Sikorsky dipped below the water level, where it was bashed by the waves. Water flooded through the open door. The tail pointed straight up into the air and then disappeared beneath the waves.

Tyler kept staring at the place where the helicoper went under. Each passing second without seeing the other passengers stretched for an eternity.

Then when it seemed like they couldn't possibly make it to the surface alive, three more survival suits popped up and bobbed on the waves. Seven survivors. With five passengers and two pilots, that meant seven for seven. They'd all made it.

Tyler clapped his hands together and yelled, "Yes!" He slapped palms with Dietz, who was grinning from ear to ear.

"Those lucky sons of bitches!" Dietz

yelled, staring at the people floating in the water.

Tyler shook his head at their good fortune. He'd seen the results of a couple of helicopter crashes in Iraq. No survivors in either of them. But for the Sikorsky passengers, it wasn't over yet.

"That water must be freezing," he said. "They won't last long, even with the survival suits."

Dietz's grin disappeared. "I'm sure Finn's on the phone with the Coast Guard by now —"

Tyler cut him off. He could feel the time pressure already. "They're too far away. Remember the fog?"

"Then how do we get them out?" he asked. "You mean they lived through the crash, but they're going to die in the water?"

"Not if I can help it."

Tyler knew he was the only one on board Scotia One with expertise in aviation disasters. He had to convince the rig manager, Roger Finn, that they couldn't wait for the Coast Guard to send a rescue helicopter. That might be tough, since Tyler had been hired by the platform's parent company and Finn barely tolerated his presence on the rig.

"Keep an eye on them," Tyler said to

Dietz, and sprinted back across the landing pad in the direction of the stairs.

"Where are you going?" Dietz yelled after him.

"To the control room!" Tyler yelled back.

Hurtling down the stairs, Tyler had just the slightest moment when he thought maybe he shouldn't get involved. It was his instinct to swoop in and insert himself into the situation, but no one was depending on him for help. It wasn't his responsibility. The oil rig crew and the Coast Guard would handle it. They would save the passengers.

But Tyler thought about what would happen if he were wrong. There were seven people struggling to stay alive out there, including Dilara Kenner, whom he had personally invited to the rig. If those passengers died and he hadn't done everything he could, their deaths would be on his head even if nobody else knew it. Then he would be plunged back into more months without sleep for days at a time, his mind needling him with all of the things he should have done. The thought of those sleepless nights was what kept his feet moving.

FOUR

Captain Mike "Hammer" Hamilton leveled his F-16 at thirty-five thousand feet, and his wingman, Lieutenant Fred "Fuzzy" Newman matched his course. After scrambling from March Air Force Base just east of LA, they had both lit their afterburners to get out over the ocean before the airplane they were intercepting crossed the coast. Now the private 737 designated N-348Z was clearly visible on Hammer's radar. They were closing at a relative speed of two thousand miles per hour.

"Two minutes to intercept," Fuzzy said.

"Copy that," Hammer said. "LA Control, this is CALIF three-two. Any more comm traffic from the target?"

"Negative, CALIF three-two. Still nothing." During the briefing en route, Hammer was told that all communication had been lost with an airplane that had turned back from a course to Honolulu. When it had

41

turned around, it was to get medical attention for some passengers who had gotten sick. Then the pilot's communications had become increasingly distressed. Apparently, everyone on board, including the flight crew, had come down with the mysterious illness.

The communications became increasingly erratic and strange, as if the pilot were succumbing to some kind of madness. His last communication had been so odd that LA Control had played it back for Hammer. It was the eeriest radio call he had ever heard.

"Flight N-three-four-eight Zulu, this is LA Control. Your last message was garbled. Say again."

"I can't see!" the panicking pilot said. *"I'm blind! I can't see! Oh, Jesus!"* Hammer had never heard a pilot lose it like that.

"Are you on autopilot?"

"Yes, on autopilot. Oh God! I can feel it!"

"Feel what? N-three-four-eight Zulu? Feel what? What is happening?"

"I'm melting! We're all melting! Make it stop!" The pilot screamed in obvious pain, and then the communication abruptly terminated. That was an hour and twenty minutes ago.

"Have they made any move to descend?" Hammer asked. Since 9/11, the primary mission of his Air National Guard wing was homeland defense. Standard operating procedure was to intercept all aircraft that had lost communication. If there was any indication that the aircraft was in the control of terrorists and suspected of being used as a weapon, there would be no choice but to take it out. But from what he'd heard, Hammer didn't think that's what they were dealing with. No way a terrorist could make a pilot act like that.

"Negative," the controller said. "They haven't deviated course or altitude."

"Copy that. Intercept in one minute. You heard him, Fuzz. When we get there, we'll circle around and pull alongside, see what we can see."

Hammer spotted the bright blue 737 in the distance, and it quickly filled his windscreen. He and Fuzzy shot by and banked around, reducing their throttles to half what they were. They nudged forward until they were flying even with the 737, Hammer on the port wingtip and Fuzzy on the starboard wingtip.

"LA Control," Hammer said, "we have intercepted the target. It is flying straight and level at flight level three-fifty. Air speed five hundred fifty knots on course zero-seven-five." If it stayed on that course, it would fly directly over Los Angeles.

"Copy that, CALIF three-two. Describe what you're seeing."

"The plane seems to be in good shape. No damage on my side."

"None on mine, either," said Fuzzy.

"I can't see any movement inside. I'll move a little closer to get a better look."

Hammer nudged the F-16 forward and starboard until his wingtip was in front of the 737's. Anybody on board would surely see him. Those still conscious would be pressing their faces against the windows, but none did.

"Any signs of life, CALIF three-two?"

"Negative." The bright sunlight streaming through the starboard windows was visible through the port windows, allowing Hammer a clear view of the seat backs. According to the briefing, the plane had the movie star Rex Hayden and his entourage on board. He expected to see heads lolling backward in some of the seats, but he couldn't see a single person. Strange.

"Fuzzy, you see anything from your side?"

"Negative, Hammer. It's as quiet as a . . ." The next intended word must have been "cemetery" because Fuzzy stopped himself abruptly. "Nobody on the starboard side as far as I can see."

"LA Control," Hammer said, "you got your info wrong. This is an empty flight. Must be a ferry."

After a pause, the controller came back. "Uh, that's a negative, CALIF three-two. Manifest shows twenty-one passengers and six crew."

"Then where the hell are they?"

"What about the pilots?"

Hammer pulled farther ahead until he had a view straight into the cockpit. The windows were clear. Large-jet pilots wear a four-point belt. Even if the pilots were unconscious, the seat belts would keep them upright.

Instead, Hammer saw a disturbing sight. The belts were connected, but slack. The cockpit was empty. If what they were telling him was correct, twenty-seven people had simply vanished over the Pacific.

"LA Control," he said, hardly believing his own words, "there is no one on board the target."

"CALIF three-two, can you repeat that?"

"I repeat, N-three-four-eight Zulu is completely deserted. We've intercepted a ghost plane."

FIVE

Tyler's heart was pounding by the time he reached the Scotia One control room, a state-of-the-art facility that allowed control of every aspect of the rig's operations, including all the pumps and valves on the platform. It also served as the rig's communications station.

Three men sat at terminals, busily going through their emergency checklists while Finn barked into the phone. He was a squat man with hair the color and consistency of steel wool, and his voice boomed with the authority of a drill sergeant. Tyler listened while he caught his breath.

"We've got seven in the water . . . Yes, an explosion . . . No, our standby ship left yesterday to help with a spill at Scotia Two. They have survival suits on . . . When? . . . Okay, we'll sit tight until then." He hung up the phone.

Tyler made a beeline for Finn. He heard

46

the urgency in his own voice. "We can't sit tight."

Finn nodded at the clock on the wall. "Coast Guard is going to get a rescue helicopter into the air in five minutes. At top speed, they'll be here in less than two hours. So we wait until then."

"The fog is rolling in," Tyler said, shaking his head. "By the time the Coast Guard helicopter gets here, visibility will be zero. In those kinds of conditions, the helicopter could fly right over them and never see them."

"If you have any suggestions," Finn said with undisguised annoyance, "I'll be glad to hear them, but I don't know what else we can do."

Tyler rested his chin on his fist as he thought. He knew that few survivors were found more than an hour after a crash at sea.

"How about the standby ship?" he said.

Finn snorted. "Don't you think I thought of that? It'll take over six hours for it to get back from Scotia Two. It's our only ship." Scotia Two was One's sister platform forty miles to the north.

Tyler thought back to when he was leaning on the landing pad railing. He snapped his fingers. "When I was up on deck, I saw

47

a yacht about five miles away. They should be able to mount a rescue."

Finn shot an angry look at one of the men. "Why didn't I know that?"

The man shrugged meekly, and Finn spat into a wastebasket in response. "Send out the distress call," he said.

The SOS went out on the radio. Seconds passed. Tyler listened intently for a voice to respond on the control room speakers, but all he heard was dead air. No reply from the yacht.

"Try again," Finn said after a few more ticks of the wall clock. Still nothing.

"They must have seen the helicopter go down," Tyler said, frustrated by the silence. The yacht was the survivors' best chance. "Why aren't they answering?"

Finn threw his hands up in disgust and sat. "Their radio might be out. Doesn't matter. They aren't answering. We'll have to wait for the Coast Guard helicopter and hope it can find them in the fog."

Tyler remembered wearing the same survival suit on his flight to the platform. They were Mark VII suits. Capable safety gear, but not the newest. Not good enough.

Tyler shook his head again. "The beacons on those suits are only accurate to within a mile," he said. "That's not precise enough

48

in pea soup fog. What's the water temp today?"

"About forty-three degrees Fahrenheit," Finn said. "The suits are rated for up to six hours in the water at that temperature."

"The suit ratings are for ideal conditions in calm weather," Tyler said, losing his patience. "Those people are probably injured, and they're being battered by waves out there. If we wait, that helicopter won't find anything but dead bodies."

Finn raised his eyebrows and gave Tyler a look that said, *And what do you want me to do about it?*

Tyler paused while his mind went into overdrive. He mentally checked off Scotia One's facilities and capabilities one by one, his head nodding imperceptibly as he thought. He churned through the multiple possibilities but returned over and over to the only choice. He fixed his eyes on Finn.

"You have an idea," Finn said.

Tyler nodded. "You're not going to like it."

"Why?"

"We have to go get them ourselves."

"How? We don't have any boats."

"Yes, we do. The free fall lifeboats."

For a moment, Finn was speechless at the suggestion. Then he shook his head. "No.

It's too risky. They're only a last resort if we have to abandon the rig. I can't authorize them to be used that way."

Scotia One was equipped with five fifty-person, totally enclosed lifeboats suspended seventy-five feet above the water. Tyler had consulted on their installation on another oil rig and had even seen one launched.

The unique feature of these lifeboats was that they were aimed at a thirty-degree angle facing toward the water. There were no rope davits to lower the lifeboats slowly to the surface of the water. When the lifeboat was full and watertight, the operators pulled two levers, and the lifeboat slid down a ramp and into space, falling all the way to the water below. It was the only way to evacuate a burning oil platform quickly.

Tyler bent down and gripped the arms of Finn's chair, looming over the rig manager. Tyler's build was the product of good genes and a regular regimen of push-ups, sit-ups, and running, which he could do anywhere in the world he was working. He knew he couldn't intimidate a hardened guy like Finn, no matter how small the man was compared to him, but he could use his size for emphasis.

With a low growl, Tyler said, "Come on, Finn. You know it's their only shot. If we wait, those people are going to die."

Finn stood and got in Tyler's face as much as a man six inches shorter could. "I know what's at stake, dammit!" Finn yelled. "But no one on board has ever launched one of those lifeboats before."

This argument is taking way too long, Tyler thought. It was time the crash survivors didn't have. Finn wasn't going to approve this without someone pushing him. Tyler couldn't stand here and wait for seven people to drown, so he lied.

"I've made a drop in one," Tyler said steadily. "That's what made me think of it."

Finn looked dubious. "You have? Where?"

"Gordian tested one two years ago. They needed volunteers to try it out." It was true Gordian had done an open-water evaluation, which Tyler had supervised, but he hadn't actually ridden in the lifeboat. It had been deemed too dangerous at the time.

Finn raised an eyebrow. "Are you volunteering?"

Tyler didn't blink, but his heart was racing. "If that's what it takes. I signed the waiver just like everyone else, and I saw where they went down."

Finn looked around the control room at the three operators, who stared back at him, then he looked out the window toward the rapidly approaching fog. Finally, he turned back to Tyler.

"Okay, you've convinced me," Finn said, putting his hands up in defeat. "We'll use a lifeboat. How many men do you need?"

Tyler fought to keep his heart rate down as he thought about the mission and remembered the saying about the duck. Calm on the surface, but paddling like hell underneath.

"Three men total," Tyler said. "One to pilot the boat and two to pull people out of the water. Grant should be one of them. He'd never forgive me if I left him behind."

Grant Westfield was not only the best electrical engineer Tyler had ever worked with, he was also an adrenaline junkie — rock climbing, sky diving, wreck diving, spelunking, anything that got the blood pumping. Tyler enjoyed joining him sometimes, but Grant was fanatical. He'd jump at the chance to launch a free fall lifeboat, something few others have ever done. And if Tyler was going to do this, he wanted the person on this rig he trusted most going along with him.

"All right, Grant goes," Finn said. "I'll send Jimmy Markson with you. We can't pull the boat back up again, you know. Not in this weather. Our crane might snap."

This is getting better by the minute, Tyler thought. "We'll use the personnel basket," he said. The basket was a six-person rig used to lift people from ships to the platform.

"I'll tell the other two to meet you down at the lifeboats. Get a survival suit along the way, just in case. I don't want to lose anyone if one of you guys goes in the water."

That sounded like a fine idea to Tyler. "I know where the locker is."

Finn snatched up a phone, but Tyler didn't stay to hear the call. After grabbing a survival suit from an emergency station, he followed the lifeboat evacuation signs, bounding down the stairs two at a time.

On the lowest deck, where the lifeboats were perched, Tyler dropped his bomber jacket onto the grating and donned his suit while he waited for Grant and Markson. Each of the five boats was painted a bright orange so they could be spotted easily at sea. They were streamlined like bullets, and the only windows were rectangular portholes in a cupola at the rear where the helmsman sat. The portholes were made of super-strong polycarbonate — the same material used to make bulletproof windows — instead of glass so that they would withstand the impact of the fall. The sole opening was an aluminum hatch at the aft end.

The boats pointed down at the ocean and rested on rails that would guide them when released. At the end of the rails, it was a seventy-five-foot plunge to the water, where the boat would dive under and then surface three-hundred feet away, propelled to ten knots by the momentum from the fall. A powerful diesel could drive the boat at up to twenty knots once it resurfaced.

With his suit secured, Tyler flung open the hatch of the first lifeboat and peered inside. Instead of a flat aisle down the center of the boat, stairs led down past seats that faced backward. The only seat facing forward was for the helmsman, and that wouldn't be occupied until after the drop was complete. Two levers on either side of the boat's interior had to be pulled simultaneously to initiate the drop, so that a panicked crewman couldn't single-handedly launch the boat before it was filled with evacuees. Safety devices ensured that the rear hatch was closed before it could drop. If the hatch were left open, when the lifeboat went under after the initial drop, water would flood in, and the boat might never resurface.

Tyler heard a clatter behind him. Two men hurried down the stairs. Both were black, but that's where the similarities ended. The one in the lead had an ebony complexion and was a couple of inches taller than Tyler, but he was lanky, and the survival suit hung from him like a coat hanger. That must have been Markson. He was in his late forties, and his face was smudged with oil, which did nothing to cover his apprehension.

The second man, who had a shaved head and mocha skin, struggled with the zipper on his survival suit. Grant Westfield, four inches shorter and fifteen years younger than Markson, still had the muscular 240-pound frame of the wrestler he used to be. He must have picked a size too small. Tyler smiled in spite of himself.

"Need some help there, tiger?" Tyler said, not bothering to hide his amusement. "Maybe you need to lose a few."

Grant zipped the suit to the top and scoffed. "These things weren't built for someone with my impressive physique."

"Just don't flex too hard and rip it. Wouldn't make a great fashion statement."

Grant pursed his lips. "I'll have you know that torn survival suits are the latest rage in Milan."

Tyler heard Markson chuckle uneasily. The joking probably sounded out of place to him, but Tyler liked it. It had been the way he and Grant lightened the mood in hairy situations ever since their army days.

"Glad you could join the party," Tyler said.

"Are you kidding? I wouldn't miss one of your crazy stunts. They tell me that you're raring to launch one of these babies." Grant seemed a lot more enthusiastic about this than Tyler was.

"*Raring* may be too strong a word, but somebody's got to do it. Might as well be us."

"You got that right," Grant said, eagerly eyeing the massive lifeboats. "I haven't ridden a roller coaster in months."

Tyler turned to the other man and held out his hand. "And you're Markson?"

"That's right, Dr. Locke."

"Call me Tyler."

They shook hands. "I'm a diver and a welder. I'm fully qualified on the lifeboats." He was a tough guy, but there was a slight quaver in his voice.

"Glad to have you along," Tyler said. He gestured at the open hatch. "Shall we?"

Grant got in first and belted himself into one of the seats. The four-point seat belts barely stretched over his huge frame. Tyler followed him in, and then Markson closed and dogged the hatch behind him. Tyler chose the seat next to the port release lever and cinched his own belts tight.

"We're set for launch," Markson said. "Are you guys ready?"

"Ready," Tyler said.

"Oh yeah!" Grant shouted, pumping himself up, just like he did in his wrestling days. "Let's see what this baby can do!"

Markson gripped the lever in his hand and Tyler did the same. Then he yelled, "Three . . . two . . . one . . . launch!" Tyler yanked his lever down. A red light glowed, indicating that the release mechanism had been activated, and he felt a clunk as the hydraulic clamps sprang open. There was no turning back now, so Tyler forced himself into mission mode, just like when he was in the army. Precision, decisiveness, and calm were his watchwords from now on.

The boat began its slide down the rails. The movement was anticlimactic. It was as if the boat were being lowered at a lakeside boat ramp off its trailer. Then the lifeboat bow dipped downward, and Tyler's stomach leaped into his mouth.

With some goading from Grant, Tyler had gone bungee jumping one time, so the feeling was familiar. His entire body floated out of the contoured seat. The weightlessness seemed to last forever. Then the impact came.

The crash of fiberglass splashing into the water boomed from all directions. It felt like the lifeboat hit concrete. Tyler's head slammed backward against the cushioned headrest. The sense of weightlessness was replaced by the crush of deceleration. The angle of his seat changed drastically as he saw water wash over the helmsman's portholes.

Tyler was thrown against his seat belt and rocked side to side as the lifeboat made for the surface. Water streamed down the cupola window, and he could see the gray sky out of the window. The lifeboat leveled out. Grant whooped in delight from behind him, but Tyler was just glad they had made it down in one piece.

"Woohoo!" Grant yelled, laughing. "Can we do that again?"

"Not with me, you're not," Tyler said, unbuckling himself.

"Oh, you know you loved it."

"Tell that to my stomach. It's still back on the oil rig."

Markson took the helmsman's seat. Although the waves pummeled them, the lifeboat was as seaworthy as a cork. But anyone swimming in that would be fighting for their lives. Tyler flashed again to the memory of Dilara's photo and pictured her struggling to stay afloat. Markson fired up the diesel, and Tyler pointed him in the direction of the crash. With the fog getting thicker by the minute, they had to hurry. Their chances of rescuing the survivors were quickly dropping toward zero.

SIX

Dilara Kenner struggled to keep the unconscious helicopter pilot's head completely out of the water, but the waves crashing over them made that impossible. At least the survival suits were buoyant. The best she could hope to do was to make sure that he didn't float away. The copilot, a baby-faced blond named Logan, tried to help, but his arm was broken, so it was all he could do to keep from inhaling seawater.

She had lost sight of the other passengers, four men who looked like they were oil workers on their way out for a three-week stint on the rig. They had been swept away by the waves, so she wouldn't be getting aid from them, either. Before she and Logan stopped talking to conserve their energy and to avoid swallowing more seawater, the copilot had told her that the oil platform had no helicopter. The nearest one was two hours away in St. John's.

It seemed hopeless, but Dilara had thought the same thing when she ran the Los Angeles marathon. The idea of running twenty-six miles without stopping was too daunting, an apparently impossible task. But by focusing only on putting that next foot down, she eventually reached the end.

So she focused her mind not on waiting for the helicopter to arrive in two hours, but instead on keeping herself alive for the next minute. The most pressing problem distracting her was the water that was seeping into her survival suit, which had snagged on a jagged piece of metal as she escaped the sinking helicopter. She could feel her limbs starting to numb.

"I'm getting tired," Logan said after ten minutes of being pummeled by the waves. "I think my suit's losing flotation."

Dilara was on the ragged edge herself, but she knew that giving up was death. "You're going to make it, Logan. Don't waste your breath talking. Just keep your head up."

"Fog's coming in. Won't see us."

"I don't care. They'll find us."

"My legs are cramping."

"Logan, I'm holding up your pilot and me," she said, trying a different tactic. "Are you saying you can't keep up with a girl?"

Logan saw what she was doing and smiled weakly.

"Good," Dilara said, seeing that her little pep talk worked. "You're not wimping out. I like that."

"I'll be here as long as you are."

"That's good to hear. I didn't come all this way to give up now."

The terrible irony of the crash was that she had thought her entire ordeal was almost over when the crash had happened. Sam and his cryptic words had just been the start of it.

Hayden. Oasis. Genesis. They didn't mean anything to her. And his claim that her father had actually succeeded in his life's pursuit . . . it was mind-boggling.

The idea that Sam had been poisoned seemed ridiculous to her. The thing that nagged at Dilara was that Sam was an expert in pharmaceuticals, so if anyone would know he was being poisoned, it would be him. But why would someone want to poison him? She wanted to believe him, but the whole story was incredible.

What convinced her was an incident that happened on the way back to her apartment.

She had noticed a hulking man in a black trench coat on the shuttle bus. He had looked at her several times, and Sam's words echoed in her mind.

You have to go . . . or they'll kill you, too.

She thought she was just being paranoid but nevertheless asked the bus driver to stay by her car until she safely drove away. She exited the lot onto Sepulveda, a six-lane boulevard leading from LAX to her studio in Santa Monica. The traffic was relatively light going north, so she had the left lane all to herself.

A large black SUV pulled even with her tiny Toyota hatchback. The SUV suddenly swung over and bashed into her car, pushing it into the oncoming lanes.

The SUV had deliberately waited until the other direction was full of traffic. Dilara slammed on the brakes and tried to resist the SUV's push, but it was twice as heavy as her own vehicle. A pickup truck was heading right at her, and instead of continuing to resist, she hit the accelerator and swung the Toyota as far to the left as she could. Screeching tires and honking horns erupted around her. It was only through luck that she merely grazed the pickup and weaved her way through the rest of the traffic before skidding to a halt in a strip mall parking lot.

The SUV sped off, leaving a tangle of

vehicles and rubber smoke behind it. Dilara guessed that the SUV had followed her from the airport. The windows had been tinted, so she couldn't see if it was the man in the trench coat, but the occupants must have been cohorts of the businesswoman who had poisoned Sam.

You have to go . . . or they'll kill you, too.

She could just blow it off and return to her normal life, as if Sam were loony, but her gut was telling her that what Sam told her was not the rambling of an old person with dementia. People were trying to kill her. She had no proof, but she was sure of it. If she went on as usual, she'd be dead within a day.

Eventually her tremors subsided enough for her to drive. She tried going to the police, but that had been a dead end. The detective she spoke with took her statement, an extended version of the one she'd given at the airport, but she could tell he thought her story was ludicrous. Her friend Sam Watson hadn't really died of a heart attack, but had been poisoned? Billions of people's lives were at risk, and someone had deliberately run her off the road to get her out of the way? Even to her, it sounded crazy. But all she could think of was the SUV deliberately ramming her and Sam's words.

You have to go . . . or they'll kill you, too.

Dilara couldn't go back to her apartment. It was the logical place for her pursuers to wait for her. If she couldn't go home, she was on the run, and she always would be until she could figure who was after her and why.

Dilara went to the closest branch of her bank and withdrew every penny in her account. Credit cards were too easy to track, and finding Tyler Locke would require travel.

Gordian Engineering hadn't been hard to track down. She went to a library and looked them up on the Internet. The company's named derived from the Gordian knot, the impossibly complex tangle cut by Alexander the Great. Apparently, Gordian was the largest privately owned engineering firm in the world, one that provided consulting services to everyone from Fortune 500 corporations to the U.S. military. Each of its senior engineers were partners, reminding Dilara of a law firm. The company's specialty was failure analysis and prevention, and the Web site cited dozens of areas of expertise — vehicle and airline crashes, fires and explosions, structural failures — the list went on and on.

She used the site's search engine to find

Tyler Locke. His title was chief of special operations, and his experience was exceptional. Majored in mechanical engineering at MIT. PhD from Stanford. Former captain in the U.S. Army commanding a combat engineering company. Expert in demolition, bomb disposal, mechanical systems, accident reconstruction, and prototype testing. Impressive credentials.

Dilara had never heard of the term "combat engineer." A military Web site told her that they are the soldiers who build bridges and fortifications, clear land mines, and defuse bombs, all while under enemy fire. She looked for a more comprehensive service history for Tyler, but she couldn't find out how long he had served or in what war, just that he'd been decorated with multiple medals, including the Silver Star and Purple Heart. With his background and experience, it sounded like he'd been in the business for thirty-five years. There was no photo, but from her experience with engineering professors at UCLA, she imagined a bald, paunchy man in his fifties wearing a white short-sleeved shirt and a pocket protector.

It would be too easy for Dr. Locke to dismiss her story over the phone. She had to see him in person.

When she found out he was on an oil rig in Newfoundland, she thought it was a great place to meet — thousands of miles from LA, no easy access for the people after her. She'd had to reserve her seat on the helicopter ahead of time — a requirement to fly out to the rig; she couldn't just walk up to the counter and buy a ticket to a private oil platform — but otherwise she was as careful as she could be not to leave a trail. She flew into the airport in Gander, 150 miles from St. John's, just in case they were waiting for her at the St. John's airport. After a three-hour bus trip from Gander, she got to the heliport just in time to don her survival suit and board the helicopter.

When Dilara got into the air, she finally relaxed. Maybe she would have some answers soon. She had been looking at the enormous oil platform out the side window when the thud of an explosion came overhead. Alarmed shouts erupted from all the passengers, including herself. The pilot had calmly compensated for the loss of control on the way down, keeping the helicopter upright all the way until they slammed into the sea.

It took a few seconds for Dilara to shake off the cobwebs after they hit the water. One of the other passengers threw open the sliding door. The pilot was slumped in his seat, unconscious. Dilara could see that the copilot's arm was pointing at an awkward angle. Before she could ask the others for help, they all jumped out of the helicopter. She sloshed through the water pouring in through the open door. They would only be afloat for a few more seconds.

She yanked the seat belt off the pilot. By that time, the water was above her waist, and the pilot floated out of his seat. The copilot, wailing in agony every time his arm hit something, staggered to the door. She wrestled the pilot to the exit just as the helicopter sank beneath the surface. With one last kick, she propelled both of them out, and the three of them rose to the surface.

Now, as she struggled to keep the pilot's face up, she resolved to find the people responsible for this, the same people who had murdered her father. Something that Sam had told her was so important to them that they were willing to kill. She had to find out what it was, and this Tyler Locke guy was going to help her. They didn't realize it yet, but they would find out that they had messed with the wrong woman.

A new noise penetrated the growing gloom. An engine. She whipped her head around. The wind made the direction of the sound hard to pinpoint. Then she saw it. An odd orange vessel shaped like a bullet. It came to a stop and bobbed on the water about six hundred feet away. A hatch opened on the back, and she could see a figure step through and begin hauling people on board. The other helicopter passengers.

She lifted the arm she wasn't using to support the pilot and waved it madly, kicking to keep herself upright.

"Over here!" she yelled. A sense of relief swept over her, and she let out a cry of joy. They were going to make it.

Logan tried to join her shouting, but he was too weak. His head dipped under the water every few seconds, and each time he came up sputtering. If they didn't get here quickly, Logan would go under and wouldn't come back up.

She yelled more loudly, but she couldn't see any response. The boat bobbed in and out of her view, the hatch on the back no longer toward her. For a second, she feared they were leaving, but then the boat grew larger. It was approaching. They had seen her.

The boat pulled alongside and stopped when the aft end was even with them. She had been paying so much attention to the lifeboat that she'd forgotten about Logan. The hatch flew open, and a tall man with tousled brown hair looked around for a moment before diving into the water right about where she'd last seen Logan.

He stayed under for what seemed like hours but must have been only a few seconds. He surfaced, holding Logan under the chin. He handed Logan to a massive black man standing in the hatch who hauled Logan up like he was a doll.

Next, the swimming rescuer took the pilot from her and passed him up into the boat.

He turned to Dilara and, in defiance of the cold weather lashing at them, smiled. "Your turn, young lady." He didn't seem bothered at all by the cold water, simply focusing his blue eyes on her. She found the effect oddly charming considering their circumstances, and it put her at ease.

Dilara reached up to the black man, who hoisted her up with one motion. Instead of taking the closest seat, she went back to see if Logan and the pilot were okay. Logan breathed raggedly between bouts of vomiting seawater, while a third rescuer bent over the unconscious pilot.

"Is he going to be all right?" she asked through chattering teeth.

The third rescuer nodded. "He's got a

pretty nasty bump, but he's still alive."

"Thanks to you," said a voice behind her. She turned to see the man from the water dogging the hatch closed. She sank into a seat, exhausted and shivering uncontrollably. The man took a wool blanket from a storage bin and draped it over her. The warmth of the blanket felt wonderful.

"How are you doing?" he asked. In the better light of the boat, Dilara could see a thin white scar trailing down the crease of his neck. His eyes seemed to be boring into her own. He took her hands and rubbed them with his own.

"You don't have an espresso machine on this boat, do you?" she replied. Her teeth snapping together made her sound like she had a stutter. "Because I could use a double-shot about now."

The man showed that bright smile again, but Dilara could see he was just as cold as she was.

"Our barista is out right now, but we'll get some nice hot java in you soon," the man said. "You must be Dilara Kenner."

She cocked her head in surprise. "That's right. I didn't expect a personal welcome. And the tall, dark, and rugged stranger who saved me is?"

"Well, I don't know which one of us

71

you're referring to, but the he-man over there is Grant Westfield, the man you saved is being attended to by Jimmy Markson, and I'm Tyler Locke."

Instead of the fifty-five-year-old she'd been expecting, he was a man in his mid-thirties, not much older than she was, and looked more like a brawny fireman than a nerdy engineer. She coughed and said, "Dr. Tyler Locke?"

"I don't think there's a need to be formal. I prefer Tyler, but Ty works, too."

"What are you doing out here?"

"I might ask you the same thing."

The shock and exhaustion must have taken its toll. Before she could stop herself, the words tumbled out of her mouth.

"I want you to help me find Noah's Ark."

SEVEN

For an hour, Captain Hammer Hamilton had been trying to raise someone on the radio of the private jet, but it was useless. All he got was static. Not that he expected anyone to answer. The only radio was in the cockpit, which he'd been staring at since he'd rendezvoused with the 737. The plane simply cruised along on its course with Hammer and Fuzzy shadowing it, passing over LA without incident. A mile away, the KC-10 tanker that had already refueled them once stood by in case they needed a refill, which would depend on how far the 737 made it.

Hammer had never seen anything like it. The closest thing he could recall was the private jet of Payne Stewart, the golfer. It was a Lear 35 that had leaked its cabin air soon after takeoff from Florida. Everyone on board had died of hypoxia, but the jet kept going on autopilot. It didn't stop until it ran out of fuel over South Dakota and crashed into a field.

Fighters had been sent to intercept Stewart's jet, but the windows had frosted over, so they couldn't see the plane's interior. Frosted windows suggested a loss of pressure. The poor bastards on board probably never knew what happened, and the NTSB never got to hear the pilot's last words. The cockpit voice recorder only tapes the last thirty minutes of flight, which in the case of Stewart's plane was long after they had succumbed.

The difference today was that the pilots had vanished. The windows weren't frosted, which made an oxygen leak unlikely. Hammer could clearly see that no one was in the cockpit. He didn't care what kind of emergency had happened on the plane, no way would both pilots leave their seats.

Of course, it could all be an elaborate ruse. Another possibility was that there were hijackers on board, and they had done something with the crew and passengers. But what? Herded everybody into the back of the plane where there were no windows? The hijackers would still need to fly the plane, and Hammer had seen no one in the cockpit.

He supposed the passengers could be

dead. Shot, or maybe gassed. But still, most of the passengers would be visible slumped over in their seats, maybe even some blood on the windows. Hammer had seen the plane from both sides. All the window shades were wide open. Nothing. Not one person.

If hijackers *had* taken over, what was all that business from the pilot? They were melting? He was blind? Why would hijackers make him say something like that?

If there was anybody on the plane, even hijackers, Hammer was sure he would have heard from them or seen them by now. Something else was happening, but he didn't know what it could be. And with no one on board, the airliner would simply do what Stewart's private jet did: fly in a straight line until it ran out of gas.

"LA Control," he said, "what's the latest on that fuel estimate for N-three-four-eight Zulu?

"CALIF three-two, it got about fifteen hundred miles out when the pilot decided to head back. Flights were reporting a pretty strong easterly headwind, so they probably burned more fuel going out than coming back. They also sat on the runway for forty minutes, so we're guessing they should be on fumes in about ten minutes."

Hammer checked his flight map. The airliner would be over northwestern Arizona when it went dry.

"CALIF three-two, you're sure no one is on board?"

"As sure as I can get without going over there myself. It's a derelict."

He knew why they were asking. His standing orders, revised after 9/11, were to use his judgment on whether the aircraft posed a risk to populated areas. If it did, he was authorized to shoot it down. He just thought he'd never be in that situation.

"CALIF three-two, let us know if N-three-four-eight Zulu makes any course corrections or altitude changes."

"Copy."

All Hammer could do now was follow the airliner and keep trying the radio. Fifteen minutes passed and then he saw what he feared. Seventy miles southeast of Las Vegas, when they were just passing over Lake Mohave into Arizona, the exhaust from the port engine abruptly stopped.

"LA Control, I've got a flameout on the target's port engine," he radioed. "How about you, Fuzz?"

"Starboard engine is still running," Fuzzy replied. "Starboard tank must have a few extra gallons in it."

By increasing power to the starboard engine, the autopilot would be able to maintain airspeed and altitude, but it would gulp the remaining fuel quickly. Two minutes later, Fuzzy radioed.

"Hammer, the starboard engine just cut out."

With the thrust gone, the 737 lost speed rapidly. It had become a 150,000-pound glider. A moment later, LA Control came on the line.

"CALIF three-two, we're showing a decrease in speed for N-three-four-eight Zulu. Can you confirm?"

"Affirmative. She's flying silent. Fuel must be gone."

"Be advised, the trajectory will take N-three-four-eight Zulu over uninhabited land."

Hammer breathed a sigh of relief. He wouldn't have to make the decision between shooting down the airliner and letting it hit a residential area. "Acknowledged."

All he could do now was watch the plane's final few minutes.

Modern airliners were built with huge wingspans that allowed them to glide for long distances, even without power. Using the hydraulic flight systems, a human pilot could keep the plane on an optimum glide path.

Hammer remembered a 747 that lost power after it flew through the ash from a volcanic eruption over Indonesia. All four engines were snuffed out by the dense ash cloud, and it took the pilot fifteen minutes to get them restarted. When he finally did, the airliner was at an altitude of less than two thousand feet, but with a wingspan wider than a football field, they were able to glide during their frantic efforts.

Without a human pilot to take over, the powerless 737 wouldn't glide for long. The autopilot did what it was designed to do: maintain altitude and heading, sacrificing speed to stay at thirty-five thousand feet. Hammer could see the elevators in the tail lower as the autopilot compensated for the loss of velocity. He had to throttle back to keep pace with the slowing airliner. When he neared two hundred knots, he was close to the F-16's stall speed.

"Fuzz, we can't fly alongside anymore. Stay on me."

Hammer increased his speed and went into a wide circle around the 737, Fuzzy on his wing.

A minute later, with the autopilot no longer able to compensate for the loss of speed, the 737 began to porpoise up and down. The nose would pitch down to gain speed, then pitch back up in an attempt to regain altitude. The third time the nose pitched up, the airliner reached its stall speed of 160 knots.

"This is it," Fuzzy said.

Hammer and Fuzzy banked away to give the airliner more room. Abruptly, the 737 flipped over, as if it were starting a Split S maneuver and then began to spin wildly, its nose pointed straight at the ground.

Hammer tried to keep his voice professional, but he had never seen the death of an airplane before. He felt frustrated that all he could do was be a witness.

"LA Control," he said, "the target just went into a dive. It's in a severe descending spiral and will soon impact the ground. Fuzzy and I will follow the target in emergency descent."

"Copy, CALIF three-two. Keep us advised."

"Keep your distance, Fuzz," Hammer said. He was afraid the plane would break apart.

"Roger that."

Hammer narrated for LA Control as they descended. When the 737 plunged below five thousand feet, the ground seemed close enough to touch. Hammer struggled to keep his voice calm, but the adrenaline was making it impossible.

"The target is still spinning . . . still intact," he said. "Below three thousand feet now . . . Two thousand. Damn, they build strong planes. Approaching the ground . . . My God!"

Hammer pulled up on the stick, but he kept looking at the stricken airliner as it finally met its doom.

One second, it was a 737 just like any other he had flown in on countless trips, then it plowed into the desert floor and became a churning mass of metal and dust. The 737 was torn apart by the impact, flinging pieces high into the air, its two massive engines tumbling away from the rest of the wreckage. No fuel was left to ignite any fires or explosions. The debris simply ran out of momentum and came to a stop, obscured by the cloud of desert sand thrown into the air by the impact.

There were no structures of any kind in sight, but in the distance, Hammer could see a lone ribbon of concrete plied by a few vehicles. According to his map, it was U.S. 93, northwest of Chloride, Arizona.

Hammer circled the crash site with Fuzzy on his wing.

"That was a hell of a thing to watch," Fuzzy said.

Hammer didn't reply. What could he say? He'd just watched a plane that took off with twenty-seven souls auger into the ground.

He relayed the exact coordinates to LA Control.

"Copy that," LA Control replied. "We've already got emergency vehicles en route."

Not that it would do any good. No one could have survived that crash.

"CALIF three-two returning to base," Hammer said. He dreaded the debriefing. It would be a long and dismal one.

As he turned his F-16 back home, Hammer took one last look at the wreckage of flight N-348 Zulu, soon to be pored over by accident investigators. He didn't envy them because this investigation would be like nothing they'd seen before. For once, the question wouldn't be why the plane crashed. That was obvious. The question would be, what could make a planeload of people disappear?

EIGHT

By the time the lifeboat got back to Scotia One, night had fallen and fog shrouded the rig. Because seas in the North Atlantic are so dangerous, the rig's lowest level was seventy feet above the water to minimize the chance that waves would damage the platform. In the reduced visibility and rough seas, it was difficult to keep the lifeboat directly under the personnel basket, and it took more than thirty minutes to lift everyone up safely.

Tyler was looking forward to stripping out of the wet survival suit, but he couldn't let anyone else be the last one out of the lifeboat. It was partly his military training and partly his innate sense of responsibility again. It just wouldn't sit well with him to ride up to safety while others were still on the boat. Before he climbed into the basket, he closed the hatch so that the lifeboat could be salvaged at a later time. There was no way to tie it up to the rig, so it floated out into the open ocean.

The pilot had regained consciousness and was carried to the platform's infirmary accompanied by the copilot. After an examination, the rig's doctor found that the pilot had suffered only a concussion that could wait for treatment on the mainland, so the Coast Guard chopper, which had been cruising in the vicinity on standby, returned to St. John's instead of attempting a risky landing in the fog. The doctor also treated the copilot's broken arm, and the rest of the passengers suffered only mild hypothermia. Tyler was amazed that no one was seriously injured. He'd only been in the water for a minute, but he was still shaking off the chill.

Dilara Kenner declined to see the doctor and seemed to regard everyone warily. Other than insisting on talking with Tyler, she had been tight-lipped since mentioning Noah's Ark. He offered to meet her for breakfast the next morning, but she said she had to talk to him right away. All she wanted was a shower and some fresh clothes.

Tyler and Grant escorted her to a guest cabin where Tyler supplied her with a jumpsuit and boots. While she refreshed herself, Tyler retrieved his bomber jacket, then went

83

back to his own room and got into a dry shirt and jeans. He met Grant outside Dilara's cabin and told him what Dilara had said on the lifeboat.

"Noah's Ark, huh?" Grant said. "Now that's out of left field. Is there something you haven't told me about your past? Doing a little archaeology on the side?"

"Not unless you count that time I was looking for something to eat in your refrigerator."

"That moo shu pork *was* disgusting. Or was it General Tso's chicken?"

"I think it was an entirely new life-form. I was scarred for life. Some of that stuff was old enough for your fridge to be considered an historic landmark."

"So if she isn't here to pick your brain about archaeology, what's her angle?"

"Hell if I know," Tyler said. "She doesn't seem like a nut to me, and her credentials check out."

"She's nervous about something. Wouldn't say squat to me."

"You better let me talk to her alone. I'll fill you in later."

Grant and Tyler had been friends since they served in the army together, Tyler as a captain, and Grant as his first sergeant before leaving to join the Rangers. A few

84

years after Tyler was honorably discharged and had started his engineering consulting firm, he convinced Grant to leave as well and become a partner in the firm, which had since been merged with another company. They'd been working together for two years now, and Tyler trusted him with his life, but he sensed Dilara might not be as open with both of them listening to her.

"No problem," Grant said. "I've still got work on that ballast problem. Should be able to solve it by tomorrow. That'll give you two time to get acquainted."

Dilara stepped out of the guest room, and despite the dark circles under her eyes, she wasn't the bedraggled form Tyler had rescued. Her hair was tied in a ponytail, and although her cheeks were still ruddy from the cold and wind, she had a golden tan that suggested long periods of time spent in the sun, or a Mediterranean background, possibly both.

Tyler could tell she was hiding her weariness just below the surface and wouldn't be surprised to see her collapse right in front of them. Treading water while holding up a man twice her weight must have been exhausting.

He had picked out her clothes and had guessed her height well — about five foot ten — but the jumpsuit was baggy. Her survival suit had been so bulky, he hadn't realized how slender she was. The belt was cinched to its limit.

"If you want," Tyler said, "I can find you something that fits a little better." Grant, who was standing behind Dilara, raised his eyebrows and nodded as if he'd like to see her in something tighter. Tyler tilted his head, and Grant got the hint.

"I've got some things to take care of," Grant said. "Nice to meet you, Dilara." He winked at Tyler as he left.

"How about that coffee you promised?" she said.

"Are you sure you wouldn't like to rest first? You look dead on your feet."

Dilara straightened up and took a deep breath. "Believe me, I've been through worse plenty of times. Once, I hiked through the Sahara for two days with no water after my truck broke down. I can stay awake a little longer. But I wouldn't say no to a cheeseburger to go with that coffee."

"You got it." He pointed her in the direction of the mess hall. Dilara strode ahead of him with the purpose of someone who didn't like to waste time. Tyler didn't know what was going on with this woman, but he liked her toughness.

A few stragglers from dinner lingered in the mess hall, a cafeteria-style facility with a made-to-order grill and a carpeted eating area with long laminated tables. It reminded Tyler of a corporate dining hall. He poured two steaming cups of coffee and ordered burgers for both of them. They found an empty table in the far corner of the room. Dilara settled into a chair across from Tyler and eyed the people around her. Satisfied that no one was listening, she turned back to Tyler.

"I appreciate your friend letting us talk alone."

"I trust Grant with my life. He saved me when I got this." Tyler pointed at the scar on his neck. "But I asked him to give us some space. I got the feeling you'd want some privacy."

Dilara squinted, apparently searching for a memory. "He looked familiar to me. Where have I seen him before?"

"When he was at the University of Washington, Grant was a three-time NCAA freestyle wrestling champion. After that, he went pro for three years."

The light went on in her eyes. "He's The Burn! The guy who left it all behind to join the army after 9/11."

"The same. Doesn't bring it up much, and

most people don't recognize him without the dreadlocks."

"That's amazing! I don't know anything about wrestling, but even I've heard of him. I even knew his catchphrase." She switched to a gravelly voice. " 'You're going to feel The Burn!' "

Tyler laughed. "Great impression, but it works even better if you grimace."

"What's he doing here? Didn't he want to go back into wrestling?"

"No, it was too much punishment on his body after years in the army, so he's out of the scene now. But next time you see him, ask him about his signature moves. He loves talking about them."

She seemed to be stalling with the small talk and paused when Tyler didn't go on. He let the silence grow.

"You want to know why I'm here," she finally said.

"You've certainly piqued my curiosity."

"Look, I'm not some kook."

"I don't think you are."

"I made a mistake earlier mentioning Noah's Ark so quickly. When I was drifting in that ocean, all I could do was think about why I came out here. So when I heard your name, I just blurted it out."

"So your original plan was to butter me

up first and *then* ask me to help you find Noah's Ark?"

"It sounds even goofier when you say it. Look, I didn't want you to think I was some kind of crazy person."

"You seem sane enough to me."

"The problem is that I'm not even sure you can help me. All I have are a few words that a family friend, Sam Watson, told me." She said the name as if Tyler might recognize it. "Do you know Sam?"

Tyler shook his head. "Should I?"

"I thought you might. He said to find you."

"Why?"

"Sam said, 'Tyler Locke. Gordian Engineering. Get his help. He knows Coleman.' "

"The only Coleman I know," Tyler said, bewildered, "is John Coleman at Coleman Engineering and Consulting. He's another engineer. We compete for work occasionally, but I haven't talked to him in over a year."

"So you don't know what the connection between you and Coleman is?"

"Not a clue. Did your friend mention anything else?"

"A few random words. Hayden. Project. Oasis. Genesis. Dawn. Do they mean anything to you?"

Tyler thought about them, but nothing was familiar. "Beyond the obvious, none of them are jogging my memory. But you're saying all of this has something to do with Noah's Ark?"

"Right."

"And me?"

"Yes."

Tyler had to admit this all sounded weird to him. What could Noah's Ark possibly have to do with him?

"Why didn't this Sam Watson contact me himself?"

"He wanted to talk to me first. You see, my father was an archaeologist, too. Hasad Arvadi. Do you know him?" She looked at him expectantly.

Tyler shook his head, and she sat back in disappointment.

"Turkish?" Tyler asked.

"Very good. I'm impressed."

"I spent some time at Incirlik Air Base." Incirlik was the United States' main base in Turkey and was a staging area for many flights into Iraq. "Your first name sounds Turkish, too. Does it mean anything?"

She blushed. "It means lover." She quickly went on. "He was one of the few Turkish Christians. He emigrated to America long ago, but he used his connections in Turkey to get access to Mount Ararat. In the past, it was very difficult to get permission to explore the region. His life's work was to find any remaining evidence of Noah's Ark. Most of the archaeological community thought he was a nut, obsessed with unproven theories, but Sam said he found it."

Tyler had to stifle a laugh. "He found Noah's Ark? The actual Noah's Ark?"

"I know. It sounds ridiculous, but that's what Sam said. He said to me, 'Your father's research started everything. You must find the Ark.' "

"If someone had found Noah's Ark, I think I might have heard that little bit of news."

"You wouldn't have if the discovery was never made public. My father's been missing for three years. Sam said someone murdered my father because of Noah's Ark. I believe him."

"Why?"

"Because of this." Dilara showed him a locket that hung around her neck. She opened it to reveal a beautiful woman with dark brown hair. Except for the lighter skin and hair, it could have been a picture of Dilara. Tyler nodded in appreciation.

"That's my mother," Dilara said. "She died when I was thirteen. My father was from Ankara, and my mother was an Italian-American from Brooklyn. He met her when he moved to New York for a teaching position at Cornell. They were an unusual pair, but they were very much in love."

That explained Dilara's exotic looks. "What's the significance of the locket?" Tyler asked.

"My father never took this off. But I received it in the mail as a birthday present during the time he went missing. I think he knew he was in trouble. I think he wanted me to have it before he was killed."

Tyler shook his head. "Look, I'm sorry about your father, but I still don't see what this has to do with me. Where is Sam now?"

"He's dead. They killed him right in front of me."

"They?"

"The people who are trying to kill me."

"There are people trying to kill you," Tyler said dubiously, as if he were responding to a mental patient who'd just told him she was abducted by aliens.

"Yes, there are people trying to kill me," Dilara said, obviously exasperated by his tone. "That's why the helicopter crashed. That was no accident. Someone brought it down on purpose."

NINE

With the press of a button, Sebastian Ulric turned off the bank of TVs showing every news channel's coverage of the Rex Hayden plane crash. He stood and walked out onto the aft deck of his luxury yacht, *Mako,* a craft so big that it boasted its own helipad and submarine. Fifteen miles away, the hills of Palos Verde stood out from the smog clinging to Los Angeles and Long Beach. A slight breeze ruffled his blond hair, but that was the only thing out of place on an appearance blessed with attributes that he used to charm his followers: intense green eyes, a tanned, muscular frame, and a strong jawline that echoed his strength and determination. Ulric knew he cut the figure of a natural born leader, and these latest events forced him to assume that role yet again. He closed his eyes and reached out with his mind, hoping to find guidance for his next step.

"This is only a minor setback, sir." Dan Cutter had followed him outside. Always the servant, Cutter. Always wanting to please. He was a tactical genius, but he could never see the big picture.

Ulric turned and smiled at Cutter. The army veteran was a giant of a man with a forehead that bulged like those on the Beluga whales at SeaWorld. He had the physique of an alligator wrestler, and a craggy face that betrayed years on dusty battlefields. Yet, he now had the downtrodden appearance of a mutt that had disappointed its master.

"You think I'm upset?" Ulric said. "On the contrary. I'm elated."

"Elated, sir?"

"Of course. Look out there and tell me what you see."

Cutter paused, as if it were a trick question. "LA, sir," he said firmly.

"Right. You see a city. But it's a city rife with crime, misery, greed, unhappiness, debauchery, wickedness. All the sin the world holds can be found in that city. And this is one of the richest cities in one of the richest countries on earth. Now take its woes and multiply them a millionfold. That microcosm of sin is magnified beyond belief. Beyond reckoning. It staggers the

94

mind that for all the great things that we have accomplished as a species, we have done even more to debase ourselves to such a low level. Do you know what I see?"

"No, sir."

"When I look at that city, I see a blank slate. I see a new beginning for humankind. It's just one of the thousands of places we will be able to reclaim for the righteous among us once the New World is upon us. And now I know my vision will be a reality. Our demonstration was a success. Our people will believe. They will see that it can be done, that I have delivered on my promise to them."

"What about the airplane? It was supposed to crash into the ocean when it overflew Honolulu. Now that it's lying in the desert, they'll have recovery teams combing through the wreckage."

"As you said, a minor setback."

"But the device may have survived the crash. We expected it would be lost at sea. If the device is recovered, the evidence could lead back to us."

Ulric had to admit the remains of the device could be a problem. He was the chairman and chief technology officer of Ulric Pharmaceuticals, whose revolutionary methods for vaccine production had taken the market by storm, lifting its stock and Ulric's net worth into the stratosphere. Of course, taking a few shortcuts on FDA approvals and greasing the right palms made things go more smoothly. His combination of money and connections in the medical industry had made construction of the device possible, but some of the components had been highly specialized. There was a slim possibility they could lead the investigators back to Ulric Pharmaceuticals.

The carefully orchestrated planning for Ulric's New World operation was three years in the making, and Friday was a critical date. There was no way to shorten the timeline, and Ulric couldn't take the chance that they might be compromised at this critical juncture. They had to get the device back.

"Can you retrieve it?" Ulric asked.

"Yes, but it'll take some time to infiltrate the crash site. By that time, they'll have taken all of the luggage to a central facility for sorting and analysis. It will be easier and cleaner to find it there. That is, if the device wasn't destroyed."

"We can pray that it was."

"Of course."

"And the other matter?"

"We have a problem there as well."

"Oh?" Ulric hadn't heard about this. He

assumed it had been settled.

When he'd been informed that Sam Watson, one of his star scientists, had discovered their plans, the first priority had been to make sure he didn't pass on this information to anyone else. Watson had been a faithful member of the Church of the Holy Waters, but he hadn't been in Ulric's innermost circle, the only ones who knew the entire plan. He must have grown suspicious about the true nature of his work and broke into some key files that contained details of the operation. Security discovered the leak, but Watson fled. He didn't escape with any hard evidence, but he knew enough to be a danger. Since his work was essentially finished, Ulric had no more use for him and ordered his termination.

But before Ulric's security team could carry out the order, Watson had phoned someone. What was said, they didn't know, but Ulric was sure it wasn't the police, or Watson would have been in their custody within hours. Still, he could have mentioned something critical. They couldn't take him out until they knew whom he had spoken to, so they kept him under surveillance and waited until the meeting.

Watson's assassination went off as planned, but he managed to convey something to the woman, Dilara Kenner, who had escaped after she narrowly avoided being killed by the SUV. They lost her trail until a search of airline databases showed her reservation with Wolverine Helicopters in St. John's, Newfoundland. At first, her trip to an oil platform in the middle of the Atlantic was puzzling. Searching the names of the people on the rig registered with the Canadian Coast Guard, they discovered who she might be meeting on board. Tyler Locke, a one-time contract employee of Ulric's who had been more trouble than his reputation had been worth.

Once Ulric knew Locke was involved, it made sense. They had to stop her before she could talk to him. Killing her outright would have raised too many questions, especially by Locke, so they'd had to make it look like an accident.

"She's not dead?" Ulric asked.

Cutter shook his head.

"What happened?"

"The explosive on the helicopter wasn't powerful enough. My men on the yacht set it off, but it only damaged the engine. The passengers got out before it sank. The standby ship was gone, but according to radio broadcasts we intercepted, Tyler Locke used one of the free fall lifeboats to save them. No way they would have survived until a Coast Guard helicopter made it out there."

"Tyler Locke. Still can't keep himself out of trouble. Well, now we have a much bigger problem. We have to assume she's told him what she knows. Is the yacht still in place?"

"They're waiting for my orders."

"What are our options?" Cutter always had a backup plan, and he didn't disappoint.

"We already have a plan in place. My men are prepared to take out the entire rig."

"It has to look like an accident," Ulric said. "Tyler's murder would open up even more questions."

"It'll look like negligence on the part of the oil company. With over two hundred deaths, a billion-dollar oil platform destroyed, and oil flowing into the North Atlantic, they'll have their hands full. A full-scale investigation will take weeks."

Ulric smiled and looked out at the smog, which would soon be a distant memory.

"Excellent," he said. "By the time they find out what really happened, it will be far too late to stop us."

TEN

While they waited for their food, Tyler listened intently to Dilara's story about Sam Watson's death and her subsequent car crash, stopping her only to clarify. She wasn't lying, that much he was sure of. Which left him with what? That either she was the victim of a bizarre set of co-incidences, or that he was somehow con-nected to some vast conspiracy bent on kill-ing this lone woman. Neither option seemed likely, so he withheld his opinion.

The cheeseburgers arrived still steaming hot from the mess grill. Dilara and Tyler interrupted their discussion to dig into them.

"This is amazing," Dilara said after one bite. "Am I delusional from the cold, or is this the best burger I've ever had?"

"Gotta keep the workers happy, so the ingredients are top-notch. They're out here three weeks at a time. The company would have a riot on their hands if they served crummy food."

Dilara chewed in silence. The food and coffee brought a brightness back to her eyes.

"You didn't take the bait about me being delusional," she said. "You think I am, don't you?"

"Honestly, I don't know what to think," Tyler said. "You don't seem delusional to me, but then again, I haven't known you that long."

"Are you going to help me?"

"I'm not sure what you're asking me to do."

"I'm not either, but I know people are trying to kill me and that the secret to this whole thing will be revealed if we can find Noah's Ark. You're involved somehow. Sam was sure of it."

Tyler put up his right hand. "I swear I don't know where Noah's Ark is. Scout's honor." He couldn't help but be slightly sarcastic. Or maybe excessively sarcastic. He wasn't a good judge of his own level of sarcasm.

"Believe me, I get that. But whoever tried to kill me doesn't want me to talk to you. There must be a reason."

Tyler sighed. She wouldn't give up until he gave her something. "I'll have my guys

101

look into Coleman Engineering, but I have a job to finish here, and then I have to be in Europe in two days for another job."

"You have to cancel it."

"Listen, I'd like to help you —"

"What about the helicopter? You said yourself that the crash seemed odd."

Tyler shrugged. "It could have been some kind of explosive device, but it also could have been a fractured turbine blade or some other mechanical problem. The water here is over a thousand feet deep. It'll take weeks, if not months, to recover the helicopter."

"We don't have that kind of time! It's already Saturday night. Whatever is going to kill billions will be set in motion this coming Friday."

"Look, you're welcome to stay on board as long as you need. I've already okayed it with the rig manager. But if there's no connection with Coleman, there's nothing else I can do. You'll have to take it up with the police."

For the first time, discouragement crept into Dilara's voice. "I already tried that in LA. They said Sam died of a heart attack, and they said the SUV that slammed into me was probably just a drunk driver."

"Maybe he was."

It was her turn to be sarcastic. About

medium level. "So I see a man die in front of me, I get into a car accident that could have killed me, and then I barely escape a helicopter crash with my life, all in the span of three days? Come on. I can see you don't believe that."

Tyler had to admit: this woman was tenacious. "I've never been a fan of coincidences, but I've seen them before. Still, that's a nasty run of bad luck."

"I'm not planning to play blackjack anytime soon. I just need some help."

Tyler popped the last bite of his burger into his mouth and waited to speak until he'd finished it.

"Okay, I'll check it out myself," he said, "but I can't promise anything. I'll talk to John Coleman tomorrow. Maybe he knows something about this."

"Thank you," Dilara said, obviously relieved to have someone else on her side. Tyler was interested to hear what Coleman had to say, but he didn't expect much. His guess was that Sam Watson had been wrong about Tyler. Perhaps it was John Coleman who was involved in all of this.

Dilara finished her burger, and the fatigue finally overtook her. Tyler escorted her back to her cabin and told her he'd let her know the minute he heard anything, but since it was a Saturday, he didn't expect any information until at least the next morning. Then he retired to his own cabin. Tyler wanted to get some information about Coleman before he contacted him, so he sent an e-mail back to Aiden MacKenna at Gordian's Seattle headquarters, which was four and a half hours behind Newfoundland Time. After it went out over the rig's wi-fi system, Tyler passed out on his bunk, exhausted from the day's events.

At 1:15 in the morning, a chime from his laptop woke him. Feeling rested from a few hours of sleep, he turned the computer toward him and saw that he had an instant message. It was from Aiden, Gordian's top expert in information retrieval. Tyler often used his services to salvage electronic data from disaster sites, but Aiden was a renaissance computer whiz and could tackle almost anything Tyler threw his way. Tyler wasn't surprised to see that he was checking his e-mail at eight-forty-five on a Saturday night.

Tyler, my man, I've got your answer. You awake? the message said.

I am now. Where are you? Tyler replied.

At home, playing Halo and shooting Red Bull with some nerds from the office. I'm kicking ass, BTW. I would have answered you sooner, but I just saw your message.

What did you find out?

You haven't heard from John Coleman in a while, have you?

Not for six months. Why?

He's dead. Freak accident.

Dead? John Coleman was only in his fifties and seemed to be in perfect health.

What happened to him? Tyler typed.

Instead of a reply, the computer window said, *Connection lost.* Great timing. Just when they were getting to the good part.

Tyler checked his connection to Scotia One's wi-fi network, but it was showing 100 percent. He tried to pull up Google, but all he got was an error page. That meant the rig's connection to the Internet was down.

Scotia One was equipped with a satellite antenna that served as its connection to the outside world. The workers on board could use it to surf the Web and send e-mails when they weren't working. It also served as a backup to the platform's radio. There could be only two explanations for why the connection was down. Either there was some kind of internal glitch, or the antenna itself was disabled.

Tyler looked out the window. The fog was still heavy, but through a brief opening in the murk he could see that the sea was

105

relatively calm. The conditions made a mechanical failure unlikely. With no storm to damage the equipment, the antenna should be intact. It must have been some kind of electrical or software problem.

He picked up the phone and called the control room. It was answered by Frank Hobson. Tyler remembered him as a timid man with black horn-rimmed glasses who always worked the graveyard shift alone.

"Hi, Tyler," he said in a reedy voice. "What can I do for you?"

"Frank, I'm having some trouble with the Internet. When will it be back up?"

"I didn't even know it was down. You're probably the only one up at this hour using it. Let me check." Tyler heard tapping on a keyboard. "Yup, it's out here, too."

"Can you isolate the problem? I was messaging someone and got cut off."

Hobson paused. More tapping. "The software checks out. Maybe it's a mechanical problem. Might be the satellite dish. I'll have to call someone to look at it."

"I can do that for you." Tyler was awake now and eager to get the rest of the story from Aiden, so he thought he might as well get some air.

"You know where it is?"

"Yeah, Grant and I were working on it a

106

couple of days ago when we were trying to diagnose that electrical problem. If it looks like an electrical glitch, I'll haul Grant out of bed."

"Thanks."

"No problem."

Tyler hung up, stood, and stretched. He threw on his jeans and jacket and headed outside.

The night air was crisp, and the ever-present smell of oil flowed over him with the breeze. Even this late, workers roamed the rig, oil production being a twenty-four-hour job. Visibility was limited to thirty feet. The screech of some sort of grinding tool pierced his ears every few seconds.

Tyler stepped onto the catwalk that led to the top of the habitat module, where the satellite dish was located. Ahead of him, barely visible through the haze, Tyler could make out the figure of a man dressed in a black jumpsuit disappearing into the mist toward the lifeboat evacuation stairs. He had something slung over his shoulder, but Tyler couldn't make out what it was before he was gone. Maybe he had already fixed the dish. Tyler called out twice, but the man didn't respond. Must not have heard him over the grinding noise.

Tyler reached the stairs and climbed up to

the antenna cluster that formed Scotia One's communications link. The satellite dish was about six feet across, pointed at a geosynchronous satellite, and the radio antenna was thirty feet tall, with plenty of power to reach St. John's two hundred miles away. Neither was damaged.

He trailed the wires leading from the dish, and an iciness knotted his stomach when he saw the problem. The wires had been cut and a section removed. Whoever had done it was skilled. Tyler followed the wires from the radio mast and found the same thing. The wires ended in a control box, which had been smashed. Someone didn't want them in touch with the outside world.

Tyler could think of a few reasons why someone would go to all that trouble, and none of them had a happy ending. He rushed down to the control room and burst through the door, startling Hobson, the only man inside. His thick glasses magnified his eyes to a cartoonish size.

"We have an emergency," Tyler said curtly. "Someone cut the wires to the antennas and destroyed the control junction."

Hobson leaped out of his chair. "What? Who would do that?"

"Get Finn and tell him there's an intruder on the platform."

"An intruder?" Hobson said, recoiling at the thought.

"I saw him a few minutes ago. At the time I thought he was a rig worker wearing an outfit I hadn't seen before, a black jumpsuit." The intruder must have known it wouldn't take much time for the crew to discover the destroyed equipment, which meant he wasn't going to be on board much longer. Tyler had to catch him before he got away, and for that he needed Grant's help. For all Tyler knew, there were multiple intruders, and they were heavily armed. That notion disturbed Tyler, but it would terrify Hobson, so he didn't mention it.

"How could anyone get on board?" Hobson asked.

"Maybe he climbed up. Doesn't matter. Before you call Finn, get Grant Westfield and tell him to meet me at the lifeboats. Quietly. You know his cabin number?"

Hobson nodded. "Should I activate the alarm?"

"No. That'll tip off the intruder that we know he's here." Tyler needed to find out why this guy would want to cut off their communications. He wished he could get his hands on a gun, but an oil platform was the last place where they would let him bring his trusty 9 mm Glock, and they certainly didn't stock shotguns on board.

He had to hope he and Grant would be able to handle the situation. In a battle, Tyler preferred staggering force against an overmatched opponent. If there were two armed intruders, he and Grant could take them. They had been up against worse odds than that before. But if there were three or more, they could have real problems, so some kind of weapon might make a difference.

Hobson snatched up the phone and dialed. Tyler went to the door, but before leaving, he said, "Frank, tell Grant to stop at the toolroom and pick up two big fat wrenches."

ELEVEN

Tyler crept down the stairs until the lifeboats were in view. He felt naked. No gun. No situational intelligence. No plan. Although he could improvise with the best of them, he'd rather put together a well-thought-out plan of attack that — like all army operations — went to hell *after* the mission started. Instead, he'd already skipped to the second part, which made the hair on the back of his neck stand at attention.

Through the fog, he saw the man in the black jumpsuit hunched over the hatch of the rightmost lifeboat, attaching something to it. He was in his thirties, dirty blond, medium build, no visible tattoos. A silenced Heckler & Koch MP5 submachine gun hung from his shoulder by a strap. He seemed to be alone. Visibility was now over thirty feet, and a lot of open space separated him from Tyler. It would be almost impossible to sneak up on him.

Tyler felt a tap on his shoulder. Fists up, he whirled around to find Grant crouching behind him. For a big man, Grant was as light on his feet as Fred Astaire. Tyler was glad Grant was on his side.

Grant was carrying two heavy pipe wrenches, both two feet long. Big enough to be good weapons, but not so large that they'd be unwieldy. Good man. Grant handed one to Tyler, who rested it on his shoulder.

Bad guy, Tyler signed to Grant using American Sign Language. *We need a distraction.*

What did you have in mind? Grant signed back.

Tyler's grandmother was deaf and had taught him ASL soon after he learned to talk. When he joined his combat engineering unit, Tyler saw how useful it could be in situations requiring stealth and added it to their normal repertoire of tactical hand gestures. Grant had picked it up quickly.

I just need a few seconds, Tyler signed. *Get around to the other staircase and act like you're talking to someone.* At least he now had a plan. Not the most elegant plan, but the intruder wouldn't expect that he'd been discovered, so it should work.

Give me thirty seconds, Grant signed and

went back upstairs. Tyler got a firm grip on the wrench.

The intruder finished his task at the lifeboats and moved to the railing, where Tyler for the first time saw a claw hooked to the side of the rig. The intruder started to climb over the railing, then stopped. Tyler heard Grant stomp down the other staircase, his voice animatedly raised in some non-existent argument. The intruder turned to see who was coming.

He looked at the railing again, as if considering whether he could make a quick getaway. Then he looked back at the staircase and seemed to decide against it. The submachine gun came off his shoulder and pointed in Grant's direction. He raised the weapon to his eye and waited. With the intruder's attention distracted, Tyler saw his chance.

He padded down the stairs, careful not to make a sound, and tiptoed up to the intruder. When he was still six feet behind the intruder, Tyler raised the wrench over his head, but he hadn't thought to tighten its jaw. The loose mechanism rattled with an audible clink. Tyler froze, but it was too late. His plan had already gone to hell.

The intruder spun around. Tyler, his surprise attack up in smoke, rushed him.

The intruder pulled the trigger as he swung the gun toward Tyler, intending to cut him down in a scythe of bullets. Nine-millimeter ammunition ricocheted off the surrounding metal. Shell casings rattled off the grating. Tyler was close enough to smell the gunpowder puffing through the silencer's baffles.

Before the intruder could get the barrel of the gun all the way around, Tyler parried with the wrench. The muzzle was so close to his head that he could feel the hot gases singe his hair. Even silenced, the gun was roaring like a jackhammer in his ear; without the silencer, Tyler would have been deaf for a week.

Tyler knocked the gun aside. The intruder lost his grip, and it dangled from his shoulder. Tyler tried to grab the weapon, but it dropped to the grating. The intruder kicked it, and it fell over the side to the sea below.

So far, the encounter had lasted all of three seconds. Grant by now had raced to help Tyler. With the wrench, he swung at the intruder from behind, but the man saw Grant at the last second and ducked to take the impact with his left shoulder. That move alone told Tyler the intruder was something special, probably ex-military, but it didn't keep the bone from cracking. The intruder howled with pain.

The force of Grant's hit threw both the intruder and Tyler to the railing. The intruder's right hand dropped to his side and retrieved something from his pocket. Tyler expected a knife or a pistol, but the intruder held a cylinder with a button on the end. A detonator.

Before Tyler or Grant could wrestle it from him, the intruder pushed the button. Bright flames gushed on the hatches of the four remaining lifeboats. Tyler and Grant tackled him to the catwalk grating and wrapped their arms over their heads to shield themselves from the heat. The intruder struggled, but Grant put an end to that with an elbow to the gut. After a few seconds, the flames died down.

They pinned down the intruder's arms and legs, but he no longer resisted.

"Who are you?" Tyler demanded. "What are you doing here?"

Despite the pain, the intruder smiled. "God only knows." Then he bit down hard.

"Poison!" Grant yelled. He jerked the intruder's mouth open and pulled out the capsule, but it was too late. In seconds, the man was dead. Cyanide.

In the sudden silence, Tyler heard a motor revving below them. He went to the railing but couldn't see the boat, which sounded like a Zodiac, speed away. Tyler noted that it seemed headed toward the yacht he had seen earlier.

Grant wasn't breathing hard like Tyler was, but he could see the fire in Grant's eyes. His friend was juiced.

"What the hell is going on?" Grant said.

Tyler shook his head. "Don't know. But whatever it is, we better find out quick. I don't think what he came here to do is finished yet. You search him. I'll take a look at the lifeboats."

Tyler kept his distance as he inspected the damage. The hinges and latches on all of the lifeboats were still glowing, melted shut by an incendiary, probably Thermate-TH3. There was no way to get into them now. From a professional standpoint, Tyler admired the guy's work. Fast, efficient, effective. On a personal level, Tyler wanted to wring his neck, not only for wrecking the lifeboats, but also for killing himself before answering Tyler's questions.

"Why go to all this trouble to disable the lifeboats?" Tyler said.

"I think I know why," Grant said. "Quick. You need to look at this."

Tyler turned and saw Grant holding a large plastic case.

"What is it?" Tyler said.

Grant opened it. The inside of the case was lined with foam. There were three slots in the foam. All three were empty.

"Smell," Grant said, holding it up. Tyler sniffed the foam insert. He recognized the smell immediately. The chemical DMNB and a hint of motor oil. The odor reminded him of his army days. His stomach did a somersault. Suddenly the cheeseburger wasn't sitting so well anymore.

"At least now we know," he said.

"Think they used timers?" Grant asked, his customary humor gone. So was Tyler's.

He nodded. "Got to. Remote detonators would be too unreliable and might be set off by equipment on board the rig."

If the intruder had used timers, he would want to make sure he was off the platform before . . .

Tyler reached down and picked up the dead man's wrist. As he feared, the intruder's digital watch was counting down.

"We've got exactly thirteen minutes left to find them," Tyler said, synchronizing his own watch.

DMNB and motor oil were the volatile components of composition C-4, a plastic explosive manufactured in the United States and used by the military. Somewhere on the

117

oil platform, the dead intruder had planted three bombs.

TWELVE

Leaving the dead man behind, Tyler and Grant bolted for the control room. Tyler couldn't help sneaking a few peeks at the timer ticking inexorably down on his watch. He almost tripped during one glance, which reminded him that he hadn't disarmed a bomb since his army service. When they did find the bombs, one stupid little mistake like that, one moment's distraction, and he wouldn't have time to say "oops" before he was blown into tiny pieces. He had to stay focused.

In the control room, they found Finn badgering Hobson, who had his head turned to avoid the spittle showering his face. When Finn saw them enter, he let up on Hobson and shouted at Tyler.

"What's all this about the antenna wires being cut, Locke? And what's going on with the lifeboats?"

"The lifeboats are crippled," Tyler said.

He looked at his watch again. "We've now got exactly twelve minutes and twenty-five seconds to find three bombs somewhere on this rig."

Finn nearly tore his hair out. "Bombs? Are you serious?" Tyler could sympathize. First a helicopter crash, now this, all in one day. It was a ridiculous coincidence. Then it hit him. It wasn't a coincidence at all. This was about Dilara. Someone wanted her dead, just like she'd claimed, and now Tyler felt like an idiot for not believing her.

"There's a corpse on the lifeboat deck," Grant said. "That serious enough for you?" He showed Finn the backpack he'd taken from the intruder and pointed to the three empty slots in the case.

"You have got to be kidding me," Finn said, his face drained of color. He turned to Tyler. "Okay. You're the bomb expert. What do we do?"

The weight of responsibility came crashing down on Tyler's shoulders, but the army didn't spend hundreds of thousands of dollars training him to be a captain for nothing. They got their money's worth. He took a deep breath. Precision, calm, decisiveness.

"First," he said, "muster everyone to the safety block." The safety block, located under the helicopter pad, was the last-ditch safe haven for those who couldn't make it to the lifeboats. It had blast resistant walls and a separate air feed.

"Done," Finn said and slammed his hand on a huge red button. Three short horn blasts blared across the rig, followed by the sound of a woman's voice.

"This is not a drill. Proceed to the safety block on deck seven. This is not a drill."

"Second," Tyler said, "close the sea line valves."

"I'm not authorized to do that unless there's a fire," Finn said.

"In a few minutes, there will be unless we find those bombs."

Tyler could see Finn mentally weighing the consequences of taking that action. Closing the valves that controlled the flow of oil from all of the rig's well heads to the ocean-floor pipeline was a major decision. It would take days to start production again once they were closed.

"You're sure there are bombs?" Finn asked.

"Positive," Tyler said. He had detonated and defused so many explosives in his life that the smell of C-4 was as recognizable to him as antiseptic was to a doctor. "And you don't want to find out the hard way that I'm good at my job." Another glance at his watch. "We're at eleven minutes and forty-five seconds."

Finn reluctantly nodded at Hobson. Hobson punched the emergency stop button, which shut off the sea line valves.

"They're shut down," Hobson said, "but we're still getting gas from Scotia Two. With the radio down, we can't reach them to tell them to shut it off." Natural gas from Scotia Two was fed through Scotia One and then on to the pipeline to the coast.

Now Tyler understood why the intruder had first put communications out of action. It would not only make any rescue calls impossible to send, but it would also make them unable to notify Scotia Two to shut off the gas supply. Any fires that were started by the explosions would be fed by three tons of natural gas per minute, reducing the entire rig to slag.

The disabled lifeboats were the crucial part of the intruder's plan. He wanted to make sure no one would survive. Anyone who didn't die in the initial blasts or resulting fires would be killed by the fall overboard or by hypothermia in the cold North Atlantic. It would look like an accident to investigators when it was all over.

The intruder knew exactly how to destroy the oil platform so that every single person on board would die, and Tyler realized that he might have stumbled into some luck. Knowing the intruder's goal might be the key to finding the bombs before they detonated.

"This platform is huge," Finn said. "How can we possibly find three bombs in less than twelve minutes?"

Tyler didn't respond. Time slowed as he tried to put himself in the head of someone wanting to destroy Scotia One. It was something he had done many times in the army when he was looking for improvised explosive devices in Iraq. Try to think like the enemy. Where would Tyler put the bombs if this were his demolition mission?

Another glance. Eleven minutes and ten seconds.

"Okay," Tyler said. "All we have time for is a targeted search. We'll take walkie-talkies. Grant, you check the Scotia Two gas line, starting with the main valve. If that guy knew that we couldn't shut down Two's feed, that would be the best place to start a fire. Finn, the second one is probably at the pumping machinery for the firefighting system. He'd want to disable that at the same time."

"What about the third bomb?" Grant said.

"I'll take the safety block. If I wanted to

kill everyone on board, that's where I'd put it."

"But I just sent everyone there!" Finn yelled.

"If the third bomb isn't there, that's the safest place on the rig. If it is there, it won't matter where people go."

Finn shook his head as he distributed the walkie-talkies.

"Let me know when you find it," Tyler said to Finn, "but don't touch it. It may be booby-trapped." He took off his watch and tossed it to Hobson, who bobbled it like it was white-hot.

"What's this for?" he said.

"Call out on the walkie-talkie at every minute mark," Tyler said. It would keep them all informed about the time left, but in reality, Tyler just didn't want the distraction of looking at his watch anymore. "And when you get down to four minutes, head to the safety block. You don't want to be here if the bombs go off."

"All . . . all right," Hobson stuttered.

Tyler followed Grant and Finn out of the control room and then sprinted toward the safety block. Masses of people were already herding in that direction, slowing him down.

"Coming through!" he yelled. "Make a hole!"

124

He pushed past one woman and saw that it was Dilara. She looked bone-tired and terrified.

"What's happening?" she asked, trying to keep up with him.

"We have a situation," Tyler said, deliberately not using the word *bomb* for fear of panicking those around him. But Dilara was persistent and latched on to his arm.

"What kind of situation?"

"Can't say."

"It's them, isn't it? They've sabotaged the rig." A few passersby murmured in response.

Tyler pulled her aside and put his lips next to her ear. "Look, I believe you now," he whispered. "There are people trying to kill you. And now it looks like they're trying to kill the rest of us with you."

"Oh my God!" she said loudly, drawing more stares. "I'm right?"

"Keep quiet! The last thing we need is a panic. There are bombs on the platform."

"Bo—" Dilara began to shout before Tyler clamped his hand over her mouth.

"Just stay with me. I might need an extra pair of eyes to find it." She still looked scared, but she nodded, and Tyler released her.

Hobson's trembling voice came over the

walkie-talkie. "Ten minutes."

Tyler led her past the others streaming toward the safety block. The block's ordinary purpose was as a massive storage room underneath the helicopter deck, but it doubled as a safe haven in emergencies. Blast walls surrounded the room, and the door was heavy-gauge steel. The safety block was fed by an air system that would protect those inside from smoke emanating from fires on the rig. The room was so well protected, Tyler was sure a bomb would be inside it.

More than a hundred people already crammed the safety block. The room was big enough to fit every worker on the platform. If the C-4 went off inside here, the effects would be catastrophic.

"Start on that side and work around to me," Tyler said to Dilara. "I'll take the other side."

"What am I looking for?"

"It'll be about the size and shape of a brick. Check inside any drawers or lockers."

"What if I find it?"

"Just call me over. And for God's sake, don't touch it."

"I'm not insane," Dilara said, and began throwing open locker doors.

Tyler quickly ran his eyes from floor to

126

ceiling and over every piece of stacked equipment. The intruder wouldn't have moved anything to set it. He'd simply choose an out-of-sight location because he didn't expect a thorough search. Storage lockers abounded, containing all kinds of survival suits and other safety equipment, and Tyler felt sure that was where the intruder would have hidden the bomb. He rooted through each one, tearing everything out.

His walkie-talkie squawked.

"Ty, this is Grant. I found one, right next to the main gas line."

"What does it look like?" Tyler said into the walkie-talkie as he continued to search.

"Black, rectangular, twelve by four by four inches. LED readout matching our dead man's timer. The detonator casing is wrapped around the C-4."

That wasn't good. It would make the bomb trickier to disarm.

"Mercury switch?" Tyler said. Some bombs were activated by a motion sensor.

"Uh . . . nine minutes, guys," Hobson said.

"Thanks, Frank," Tyler said. "You're doing great."

"Negative on the mercury switch," Grant said. "He couldn't have placed it where it is and then armed it. Guess he thought vibrations might set it off prematurely. It's just lying there, hidden under a pipe. No attachment to the rig."

That was good. Meant it could be moved. But they couldn't simply dump it over the side of the platform. The wave action might land it on a feed pipe, causing a gas explosion underneath the platform, or the bomb might fall next to one of the support pillars. If one of those gave way, the entire rig might topple into the ocean. Neither was a pleasant thought.

"Disposal?" Grant said.

"I'm thinking about it. Go help Finn find the second one."

"On my way."

Tyler continued searching as fast as he could. He was halfway along the wall when Hobson called out, "Eight minutes." Tyler cursed under his breath and kept going. Maybe giving Hobson the watch was a bad idea. Then he heard Dilara yell to him from across the room.

"Tyler, come here!"

He rushed over, drawing attention to the area. By this time, people had already seen Dilara's find and started speculating about what it was, but Tyler didn't have time to calm them down.

"I think I found it," Dilara said, pointing

at the object.

It was just as Grant had described. The C-4 was hidden behind some gas masks on the top shelf of a storage locker. After a cursory inspection, he couldn't see any sign of a mercury switch. He pulled the bomb out to examine it.

"Seven minutes left," Hobson said. The calls seemed to be coming faster, but Tyler tried to ignore it and focus on the bomb.

He hadn't seen anything so sophisticated since he'd left the army. The brick of C-4 was enough to destroy the entire safety block. The detonator was clamped to the top of the brick and wrapped around the explosive. If he tried to remove it, the bomb might explode. By prying open the case, Tyler might be able to disarm it, but he couldn't disarm all three bombs in less than seven minutes.

He got another call on the walkie-talkie from Grant.

"Ty, I'm with Finn. We found the second one. It was under the main diesel generator for the firefighting system right where you thought it would be."

"Good. I've got the third one."

"Disarm them?"

"Oh my God!" Hobson said. "Only six minutes now!"

129

"Not enough time," Tyler said.

The only other choice was to get rid of the bombs. He had to figure out a way to get them far away from the rig. Then he realized the means had been staring him in the face.

"Grant," Tyler said into the walkie-talkie, "you've still got the case?"

"The first two are already in it. They won't rattle around in there."

"Good. I've got an idea."

THIRTEEN

Tyler told Grant to meet him at the lifeboat station with the two bombs. Then he searched for a heavy metal bar, preferably an ax, something that he could use as an impact tool.

"An ax!" he yelled to the crowd. "A crowbar! Anything heavy!"

A man in a blue jumpsuit and tool belt answered him. "How about a hammer?" he said. He raised a handheld sledge and handed it to Tyler.

"Perfect," Tyler said. He turned to Dilara. "Stay here."

"But . . ."

He leaned over and whispered, "If this bomb blows up, the safest place on the rig is right where you're standing."

She wasn't comforted. Her face was etched with fear.

Tyler smiled. "Don't worry. I've got a plan."

That seemed to help. She didn't protest further.

With the sledge in one hand and the bomb in the other, Tyler flew through the exit and down the stairs. One flight down, he heard Hobson's voice bleat from the walkie-talkie on his belt. "Five minutes!"

Tyler reached his target, the chemical storage room. He threw open the door to see shelves lined with chemical bottles. Glass, plastic, and metal containers were haphazardly stacked in no discernible order. He ran his fingers over the labels, searching for a bottle of acetone, the chemical in fingernail polish remover. On the rig, it was used as a heavy-duty degreaser.

"Four minutes!" Hobson said. "I'm heading to the safety block!"

Tyler was beginning to think his plan might be screwed. He saw bottles of ammonia, benzene, hydrochloric acid, ethylene glycol, but no acetone. One of those other chemicals might work, but the only one he was sure of was acetone, and he couldn't find it in this mess. He'd seen plane crash sites that were neater.

If he heard Hobson call out "three minutes" before he found the acetone, he'd have to take a chance with the benzene or ammonia.

Tyler started shoving containers aside, looking in the back rows. He knew it was here. Then he saw a capital *A* on a plastic sixteen-ounce bottle. He twisted it around and saw the word ACETONE. He breathed easier now that it was in his hand.

"Three minutes left!"

Tyler stuffed the acetone into his pocket and took off for the stairs, the grating clanging under his feet.

The lifeboat station was five levels below the safety block. He made it there just as Hobson said, "Two minutes." Grant and Finn were waiting for him.

"Glad you could make it," Grant said cheerily, but Tyler could see the faint lines of tension around his eyes.

Although Finn's face was white, he still had some of his bluster. "Where the hell have you been?"

"In your moronically organized chemical storage room," Tyler said as he placed the third bomb in the case. Grant snapped it shut.

"Now what?" Grant asked.

"We're going to put the bombs in one of the lifeboats and launch it." The boats could be launched from the outside as well as inside. He handed the sledge to Grant and removed the acetone bottle from his pocket.

"In one of the lifeboats?" Finn protested. "But the doors are welded shut. How do we get the case inside?"

"Through the cupola window."

"One minute!" Hobson shouted. This was getting a lot closer than Tyler wanted.

"The windows are made of polycarbonate, genius," Finn said. "They're unbreakable."

From his belt, Tyler plucked his Leatherman tool — a sort of Swiss Army knife on steroids — and opened the saw blade, which he dragged across the window to score the surface.

"Normally, it *is* unbreakable," Tyler said as he unscrewed the top of the acetone bottle and carefully poured the contents along the top of the small port cupola window. "But when you treat it with acetone, polycarbonate crystallizes."

He dropped the bottle and smeared the acetone over the entire window with his hand to make sure it was covered with the liquid. Tyler took the hammer from Grant and counted to ten, giving the acetone time to be absorbed through the scoring marks he'd made.

"What are you waiting for?" Finn shouted.

Tyler ignored him and kept counting down. On one, Tyler raised the hammer and

134

swung it with all his strength at the window. The pane of polycarbonate shattered like glass into the lifeboat.

"Voilà," Tyler said more calmly than he felt. He tossed the case through the window.

"Thirty seconds!"

Tyler took hold of one of the two launch levers on the outside of the lifeboat. Grant grabbed the other.

He nodded at Grant. "Ready . . . now!"

They both yanked simultaneously. The clamps released, and the lifeboat began its slide down the rails. It accelerated and then dropped into space. After falling gracefully for two seconds, it hit the water with a tremendous splash.

The entire boat disappeared beneath the water. For a moment, Tyler couldn't see it as he peered through a break in the fog. The lifeboat resurfaced again a hundred yards from where it had gone under, and Tyler breathed easier. He had specifically chosen that window because it was the smallest. No doubt the lifeboat had taken on water, but it wasn't enough to sink it. The forward momentum from its slide down the rails continued to push it away from the rig at ten knots.

"Behind the lifeboat!" Tyler yelled. They had no sooner retreated to the safety of a huge lifeboat when a tremendous roar ripped the air. The rig was briefly lit by a flame shooting hundreds of feet into the air. Bits of orange debris rained down around them.

When the hail of lifeboat hull abated, Tyler got up and looked around the side. Fragments of burning fiberglass and metal littered the sea, but no large pieces of the lifeboat were left, and all traces disappeared as the fog descended again.

The intruder hadn't been playing around. Any one of those bombs would have been strong enough to blow up half the platform and ignite a blaze that would have been impossible to put out.

"Well," Tyler said as the adrenaline drained from his system, "that was interesting." He leaned back against the railing, suddenly exhausted.

"That may be the biggest understatement I've ever heard," Finn said. "You must have ice in your veins. I nearly crapped my pants." He pointed at the dead man still sprawled on the catwalk. "Who is that guy? A terrorist?"

Tyler stared at the body. "I don't think so," he said. "Someone seems to want Dr. Kenner dead. And I'm guessing they want me dead now, too."

"Why?" Grant said.

"That's what we're going to find out."

"That was a hell of a close thing. That guy sure knew what he was doing."

"True, but he made two mistakes."

"Which were?"

"First," Tyler said, "he shouldn't have tried to kill me. Gives me a personal stake in Dr. Kenner's problem. It also just pisses me off."

"If it makes you feel any better," Grant said, "he didn't finish the job. You're still alive."

"That, my friend, was his second mistake."

FOURTEEN

It took two hours for one of the rig's electricians to rewire the radio antenna, but because of the destroyed junction box, the satellite linkup wouldn't be fixed until Sunday evening, which was when the fog was supposed to lift. With Grant's help, Tyler used the time to complete Gordian's consulting work on the platform. The job kept his mind occupied, since he couldn't continue the conversation with Aiden MacKenna and find out more about Coleman until the Internet hookup was back online. While Tyler and Grant worked, Dilara could only wait in her cabin and stew.

At 10 P.M. the satellite connection was finally repaired, allowing Tyler to rearrange his travel plans. At the same time, the fog dispersed, and a helicopter left from St. John's, bound for Scotia One. When it took off from the oil platform, Tyler planned to be on it with Grant and Dilara for the return to Newfoundland. Gordian's private jet was en route from New York and would meet them at St. John's to take them back to company headquarters in Seattle, where he could investigate the incidents of the last few days. Since the rig was in international waters, the oil company would be responsible for its own investigation. In the meantime, they were having new hatches rushed from the manufacturer to make the lifeboats functional again.

His work on the rig done, Tyler turned his focus back to the bizarre incidents of the past day. He joined Grant and Dilara to wait in his cabin for the helicopter to arrive. He had to find out why mild-mannered archaeologist Dilara Kenner had drawn two attempts on her life in the span of twelve hours.

As Tyler expected, the intruder had carried no identification. The body was taken to cold storage after Tyler had taken digital photos of the man's face and close-ups of his thumb and index fingerprints. The wi-fi system was now up and running, as were the telephones. He loaded the photos onto his laptop and e-mailed them to Aiden MacKenna so that he could start tracking down who this guy was. Tyler spoke with Aiden while Dilara, who was now convinced

139

that Grant could be trusted, filled him in on the story she had told Tyler the previous day.

"I sent you a photo and some prints," Tyler said into the phone. "Let's get an ID on this guy."

There was a slight pause before Aiden's answer. Aiden had gone deaf five years ago from meningitis. Aiden had seen Tyler signing at an engineering conference and introduced himself, and Tyler ended up recruiting the Irishman to Gordian. One of the toys Aiden had, courtesy of another Gordian contract, was a speech-to-text translator. Since his deafness hadn't affected his ability to speak, it allowed him to talk on the phone with anybody. The only drawback was the milliseconds required for the software to convert the spoken words on the phone to printed words on his computer.

"Opening the photo now," Aiden replied in a thick brogue. "Good lord! He looks like he's had a few pints too many."

"He's dead. Tried to turn us into flambé." Tyler gave him the quick summary of the previous day's events.

"Sounds dreadfully boring," Aiden deadpanned.

"Yeah, it's been a real yawner here."

"I don't suppose your dead ninja wannabe

140

had a wallet on him."

"No, but he had an ex-military vibe. I'd start there."

Because of the work Gordian did with the FBI and the military — investigating plane crashes, evaluating new weaponry, assessing terrorist threats on infrastructure targets — the company had access to confidential databases not available to many other companies. Like Tyler, Aiden had a top military clearance.

"And see if you can find out whether there was a Lürssen or Westport yacht in the area today. Eighty-footer. It's got to be connected."

"Can't be too many of those cruising the North Atlantic."

"Now what's this about Coleman?" Tyler asked. "You left me hanging."

"Right. I was all ready to blow your mind, but you took the air out of my plan."

"You said he was dead. When?"

"Three weeks ago."

"How?" Like Gordian, Coleman's company was based in Seattle. Tyler was sure it had been front-page news there, but he had been on the road for the past month and hadn't read any newspapers.

"You're going to love this," Aiden said. "An explosion. Seems he and three of his top engineers were consulting on a demolition project. An electrical short detonated the dynamite early. All four were turned into hamburger."

Another coincidence. Tyler didn't like it.

"Have Jenny set up an appointment for me tomorrow afternoon with whoever is left at Coleman's company. I want to get more details about this supposed 'accident' when I get back to Seattle."

"So you're not going to be working on the Rex Hayden crash?"

Tyler frowned at the mention of Hayden's name. "What crash?"

"Forgot you were out of the loop out there. Hayden's plane took a dirt bath outside Vegas. No survivors."

"When?"

"Yesterday afternoon. Weird stuff. Plane turned back from a flight to Hawaii, overshot LA, and ran out of fuel over the Mojave. It's been all over the news. You'd think the president's plane went down. Then again, Hayden's probably more famous than the president."

It couldn't be a fluke that Hayden was one of the names Sam Watson said to Dilara before he died.

"Gordian won the NTSB investigation contract," Aiden said. "Judy Hodge got

142

there yesterday with her team, but I figured Miles would want you on the case because it's so high profile."

It didn't surprise Tyler that Miles Benson, the president of Gordian and the smartest man Tyler had ever met, had already been contacted to help with the investigation. Gordian had consulted with the National Transportation Safety Board on many of the highest-profile plane crashes of the past ten years — TWA flight 800, the American Airlines crash over Brooklyn a year after 9/11, and NY Yankees pitcher Cory Lidle's flight into a Manhattan high-rise. Gordian was the most capable company to assist in the probe of a crash involving a star as big as Rex Hayden.

The dead bodies were piling up fast. First Coleman, now Hayden. Both mentioned by Sam, and both pushing daisies. Tyler didn't like the pattern, because his name was in there, too. The evidence was fresher on Hayden's death, so that was Tyler's first priority.

"Tell Judy we're joining them at the crash site," he said to Aiden. "We'll make a stop in Vegas before we come back to Seattle."

"If you pop into a casino, put a hundred on Ireland to beat Germany in what you call soccer."

143

"Sorry, Aiden. You know I never gamble. Might use up all my luck."

Tyler hung up and stared at Dilara with curiosity. What a beautiful archaeologist and Noah's Ark had to do with the deaths of an engineer and a world-famous movie star was a question he never expected to be asking himself. The answer had to be even stranger than the question.

"You, Dr. Kenner," he said with a smile, "are a trouble magnet." He winked at her.

She smiled back at both of them. "Then it seems like I'm in good company."

"Speak for yourselves," Grant said. "I consider myself more of a trouble*maker.*"

"I can vouch for that," Tyler said.

The muffled roar of helicopter blades penetrated the walls. Tyler glanced out the window and saw the Super Puma heading for the landing pad. He waited breathlessly for a puff of smoke from the chopper's turbine, but it glided in safely. He didn't think they'd try blowing up another helicopter, but he'd feel better once they reached Newfoundland safely.

"Our ride is here," he said. "Time for a change of scenery."

As they walked to the helicopter pad, Tyler made one last phone call to arrange for the jet to divert to Las Vegas and have a

Jeep waiting for them at the airport. He wanted to see the Hayden crash site for himself.

FIFTEEN

The news about the failed assassination of Dilara Kenner and Tyler Locke didn't reach Sebastian Ulric's ears until the next evening. He had spent his Sunday flying back from LA to make an inspection of his facility on Orcas Island in the San Juan Islands off the coast of Washington State. The fifty-seven-square-mile island was home to 4,500 people and a bustling tourist trade, which meant visitors to Ulric's facility could come and go without attracting undue attention.

He ate dinner with Svetlana Petrova on the veranda of the facility's mansion and enjoyed the cool October breeze, a luxury he would be able to enjoy for only one more week. She was dressed in a sheer top and miniskirt, showing off her assets to full advantage. She looked faintly like the businesswoman she had pretended to be when she poisoned Sam Watson. Ulric only wished she had been part of the mission to follow Dilara Kenner out of LAX and kill her before she had caused all this trouble. Petrova certainly wouldn't have left the job unfinished.

The building where they were eating was one of five on the four-hundred-acre property. Huge old-growth pine trees ringed the densely wooded property.

Dan Cutter sat stiffly in a chair at the opposite end of the table. He didn't eat, only sipping from a glass of water. Petrova listened to the conversation in silence. Ulric had met her when she had been trafficking black market pharmaceuticals into Moscow for the Russian Mafia. He saved her from that lifestyle and brought her to the United States. Her parents had been nuclear scientists who were killed in the Chernobyl disaster, so she shared a kindred spirit with Ulric's vision for a better world.

"Why did it take so long to notify me?" Ulric asked.

Cutter shifted in his seat, the discomfort apparent. "The operative in charge didn't want to call with the bad news until it was confirmed that they had both survived."

"His name?"

"Gavin Dane. He claims that our man on the platform was overpowered when he was installing the Thermate on the lifeboats.

Locke must have discovered the bombs we planted and put them on a lifeboat."

"Good old Tyler. Resourceful as ever. Your operative should have sent more than one person on board."

"He felt stealth was more important than numbers."

"Did you warn him how intelligent Tyler is?"

"Yes, but he had operational authority. It was his call."

"Then he is an idiot and careless. Those are two characteristics we don't want to carry over into the New World."

"I agree."

"First, Barry Pinter loses a prime opportunity to kill Dilara Kenner when she left the airport, now this. Two major mistakes in three days. I'm not used to that kind of failure rate. Especially not this close to the end. Have there been any more leaks besides Sam Watson?"

"No. He appears to be the only one who was in on it."

"Still, we can't have the rest of our people getting it into their heads that they can back out now. Not all of them may have the nerve to follow through. Not without a little reinforcement."

Ulric's mother died at a young age, but

she had been the one to instill in him a sense of righteousness and purpose, assuring him until her untimely death that his unique intellect was a sign from God that Ulric was meant for greatness.

Ulric's father, a simpleton and a drunk, had given him only one gift, and that was to show him the value of discipline.

"What do you have in mind?" Cutter said.

Ulric had just the method. He stood abruptly and whispered to Petrova, who smiled her agreement at his plan and nodded. She gave him a long kiss, then stood and walked into the house.

"Come with me," he said to Cutter. "And have Olsen meet us in the observation room."

Ulric walked down the stairs from the veranda and out under the cloudy skies typical of the Pacific Northwest. The house, a massive Tudor-style mansion, was used to host the new disciples of his religious organization. Next to it stood a hotel housing the estate's 250 workers. The three other buildings were identical square structures three-hundred feet on each side and fifty feet tall. The unassuming buildings looked like airplane hangars, but the only aircraft on the property were three helicopters lined up on landing pads outside the hotel.

149

Stretching into the small harbor on Massacre Bay was a dock long and wide enough to handle any large equipment he wanted to bring in.

He strode toward one of the hangar-style buildings and walked through a door where he was met by a guard in a small antechamber. He sat at a desk behind two-inch-thick bulletproof windows. Ulric placed his hand on the biometric scanner.

When it showed green, the guard nodded and waited for Ulric to utter the password, which was changed weekly. Nobody — not even Ulric — was allowed in without the proper password. There were two passwords, both randomly generated: a safe word and a warning word. If Ulric gave the warning password, the guard would know the person with him was coercing him. The guard would let Ulric in, then shoot his companion in the head as he walked through the door.

The warning word this week was *Heaven.*

Ulric said the correct password: *"Searchlight."*

The steel door slid open. Ulric and Cutter passed the guard's desk to a four-way intersection. At the ends of eighty-foot halls to the right and left were doors that led to emergency stairwells. Ahead of them was a door that led to the main part of the warehouse. Ulric turned right and stopped at the call button for the two elevators. He pushed it, and the left door opened immediately. He and Cutter got on.

The elevator's control panel listed seven floors, all underground, plus the ground level. Ulric inserted a key into the panel and turned it. An LCD panel lit up, and he typed a pass code into the touch screen. The elevator doors slid closed, and they glided silently toward the fifth level, which was accessible to only a few select people. The doors opened a few seconds later to reveal a clean white hallway a hundred feet long directly in front of him, plus two eighty-foot hallways to either side identical to the ones on the ground level. All seven floors of the underground facility were designed in the same T-pattern, with a stairwell at each of the three ends, east, west, and north.

Ulric walked down the long hallway and stopped at a set of double doors halfway down. He walked through the doors into a vestibule and then opened another set of doors to reveal a chamber with a fifteen-foot-long window on the opposite side. An operating panel lined the bottom of the window. The chamber was used for observing the effects of their experiments in safety.

Howard Olsen, one of Cutter's security operatives and a fellow army vet, stood at attention when Ulric entered. He was typical of Cutter's recruits, a religious idealist who had joined one of the army's more fanatical underground faith groups. Like the other soldiers Cutter had found for Ulric, Olsen had little hope for the future of the human race after what he'd seen in Iraq and Afghanistan and had gladly joined Ulric's Church of the Holy Waters when he had been dishonorably discharged for going too far in battle, killing two supposedly innocent civilians. Ulric knew there was no such thing as *innocent* in this world.

"Olsen," Ulric said. "You need to hear this."

Olsen didn't respond. Like a good soldier, he only answered when asked a question.

"How many do you think we can fit in here?" Ulric asked Cutter.

Cutter looked around the observation room. "At least twenty-five."

"That's enough. We've had too many mistakes and too much compromised loyalty. We're going to have a demonstration."

"Of what?"

Ulric glanced at the window, and Cutter followed his gaze. A look of understanding crossed his face when he realized what Ulric was planning.

"Sam Watson is already dead," Ulric said, "but we still have Gavin Dane and Barry Pinter. They were careless and will be a liability in our future plans. Bring them here. Immediately."

"Who should observe it?" Cutter asked.

"Bring everyone who knows the full extent of the plan. They need to see what will happen to them and their spouses if they try to back out now."

Every one of his followers was ready to die for the cause, but most knew only that a wonderful New World would begin in five days and that they were chosen to be a part of it. For security purposes, only a select few knew what the New World really meant. Sam Watson proved that security might have been put at risk.

Ulric turned back to Olsen, who seemed confused. He was not one of the select few.

"Pinter and Dane," Ulric said, "are going to die in the room right behind that window because they did not accomplish their missions. Now I have a mission for you. I have discovered that Tyler Locke is going to Seattle. He rearranged his travel plans, so he obviously suspects something. I don't know what it is, but at this point, it can't be much. However, he is a very resourceful

153

man, and with time, he will find out more. Your mission is to kill him."

"Yes, sir," Olsen said. "Understood, sir."

"I want to make sure it is perfectly clear. I don't want to see you back here until Tyler is dead. Because if I do, you'll be the next one going into that room. And what happens in there is far worse than you can possibly imagine. Either Tyler dies, or you do. Understood?"

For the first time, Olsen's steely demeanor wavered. He took a quick glance at the sterile room and licked his lips.

"It's clear, sir. Locke is a dead man walking."

SIXTEEN

Gordian's Gulfstream jet left St. John's at one in the morning, Newfoundland Time, thirty minutes after the helicopter arrived from Scotia One. There was room for up to twelve people, but Tyler, Dilara, and Grant were the only passengers. Because of all the out-of-the-way locations where Gordian's staff worked, Gordian kept three of the Gulfstreams in its fleet. The fees Gordian charged more than covered their use, and the firm had been able to buy them for a song in a government sale of confiscated drug smugglers' property.

Grant was already asleep in the back, and despite a nap in the helicopter, Tyler felt his own eyes drooping. Dilara, on the other hand, seemed wide-awake. She had just returned from the plane's lavatory, where she had changed into a jacket, blouse, jeans, and boots that Tyler had arranged to be waiting for her on the tarmac. He wanted to ask her some more questions before he snoozed.

"Thanks for the clothes," she said. "I felt like a prison inmate in that jumpsuit."

"I don't think anyone would mistake you for an escaped convict, but I do think your new duds suit you better."

"And I never thanked you for rescuing us in the lifeboat. From what I heard, it was all your idea."

"Yeah, my crazy ideas sometimes actually work."

She looked back at Grant and shook her head. "How can he sleep like that after everything that's happened?"

"An old army axiom," Tyler said. "Sleep when you can because you never know when the next chance will be. He's just sleeping ahead."

"Sleeping ahead. I wish I could do that."

"You should try. We've got an eight-hour flight ahead of us. But first, how about we chat?"

"Okay. Tell me something about yourself."

Tyler grinned. "Like what?"

"Who was your boyhood hero?"

"Easy. Scotty from *Star Trek*."

"The engineer?" She laughed, a rich, throaty sound that Tyler found infectious.

"What can I say? I'm a true geek at heart.

Kirk was the hero, but Scotty was always the one saving his butt. And you? Don't tell me it was Indiana Jones."

Dilara shook her head. "Princess Diana. When I was young, I was a girly girl. I loved the dresses. But my father kept dragging me around the world, and archaeology became my passion."

"And Noah's Ark?"

"My father's passion."

"Sam Watson said your father actually found it."

"You don't believe him."

"I'm a natural-born skeptic. So no, I don't."

"Which part? That the Ark existed or that my father found it?"

"That a four-hundred-fifty-foot-long ship carried all of the world's animals two by two upon waters that flooded Earth."

"Many people believe the literal story in the Bible."

"And I'm sure you know," Tyler said, "for many reasons, it's simply not possible. At least, not without miracle after miracle. The story of the Ark took place six thousand years ago. At that time, wood was the only construction material used in boat making. The longest wooden ship ever made, a Civil War frigate called the *Dunderberg,* was three hundred and seventy-seven feet long."

Dilara looked dubious. "You just know that? What, are you a walking encyclopedia?"

"At the risk of bursting my aura of omnipotence, I'll admit I did a little research once we had the Internet connection back up."

"So you're saying Noah's Ark couldn't have been longer than three hundred seventy-seven feet?"

"From an engineering standpoint, a purely wooden ship bigger than that is untenable. Without the iron frames and internal bracing that nineteenth-century ships had, a ship the size of Noah's Ark would flex like a rubber band. It would have sprung leaks in a thousand places. Not to mention that in a raging storm like the Flood, wave oscillations would have snapped the frame like a twig. The Ark would have sunk in minutes. Good-bye human race."

"Maybe it was smaller than the Bible claimed."

"The size is only the first problem," Tyler said. "Do you know how long it takes for wood to rot completely away?"

"In a desert climate like Egypt, thousands of years. We find wooden artifacts in Egyptian tombs all the time."

"And in a rainy climate?"

"Several hundred years if the wood isn't maintained," Dilara said. "Certainly less than a thousand years, even in alpine conditions."

"Exactly. Noah's Ark was supposed to have landed on Mount Ararat, which gets substantial amounts of precipitation. Just look at all the collapsing barns from a hundred years ago. If those barns are already rotting, any traces of the Ark would have disappeared thousands of years ago."

"Believe me, I know all the arguments against it. My father believed in the Ark, but he didn't subscribe to the literal interpretation because of the logical problems with the story as it's given in the Bible. For example, there are thirty million species in the world, meaning Noah would have had to load fifty pairs of animals per second to do it in seven days, even if he could fit them all in a boat that size."

"Which he couldn't have, even if the Ark had been ten times bigger." They were getting on a roll now, each of them feeding off the other.

"Then there's the problem of the amount of food and water the Ark would have had to carry," Dilara said. "This is one of my personal favorites. One elephant alone eats

159

a hundred and fifty pounds of food a day. So if you have four elephants, two Asian and two African, for just forty days that's twenty-four thousand pounds of food, which also comes out the other end. Now add in rhinos, hippos, horses, cows, and thousands of other animals. Eight people feeding all those animals and cleaning up after them would have been impossible."

"Not to mention smelly. And let's not forget the fact that it would take five times the amount of water there is on Earth to cover all of the continents. Melting the polar ice caps might put Florida under water, but no way would the oceans cover mountains."

Dilara looked impressed. "So you know some of the arguments against literal interpretation."

"Not really," Tyler said. "But I know science."

"Not everyone takes the Bible literally. Some people see the story as an allegory. But even allegories usually have their bases in fact, so alternative theories have been proposed to explain the Flood story. Did you know that the Bible's story was not the first?"

"I know that Flood stories are a common theme across many cultures."

"But the Bible's story specifically seems

to come from a tale told a thousand years before the Bible was even written. In 1847, archaeologists discovered cuneiform tablets that told the epic of Gilgamesh. Its story of the Deluge is remarkably similar to the one in the Bible, so some historians think the Jewish scholars who wrote the Old Testament based the story of Noah on Gilgamesh."

"You still have the problem that, scientifically, it ain't possible."

"Not literally, as written in the Bible. But in 1961, Bill Ryan, an oceanographer at the Woods Hole Oceanographic Institute, discovered that the Mediterranean burst through a dam in the Bosporus Strait sometime around 5600 B.C. Until that time, the Black Sea had been a freshwater lake four hundred feet below sea level. When the dam burst, a waterfall fifty times greater than Niagara Falls filled in the entire Black Sea in a matter of months. Now imagine being a farmer living on the shores of the Black Sea at that time."

"I guess you'd have to take all of your family, animals, and belongings and hightail it out of there."

"Possibly by boat," Dilara said. "With embellishment and a few added miracles, it could have turned into the story of Noah."

161

"I'll buy that. But it still doesn't explain how your father found the Ark, how he would even know it *was* the Ark, how it survived all those millennia, or most important, what it has to do with the impending death of billions of people, as your friend Sam Watson claimed."

Dilara sat back in her seat and looked out the window. She unconsciously stroked her hair as she thought. Tyler caught himself staring at her, and he looked away just before she turned back.

"You're a real optimist," Dilara said. "Is the glass always half empty with you?"

"With me, the glass is too big. I'm just trying to zero in on the answer. It's the way I work."

"So how do we get those answers?"

"Sam said the name Hayden. It must have something to do with Rex Hayden's plane crash. I've arranged for us to get a firsthand look at the crash site. I'm guessing the plane was somehow brought down intentionally."

"Another bomb?" Dilara's eyes looked as wide as they did when she found the bomb on the rig.

"No, it ran out of fuel and crashed. I don't have many details yet, but I always like to see the crash site itself before we listen to the flight recorder and start the laboratory

162

analyses. Then we're going to Seattle."

"Why?"

"That's where Coleman's company is based. There might be something at his office that can shed light on everything that's happened. We'll swing by Gordian headquarters. I've got to talk to my boss and let him know what's going on. We also have a computer data recovery guru who's the best I've ever met. He should be able to help us with our research."

"You seem pretty gung ho about this now."

"A near-death experience will do that for you."

"Now that I survived the attempt to blow up the oil platform, do you think they'll stop trying to kill me?" Dilara's voice sounded more frustrated than anything, maybe because she and Tyler still had no idea who "they" were.

Tyler shook his head. "Sorry, but they seem like the persistent types. That's why you're staying with me from now on."

"You don't think I can take care of myself?"

"Oh, I have no doubt that you can. But if we're going to solve this thing, we need to stick together. Remember, they want to kill me now, too. Maybe even Grant, but they better not even think of going after him."

163

"Why?"

"They'd be on the wrong end of a whupping if they tangled with Grant. He's the real deal. He's a black belt in Krav Maga and an expert in any weapon you can think of."

"Not to mention that he's huge. What's Krav Maga?"

"An Israeli form of martial arts. With his wrestling moves, it's a lethal combination."

"He was in Army Special Forces, I bet. What branch? Delta?"

"I could tell you, but he'd have to kill me."

"I remember seeing him on TV one time. He was intense. In person, he's got such a friendly face."

"Normally. But he's the scariest son of a bitch I've ever seen when he's mad."

She leaned over to him. "And what about you? You know Krav Maga?"

"Grant's taught me a few moves. I can handle myself."

"I've noticed." She held his eyes a few more seconds then sat back. "Then I'd better stick with you."

"While we're trying to figure all this out, is there someone we should keep informed? That you're safe, I mean?"

She shook her head. "No one."

"What about Mr. Kenner?" Tyler glanced

at her ring finger. It was bare, no tan line.

She followed his gaze and splayed her fingers. "Right. You know my maiden name is Arvadi."

"Didn't seem relevant until now."

"I got divorced two years ago," she said. "Another archaeologist. You know how it goes when two people don't see each other much, traveling all over the world separately. Not enough time together. I decided to keep the name, since I'd already established my credentials with it." She paused. "How about you? Any family?"

"A younger sister. We were air force brats. My father's still in active service, a general. Runs the Defense Threat Reduction Agency. I don't see him much now. He didn't care for my choice of career. Sounds like you and your dad were a lot closer than I am with mine."

"Married?" Dilara asked. Her tone was curious, but neutral.

He shook his head. "Widower." He didn't elaborate. The silence grew heavy.

"Well," Dilara said, taking the hint, "I think I will get some sleep."

"You can have my seat," a deep voice said from behind Tyler. He turned to see Grant standing behind him. "It's already nice and warm. And Tyler told me you wanted to know about some of The Burn's signature wrestling moves. When you wake up, I'll tell you about the Detonator. I used that one to win my first match."

"I can't wait to hear about it," she said with a laugh and moved to the back of the plane.

Grant took her seat.

"I like her." He lowered his voice. "So . . . it sounded like you two were hitting it off." He winked. Sometimes Grant went overboard pushing Tyler to find someone after his wife died.

"Just making conversation," Tyler said. He glanced back at Dilara. She was already curled up in the seat, her eyes closed, a blanket wrapped around her. It was the first time Tyler had really seen her vulnerable, and he felt an overwhelming surge of protectiveness flow through him. He turned back to see that Grant had a silly grin on his face.

"You know about my girlfriend?"

"The woman you met two weeks ago in Seattle is now your girlfriend?"

"Tiffany," Grant said. "She's perfect."

"You've been on what, two dates?"

"I know it's early, but she has all the qualities of the future Mrs. Westfield. Know how we met?"

Tyler smiled. "At the strip club?"

"At the athletic club. She just works at a strip club."

"Bouncer?"

"Waitress," Grant said, feigning annoyance. "Putting herself through nursing school. She's petite but strong."

"I hope she's not too petite. You could crush her."

"You should see her on the bench press. Wow! I noticed her. She noticed me. For a few days, no talking, just looking. But we finally made a connection one day. Know how?"

"How?"

"Just making conversation."

Tyler looked at Dilara again. She was fast asleep.

"There's nothing going on," he said.

"All right." Grant didn't sound convinced.

"You're going to be a pain in the ass about this, aren't you?" Tyler said.

"Oh yeah," Grant replied.

Tyler sighed. It was going to be a long flight.

SEVENTEEN

After landing at McCarren International in Las Vegas, Tyler, refreshed from four hours' sleep, took the keys to a rental Jeep that was delivered to the Gordian jet and got into the driver's seat. A GPS navigational unit sat on the dashboard in front of Grant. In a few minutes, they were on Highway 93, which would take them all the way to the crash site.

"How far away are we?" Dilara asked from the backseat.

"Judy Hodge, the lead Gordian engineer on site, said it was about eighty miles," Grant replied. "Smack dab in the middle of nothing. Luckily, it's only about a mile off ninety-three on flat ground. If it had been in a canyon or on a mountain, the recovery would take ten times as long."

"How long *will* it take? To figure out what happened, I mean."

"Usually months for the initial findings,

and years for the final report."

"Years? Sam said we had until Friday, and it's already Monday morning!"

"Because this doesn't look like an accident," Tyler said, "I'll convince the NTSB to put a rush on the investigation. Grant, I want you to take over here."

"Oh, you are mean," Grant said. "To Tiffany, that is."

"She'll live without you for a few more days. We'll ship all of the wreckage back to the TEC. Put it all in hangar three."

"What's the TEC?" Dilara asked, pronouncing it as a word, like Tyler did.

"Gordian's Test and Engineering Center. It's in Phoenix, so it won't take long to move the wreckage there. It's a five-thousand-acre facility built way out in the desert twenty years ago. Phoenix grew so much in that time that it's now right outside the suburbs. We have a seven-mile oval test track, a dirt obstacle course, a skid pad, both an indoor and an outdoor crash test sled, and extensive laboratory facilities. There's also a mile-long runway and five hangars for flight testing."

Tyler knew he rhapsodized like a proud father when he described the place, but he couldn't help it. It was Gordian's crown jewel.

"So you test for the car companies?" Dilara said. "I thought they had their own
tracks."

"They do, but a lot of companies want
independent testing. Insurance companies,
lawyers, tire companies. Our biggest client
is the U.S. government. We can test virtually anything on wheels. Everything from
bicycles to heavy trucks. In fact, they're going to be putting a mining truck through its
paces day after tomorrow."

"Sounds like you enjoy that kind of stuff.
Do you get to drive it?"

"Sometimes, if I get the chance. This truck
would be especially fun."

"A truck? You're kidding. Why?"

"It's a Liebherr T 282B, a truck that's
twenty-five feet tall with an empty weight of
two hundred tons."

"That's four hundred thousand pounds,"
Dilara said. "I can't imagine something that
size."

"It's the biggest truck in the world. Essentially a three-story building on wheels.
When fully loaded, it weighs twice as much
as a 747 at takeoff. The tires alone are
twelve feet in diameter and weigh more than
any car you've ever driven. A Wyoming coal
mine asked us to test it for them to see if
they want to buy it. Our fee is worth it when

you're thinking of buying twenty of them at four million a pop."

"Sounds incredible."

"Unfortunately, since we're going back to Seattle, I'll have to wait to take it for a spin."

The rest of the ride passed silently. Soon they were past Hoover Dam and into Arizona. The harsh desert terrain was dotted with only a smattering of trees. The air shimmered from the heat, the temperature already into the nineties.

Twenty-six miles north of Kingman, the GPS unit indicated they were at the turnoff, and Tyler wheeled the Jeep onto a dirt access road. In another minute, they approached a cluster of vehicles. Thirty vans topped with satellite dishes dotted the sparse landscape. Reporters stood in front of cameras, broadcasting what they knew about the crash that had taken the life of one of the world's best-known celebrities.

They drove past the vans to a roadblock of three Arizona State Police cars. A trooper waved them to a stop.

"No press past this point," the trooper said.

"We're not journalists," Tyler said. "We're with Gordian Engineering." He handed the trooper his ID.

The trooper took a quick look at it, then

handed it back. "They're expecting you, Dr. Locke. You'll find them about a half mile ahead."

"Thanks."

Tyler continued on until he reached another set of vehicles. This group was dominated by police cars, fire engines, and coroners' hearses for evacuating the bodies, but they were also accompanied by three army Humvees and a hazardous materials tractor-trailer. Next to it, two people in bio-hazard suits bent over a grim row of black bags that must have contained the remains they had recovered so far. Tyler couldn't guess what the hazmat unit was there for. The plane shouldn't have been carrying any dangerous chemicals, and any fuel would have burned up long ago.

A van sat apart from the other vehicles. On its side was the Gordian logo, a mechanical gear surrounding four icons that represented the firm's areas of expertise: a shooting flame, a lightning bolt of electricity, an airplane superimposed over a car, and a stylized human figure.

A trim woman in her thirties stood next to the van and spoke into a walkie-talkie. Judy Hodge looked up when she heard the Jeep approaching. She wore a Gordian baseball cap, tank top, jeans, and latex gloves. When she saw that it was Tyler, she put the walkie-talkie on her belt and came over to the Jeep.

Tyler hopped out and shook her hand. She nodded at Grant, and Tyler introduced her to Dilara.

"Good to see you, Judy," he said. "Looks like a real circus back there."

"The police have already caught two reporters who snuck past the barricade," Judy said. "Plus, we've had to fend off souvenir hunters. I'm glad we have G-Tag. We need to get this stuff off-site as soon as we can. I never knew how crazy Hayden's fans could be."

G-Tag was a method for processing airplane wreckage that had been developed by Gordian. Each piece of wreckage was photographed with a digital camera, and its exact GPS location was recorded. Then a bar code was printed with a unique ID number and attached to the wreckage. The data was automatically sent to Gordian's central computers, providing a detailed map of every piece of wreckage as it had been found. The G-Tag system reduced the amount of time needed to document the wreckage by a factor of ten from the previous manual method and meant they could start removing wreckage from the site

173

within hours, preserving the debris from the elements.

"Have you started shipping wreckage to the TEC yet?" Tyler asked.

"The first tractor-trailer will arrive in an hour. We'll have twenty of them running back and forth to the TEC. The main concentration of wreckage is over there." She pointed at a spot where workers were massed. Tyler could see only a few large pieces, including what looked like an engine.

"When I'm done here, I'm heading back to Seattle with Dr. Kenner. We've got to rush this investigation. Judy, you'll stay here on-site until it's cleared. Grant's going to take care of processing the wreckage back at the TEC. Now tell me about the crash."

While they walked, Judy told them about the plane's ghost flight back to the mainland. She'd received an electronic copy of the fighter pilots' report and related its contents to them. Tyler saw dozens of pieces of metal, luggage, and assorted unidentifiable detritus already tagged with flags for removal.

Tyler stopped at a three-foot-square section of fuselage centered around a blown-out window. He knelt down to look at it as they talked.

"Any signs of explosive decompression?"

174

"None. The plane was completely intact until it hit the ground."

Through the empty window frame, Tyler saw something white underneath the fuselage catch the sunlight.

"Do you have any more gloves on you?" Tyler asked. They might have missed a separate piece of wreckage under the fuselage section, which was tagged and flagged, meaning it had already been photographed.

"Sure," Judy said and handed him a pair of gloves.

"So we might be looking at a slow oxygen leak?" Tyler said as he donned them.

Judy gave him a quizzical look. "No. Wait, I thought you knew . . ."

"Knew what?" Tyler said as he turned over the fuselage piece. He stood up in surprise when he saw what was under it. A gleaming white human femur, probably male.

It wasn't unusual to find body parts strewn about with the wreckage, but it was strange to find a bone. Especially one that looked as if it had been picked clean by scavengers, even though there was no possibility that coyotes had gotten to it under that piece of fuselage.

Judy spoke into her walkie-talkie. "We've got another one over here," she said.

Tyler heard someone reply that he was on his way.

"This isn't the first bone you've found?" He bent over for a closer look.

Judy shook her head and started to speak. "We —"

Before she could say more, a voice behind Tyler said, "Don't touch that!"

He turned to see a man fully garbed in a biohazard suit approach. He took a photo of the bone, then gingerly picked it up and placed it in a plastic bag. After he marked it, he left without saying another word.

"I'm sorry," Judy said. "I thought you'd been briefed."

"We just got the basics from Aiden MacKenna before we headed out here," Tyler said. "What the hell is going on, Judy?"

"That bone is why the hazmat team is here. Because of the condition of the remains, the FBI was worried about biological or chemical residues. The closest team was an army unit from Dugway Proving Grounds in Utah. Didn't find anything. They gave us the all-clear to start our processing yesterday afternoon."

"How many bodies have you recovered so far?"

"None."

"What?" Tyler said, incredulous. "You

must have found some by now. According to the manifest I saw, there were twenty-seven people on board."

"We've found remains from at least twenty people, but no bodies."

"By remains, you mean hands, torsos, things like that?"

"No. That row of bags you saw before contains nothing but bones."

Tyler was speechless. Grant looked like he felt — completely shocked.

"How is that possible?" Tyler finally asked.

"We have no idea," Judy replied. "All we know is that before the plane crashed, something reduced every single person on board to skeletons."

COLEMAN

EIGHTEEN

It had taken eight hours for Gavin Dane to return to Washington once the yacht had docked in Halifax. Ulric made sure that the leader of the failed mission on Scotia One had been told only that he was to appear immediately at the Orcas Island compound. Surely he expected a dressing-down for his failure, but he didn't know how harsh it would be.

Barry Pinter, who had been given the task of eliminating Dilara Kenner as she left the airport, had already arrived at the compound and was helping with the last preparations for the upcoming days. Cutter was bringing them both down, now that the observers were ready.

A retinue of Ulric's top scientists and operatives gathered nervously in the observation room. Other than a few murmurs, they were quiet. They knew something important was about to occur, but they didn't know the nature of it. Ulric, who stood at the window next to Petrova, watched them. Good. They were in just the frame of mind he wanted. He pushed a button on the control board.

"Let's begin," he said into the microphone.

A door opened inside the test chamber, silencing the last whispers. Cutter led two men into the steel gray room. The first was Gavin Dane, a compact man with a crew cut and a tight-fitting black T-shirt that showed off a lean physique.

The second man was Barry Pinter, about a foot taller than Dane and at least fifty pounds heavier. He walked with the grace of a cat. Both men were veterans of army special ops units: Dane with the Rangers, Pinter with the Green Berets.

Ulric looked at both of them dispassionately. He didn't enjoy having to do this, but it was necessary. It was a shame to part with them, but the project had reached a critical point, and he couldn't take any chances. He needed to make examples of them.

Cutter left the room and closed the door behind him. A bar slammed down, the unmistakable sound of the door being locked. Dane and Pinter, who knew each other from previous operations, looked at each other, the confusion now turning to alarm. Then they surveyed the room, which they had never seen before.

The test chamber's floor was made entirely from steel grating. Ulric had it forged from carbon steel that was exceptionally resistant to high temperatures. Above them, the ceiling was another grating that fed into a sophisticated venting system comprising fourteen advanced filters. The sides of the room were inch-thick steel, and the observation window was made of a high-tech polymer that allowed it to be extremely thick without distorting the view.

The only object inside the chamber was a full-face gas mask lying on the floor.

Ulric keyed the microphone so that Dane and Pinter could hear what he was about to say to the observers.

"Good afternoon, ladies and gentlemen. You are obviously wondering why everyone is here today. That's good. Curiosity is one of the reasons I have recruited you for this epic journey. As you all know, we are very close to embarking on this voyage. Unfortunately, I am aware that some of the people involved with this project may be having second thoughts."

Everyone in the gathered group was stone-faced. None wanted to betray any thoughts of that kind, especially if they were, indeed, harboring them.

"I understand that feeling. This is a huge undertaking. One that will change the face of this planet. A change that I — that we — believe will ultimately save the human race. But sacrifices will have to be made. From all of us. And I think that some of you may be having trouble facing that reality."

Ulric glanced into the chamber, and he could see fear on the faces of both Dane and Pinter. He noted that they were both surreptitiously eyeing the gas mask.

"Therefore, I thought it was important that we reinforce our resolve for the task ahead. That we can brook no wavering, no second thoughts, no betrayal, no failure. We must stay focused on the task at hand. And so I have brought these two men here today." Ulric waved his hand at the window. "Two men who have failed us, all of us, and put everything we have worked for at risk."

He turned to the window. "Gavin. Barry. You are going to show these people why it is so important for each and every one of us to do our jobs with utmost competence. You will show them what's at stake."

Pinter ran to the door, prying at it, trying to find purchase to open it, but it was useless. The door was triple bolted and sealed. There was no way to open it from the inside. Dane simply stood there, stoic, waiting to hear what was next.

"There is only one gas mask for a reason," Ulric continued. "In sixty seconds, the test chamber will be flooded with Arkon-B, a form of the biological agent that will make our New World possible. Whoever is wearing the gas mask will be spared its effects. The other . . ."

That was all it took. Pinter lunged for the mask, but Dane, who had always been the smarter one, knew the most effective strategy was to disable the other man. He sidestepped Pinter and chopped him on the back as he went by. Pinter fell to the floor and, realizing his mistake, popped back up and faced Dane in a fighting stance. Both men were skilled in martial arts, but Pinter had the size advantage. They stood there, assessing each other.

Ulric glanced at his watch.

"Fifty seconds," he said to spur them on.

The words had the intended affect. Dane leaped into the air and spun around, his leg kicking out. Before it could connect with his head, Pinter ducked and threw his arm up to block it. The impact sent them both sprawling. Pinter was the first to recover and ran over to Dane, who was still on his back. Pinter lashed out with his leg, trying to hit Dane in the side. Dane grabbed Pinter's ankle and twisted it around, using Pinter's momentum to propel his body over Dane. While Pinter was in midair, Dane kicked at his groin.

Pinter crumpled to the ground, moaning in pain, but he wasn't finished. Dane coiled to strike a killing blow to Pinter's neck. Pinter countered with a punch to Dane's face, sending him reeling. Both of them sat on the floor, regrouping for the last battle.

"Thirty seconds," Ulric said. With two men like that, it would never occur to them to work together and share the mask. It was an unfortunate example of why his New World was necessary. The basest human selfishness was on display right in front of them. A fitting demonstration given the circumstances. Ulric just hoped that one wouldn't kill the other. Then he would have to send Cutter in to take the mask away from the victor.

Dane and Pinter circled around each other. Pinter had a noticeable limp that he was attempting to hide, while blood flowed freely from Dane's nose.

Cutter, who had now returned to the observation room and stood at Ulric's side, whispered to him, "What would happen if the winner had a cut?"

Ulric hadn't considered the possibility that the winner would have exposed wounds on his body, but it would make an interesting test to see how virulent the Arkon-B was, to see if it could enter the bloodstream in that way.

"I suppose we might be about to find out."

Dane and Pinter went at each other with a furious set of blows that was hard for Ulric to follow. Then Pinter positioned himself so that he could get Dane in a headlock. He squeezed Dane's throat, and this looked like it might be the decisive move.

"Fifteen seconds," Ulric said and nodded at the operator at the control board. The operator's finger hovered over the button that would release the Arkon-B.

Dane's face was now turning a shade of purple. It was almost over. Then with a last bit of effort, Dane angled his body slightly and kicked backward, striking Pinter at the knee. Pinter howled in pain and released Dane, who immediately struck at the other leg. Pinter screamed and went down holding both legs. From what Ulric could see, it looked like a dislocated right knee and a broken left leg. Pinter wouldn't be walking again.

Dane stood there, staring at Pinter to see if he could finish him off safely, forgetting about the time limit. Ulric started counting down. "Ten, nine, eight . . ."

Dane looked up at the speaker, then scrambled for the mask.

"Seven, six, five . . ."

He grabbed it off the floor and slipped it over his head.

"Four, three, two . . ."

As Ulric said "one," Dane cinched the straps tight and turned his attention back to Pinter, who was still crumpled on the floor. He stared at Dane with a look of pure hatred.

Ulric again nodded at the operator, who pressed the button. A whoosh of air could be heard in the test chamber. Dane and Pinter looked down at the floor. A continuous blast of air buffeted their clothing toward the ceiling.

Ulric could sense the others in the room holding their collective breath. He knew they wouldn't have to wait long. The Arkon-B used in Hayden's airplane was exactly the same composition as the agent flooding over Dane and Pinter now, but the concentration had been one-hundredth what it was in the test chamber because the delivery device on the plane had to be small and portable. That's why it had taken so long to take effect and why they had selected an overseas flight. By the time anyone on Hayden's plane knew what was happening, they should have been too far from shore to return in time.

Pinter had pulled himself over to a wall and leaned against it. His face was a rock, but Ulric could see the fear in his eyes. Dane retreated to the opposite side and kept a wary eye on him in case he made a try for the mask. Even if he did, it was too late for Pinter. He'd already been exposed. It was now simply a matter of time.

As Ulric expected, the first effects were evident in only two minutes. Pinter began to cough, just one or two at first, then almost constantly. His lungs had been the first organs to be attacked, and the Arkon-B would now be coursing through his bloodstream.

The cough turned into a hoarse hacking, and a trickle of blood started to drip from his mouth. Pinter felt the wetness and wiped at it. He saw the blood and was suddenly gripped with terror.

"Please! I'm sorry!" he screamed between coughs. "Please! Help me!" He looked at Dane, who watched him with wide eyes.

The trickle of blood from Pinter's mouth

became a torrent, and gasps of horror and muffled cries erupted from the observers. Pinter's skin began to slough off, in flakes at first, then entire pieces. Pinter was dissolving in front of them.

He could only moan in agony now. Then his hand flew to his throat, and he gasped for air. No doubt his lungs were filled with fluid. He was drowning in his own blood.

Death took only another thirty seconds. With a final gurgle, Pinter succumbed, his eyes staring at Dane. His head fell backward against the wall, removing a large patch of skin, and the back of his head left a smear of blood as his body pitched over onto the floor.

Some of the observers cried out or even wept in disgust and fear, but Ulric raised his hand, silencing them. They weren't done.

As they watched, Pinter's body continued to deteriorate, as if they were watching a time-lapse video of a rotting corpse decaying. The sores all over his body expanded to holes, and gore oozed out over the mesh floor, the liquid dripping through the gaps in the grating. The blood on the wall quickly disappeared, as if it were water evaporating on a hot skittle.

Ulric took a look around the room, and

everyone's eyes were riveted in terror on Pinter's disintegrating body. A few of them looked like they were about to faint. One woman vomited into a wastebasket. The demonstration was having its intended effect. Anyone in this room who was even thinking about following in Sam Watson's traitorous footsteps wouldn't consider it now.

Every cell of Pinter's flesh was attacked, and within another three minutes, nothing was left of him except his bones, picked clean, as if he'd been consumed by a ravenous school of piranhas. His skull, which had been a human face a mere five minutes before, grinned at the observation window in a perverse leer.

The operator pressed the button again, and the whoosh of air stopped.

"And that concludes today's demonstration," Ulric said. "I'm sure everyone found it instructive. If you don't want to be part of the masses that will be exposed to Arkon-B in five days, you will do nothing to jeopardize our carefully laid plans. Am I understood?"

A few of them said "yes" immediately while the rest nodded eagerly.

Satisfied, Ulric said, "You may go." He nodded at the woman who had vomited.

"Take the wastebasket with you."

They filed out quietly, still dumbfounded by what they had witnessed. Inside the test chamber, Dane yelled through his mask and pounded on the door.

Ulric let the last of the observers exit and closed the door behind them. The only ones left were the operator, Cutter, Petrova, and Ulric.

"What about Dane?" Cutter asked. "Should I let him out?"

The operator, who knew how Arkon-B worked, raised an eyebrow at Cutter. Cutter was aware of many of the biological agent's properties, but he didn't realize how virulent it was.

Ulric shook his head solemnly. "I'm afraid we can't. Although Gavin is wearing the mask, he has been exposed as well. Arkon-B can be absorbed through the skin, albeit much more slowly than through the lungs. We can't allow him to leave the chamber now that he's been infected. He'd be the death of us all. There's only one thing we can do for him now."

Ulric glanced at the operator, who muttered something under his breath, maybe a prayer. He flipped up a safety panel and positioned his finger against a red switch marked STERILIZE.

192

"This will spare Gavin from what Barry went through," Ulric said. He nodded at the operator. "Go ahead." The operator flicked the switch.

Flames shot up through the grating, leaping all the way to the ceiling. Dane screamed as the fire bathed him, and he danced around in agony for only a few seconds before he fell to the floor, his body quickly vaporizing. Ulric saw that the temperature in the chamber had already shot up to a thousand degrees and was rising. Soon nothing organic would be left in the chamber, with even the bones being sucked up into the ventilation shafts as ash to be filtered out and disposed of safely.

"Another two minutes," Ulric said to the operator. They needed to be sure that all the Arkon-B was destroyed. How ironic, Ulric thought, that just a few feet away was the deadliest substance in existence, and yet in five days, where he was standing would be the safest place on Earth.

NINETEEN

The flight from Las Vegas to Seattle hadn't taken much longer than the road trip back from the crash site to the airport, so it was only two in the afternoon when Tyler and Dilara landed. He led her from the Gulfstream to Gordian's facility at Seattle's Boeing Field. With three jets, Gordian rated a designated ramp at the airport just south of the city's downtown.

The early October day was unseasonably warm and uncharacteristically bright. The clouds that seemed ever present in the winter hadn't yet arrived, revealing a great view of the Olympics and Mount Rainier sparkling in the distance.

Tyler stopped at a sleek red sports car and opened the tiny trunk. He tossed his bag inside, then unhooked a cord from the car.

"What's that for?" Dilara asked.

"The battery charger," Tyler said, climbing into the driver's seat. Dilara got in the passenger side. "This is a Tesla. Completely electric. Fully charges in four hours."

He pushed a button to start the car. A polite ping announced that the Tesla was operating, but otherwise the car was silent. Tyler put it into drive and eased it out of the lot. When he was on Highway 99, he floored it. The Tesla leaped forward like it was launched from a catapult. Within seconds, they were cruising at eighty.

"So you *do* get to try out your toys," Dilara said.

"Not a bad perk, is it? We're testing a second one down at the TEC. They let me borrow this one for everyday driving. I get to keep it for a while, as long as I give them feedback on how to improve it for the next version."

One of Tyler's side hobbies was testing and reviewing cars on a freelance basis. His personal vehicles — the ones he actually paid for himself — were a Dodge Viper, a Porsche Cayenne SUV, and a Ducati motorcycle, but he loved driving the newest thing on wheels. The Tesla was his for a few more weeks. Then he'd move on to something else. Maybe the new Ferrari coming out next month.

The Seattle skyline approached quickly. Dilara watched a ferry coming into Elliott

Bay as Tyler sped along the Alaskan Way Viaduct. He said little, letting her take in the sights as he tried to make sense of what he had learned in the Mojave.

They had stayed two hours at the site, speaking with the head of the army's bio-hazard crew, but Tyler hadn't been able to get much more out of them about the possible cause of the disintegrated bodies. The army scientist speculated that it was some kind of biological agent, but he couldn't find any of it in the bones or wreckage. Given that none of the LA ground crew had suffered a similar fate, the scientist assumed that the flesh-eating bug had been dispersed midflight. That meant they might be able to find the source of it among the wreckage.

Tyler had told Judy to send everything they found back to the TEC, and Grant would start going through every piece of luggage and onboard equipment as quickly as possible. Tyler didn't know what they should be looking for, but he wanted to see anything that looked unusual. When he was done in Seattle, he'd head back down to Phoenix to monitor their progress.

Tyler took the Seneca exit and wound through downtown Seattle until he reached Gordian's building across from Westlake Center, a shopping mall and tourist spot for the city's many visitors. The famed monorail, which shuttled between Westlake and the Space Needle, cruised to a stop overhead just as Tyler turned into the Gordian parking garage.

He stuck his ID into the card reader to open the garage's steel door. A sensor in the floor made sure only one car went through for each ID. Tyler parked in his reserved space and led Dilara to the elevator. He placed his hand on a biometric scanner. It beeped its acceptance of his ID, and the elevator doors whisked open.

Dilara raised her eyebrows at the security but said nothing.

"We do a lot of government work," Tyler said and left it at that. Gordian's highly secret military contracts dictated the extra levels of security. The tourists who swarmed outside had no idea they were walking past one of the most secure facilities in the entire state of Washington.

A few seconds later, the elevator opened at the twentieth floor to reveal a lobby reminiscent of an upscale law office. Muted paint complemented dark woods and plush chairs in the waiting area. A receptionist sat at a fine mahogany desk that stood in front of a glass door. Dilara signed a form to get an ID badge and clipped it to her collar.

197

Tyler walked her to his office. The floor-to-ceiling windows showed off the view of Puget Sound to great effect. The room was sparsely decorated because he spent so little time there. A pile of his noncritical mail and a phone were the only things on his desk. No need for a desktop computer because he kept his laptop with him. A bookshelf held a collection of engineering texts and car magazines, and the wall was covered with pictures of race cars and photos of Tyler standing next to men in racing uniforms.

"You're a car nut, I see," Dilara said. She looked more closely at some of the photos. Tyler noticed that they were the ones that featured him with one arm around the same woman, a beautiful blonde, in all of them.

"That was my wife, Karen," he said.

"She's gorgeous." Dilara faced Tyler, her eyes showing the condolence he'd seen many times. "When did she pass away?"

He always dreaded the inevitable questions, but at least he was now able to talk about it without choking up. "Two years ago. Car accident. Her brakes failed, and she got broadsided at an intersection."

"I'm very sorry."

"Me, too," he said. He let the pause go on slightly too long. He cleared his throat. "If you don't mind waiting here, I'm going to talk with my boss. I may ask you to come in, but I'd like to talk to him first. If the phone rings, it'll be me, so go ahead and answer it."

"Sure. I'll just take in the view."

Tyler left her and walked to the end of the hall, where he knocked on the door of Miles Benson, Gordian's president and CEO. He heard a gravelly voice yell, "Tyler, get your butt in here!"

The receptionist must have told Miles that Tyler was there. He wasn't even in the room yet, and it sounded like he was off to a great start.

Tyler opened the door to Miles's expansive office. The room was comfortable, but it was all-business. In the middle of the room was an eight-person conference table. To the side were a couch and chair, with an empty space where a second chair would have been appropriate. At the far end sat a massive desk. Behind it was a weathered man with a flat-topped crew cut he retained from his days in the army. Miles Benson waved Tyler over but continued typing at his keyboard. When he was done, he looked up at Tyler, raised an eyebrow at him, and grabbed a folder from his desk. Then he began to rise, something visitors rarely expected, since they almost always knew

that Miles Benson was a paraplegic, paralyzed from the waist down in an industrial
accident.

Tyler had seen him do it so many times,
but the process still amazed him. He rose,
still sitting, courtesy of his iBOT chair, a
motorized wheelchair developed by the
maker of the Segway. The chair normally
moved around on four large wheels, but
whenever he felt like being twelve inches
higher, Miles would activate the gyroscopic
control that pivoted the seat so that it balanced on just two of the wheels. Computers
continually adjusted the wheels so that it
wouldn't tip over. The effect was disconcert-
ing at first, but Tyler had quickly gotten
used to it. He sat on the edge of the conference table so that his eyes were level with
Miles's.

Miles fingered the controller, and the
iBOT deftly swung around the desk. He
shook Tyler's hand with a grip that could
crush steel. Tyler knew he lifted weights
daily and exercised with a racing wheelchair.
Miles wasn't the type to let a little thing like
paralysis slow him down.

"How was the marathon?" Tyler asked.

"Won my age division," Miles, who was
sixty-two, replied proudly. "I would have
come in first for everyone forty and up if I

hadn't gotten a blister on my left hand in the twenty-third mile. Some son of a bitch from the Special Olympics passed me with a mile and a half to go."

"I think you mean Paralympics."

Miles grunted. "Whatever. All I know is that he was twenty years younger than me, and that he was an ass. Looked over his sunglasses as he went by me and winked. I almost ran him off the road."

"What stopped you?" Tyler said with a smile.

"The same thing that's stopping me from tearing you a new one for abandoning the Norway job — my good-natured heart. That's a half-million-dollar contract you let go."

Miles was more than Tyler's boss. Miles had been his mentor in his college years, driving him to excel in engineering school when he was Tyler's professor and academic adviser at MIT. After Tyler left the military and earned his PhD, it had been Miles who had advised him to start his own engineering consulting firm, which Tyler called Gordian Engineering. When the grind of administrative and sales work had gotten to Tyler, Miles had convinced him to merge Gordian with Miles's own company, which he had founded when he left MIT. The combined firm took on the Gordian name, and Miles assumed leadership of the combined company. Even though Miles was a stellar engineer, his true expertise was in sales and hiring, and with Tyler able to concentrate his engineering skills on fieldwork, the company had doubled in size annually.

So even though Miles's words would have seemed sharp to anyone else, Tyler knew that he didn't really mean it.

"I know you had a good reason," Miles continued.

"The job's not abandoned. Just delayed. We were able to finish up the work on Scotia One."

"From what Aiden told me, you saved their bacon a couple of times."

"Unfortunately, the only reason they were in trouble in the first place was because of me. And Dilara Kenner."

Miles tossed the folder he'd been holding onto the conference table. "That's for you. I already looked through it. I had Aiden gather up everything he could on Dr. Kenner. She has a pretty impressive background."

"She's pretty impressive in person, too."

As Tyler perused the contents of the folder, he explained to Miles the events of the last forty-eight hours. When he was through, he looked for some response from Miles, who was as inscrutable as ever.

"How do you think this is all related?" Miles finally asked.

"Good question. Coleman and Hayden are linked somehow, and somebody has gone to a lot of trouble to get Dilara Kenner and me out of the way so that we won't find out how. The next job is to discover what their connection is to Genesis, Dawn, and Oasis. I'm hoping that if we know what they have in common, we'll know how finding Noah's Ark can prevent the death of a billion people. In the meantime, I think it's time we involve the FBI on this."

"I agree," Miles said. "It sounds like you're on to something here. I know the local special agent in charge. I'll give him a call. What about your father? You said you thought the guy who tried to bomb the rig was ex-military. Maybe General Locke could help us with this."

Tyler stiffened. The thought of running to his dad for help was horrifying. When times had been lean at Gordian, Miles had pushed Tyler to get his father to steer some military contracts their way, but Tyler had steadfastly refused.

Not if my life depended on it, he thought, but he said, "That's not a good idea."

203

Miles frowned. "You sure? He's well connected and could grease the skids for us getting information."

"We can handle this on our own."

Sherman Locke was a two-star general in the air force, an enlisted man who had worked his way up through Officer Candidate School. When Tyler's mother had left them when he was four, his maternal grandmother had raised Tyler and his newborn sister. Their father had been a stern disciplinarian, and nothing Tyler did ever seemed to be good enough. He was once grounded for three months for getting a B in high school, the only time it happened.

Tyler never considered the Air Force Academy an option because his poor eyesight at the time — since corrected by laser surgery — meant he was ineligible for pilot training. Instead, he wanted to go to West Point. The General, as Tyler called his father, wouldn't support his application. The General never would tell Tyler why, but he guessed it was because his father didn't think he was tough enough for it. In defiance, when Tyler matriculated at MIT, he immediately enrolled in the Army Reserve Officer Training Corps over his father's objections.

From that point on, Tyler made sure to

make his own way, both in the military and in private life. Getting help from his father was anathema. Their relationship had been cool ever since, even when Karen tried to mediate and bring them back together. Then she died, and the wall between them went up again.

Miles obviously didn't think Tyler was making the right call. Tyler could see it on his face, but he couldn't think of anything that would change his mind.

"All right," Miles said after a pause. "It's your decision. You're keeping Dr. Kenner with you at all times? She seems to be critical to this whole thing."

"She's in my office now. I don't plan to let her out of my sight."

"Ask her in here," Miles said. After Tyler made the call, Miles said, "What's your next step?"

"After we stop off at the computer shack to talk to Aiden, I'm going to take Dilara over to the Coleman offices and see if we can't find out the connection there."

A knock at the door. This time, Miles changed his voice to a pleasant invitation. "Please come in."

Dilara entered. Even though Tyler had never told her about Miles's condition, she didn't show the slightest amazement at the sight of him sitting in his wheelchair three feet above the floor. She walked right over to him with her hand outstretched.

"Nice to meet you, Dr. Benson," she said.

"Your photos don't do you justice, Dr. Kenner. And please call me Miles."

"Thank you, Miles. And I'm Dilara. I assume you've heard my story."

"Yes. Tyler says you've been through a lot in the last few days."

"Yes, but at least I got some new clothes out of it." Miles smiled at Tyler, as if to say he was right. She *was* impressive.

"Tyler thinks there's much more to uncover here," Miles said. "He has Gordian's full resources to pursue this."

"Thank you for your help."

"Well, this isn't just out of the goodness of my heart. Scotia One has already talked to me about replacing the lifeboat he blew up, so I want to know who to bill. The contract for investigating the Hayden crash will cover part of the expense. But most of all, I'm an old soldier, and I tend to take it personally when someone tries to kill one of my own."

"I do, too," Tyler said. He stood. "Shall we go see what Aiden can tell us?"

"Keep your eyes open out there," Miles said.

"Don't worry," Tyler said. "Dilara can handle herself."

"I know. She's not the one I was talking to."

Howard Olsen stood fifty feet from the Gordian building's entrance, hovering at a bus stop to avoid suspicion. Since he hadn't known how Tyler Locke was arriving in Seattle, the best place to intercept his targets was at the company headquarters, and his plan had been correct. He'd seen Locke and Dilara Kenner arrive in a red sports car thirty minutes ago, but the garage gate had prevented him from following them in and finishing the job right then and there.

He'd scouted the building thoroughly, but there was no way for him to get in undetected without more advance work. His next opportunity would be to tail them when they drove out of the building. His partner, Cates, was waiting in a car around the corner. There was no place to park within view of the garage exit, so Olsen would call Cates when he spotted Locke's car emerging. Then it would be a simple matter of following them and waiting until they stopped at a light. Olsen and Cates would pull up next to them and spray them with the two MP5 submachine guns that were in the car. They'd be dead before they knew what was happening.

TWENTY

The computer shack, like the rest of Gordian, was not what Dilara had been expecting. She thought it would be some drab box filled with cluttered computer equipment and wires all over the place. Instead, she found a sleek high-tech center that could have served as the bridge of a futuristic starship. Colorful flat panels sat on ergonomically correct desks spaced at discrete intervals around the room. Through a huge window at the opposite end, she could see an entire wall covered with a screen the size of the JumboTron at a football stadium.

Everything she saw continued to confound what she thought she knew about engineers. Tyler Locke was this swashbuckling adventurer, his company was on the cutting edge of technology, and every person she met defied the nerd stereotype. She had been taken aback seeing Miles Benson's wheelchair solidly perched on two wheels, but she thought she hid it well.

"That's our previsualization facility," Tyler said, pointing at the JumboTron. Two men slumped on a couch, wildly swinging controllers and blasting away at life-size aliens in some video game. "Before we go to work on a difficult project, we like to storyboard scenarios or display engineering schematics. When the previz isn't in use, we let our guys blow off steam with it."

Other than the two game players, only one person was in the computer shack, typing at a computer.

"It's Monday," Dilara said. "Where is everyone?"

"Could be a meeting going on, but most of our engineers don't have regular hours, so workweeks are relative. We're driven more by deadlines and when the clients need to see us. Sometimes this room will be packed on a Saturday night if we're finishing up a project."

The room's lone occupant, a shaggy-haired man in his twenties, peered intently at a monitor while his hands flew over the keyboard like a virtuoso playing a Beethoven sonata. His back was to them, and he was so focused on the computer that he didn't seem to notice them.

"He hates to be surprised," Tyler said with

a grin. The man at the computer kept typing. Tyler went over to the man and stood directly behind him. He raised his hands, as if he were going to grab the man's shoulders.

"It won't work, Tyler," the man said in an Irish brogue without stopping what he was doing. "I noticed you and that fine lady when you entered. You can't sneak up on me when there are twenty monitors in the room reflecting your every move."

He spun around in his chair and popped to his feet. He shook hands with Tyler and then began to use sign language. That's why he hadn't turned around when they were speaking. The man was deaf.

Tyler smirked and replied both in sign language and verbally. "Yes, I will introduce you, and no, she is not interested in that." The man, who had a handsome face and thick eyebrows that overpowered his wire-framed glasses, smiled at her roguishly. Whatever he had said, she didn't get the sense that Tyler would tell her.

"Dilara," Tyler said still looking at the man, "this is our resident computer data recovery expert, Aiden MacKenna. As you can see, he is deaf, and he has a wicked sense of humor. I'm signing to him as a courtesy, but he can read lips, and his glasses display a tiny text translation of your

211

spoken words."

Dilara took Aiden's outstretched hand. "A pleasure," he said. "And I was simply asking Tyler how long he was in town for." He spoke with a clarity unusual for a deaf person. If Tyler hadn't told her, she wouldn't have known about his hearing impairment.

Tyler threw him a disapproving look. "You're lucky that you're indispensable."

"That I am. And lucky you are that I chose you over Microsoft or Google." Aiden turned his attention back to Dilara. "So you're the archaeologist I've been hearing so much about. You don't look much worse for the wear."

"Well, Tyler has been taking good care of me." As soon as she said it, she realized how it sounded.

"Has he now? And what can I do for you both?"

"A couple of things," Tyler said a little too quickly. Dilara thought she saw his cheeks redden slightly. "First of all, what connections have you found between the items I told you about?"

Aiden dropped back into his chair. "Ah, yes. Your cryptic phrases." He plucked a Post-it note from the monitor. "Hayden. Project. Oasis. Genesis. And Dawn."

"Don't forget Coleman."

"Right. And somehow these are related to Noah's Ark?"

"You tell me."

"Well, I think we're all in agreement that Hayden refers to Rex Hayden and his unfortunate demise. Never really cared for the guy myself. His movies were shite."

"Any link to Coleman?"

"My research doesn't show any connection between Hayden and Coleman. Not that I expected to find a link between a movie star and an engineer. And I couldn't get into Coleman's files online. The office is still there, but I'm told it went dark after the top engineers were killed. To get anything from their files, you'd have to access their computers on-site."

"What about the other words?"

"Well, in isolation they were too generic to mean anything. For instance, I thought Genesis was simply a reference to the first book of the Bible. But then I put them in the order you gave them. To me they looked like phrases rather than words, so I tossed them together. Project Oasis doesn't show up anywhere. Maybe it was something Coleman worked on. But I did find something for Genesis Dawn."

Tyler snapped his fingers, as if he just figured it out as well. "The cruise ship."

213

"You're kidding," Dilara said, perplexed yet again at how all this was tied together. "A cruise ship?"

"Not just any cruise ship," Aiden said, handing them a picture of an enormous vessel. "The largest cruise ship ever built. Of course, every new cruise ship seems to be the largest ever built. Capacity for six thousand passengers and two thousand crew. Makes the *Titanic* look like a bathtub toy."

Tyler glanced at the printout and then handed it to Dilara. It looked like a promotional photo from the cruise line's Web site. The *Genesis Dawn* was shown as if it were passing the Statue of Liberty, which was dwarfed by the immense ship.

"And guess what?" Aiden continued. "She makes her official maiden voyage on Friday."

Tyler looked up sharply. "Where?"

"Embarkation port is Miami."

Dilara thought back to the wreckage of Hayden's plane and the gruesome discovery of bones. She exchanged glances with Tyler. They both realized what the implications were.

"Oh my God!" she said. "We've got to stop it!"

"What do you mean?" Aiden said, confused. "Stop what?"

"She's right," Tyler said. "The *Genesis Dawn* might be the next target."

"For what?"

"For the bioweapon that was used on Rex Hayden's plane."

"Why would they kill a shipload of people?"

"That's a good question."

"It doesn't matter," Dilara said. "We need to get them to stop the sailing."

"There's no way we're going to convince anyone to stop the maiden voyage of a billion-dollar ship without some pretty strong evidence," Tyler said. "The best we could hope for is tighter security, but with eight thousand crew and passengers to search, it'll be hard to stop the attackers unless we know what we're looking for."

"What are we waiting for, then?" Dilara said impatiently. "Let's get over to this Coleman guy's office and see what we can find."

Aiden seemed amused by her eagerness, but Dilara was too fired up to care. She was sick of being on the defensive. She wanted to start getting ahead of whoever was behind all this.

"You heard the lady," Tyler said. "We're on our way there. But one last thing. What have you gotten on Sam Watson?"

"I haven't had time to work on that yet. All I know is that he worked for a small pharmaceutical firm."

"Keep on that. We need to know how he found out about all this."

"Will do." Aiden handed Tyler an object the size of a pack of chewing gum. "That USB drive is the latest from Samsung. Should be big enough to download anything you find on Coleman's computers. Just out of curiosity, how do you plan to get in?"

"I have an idea."

"Well, good hunting." Without another word, Aiden sat back at his computer and began typing again.

As they left, Dilara said, "Aiden's enunciation is excellent."

"He went deaf only five years ago. Viral meningitis."

"Do you have many disabled people on staff?"

"Over a dozen. Finding Aiden was just a case of serendipity, but Miles is well known in the disability community. He's aggressive about recruiting them."

When Tyler and Dilara were in the elevator, he punched the button for the lobby instead of the parking garage.

"We're not driving?" Dilara said.

"Coleman's office building is only three blocks from here. There'll be plenty of people on the street, so we should be safe. They don't seem to like witnesses. But if you'd like, we can drive instead."

"Not at all. It'll feel good to stretch my legs. I'm used to being outside most of the time anyway."

They exited past a formidable front security area and into a street scene that bustled with life. The afternoon sun was shadowed by the tall buildings, but the air was still warm. They used the first crosswalk to get to the opposite side of the street and headed north.

She still wore the clothes Tyler had provided for her, and if they were going to continue to work together until Friday, she was going to need more. She slowed when she passed a store with a good selection of outdoor wear, and the collection of shirts and pants in the window was just her style. She pointed at them.

"Do you mind if we go in there on the way back?" she asked Tyler. "I usually travel light, but this is ridiculous." She waved at her current ensemble.

Tyler smiled and glanced at the store's window. "Absolutely. I'm sorry we couldn't get you more —" Suddenly, his eyes flew open in alarm, and he yelled, "Get down!"

He shoved Dilara roughly to the ground and covered her body. It happened so fast that she was too shocked to resist. Then she heard a series of quick thuds, like muffled drumbeats, and the storefront window blasted inward, showering her and Tyler with stray shards.

It only took a moment for her to comprehend what was going on. The muffled thuds were silenced gunshots. Someone across the street was shooting at them.

TWENTY-ONE

Olsen had been surprised to see Locke and Kenner emerge from the Gordian building's front door. They crossed at the light and began to walk along the opposite side of the street. He quickly reassessed the situation and realized that this was an even better opportunity to take them out. Fifth Avenue, a one-way street heading south, was only thirty feet across. From this range, he could cut them down and escape before anyone could react.

He radioed Cates to bring the car around. Within seconds, Cates came to a stop in front of him in the generic Chevy they had stolen for this operation. Olsen dove into the car and came back out with the silenced MP5 cradled in his arm. Normally, he would never attempt an assassination in the open like this with so many witnesses, but he was unrecognizable in a wig and fake mustache. By the time the police got a serious investigation under way, it wouldn't matter. Olsen would be safely back at the Orcas Island compound, and the Seattle police would be a distant memory.

He raised the MP5 to his shoulder and aimed. He couldn't have asked for an easier shot, but just as he had pulled the trigger, Locke and Kenner dove to the ground, disappearing behind a parked car. He unloaded the rest of the clip into the car, hoping the bullets would go right through it and into his targets.

Olsen realized his mistake and swore at himself. Locke had seen him in the window's reflection. In his eagerness to end the mission quickly, Olsen had stupidly lost his most important advantage: surprise. But now he was committed. He slapped a new magazine into the submachine gun. He could still finish this right here.

"Let's go," Olsen said to Cates. "Leave the car. We'll grab a new one when we need it." They had been careful to use gloves.

Cates, a bulky fireplug of a man in a skullcap and sunglasses, jumped out of the car with the other MP5. A bus screeched to a stop in front of them, blocking their view. They ran behind it and sprinted across the street, hoping to catch their targets still on the ground.

When they had a view of the opposite side again, Olsen saw Locke and Kenner throw open the door to the clothing store and run inside, past screaming customers who were flat on the ground covering their heads, some on cell phones calling 911. Olsen jumped through the window he'd just shot out and brushed aside the mannequin that remained standing. He took another shot, but the bullets chewed up some clothing racks and missed. The few people still standing in the store dove to the floor at the sight of the weapon. The targets went through a door at the opposite end of the store into the interior of the Westlake Center mall, and Olsen and Cates took off in pursuit.

Locke and Kenner went around the corner just before Olsen could shoot, and then he saw them take an escalator two steps at a time. The angle was bad, so he followed instead of firing.

The targets led Olsen and Cates up two sets of escalators, brushing past customers who were oblivious to the silenced gunshots that caused the mayhem outside the mall's interior. Squeals of fright erupted when people saw the submachine guns waving around.

Olsen and Cates were halfway up the

second escalator when the targets turned left and ran past a line of people. Olsen saw where they were headed. The monorail station was inside the mall on the third floor just off the food court, and Locke and Kenner had jumped the ticket line. The train was about to depart.

"Do you see them?" he asked Cates.

"I think they got on the monorail!"

"Get on that train!" Olsen yelled as he backtracked down the escalator. "I'll wait out here in case they get off. Take them out if you can. I'll meet you at the other station."

He stopped to make sure Cates got on and scanned the crowd. Then the train's doors closed, and it quietly rolled out of the station. As it passed, he glimpsed Locke's face in the window.

Olsen raced down the escalators. The monorail had only one other stop, right next to the Space Needle at the Seattle Center entertainment complex. He ran outside to find the Chevy hemmed in by traffic. A police car had already arrived at the scene. The officer was looking in the other direction, his pistol drawn, trying to find out what was going on. Without waiting for him to turn, Olsen shot the officer in the back.

He jumped into the squad car and hit the siren.

The monorail glided on its overhead track two blocks ahead of him, but if he hurried, Olsen could make it to the other station before the train arrived. He made a U-turn over the sidewalk and wove around the traffic in the wrong direction down Fifth Avenue. Within seconds, he'd already closed the gap with the monorail. At this rate, he'd be standing in the station by the time Locke and Kenner got there. If Cates failed to kill them, Olsen would be there to finish the job.

Tyler planned to give himself a good butt-kicking if he lived through this. He'd been careless to let his guard down, but he never expected his attackers to be so bold, shooting at him and Dilara in broad daylight with crowds of onlookers. Now that he was on his home turf, he had gotten complacent. He had a Washington State permit for a concealed handgun. He should have gone to his house first and retrieved his Glock pistol. A lot of good the permit did him now, unarmed against two professionals carrying automatic weapons.

Tyler's impulse had been to get on the train just as it was leaving and convince the operator to stop before the two-minute trip was over so that the police could arrive and drive off their attackers. Suspended twenty feet above the street, there would have been no way for their pursuers to reach them. When Tyler saw one of them dive into the back of the four-car train right before the doors closed, he knew he'd have to change his tactics.

Their sole option was to stay alive for the next 120 seconds and hope the police would be waiting at the other end. The question was how to fend off this guy for those two minutes. He and Dilara were in the lead car, with the driver only twenty feet away. Even on an October Monday, the sunny day meant that the train was filled with tourists, many of whom were loaded down with shopping bags and souvenirs. Kitschy Space Needle models and gimcracks from Pike Place Market were everywhere, but nothing that looked like it would be an effective weapon. Tyler would have to take on this guy hand to hand.

He and Dilara crouched down behind the maintenance access panel that jutted three feet across the linkage between the first and second cars. He was just as scared as he was in any combat situation he had faced in Iraq, but he tamped it down like he always did and focused on what to do next. He heard screams from the back, but no gunfire. The passengers must have seen the gun, but his pursuer was a professional. He wouldn't waste bullets on someone unless they got in his way. Tyler took a peek through a gap in the access panel and didn't like what he saw.

The gunman, now in the third car, was methodically walking through the train, checking each passenger. The tourists provided some cover, but Tyler was afraid of getting innocent bystanders caught in the crossfire. He had to do something before this turned into a bloodbath.

"Dilara, crawl toward the front," Tyler said. "Take my cell phone. Call the police and tell them that there is an armed criminal on board the monorail. Look at me and wait for my signal. When I give the thumbs-up, stand. Make sure the gunman sees you." He knew it was risky, putting Dilara in harm's way if the attacker was able to take the shot, but it was their only chance.

Her face reflected his own feelings, a mixture of fear and that sense of *not again,* but she understood immediately what he intended.

"I'm your distraction," she said.

"Right. We don't have much time. Go."

Dilara slithered forward. Tyler watched the gunman approach. The man was calm, as if he had hunted down people before and wouldn't have any trouble with Tyler and Dilara. In ten more seconds, the gunman was on the other side of the access panel. Tyler gave Dilara the thumbs-up.

Dilara stood and pounded on the train's front window. The gunman, who had been inspecting a passenger, looked up and saw Dilara. He raised his weapon and took a bead on her. The diversion worked perfectly, the gunman totally focused on Dilara. Tyler rose up in the gunman's periphery and lashed out with his leg just as the gunman fired.

The shots went up and wide, shattering the train's left side window. Screams cleaved the air. Tyler followed the blow with an elbow to the head. For a moment, the man was dazed, and Tyler reached for the gun, wrestling it from his grip.

Before he could use it, the gunman recovered and grabbed Tyler by the throat. They fell to the floor, with the gunman on top of Tyler. His hands gripped Tyler's neck like a vise, cutting off the blood flow to his brain. Tyler let go of the gun, but he couldn't force the hands to part. His vision narrowed. He tried to inhale but got nothing. The grasp was crushing his larynx. He couldn't breathe. If he couldn't get this guy off of him, he'd be dead before the train arrived at the next station.

Through his tunnel vision, Tyler saw the man turn his head in apparent surprise. An object plunged into the man's eye. More screams from the passengers. The man went slack and collapsed on Tyler.

Tyler pried the hands off his throat. He coughed until he caught his breath and heaved the man off of him. Then he could see what was sticking out of the dead man's eye. A pewter model of the Space Needle, embedded in his face up to the base. He looked up to see who his savior was and saw Dilara looking down in a mixture of shock and relief.

"I am so sick of these guys," she said, a sob catching in her throat.

"Are you all right?" Tyler asked hoarsely.

She nodded. "I didn't mean to kill him . . . I was aiming for his ear, just to knock him off you, but he turned his head and . . ." Her voice trailed off as she stared at the man, whose other eye stared back at her. She obviously had never killed someone before.

Tyler stood and put his arm around her. "You did great. You saved my life. Thank you. Is anyone hurt?" he said loudly. Several people shook their heads. He looked around at the monorail passengers, who had retreated in fear from the fight and were now staring in horror at the dead man on the floor. Although some of them were crying, nobody seemed to be injured.

He looked outside. They were entering the station at Seattle Center. Too late to stop. He had to hope the police were already there. He didn't want to be stuck on the train any longer. There was still another gunman out there, the one he'd seen in the store window. If one guy was brazen enough to go after them on the monorail, then it was unlikely the other guy would give up any more easily.

The train came to a halt and the doors slid open. He tugged on Dilara's hand. "Let's get out of here." Not wanting to be mistaken for one of the gunmen and get shot by the police, Tyler left the submachine gun where it was.

They ran down the station's exit ramp, and Tyler saw a squad car screech to a stop on the sidewalk outside fifty yards away where barriers blocked it from coming farther. He could breathe a little easier now that the authorities had arrived. More squad cars were surely right behind this one. The driver's door flew open, but the man emerging wasn't wearing a policeman's uniform. He was dressed in black. It was the mustached man from outside the clothing store. He must have hijacked a police car.

Oh, come on! Tyler thought. *Is one break too hard to get?*

He yanked Dilara's hand and dashed toward the closest cover: Seattle's famed Space Needle. The six-hundred-foot-tall tower was a concrete spire with a two-story disk on top for the viewing pleasure of the thousands who visited daily. On a clear day like today, Tyler knew it would be crowded, and that he would be putting many people in harm's way, but caught in the open as he was, he didn't have a choice. He raced up the curving ramp, pulling Dilara with him.

Tyler flung open the door and looked back. The gunman was sprinting toward them, snapping off erratic shots as he ran. A carpeted ramp led up and around to the elevators.

Tyler and Dilara wound up past a line of sightseers patiently waiting their turn. When they reached the top of the ramp, Tyler saw an elevator emptying. It was just what they needed.

They blew past the attendant, who could only yelp, "Hey!" as they passed him. Tyler

229

heard screams from the people in line, who must have seen their pursuer brandishing a gun.

"Get out!" Tyler yelled at the nonplussed elevator operator, who was guiding people to the exits. She stared at him, not sure what to do until shots from the silenced Heckler & Koch tore into the elevator wall. She dove aside, and Tyler frantically pushed the elevator's button for the observation level while Dilara pressed herself to the opposite side.

The doors were closing, but not fast enough. The gunman dove in before they slid shut. The elevator began to rise, and light flooded through the external windows that looked out on the city. Lying on the floor the gunman brought the weapon up and aimed it straight at Tyler, who for a fleeting moment realized that he was about to die. The assassin pulled the trigger.

The hammer clicked on an empty chamber. The gunman had made the classic mistake of not counting his rounds. Tyler seized the stroke of luck and pounced on the gunman. He knelt on the man's arms, but the man kneed him, throwing Tyler to the side. The man leaped to his feet and reached behind him. He withdrew a .45 caliber semiautomatic.

The man shook his head and smiled. Tyler wasn't sure, but it almost looked like the man admired him.

Dilara slammed against his arm as the assassin fired, sending two shots into the window. Tyler took advantage of the momentum shift and threw his full weight into the gunman. As the three of them wrestled, more bullets hit the glass. Tyler shoved his shoulder into the assassin's torso, lifting him up and slamming him against the window. The glass, weakened by at least eight shots, shattered outward.

The gunman fell through, but he was able to grab the metal support. He dangled there, looking up at Tyler. The elevator would reach the top in seconds, and the man would be crushed against the inside of the observation deck's elevator shaft.

Tyler instinctively began to reach out to help the man back in, then hesitated. Did Tyler really want to save him? This guy had just tried to kill him. Tyler considered leaving the man where he was, but he grudgingly realized he needed to question him. His arm shot out to grab the assailant, but to Tyler's astonishment, the man just smiled again, making no move to grab Tyler's hand.

"Why?" Tyler yelled over the rushing wind.

"All flesh has corrupted his way upon the

earth," the assassin yelled back. Then to Tyler's surprise, the man released his grip and plunged out of sight.

TWENTY-TWO

Tyler leaned against a squad car as he gave his statement to a Seattle police detective, going through every detail from the time he saw the gunman in the window reflection to the time that the man fell to a suicidal death. Dilara sat in a cruiser fifteen feet away talking to his partner. Dilara still looked shaken up by the experience and sipped a cup of coffee. Ambulances and police cars surrounded the base of the Space Needle, and police were gathering eyewitness accounts from dozens of other people.

Tyler had no doubt that the latest attempt on their lives was another link in the chain of events, and it only reinforced his belief that more deaths would be coming, particularly on the *Genesis Dawn*. Even though he had no proof, these assassins must have been involved with the same group as the man who had tried to blow up Scotia One.

233

Luckily, no one had been killed in the crosstown battle except for the gunmen. The only person injured was the policeman the mustached man had shot in the back. Initial reports said the injury wasn't life threatening.

Tyler was just wrapping up his account with the detective when a dark-haired man in a crisp gray suit approached them. He was accompanied by an attractive blonde in a similarly well-fitted suit. The man flipped open his wallet and showed the detective an ID.

"Special Agent Thomas Perez, FBI," the man said. "This is Special Agent Melanie Harris. Dr. Locke is working with the Agency on the Rex Hayden plane crash, and we have reason to believe that this attack is related not only to that disaster, but also is part of a broader terrorist plot."

That caught the police detective off guard.

"This is a homicide investigation —" he sputtered.

"No one other than the perpetrators was killed."

"A Seattle police officer was shot. We want to find out why."

"As you are no doubt aware," Agent Perez said, "the FBI has authority under the U.S. Patriot Act to take over any investigation that may involve terrorist activity. Please ask your partner to bring Dr. Kenner over here."

"This is bullshit."

"We're setting up a task force, and I'm sure your department will be involved, but for now, we need to question Dr. Locke and Dr. Kenner privately. I have full cooperation from your chief of police if you'd like to check with him."

Miles worked fast, Tyler thought, if he had already convinced the FBI to take over the investigation.

The police detective grumbled and walked over to his partner. He jerked his thumb at the FBI agents. After a few more choice words from his partner, they nodded at Dilara, and she came over to Tyler, who introduced her to the agents.

"We know about your involvement in the Scotia One incidents," Perez said. "Although that's out of U.S. jurisdiction, we've been asked by the Canadian government to lend any assistance we can in identifying the assailant. We've also been briefed by Miles Benson about your situation, Dr. Kenner. He was persuasive in convincing my superiors that there is some kind of link between these events. Dr. Locke, did you receive any verbal threats before the attack downtown?"

"I think whoever was behind this made

235

their intentions known when they crashed the helicopter and tried to blow up a billion-dollar oil rig."

"We don't know the helicopter crash was anything other than a mechanical failure."

"A couple of days ago, I thought the same thing," Tyler said and looked at Dilara. "Now I'm going under the assumption that it was brought down on purpose."

"Have you ever seen either of the men before?"

"No," Tyler said, and Dilara shook her head. "All I know is that they're completely fanatical. One of them committed suicide rather than let himself be caught, just like the intruder on Scotia One."

"Do you know why they would want to kill you?"

"I have to assume it's because of the incident with Sam Watson at LAX that Dr. Kenner witnessed and the downing of Rex Hayden's plane."

"How?"

"That's what I'm trying to find out."

Perez took a digital camera from his pocket and showed the screen to Tyler. He cycled between two shots. Each showed a close-up of the perpetrators' faces. One was of the man with the miniature Space Needle still embedded in his eye, but with the

236

skullcap removed. The second was the man who fell to his death from the elevator. The back of his head was misshapen from the impact with the ground. His mustache was gone, and his hair was now short and brown instead of the shaggy black it had been. Obviously a disguise.

"Now do you recognize them?" Perez asked.

Tyler hadn't seen either man before. He shook his head.

"This guy," Perez said, pointing at the second man, "had pictures of both you and Dr. Kenner in his pocket."

"Did they have any ID?"

"No. They were pros. We're checking their fingerprints now. Using the fingerprints Miles Benson said you obtained on Scotia One, we do have an ID on the oil rig bomber. He was a former U.S. Army Ranger. Dishonorably discharged. Went into private contracting, but we can't identify his employer. All of the C-4 was destroyed, so we can't trace it. For now, that trail is a dead end."

"Maybe you'll get luckier with these guys."

"I'm not counting on it. I'm sure they've covered their tracks. What I'm curious about is why they would try to take you out in broad daylight. That's pretty risky."

"Because they only have four days left," Dilara said. "They think we know something that would harm their plans."

"Do you?"

"Not really," Tyler said. "It's still a big puzzle to us. But we think the *Genesis Dawn* is the next target."

"Why?"

"Because of something Sam Watson told Dilara."

Agent Harris spoke for the first time. "We'll have the autopsy rechecked, but preliminary reports showed no trace of poison in Watson's system. The coroner concluded it was a heart attack."

"That's what they wanted it to look like. Sam worked in a pharmaceutical company. Maybe it was them. They might have access to untraceable poisons."

"That sounds pretty far-fetched to me," Perez said. "Why would they attack you in front of dozens of witnesses but kill an old man with an untraceable poison?"

"They're getting desperate," Tyler said. "They thought it could be contained if they killed Sam Watson and Dilara in seemingly natural or accidental ways."

"What's 'it'? Who's 'they'?"

"It all has to be related to the bioweapon on Hayden's plane," Dilara said.

"Hold on," Perez said. "We're still not sure it was a bioweapon. It could be some natural phenomenon."

"Oh, come on, Agent Perez!" Tyler said. "Did you read what happened to those people?"

"We're working under the assumption that it was a terrorist attack, although no one has claimed responsibility, but we also don't want to jump to conclusions and panic anyone. That investigation is still ongoing."

"Yes," Tyler said, "and Dilara and I are returning to Phoenix tomorrow to help with it. A lot of the wreckage has already been trucked back to our TEC facility, and our technicians are sifting through it all. We're hoping to find some kind of clue in it. We have to work fast, though. The *Genesis Dawn* sails Friday morning."

"We can have security beefed up at the *Genesis Dawn* gala and sailing," Agent Harris said, "but you're not giving us much to go on."

"What gala?" Tyler asked.

"There's a huge party for bigwigs the night before the maiden voyage. Lots of big names will be there."

That sounded like a tempting target to Tyler, but he thought the real attack wouldn't occur until the ship was at sea. It

239

fit the MO of the airplane disaster better.

"We have to stop the sailing," Tyler said. "Or at least postpone it."

"Impossible," Perez said. "Unless I have a concrete threat to the ship, there's nothing more we can do."

"We have one more lead," Tyler said.

"Let's hear it."

"Coleman Engineering and Consulting. We have reason to believe they may be involved."

"How?"

"I don't know. John Coleman and his top engineers were killed in an accident. I'm guessing the answers might still be in his records."

"What makes you think Coleman is involved?"

"Sam Watson said his name to me before he died," Dilara said.

"Can you get us a search warrant?" Tyler asked Perez.

"With what? The accusations of a dead man? The judge would laugh me out of his office."

"You don't think this shooting spree is enough?" Tyler asked.

"But how is it related? You'll have to come up with a more tangible link than Sam Watson's dying words before I can get into

240

Coleman's firm. I think our time will be more productively spent looking for the identity of the two dead assassins and seeing if they are linked to the man on Scotia One."

"So we're just forgetting about Coleman?" Dilara protested.

"Unless you have evidence to justify a warrant, yes," Perez said. "I suggest Dr. Locke focus on Hayden's airplane crash."

"But —" Dilara began, but Tyler held up his hand.

"We'll head back down there tomorrow," he said.

"While you're in Seattle," Perez said, "I want the police to provide protection for you."

"That's okay," Tyler said. "Miles Benson has hired a private firm for our security. They're on the way to pick us up now."

Perez raised an eyebrow. "Fine, then. When I know anything about your attackers, I'll let you know." He and Agent Harris walked away together.

Dilara turned on Tyler.

"How could you give up so easily?" she demanded. "Coleman could be the key to this whole thing! We need to know about Oasis."

Tyler looked directly at Dilara. "I don't

give up. We're going to get into Coleman's office tonight."

"How? Without a warrant —"

"We don't need one," he said.

"Why not?"

"I don't think John Coleman died in an accident. I knew him. He was a great engineer, very careful. Which means somebody murdered him. And anyone who could plan an oil platform disaster could have staged an accident that killed John. He may not have even known he was in danger. He wouldn't have been involved in something criminal, at least not wittingly."

"How does that help us?" Dilara pressed, sounding frustrated. "How can we get into his office?"

"You said Sam Watson told you they killed your father. Would you let someone search your father's office if you thought that person could find his murderer?"

"Of course. In a second."

"Well, let's hope your reaction is universal. John Coleman has a daughter."

TWENTY-THREE

Pharmacologist David Deal awoke drenched in sweat. His eyes fluttered open and took in the sparsely decorated room he had been confined to as part of his final initiation as a Level Ten. Other than the single bed with its thin blanket and sheet, the only objects in the room were a metal desk, a cane-backed chair, and the coveted Final Chapter of the Diluvian Manifesto, the Church of the Holy Waters's sacred text. An alcove held a sink and toilet. The thick door was the lone exit from the ten-foot-square room.

Human contact occurred only when meals were brought in three times a day during the last six days of the initiation that all Diluvians aspired to. As a faithful Level Nine, he had been deemed worthy just two days ago and had been flown out to Orcas Island for the Ritual, as it was known. There were only three hundred Level Tens in the entire church, and he felt blessed to be asked to achieve his ultimate goal.

He'd been through a process much like this for each level, but this one had been the most intense, the most spiritual. He had read and reread the Final Chapter until he had memorized it verbatim. Suddenly everything he had learned in the Bible made sense. It was as if his soul had been mired in quicksand, and the teachings of the Faithful Leader, Sebastian Ulric, had plucked it from its thrashing and soothed it with his wise and beautiful words.

He knew the isolation was an important part of the Ritual, and it didn't bother him at all. Dressed only in a pure white robe, he was able to explore the visions he saw with rapt attention.

Since he didn't have a clock, Deal didn't know how long it had been since he'd finished dinner, but he had had enough time to read the Final Chapter halfway through again. The mind-expanding power of the words filled his head until he could feel his soul transcending its normal boundaries. The light weightlessness was the first sign of the impending vision, and he fervently waited for its arrival.

Then a firework of light exploded in his brain, causing Deal to fall backward onto the bed. He opened his eyes, and the bril-

244

liant starbursts faded away. He had been told that the Final Chapter wasn't the whole Truth, that the visions were his personal insights into what the Final Chapter actually meant, and each individual Level Ten was the recipient of his own Truth. That was why he desperately wanted to see another vision, to reveal the last bits of Truth.

Then it came. The sounds, the lights, the words. They told of a new beginning for the earth, a beginning that he was to be an instrumental part of. It was the most beautiful thing he had ever experienced.

As he caressed the back of Svetlana Petrova, Sebastian Ulric watched David Deal on the three monitors, and the ecstasy on the man's face told him everything he needed to know. Another sheep had entered the fold.

"I love watching this," Petrova said in a Slavic purr from her perch on Ulric's desk. "It's so sexy. The power. The control." She ran her hand through Ulric's hair, sending a tingle down his spine.

"I thought the indoctrinations were complete," she said. "The target number was three hundred, no? We're almost evenly split between men and women. Why do we need this man?"

"He has special skills, ones that I thought Sam Watson would bring to the project. With Watson gone, I thought it was prudent to bring in someone else to replace him."

"You are truly a wise man. That's only one of the reasons I love you."

Since he had his own vision for the Church of the Holy Waters ten years before, Ulric had scoured the universities for the best and brightest scientists, engineers, and thinkers. It had been a lengthy and arduous process to recruit the men and women he felt would be amenable to the church's teachings. He had to find the right combination of intelligence and receptiveness to his philosophy.

The indoctrination process was finely honed through years of development. At the beginning, initiates didn't even know a church was involved. It was more about a common goal for a better planet, one rid of both human suffering and contempt for the Earth's natural treasures.

Then they were wined and dined and brought to one of the church's facilities in a resort destination: Maui, the Bahamas, Acapulco. There they were treated not only to a fine vacation, but also to spirited discussions about how to improve humanity's lot. If they continued to show a willingness to further the same goals that Ulric's church had, the next step was a trip to Orcas Island.

When they arrived, they were asked to sign a nondisclosure agreement so ironclad that breaking it would bring penalties severe enough to make the signatory a pauper for the rest of his life. The NDA was intended to keep malcontents from revealing the church's practices. There were no exceptions, and those who wouldn't sign were immediately escorted off the property. Ulric didn't care about them; they weren't the types who would be useful to his cause anyway.

Then came the real test — the Leveling. David Deal was in his last Leveling to Level Ten, the most mind-altering of them all. Each person progressed in Leveling at a different rate, but only the ones who showed the most promise were promoted to anything above Level Five. Ulric needed a pharmacologist in his New World. He thought it would be Watson, but he'd been disappointed when he'd found that Watson had betrayed him. Deal was his next choice, which was why the scientist was now staring in rapture at the hologram projected into his room.

It was a state-of-the-art setup, with hidden projectors in multiple corners of the room. The air was suffused with a light smoke, barely visible until laser light was played over it. The drugs that had been developed by Ulric's company and laced into Deal's food made him more susceptible to the suggestion that the images were a product of his imagination rather than technology.

All of these procedures were necessary to ensure that each person received the most deeply felt religious experience of his life. Of course, there were risks associated with such an intense process. It was during one of these sessions that Rex Hayden's brother had a seizure and subsequently died. The autopsy found a genetic defect in his heart, and Ulric had been grateful that the man hadn't survived to become a flawed member of his New World.

During the incident, one of the church members panicked and called an ambulance instead of dealing with it internally, which brought on an investigation by the authorities. But because of Ulric's well-placed connections, it never went anywhere. Ever since the incident, Rex Hayden had been relentless in trying to expose the inner workings of the church, which he felt was responsible for his brother's death. Cutter's idea to test Arkon-B on Hayden's plane had been a just method for punishing Hayden's interference.

For the rest of Ulric's adherents, the effect of the Leveling was profound. Few coming out of these rooms doubted that what they had seen was a spirit guiding them to a better life. The ones who still questioned what had happened were either excommunicated from the church, or they were disposed of in more permanent ways in the case of the most persistent troublemakers.

Somehow Sam Watson had slipped through their carefully crafted vetting procedures. That's why Ulric had been forced to buttress his flock's loyalty with the lab demonstration. One way or the other, they would obey when the time came.

A knock came at his office door. He casually flicked off the feed from Deal's room with the knowledge that his indoctrination team was almost finished.

"Come!"

Dan Cutter entered and came to a rigid halt in front of Ulric's desk. He was careful not to glance at Petrova, who was now lounging in a chair to the side of the desk.

"Sir, Olsen was unsuccessful," Cutter said.

"What happened?" Ulric asked without inflection. No need to betray his fury.

"There was a shoot-out at the Space Needle. Both he and Cates are dead, and the Seattle police and the FBI are now involved."

Ulric didn't bother to ask if his men had been captured and interrogated before they died. Neither of them would have let that happen.

"Locke and Kenner are still alive," Cutter said. "Should I have another team sent to take them out?"

Just like Cutter. Always a man of action. But sometimes inaction was the best course.

"No, it's too late now. They'll be protected. At this point, any future assassination attempts would be counterproductive. Besides, we have our contingency plan in place."

Locke was more resourceful than Ulric gave him credit for, already surviving two attempts on his life. Still, he shouldn't have been surprised. Locke was also a man of action.

"What about Friday?" Cutter asked. "Maybe we should change —"

"Nothing will be changed!" Ulric said, sharper than he intended. He calmed his voice. "We will not allow some errors in execution to alter our long-developed and well-conceived plan. And we won't let Tyler

Locke dictate how we proceed. However, we can't allow him to find the device used in Hayden's plane and decipher its contents. Is your operation ready?"

"Yes, sir. I will be conducting the mission myself along with my top man. Our intelligence suggests that a large number of pieces have already been transferred from the wreckage site to Gordian's TEC facility in Phoenix. We should be able to find the device there. We'll begin the search tomorrow morning."

"Good. Once we have it back in our possession, destroy it."

Cutter nodded, again studiously avoiding Petrova's stare, and exited.

"I like him," she said. "He's a tough guy. Like a Rambo. So is it really true what I've heard about him?"

"About his injury?" Even though Cutter had been his security chief for years, this was the first time she'd asked.

She nodded.

"It is," Ulric said. "That's one reason he's such a valued asset. Why do you ask?"

Petrova arched an eyebrow and rose from the chair. She slinked over to Ulric and settled on his lap. "You don't have to worry about the competition." She kissed him lightly on the cheek, then the forehead.

"Now, tell me about your plans for this evening." She kissed him on the lips.

Ulric knew he had chosen the perfect woman to accompany him into the New World.

TWENTY-FOUR

Julia Coleman sat in the Starbucks at the base of the building where Coleman Engineering's offices were located. Her shift at Harborview Medical Center had just ended, and she still wore scrubs. Tyler knew she was a medical resident, but little else. As he entered the coffee shop, he could see her bloodshot eyes behind her tortoiseshell glasses, and her hair was tied back in a ponytail. Her expressionless face told him everything he needed to know about the long hours she'd just pulled.

When Tyler called her, she had agreed to meet with them, but she wanted to hear why they wanted access to her father's records before she gave permission to go through them. Tyler suggested they discuss it over coffee near Coleman's office so he could get into the files as soon as he had her agreement.

The two guards from the security firm

observed Tyler and Dilara from a car parked outside. Tyler felt sure that another attack wouldn't be coming tonight, but their presence calmed Dilara.

Tyler introduced himself and Dilara to Julia Coleman, but the doctor didn't stand as she wearily shook their hands. They took seats opposite her.

"Thank you for meeting us," Tyler said. "I know you must be exhausted."

"You got my attention when you said this was about my father."

"Yes, I'm very sorry for your loss. We have come across some information that may shed new light on your father's death."

"Are you with the ATF?"

"No, I'm an engineer with Gordian Engineering. I knew your father, but I never worked with him."

"That's right. I remember now. My father spoke highly of you, even though you were a competitor." That surprised Tyler. Gordian and Coleman had always had a friendly competition for contracts, but he didn't know that Coleman had talked about him to Julia. "Are you with Gordian, too?" she asked Dilara.

"No, I'm an archaeologist."

"Why would an archaeologist know anything about my father's death? Did you

254

know him?"

"No," Dilara said, "but I may have known someone who did. Do you know a man named Sam Watson?"

Julia shook her head. "Doesn't sound familiar. Did he have something to do with the accident?"

"We don't think it was an accident," Tyler said.

"But the ATF investigation said that they had improperly connected the wiring for the explosives. It was triggered prematurely."

"Was your father the kind of man who would make that kind of mistake?" Tyler knew that working with explosives was not something you played around with. If you got careless, you got killed. John Coleman had been in the business for a long time.

"He was a perfectionist," Julia said. "That's why I always assumed it was one of the other engineers who made the mistake."

"Do you know what sort of project he was working on at the time?"

"It was a new tunnel in the Cascades. They were going through the placement of the explosives the night before the first blast was to be made. Then the accident . . . It was horrible. All of the top engineers in his firm were killed."

"Who's operating the company now?"

"No one. I'm not an engineer, and I certainly don't have time to run a business. It was a consulting firm, so nobody wanted to buy it. I didn't want to go through years of litigation from the other engineers' families, so I just settled wrongful death suits with all of them and shut it down. I haven't had time to figure out what to do with everything in the office. It's still there, but I was going to close it down next month."

"What was he working on before the tunnel?"

"Some huge project for the government. Top secret. Worked on it for three years. He couldn't tell me anything about it." Julia looked at both of them. "Are you saying my father was murdered?"

"That's a possibility."

"Why? Who would want to kill him?"

"That's what we're trying to find out, and we need your help."

Julia sat back and stared into space as the idea that her father had been murdered sunk in.

"My mother died when I was twenty," she finally said. "He was the only family I had left. I'll let you have anything in his office if you can tell me who killed him."

They threw away their coffees and followed Julia into the building. The offices were on the third floor. Julia unlocked the door and took them inside. A typical cubical farm greeted them.

"My dad's cube is in the corner," Julia said.

"Would it be all right if I turned on your server so that my computer staff can download your company data and analyze it for any clues?" Tyler asked. "I know his company probably had contracts prohibiting disclosure of information . . ."

"I'll consider you a subcontractor. If some company wants to sue later, they can take it up with the firm's lawyers."

Tyler fired up the computers and called Aiden MacKenna, who walked him through opening a port in the security system to allow remote access to the files. He told Aiden to look for any files about Project Oasis. While Aiden began his search, Tyler went through John Coleman's desk and file cabinet.

As he expected, the majority of Coleman's files were electronic. Most engineering firms drew up their project plans on computers and communicated by phone and e-mail, but there was always a need to print out blueprints, schematics, and presentations. There should be some paper trail for Oasis if he really had worked on it. Coleman's file folders were meticulously labeled by date.

Two other cabinets were stuffed until there was almost no room in them, and Dilara went through each of the files, looking for a reference to Oasis. A third cabinet, closest to his desk, was also full in the bottom drawer, but the top drawer was almost completely empty. Tyler looked at the dates on the folders more carefully. There was a steady stream of projects up until three years ago, and then suddenly only a smattering of projects were listed in the files.

"Dr. Coleman," Tyler said, "have any files been removed from the office?"

"Not that I'm aware of. Why?"

"Some files seem to be missing. Do you know the name of the project your father was working on for the past three years?"

"He wasn't supposed to tell me anything, but once when he was very tired, he let the project name slip out by mistake. He actually seemed scared when he realized what he'd done and told me not to say a word about it to anyone. The project was called Oasis."

Tyler exchanged glances with Dilara. "Dr. Coleman, can you recall anything else about Oasis?"

"All I know is that he was traveling to the

San Juan Islands constantly during that time. He must have made a lot of money on the project. After his death, I found out that his firm had deposited more than thirty million dollars recently. That's what allowed me to settle the lawsuits and keep the office while I decided what to do with it." She registered the look of surprise on Tyler's face and went on. "My father would have been disappointed if I had abandoned my medical career."

Tyler nodded, but he couldn't get over the contract size. Coleman's firm was talented, but small. Thirty million dollars would be a huge amount of money for them.

"Dr. Locke," Julia Coleman said, "I need to go home and get some sleep." She held out the office key. "Just lock the door on your way out."

"That's very generous of you," Tyler said, taking the key from her.

"I just want to know one thing. Are you going to catch the person who did this to my father?"

"We'll do our best."

"Good. I may be a doctor, but I would happily see the person responsible for his death fry."

She let herself out, leaving Dilara and Tyler alone in the office.

"I know how she feels," Dilara said. "So you think someone took the files on Oasis?"

"This stinks of a cover-up," Tyler said. "First, all of the top engineers in the firm who worked on Oasis are killed in a tragic mishap that someone as skilled as Coleman should never have let happen. Then all of the files mysteriously disappear. And to top it off, his firm was paid an exorbitant fee, probably in the hopes that the survivors would be mollified by the money. Someone came in here and stole every single piece of paper about Oasis, and I'm guessing the only reason they didn't torch the place to cover their tracks is because it would have raised questions they didn't want asked."

"What about the computer files?"

"If there's anything left, Aiden will find it."

They looked through the paper files for another hour but found nothing about Oasis. Whoever had cleansed the files was thorough. Their only hope now was something overlooked in the electronic databases. Tyler was disheartened when Aiden called with his results.

"These guys were good, Tyler. Absolutely no references to Oasis in any of the files. PowerPoint, Word, e-mail. All wiped clean of any traces. And yet they left a lot of other stuff. Probably because a straight wipe of the files would have been too obvious."

Tyler felt like Aiden told him that last bit for a reason.

"But you found something anyway," Tyler said, suddenly hopeful.

"I said they were good. But I'm better. I decided to do some peripheral searches. Since this Watson guy mentioned you by name, I used it as one of the search parameters. I found a few general e-mails between you and Coleman. A couple of requests for references, things like that. But there was one e-mail that particularly intrigued me."

"From me or to me?"

"Neither. It was *about* you."

"Read it to me."

"It's from Coleman to one of his other engineers. Quote, 'Jim, this new project is going to make us all rich. I can't believe Tyler turned it down. Sounds right up his alley. His loss is our gain. Project was called Whirlwind. Goofy, huh? These military types love their code words. The client is changing the project name, but hasn't sent it yet. I'll let you know when I get it, and then we can crank it up. Give me your picks for our team to work on this. Remember, this is a black project. No one else can know about it. John.' End quote. Am I right? Does that have anything to do with all this?"

For a moment, Tyler was speechless. Whirlwind. He hadn't heard that word in the three years since he'd signed up for the project and then been dropped by the client two months later.

"Tyler? You still there?"

Tyler swallowed. "Yeah, Aiden. See if you can find any more references to Whirlwind, and I'll get back to you."

Tyler hung up. The shock on his face must have been apparent because Dilara asked him, "What's wrong?"

He told her about the e-mail.

"So you think Whirlwind was the same project as Oasis?" she said.

"I hope to God it isn't."

"Why?"

"Because whoever is behind Whirlwind is preparing for the end of the world."

TWENTY-FIVE

After Tyler's pronouncement about the end of the world, all Dilara could get out of him was that he needed to think. She got the sense that it was how he puzzled through problems, drawing into himself. She went back to searching through the files in silence. As they expected, there was nothing about Oasis or Whirlwind.

Dilara agreed with the e-mail from John Coleman. Why did projects — particularly military operations — always have to have some mysterious name? Must be something about control and power. Men who were into that liked secret clubs, and what better way to be exclusive than to have a code name?

But something about Whirlwind had spooked Tyler. He wasn't the sort who made such bold statements without a reason. The way he had said it sent a shiver down her back, as if she were privy to some clairvoyance of a seer peering into a crystal ball. If he *was* a psychic, whatever was coming was too horrible to contemplate.

With Coleman's files exhausted, they silently turned to the files of the other engineers who had been killed. They were equally unsuccessful with those. The organization that had cleansed the files knew exactly what they were looking for.

By the time she and Tyler realized that nothing would be gained by further searching, it was nine-forty-five.

"Are you hungry?" Tyler asked.

Dilara had been so caught up in the search that she hadn't even thought of food. But as soon as he mentioned it, hunger pangs thudded in her stomach.

"Starving."

"We're done here. Do you like seafood?"

"Anything cooked. Sushi makes me gag."

"And I'm allergic to shellfish, but we'll figure something out." They locked up the office and found one of the bodyguards waiting in the lobby. The three of them got into the car with the other guard.

After a stop at the grocery store, it took ten minutes to reach Tyler's home in the Magnolia neighborhood of Seattle. She had been expecting a bachelor pad apartment in a high-rise. Instead, they stopped outside a

Mediterranean-style mansion that was perched on a cliff overlooking Puget Sound.

The bodyguards took up a post on the street outside. After Tyler disabled the alarm and made sure no one had tampered with it, he let Dilara inside. The lights inside the house were off, but moonlight flooded through floor-to-ceiling windows at the back of the house. Then he switched on the lights, and she saw a home that looked like it could have been featured in *Architectural Digest*.

Bamboo flooring extended as far as she could see. The living and dining rooms featured highly polished antiques, and an immense kitchen showed off shiny granite countertops and stainless steel appliances. The effect was sleek without being sterile, the decorations and wall hangings chosen to give the house a comfortable feeling. It certainly didn't look like the home of a single guy who was never home. The only thing that marred the effect was one white living room wall that was painted with five two-foot-by-two-foot squares, all various shades of yellow. Then it hit her. His deceased wife must be responsible for the interior décor, and the unfinished wall had been her project.

Suddenly, the house didn't seem so perfect. It felt more like a mausoleum, as if it was preserved in the state it was on the day she died.

Tyler noticed her eyeing the color swatches.

"Karen's work," he said, confirming her suspicion. His voice was tinged with regret. "She liked the sunny feeling of the yellow on a cloudy day. She never told me which one she preferred. I keep thinking I'll paint it, but I can never choose one of them."

Tyler picked up a remote, and a Vivaldi concerto wafted from hidden speakers. Dilara wandered over to the windows. A patio door led onto a deck that thrust to the edge of the cliff. The twinkling lights of downtown Seattle provided the perfect backdrop for the Space Needle. She could see a ferry plying the waters of Elliott Bay.

"On clear days," Tyler said as he unloaded the groceries, "Mount Rainier is right behind the skyline."

"It's an amazing view."

"It's the main reason Karen and I bought the house."

Again, she could hear the sadness in his tone. He went back to preparing dinner. Dilara sensed the awkwardness.

"Can I help?" she asked.

"Here," he said, showing her where the

knives and cutting board were stored. "You can cut the ends off the green beans."

Dilara watched him work. He handled himself deftly in the kitchen, smoothly choreographing his every move. A couple of times, she saw him unself-consciously nodding his head to the music. This was a man who enjoyed life, even with the grief that weighed on him at times. She couldn't deny that his attitude and competence were attractive, but those thoughts were ridiculous considering their current situation. She caught herself looking at him more than she should and focused again on the green beans.

Other than a couple of questions about where things were, they were silent. Her mind drifted back to what they had found in the e-mail message. Finally, curiosity got the better of Dilara.

"What's Whirlwind?" she asked. He stopped chopping the potatoes and looked at her. His expression was unreadable, but she got the feeling that the word itself bothered him.

"Sorry," she said. "That came out more bluntly than I planned."

He went back to chopping. "It's a top secret Pentagon project I worked on briefly."

"You mean the Defense Department is

behind all this?"

"The company that hired me, Juneau Earthworks, said it was a Pentagon project. It's the reason I was initially hesitant to tell you. But now that I think about it, I'm not so sure it *was* the military."

"I don't understand. How can you be unsure?"

"When you work on a black project, everything runs through dummy corporations like Juneau. You can't just call up the Pentagon and ask to speak to the project manager. They'd deny its existence, so there's no way to confirm that it's really a government operation. But the way these guys were throwing money around, I had to assume that they were with the government."

"What kind of money are we talking about?"

"The project was budgeted at four hundred million dollars."

Dilara whistled at the figure. "What was the project? A space flight to Mars?"

"A bunker. The reasoning was that the old nuclear fallout shelters for the government were outdated and susceptible to new types of biological and chemical attack. Instead of retrofitting the old bunkers with the latest hardware and computer systems, they wanted to build in a new, undisclosed location with everything up-to-date and upgradeable. It was going to be the most advanced bunker ever designed. It's the kind of challenge that makes any engineer salivate."

"But they fired you?"

"I was going to be the chief engineer on the project," Tyler said while he grilled the salmon. "We had just begun to get a handle on the specs and schematics. Then two months after they awarded the contract to Gordian, they pulled out. Said Pentagon budgets had been revised and there was no money to fund the project. It seemed fishy to me at the time. You don't just cancel a project worth almost half a billion dollars out of the blue. But they paid our hefty cancellation fee, and we moved on. I assumed it bit the dust and didn't think about it again until today."

"But they didn't cancel it. They just hired Coleman's firm and changed the name to Oasis."

"Apparently. We're talking about a bunker big enough to sustain over three hundred people for at least four months. Self-contained power, water desalination plant, air filtration, extensive food stores, and every amenity you'd expect at a five-star

269

resort. All built underground. It was even supposed to have room for animals and hydroponic gardens."

The mention of the animals made Dilara flash back to the man who'd dropped from the Space Needle.

" 'All flesh has corrupted his way upon the earth,' " she said.

Tyler stared at her. "That's what the gunman said just before he let go. I asked him why. Why he was after us."

"They're building a new ark. But instead of a boat, this ark is subterranean."

"What?"

"That phrase," Dilara said. "It's from the Bible. Genesis chapter six."

"The Flood story?"

"It's what God told Noah just before he decided to wash away the sins of man and beast."

"I'm not a biblical scholar," Tyler said, "but as I recall, God said he wouldn't do that again. It was a one-time deal."

"You're talking about his covenant with Noah. 'And I will establish my covenant with you; neither shall all flesh be cut off any more by the waters of a flood; neither shall there any more be a flood to destroy the earth.' "

"Sounds ironclad to me. Of course, this

group may not believe in God."

"Do you?"

"As I told you, I'm a skeptic." He stopped there and waited. He obviously wasn't going to say more.

"On the other hand, they could very well believe in God," Dilara said. "Many people take the Bible literally, and it specifically said that *God* would never again cleanse the earth."

"So if you want to get technical, somebody else could take care of the dirty work this time around?"

"I'm just saying that somebody could look at it that way."

"I've known a few people who might," Tyler said.

"But they'd have to be insane to carry it out."

"You don't think that's possible? After everything that's happened to us?"

"How could they create a flood that would destroy the world?"

"Oasis was designed to protect the occupants from radiation, biological contagion, and chemical agents. In Noah's era, a flood may have been what wiped out humanity, but I think they are planning to repeat the job this time with whatever killed the people on Rex Hayden's plane. Maybe

271

the link to Noah's Ark is an allegory."

Dilara paused. "The connection can't be simply symbolic. Sam said my father found it. The real Noah's Ark. There's more to this. I know it."

"Maybe we'll find out more from the wreckage of Hayden's plane. We can begin looking through it tomorrow when we fly down to Phoenix. In the meantime, we need a rest."

"It's just frustrating. It seems like we should be doing something."

"You should," Tyler said. "Crack open that bottle of chardonnay." He pointed to a bottle lying in the built-in wine chiller and slid the steaming salmon fillets onto a couple of plates. "Dinner is served."

Tyler poured the last of the wine into Dilara's glass. His mind felt fuzzy. He hadn't had a drink since his project on Scotia One started, so the wine had more of an effect on him than it normally would. He was glad to have the excuse to cook. Because he traveled so often, he didn't get to do it much, but when he did, he enjoyed it.

The conversation at dinner stayed away from their current predicament. Tyler told Dilara about some of his more interesting engineering jobs, and she regaled him with some of her more colorful dig anecdotes. When she got to the part about her department head and the flatulent camel, he found himself laughing out loud.

"It sounds like you're not home much," Tyler said. "I'm guessing you don't have kids."

Dilara shook her head. "No time or inclination. You?"

"No. Karen wanted kids, and I did, too — eventually — but I kept putting it off." He didn't know why he volunteered that. Must be the wine.

"I don't have the space either," Dilara said quickly. "I just live in a crummy apartment. But your house is beautiful."

"That was mostly Karen's doing. I put in a TV room down in the basement, and she took care of the rest. Ironically, the TV room is the one I use the least. I've watched a few races, and that's about it."

"Well, she had a wonderful eye. What did she do?"

"She was a therapist who worked with disabled children. She couldn't get enough of it. Always taking the extra time to help them out. That's why she was driving home so late the night she died." What was he doing? He never talked about Karen with people he'd just met. He barely talked to

273

anyone about her. It was too hard.

"When was that?" Dilara asked.

"Two years ago next month. It was a rainy night. Her antilock braking system failed approaching an intersection. She'd mentioned a few times that her brakes felt sluggish, but I was busy on a project at the time. I didn't think it was serious, so I promised her I'd look at them when I returned from my business trip. It didn't cross my mind again until that night. She slid right through a red light, and an SUV hit her doing fifty."

"How awful."

His breath caught as he relived getting that terrible phone call. "I was in Russia working on a pipeline installation when I got the news about the accident. Took me two days to get home on commercial flights. Weather and connection problems. She hung on for a day. Died while I was in the Hong Kong airport." His throat had gone suddenly dry. He swallowed and looked at the unpainted wall. "I missed saying good-bye to her by twelve hours. That's one reason we have corporate jets now."

Dilara was silent, but something about the concern in her face made Tyler go on.

"I didn't sleep well for almost a year," he said. "I combed through the accident data. Ran through it over and over in my head,

274

trying to convince myself that there was no way I could have known." He chuckled ruefully. "I mean, here I am, an expert in system failures and accidents, an engineer with three degrees, and she dies from exactly the kind of thing I'm hired to prevent."

"And could you have?"

Tyler shook his head slowly. "I don't know. The car was too badly damaged. The possibility kept me awake for a long time. I can sleep now, but her face is what I see every night when I turn out the lights."

Everyone at Gordian that he worked with knew the story, but he'd told it to only a handful of others. He supposed the death-defying he and Dilara had done together made him feel like he owed it to Dilara to tell her. He also realized that she would be the first woman to sleep in the house since Karen's death. Somehow it didn't seem right for Dilara to stay if she didn't know the history, like he would be betraying Karen.

"Well," Tyler said, "now that I've brought conversation to a screeching halt, I suppose it's time for bed."

Dilara gave him a sympathetic look but let it go.

"Where's my room?" she asked.

"Down the hall. Third door on the right. Just a minute." He popped into his bedroom and retrieved a T-shirt he'd never worn. "Brand-new. Let me know if it's not warm enough." Dilara's body type was very similar to Karen's, but he'd donated all of her clothes to charity shortly after her death. Even if he still had them, it would have been creepy to lend them to Dilara.

"Thanks for dinner," she said. "And for everything else you've done. I didn't mean for you to get dragged into such a huge mess."

"Not at all," was the only thing he could think to say.

Then to his surprise, Dilara gave him a kiss on the cheek and exited to her room. The expression of affection caught him off guard, and he didn't know what to make of it. It lingered long enough that it seemed more than just for sympathy. When he put the last dish in the washer and turned off the kitchen lights, he was still thinking about the kiss.

TWENTY-SIX

The gate at Gordian's Test and Engineering Center on the north edge of Phoenix looked like it was built to withstand a tank. A concrete guard shack stood between two huge steel grates that rode on tracks to let cars in and out. A ten-foot-tall hurricane fence topped with razor wire extended from each side of the gate and surrounded the property. Dan Cutter hadn't seen this kind of security outside of a nuclear power plant. But he didn't have to blow through these formidable obstacles. They were going to let him in.

He pulled up to the guard shack and unrolled his window, letting in the stifling heat that even at nine in the morning was already billowing from the asphalt. The man in the passenger seat, Bert Simkins, had removed his sunglasses so that he would be easily recognized from his fake ID.

"Identification, please," the guard said.

He was armed only with a 9 mm Glock in his hip holster, but Cutter knew the shack held automatic weapons.

Cutter smiled and handed him the IDs they had put together the day before. The two NTSB investigators they were impersonating were expected at the TEC, but not until later in the day.

The guard looked at each ID carefully and compared them to a preprinted list. Anticipating that, Cutter had gone to the trouble of appropriating the IDs of two people they knew would be allowed into the facility. Once the guard checked the names on the list, he looked closely at each man. This guy wasn't your average rent-a-cop. He was well trained. Cutter was impressed. But no one would be able to detect that the IDs were not genuine.

Satisfied, the guard handed them back, and the gate slid open. "Third hangar. Park on the south side."

Cutter drove through and followed the road to a tunnel that went under the seven-mile banked oval track. The track was so long that it looped around all of the buildings and test facilities, including the runway and airplane hangars. The thirty-foot-high tunnel was built so that large test materials and vehicles could be brought into the facility without interrupting track testing.

They emerged from the tunnel to see three massive buildings with multiple garage doors in each of them. Cutter had studied the layout of the TEC carefully, using Gordian's own Web site. These were the vehicle testing labs, with indoor crash test sleds, environmental chambers, and inverted drop facilities, whatever those were. Next to it was the outdoor impact sled, wet and dry skid pads, and a hundred-acre dirt track and obstacle course for off-road testing.

In the distance, Cutter could just make out a red car racing around the oval at over 100 mph. Outside the last vehicle test building, workers were talking next to the biggest dump truck he'd ever seen. On the side of the truck was the word LIEBHERR.

Cutter kept driving along the service road until five hundred feet later he approached a row of five hangars that each looked large enough to hold a 747. He parked at the third just as an eighteen-wheeler pulled past him, followed by a flatbed truck equipped with a crane. The flatbed was loaded down with a mangled aircraft engine. They must have been shipments from the crash site. These guys were working fast, which was to Cutter's advantage. The media uproar about Hayden's death had been bigger than anything since Princess Diana's. Rex Hayden not only was a huge star, but he also had cleverly parlayed his celebrity into business deals that had pushed his net worth close to a billion dollars. That had made him a formidable enemy of the Church of the Holy Waters. Cutter relished the thought of the actor dissolving in agony.

The trucks drove around the corner and out of sight.

Dozens of official-looking cars were parked in a line next to the building, meaning that Cutter and Simkins would be just two more worker bees and would go unnoticed amid the hubbub.

They got out and headed toward a door guarded by two men in police uniforms. The shirts were emblazoned with the logo of the Maricopa County sheriff's department. Each of them had an AR-15 automatic weapon at his side.

The only aspect of the mission that Cutter didn't like was that they'd had to leave their own weapons behind. If anyone spotted NTSB investigators carrying pistols, inconvenient questions would be raised. And in this heat, heavy coats would have been out of place. The light jackets they wore would have bulged from any kind of gun. Therefore, he and Simkins were unarmed.

He didn't expect the need for weapons. The mission was to find the suitcase and smuggle it out before it could be identified as the source of the bioweapon used on Hayden's plane. His plan was to use his authority as a temporary NTSB investigator on loan from the Justice Department specifically for this case to remove the luggage from the site for further analysis.

He sized up the deputies, who looked bored with the guard duty. If he did end up needing weapons, he knew exactly where to get them.

Cutter and Simkins flashed their IDs again, and the deputies let them pass. Cutter took off his sunglasses and let his eyes adjust to the dark interior.

The massive doors at the opposite end of the hangar were just closing, having already let the two trucks through. The semis idled at the far end as they awaited instructions about where to unload.

At least seventy-five people clustered at various points around the vast space. A prefabricated frame the size of an airplane fuselage was being assembled in the center of the hangar. Several pieces of the 737 wreckage were already hanging from it. The other pieces were carefully laid on the floor next to it, waiting for inspection.

The contents of the plane — seats, luggage, clothing, furniture — were all neatly placed in rows along the opposite wall. Cutter had accessed the G-Tag system through the NTSB's computer system, courtesy of the two NTSB investigators who were now lying dead in a Phoenix motel room. After a search of the G-Tag inventory, he'd found a digital photo of the steel-lined suitcase containing the device. It was still intact and on a truck bound for the TEC, scheduled to be delivered this morning. It would be found in this area.

"You take the opposite end," Cutter said to Simkins, "and work your way toward me. Try not to talk to anyone. If you spot the suitcase, don't touch it. Come find me, and then we'll look for an opportunity to remove it."

"What if it's not here?" Simkins asked.

"Then we wait for the next truck." He silently congratulated himself. This was going to be much easier than combing the desert looking for a single piece of luggage. Let the feds do the hard work, and he would simply take it off their hands here.

Cutter turned when he heard the beep of the semi backing up. At the end of the row of plane contents a hundred feet away, a black man in a tight-fitting T-shirt that was stretched over a muscular torso held up his hand. The truck stopped, and the man, who was clearly the leader, instructed two others to open the rear doors. A group of workers got in a line and began to gingerly hand out the pieces in bucket-brigade fashion while the leader yelled instructions to them.

The suitcase might have been in that shipment, but the truck's contents weren't what Cutter was paying attention to. Instead, he peered at the black man more intently. The voice. It was unmistakable. Of course, he had heard it on TV, when the man was a wrestler, but that wasn't the reason Cutter tuned out all the other noises coming from the building and focused on him.

The man turned around, and Cutter felt the old hatred flow through him. They had served together in the Rangers. Grant Westfield — electrical engineer, ex-pro wrestler The Burn, and former Special Forces soldier — was the reason Cutter no longer served the military with distinction, why he was reduced to what he was now.

Cutter turned away to avoid being noticed. There was no way Westfield would be expecting to see him here, but with Westfield in charge of this operation, the new development would significantly alter Cutter's plans.

All of a sudden, his mission wasn't going to be as easy as he had thought it would be.

TWENTY-SEVEN

Tyler watched the gray Seattle skyline as he padded through his fifth mile on the treadmill. He had set up the exercise room so that he could either catch up on his reading or simply enjoy the view while he worked out. The clouds had rolled back over Puget Sound during the night, foreshadowing the storm to come, but the Cascades were still visible. If there weren't the threat that someone was still trying to kill him, he would have gone out for a jog to Discovery Park.

His internal clock had woken him up by 7 A.M., so he had already finished some paperwork and lifted weights before starting his run. Much of his fieldwork was rigorous, so staying in shape was important to his job. Plus it gave him a respite to think. He'd had a dream about Dilara Kenner, and although he couldn't remember it clearly, he knew it wasn't entirely wholesome. That kiss on the cheek hadn't been much, but he could tell there was a spark that passed between them.

"Nice view," said a sleepy voice from behind him.

Tyler didn't startle easily, but he wasn't used to having someone in his house. His head whipped around, and he saw Dilara leaning in the doorway. He struggled to keep his eyes from bugging out at the sight of her still dressed in his T-shirt. It clung to her in all the right places and ended midthigh, revealing toned legs. He let his eyes linger for a moment and then turned back to the window. He didn't sense that she was making a double entendre on purpose, so he suppressed a smile.

"It certainly is." He tapped on the treadmill's control panel, and it ground to a halt. He used the towel hanging on the bar to wipe his forehead, and he suddenly realized that his tank top and shorts were soaked.

"Coffee?" Dilara said.

"On the counter. Breakfast?"

"I'm not a breakfast person. I'm also usually up a lot earlier than this. All the time zone changes must have caught up with me."

"I already ate. You have your coffee while I shower. When you're ready, we'll head to

the airport. Oh, and last night I had someone from my office stop by another branch
of that store you liked to get you a few
things. They're by the front door in a new
bag for you."

Dilara retrieved the bag and said, "That
was very thoughtful of you."

"I try to take care of my guests," he said
and retreated to the shower.

Once they were both dressed, they threw
their bags in the Porsche SUV, and Tyler
backed out of the garage. Two new bodyguards, who had called in earlier to confirm
that they were legitimate, waved to Tyler
and paced the Porsche from behind.

"Mind if I put on some music?" Tyler
asked.

He switched on the satellite radio, already
tuned to a classic rock station. AC/DC's
"Back in Black" thumped from the speakers.

"Let me know if it's too loud."

"A little different from the Vivaldi."

"You have to listen to rock when you drive
a Porsche."

The trip to Boeing Field took twenty
minutes, and Tyler waved off the bodyguards
once they were through the airport gates
and safely at Gordian's ramp.

The Gulfstream was already fueled and

ready to go for their three-hour hop down to Phoenix. Tyler took their bags and strode toward the plane.

He threw their bags in the cabin. Then he went outside and did a thorough preflight check of every system. He didn't think they'd try another bomb on the plane, but he wanted to check anyway.

Satisfied that the jet was in perfect operating condition, he reboarded. After he closed the cabin door, he headed for the cockpit.

"You want to sit with me?" he asked Dilara, who had already taken a seat in the passenger cabin.

He saw the surprised look he expected.

"You're the pilot?" she asked.

"I've taken a couple of lessons." Her look deepened into concern, and he laughed. "I have three hundred hours in this model and over two thousand hours total. We'll be fine."

She shook her head and took a seat in the right-hand chair. "You're a busy guy."

"I get bored easily. Sitting around ain't my thing. I'm a doer — working, playing with my cars, racing, flying. Anything that gets me out of the house."

"Is there anything you can't do?"

"I've got a lousy singing voice. Just ask Grant when we get down to the TEC. One time he took me to a karaoke bar, and since then he hasn't been able to listen to 'My Way' without laughing uncontrollably. Said I made Bob Dylan sound like Pavarotti."

"And what does Grant think of you as a pilot?"

"Oh, he thinks I'm a way better pilot than Pavarotti," Tyler said with a grin.

He spooled up the engines, and within minutes they had lifted off and were winging their way to Phoenix.

Cutter and Simkins had been at the hangar for almost three hours now, and trucks had been steadily arriving with wreckage, but they still hadn't seen the suitcase. Cutter maintained a discreet distance from Grant Westfield, and whenever he saw Westfield heading in his direction, he casually walked out of his way.

Simkins had been able to check the areas nearer to Westfield, but no luck yet. Still, Cutter had to assume the suitcase would eventually turn up. If the investigators opened it and saw the device inside, they would immediately know it was something that didn't belong on the plane, and it would be taken to even tighter security. Cutter would never be able to retrieve it after that. He needed to get it back before that happened.

Another truck pulled in, and the bucket brigade repeated. Cutter watched from behind a frame piece that hadn't been installed yet. Then he saw it. The green case he had put on the plane three days ago. It had survived, and it looked intact. Good. That would make it easier to remove.

His worry now was that bluffing his way out of the TEC with the suitcase wouldn't work if removal of anything required West-field's approval. And there was no way Cutter could bluff past him. He'd recognize Cutter instantly and know something was wrong.

Which meant he needed a different way out of the facility.

As he brainstormed a plan, he could hear a landing jet roar past on the runway outside.

The flight to the TEC had gone smoothly. Tyler taxied over to hangar two and left the Gulfstream in the hands of Gordian's maintenance crew.

The TEC was experiencing a typically busy day. In addition to the airplane recon-struction going on in hangar three, at the track pit area he could see several people hunched over a duplicate of the all-electric

Tesla roadster that he had driven with Dilara the day before. A hundred yards from it was its exact opposite: the Liebherr dump truck. It looked like they were in the final preparations before putting it through its paces.

Tyler called Grant's cell phone and found out he was still organizing the enormous pile of wreckage being delivered to hangar three. Tyler and Dilara walked over to the building to join him.

Tyler flashed his ID card at the guards and vouched for Dilara, who showed them her passport, which she'd had tucked inside her survival suit during the helicopter crash.

When they got inside, he could see that they'd been making good progress. With the unprecedented manpower Gordian had mobilized, they had been able to gather at least 40 percent of the wreckage already.

He picked out Grant supervising the unloading of a semi. Grant waved them over and continued barking at the crew.

"I love what you've done with the place," he said to Grant.

"I'm going for that jigsaw puzzle feel that's so contemporary," Grant said.

"With a bit of a Lego vibe."

"It's the latest fad at all the accident reconstructions."

"Frank Gehry would be proud. I take it that it's going well?"

"Not bad, considering I have the NTSB all over my butt for moving this stuff so quickly. But everything is tagged and photographed properly. It just meant paying overtime for three hundred people to do it."

"It's worth it, given the stakes." He told Grant about the connection with Project Whirlwind, and Dilara's theory that it might represent a second ark.

"Then I'm glad I twisted some arms," Grant said. "We've got four more trucks coming in, and then I'll shift to sorting through —"

His walkie-talkie interrupted him. "Mr. Westfield?"

Grant yanked the walkie-talkie from his belt. "Go ahead."

"This is Deputy Williams. I know you said nothing should be removed from the hangar, but these guys from the NTSB —" The voice abruptly cut off.

"Who was that?" Tyler asked.

"One of the deputies guarding the front entrance to the hangar."

Grant tried to get him back, but there was no response.

"Come on," Tyler said and ran toward the far entrance. He and Grant arrived to find both deputies lying on the ground. Tyler bent down to take their pulses, but they were dead. Their necks were expertly broken. The men had been ambushed. They were also missing their automatic weapons. Tyler was furious. These men were killed on his territory.

Grant was just as mad as Tyler was. He got on the radio as he threw the keys to his car to Tyler. "This is Grant Westfield. Put the TEC on immediate lockdown. No one goes in or out. Is that understood? We have subjects on the move who are armed and dangerous. Gamma protocols are in effect." That meant if anyone tried to ram the gates, the guards were authorized to shoot first and ask questions later.

They jumped into the Jeep, and Tyler shifted it into drive. Whoever had killed the deputies was speeding away in a sedan about two hundred yards ahead. Two security vehicles were heading toward them, so the sedan veered off and skidded to a stop next to the Liebherr dump truck. They must have realized that getting back through Gordian's massive gates would have been futile and were making a last stand at the truck.

The Gordian workers around the truck scattered when they saw the two men jump out with the machine guns spraying bullets into the air.

The gunmen climbed the stairs of the truck, and when they reached the top, they sent two Gordian workers in the cab tumbling down. Tyler suddenly understood what the intruders' plan was.

For such a huge machine, the Liebherr was surprisingly easy to drive. Anyone who could start a normal truck and get it into gear would be able to drive the Liebherr. And that's just what they did. The massive truck's two sixteen-cylinder diesels roared to life as the two security vehicles came to a stop in front of it and their occupants jumped out, aiming pistols from behind the open car doors.

"What are they doing?" Grant said.

"Making a mistake," Tyler said.

The dump truck rolled forward, crushing the hoods of both vehicles into an origami of steel. The men beside the cars dove out of the way.

Tyler pulled even with the two-hundred-ton behemoth, trying to find a way on board, when he heard the clatter of an AR-15. Bullets tore into the hood, and steam and oil spurted up, coating the windshield. The engine sounded like it was grinding itself to pieces.

Tyler pounded his fist on the dashboard

and pulled to a stop. The Jeep was destroyed. No way could they follow in it. He watched the gigantic truck as it rolled toward the security fence, which it would rip through like a damp Kleenex.

Tyler threw open the door and got out. They needed a vehicle, but the nearest ones were back at the hangar a mile away. By the time they ran back there to get another car, the truck would be long gone.

Grant, who was on the other side of the punctured hood, pointed at something past Tyler's head. "Tyler, behind you."

Tyler whirled to see the wide-eyed stares of five people who had been testing the Tesla sports car. Next to them was a trailer, but he didn't see their service vehicle. He recognized one of the men, who stood there slack-jawed.

"Del, where's your Jeep?" Tyler said.

"Fred used it to go get us some lunch," Del said.

Then Tyler's eyes settled on the Tesla.

"Del, Grant and I are going to borrow your car."

TWENTY-EIGHT

"You drive," Tyler said to Grant. "Let's toss the targa."

The Tesla had a removable targa roof, and Tyler knew the only way to catch the men in the Liebherr was to get aboard it, too, which would be easier if he didn't have to climb through the Tesla's window. He flipped a couple of latches, and Grant did the same. Then they picked up the roof section and pitched it backward where it clattered to the ground.

Grant squeezed himself into the driver's seat and punched the accelerator even before Tyler had his door closed. Except for the squealing of tires and high-pitched whine of the electric motor, the car was eerily silent, which made the roar of the lumbering dump truck even louder.

Tyler hated to see the truck damaging his beloved TEC. The Liebherr plowed its way across the dirt obstacle course, mowing down everything in its path. Even concrete and steel was no match for the huge truck. Once it got out of the TEC, no one would be safe, and there would be virtually no way to stop it.

Tyler remembered a few years back in San Diego when a psychotic had stolen a tank from a National Guard armory. Although the tank's gun was disabled, the impregnable vehicle rampaged through city streets at a stately twenty miles per hour, dozens of police cars following. There was nothing anyone could do. It destroyed homes, cars, RVs, telephone poles. The police had been reduced to watching the destruction, hoping the tank would run out of gas. The only reason the rampage stopped was because the driver stranded the tank on a concrete median. It was only then that police could assault the tank and kill the driver.

This was worse. That tank was a slow, Vietnam-era M60. Maybe fifty tons. The Liebherr 282 B weighed four times that, was twenty-five feet tall, and could reach a top speed of 40 mph. Nothing short of a precision-guided bomb would be able to stop it.

Whatever the hijackers had was worth an awful risk to obtain. That meant Tyler needed to get it back.

The local police would already be on their way to track the truck by helicopter. There was no possibility that the truck would be able to slip away. But Tyler thought the hijackers would know that and have some kind of escape plan. In the meantime, there was a two-hundred-ton truck under Gordian's responsibility that was about to blast through suburban Phoenix.

Because the Tesla was a low-slung sports car, it wasn't able to take the direct path that the Liebherr had taken. It made up for the difference with speed and handling. Grant steered it onto the smoother parts of the dirt course, careful to avoid the rubble the truck was creating.

Up ahead, the Liebherr had reached the oval track and ran across it. It bounced up a twenty-foot-high berm — built so that curious photographers couldn't spy on track testing — and then dropped over the other side. The truck was so tall that he could still see part of it above the top of the berm. Then it ripped through the outer fence. Thirty yards of hardened steel mesh were torn apart and flew up and over the truck.

They had at best two minutes before the truck reached a populated area. Unable to follow over the berm in the Tesla, Grant sped through the underground tunnel toward the main gate.

Tyler got on the walkie-talkie.

"Open the gate immediately! Grant Westfield and I are in the red car. Do not shoot! Acknowledge!"

"Who is this?" came the response.

"This is Tyler Locke! Repeat, do not shoot at the red car! That's an order!"

"Yes, sir!"

The Tesla shot out of the tunnel, and the gate was ahead, still sliding open. Grant didn't let up on the accelerator. Tyler grimaced as they whizzed through the gate, missing it by inches.

Grant wrenched the wheel around and aimed for the bright yellow dump truck, which was now a half mile ahead. There was no chance that they would lose it. It was like watching a McDonald's restaurant suddenly take off and barrel down the road.

The Tesla quickly reached 100 mph. Within thirty seconds, they caught up with the Liebherr. Looming ahead was the first sign of civilization, a warehouse district outside of Deer Valley. The truck showed no signs of slowing down.

Police cars were now following, their sirens blaring, and the few cars in front of them scattered at the sight of the approaching behemoth. Tyler used his cell phone to advise the police to stay back. He didn't want any more crushed cars, and there was nothing the police could do. Armed with pistols, shotguns, and rifles, they couldn't damage the truck in any significant way. It would take a bazooka to make a dent in the truck's twelve-foot-diameter tires. And the engine itself weighed twenty thousand pounds. Bullets would just bounce off. It would take a miracle to hit anything vital.

Grant pulled up behind the truck.

"We need to stop it," Tyler said.

"You do realize that it outweighs us by about 398,000 pounds," Grant said. "I can't exactly run it off the road."

"That's why I need to get on it."

Tyler would rather just hold back and follow safely behind, but the thought of innocent bystanders getting killed by a truck that was in Gordian's hands made him sick. If it crashed through a mall, the casualties would be horrendous.

He wouldn't have to take out the driver. The Liebherr's engine bay was exposed on both sides for ease of maintenance. Halfway up the right-side stairway, he could access the engine and shut the truck down. Then when it came to a halt, he'd let the police take over.

The driver's accomplice was the biggest

problem. Tyler would have to disable the gunman so that he wouldn't be shot while tinkering with the engine.

Tyler told Grant his plan.

"You are nuts," Grant said.

"Can't argue with that," Tyler said.

"But that's what I like about you. No fear."

Tyler glanced at Grant and gave him a wry grin. "None whatsoever. Now let's do this before I come to my senses."

Grant accelerated until he was next to the rear wheels. There was little chance that the Liebherr would be able to swing over and crush the nimble Tesla, especially with Grant driving, but Tyler braced himself for that possibility anyway.

Instead, the second gunman leaned over the platform that surrounded the cab and spanned the truck from side to side. He aimed the AR-15 and let loose a volley. Bullets pinged off the ground around the Tesla, and Grant fell back behind the truck out of the gunman's sight.

"Now what?" Grant said. "With those huge rearview mirrors, they can see which side we're coming up on."

"Then let's take care of those mirrors."

Tyler took the Glock out of its holster, glad that he'd brought it with him on this trip. When he nodded, Grant gunned the engine and pulled around to the left side. The gunman was out of sight, and before he could move to their side, Tyler popped up and squeezed off six rounds at the mirror. Two bullets hit, disintegrating it.

The gunman appeared and trained his weapon on them, but Grant was already pulling around the back of the truck to the right side. Tyler put another six shots into the right mirror.

"Nice shootin', Tex," Grant said.

The driver was now blind to what was behind him. They'd have a fifty-fifty shot at getting to the stairways at the front of the truck without being seen. At least it was better than no chance at all.

Grant whipped the Tesla around the left side and raced to the front of the truck, which had just crushed the rear ends of two cars as if the vehicles were made of balsa. Tyler instinctively ducked under the debris flying over his head, and Grant barely missed colliding with one of the destroyed vehicles.

Tyler loaded his only reserve magazine and replaced the pistol on his hip, readying himself for the jump to the stairs.

There were three stairways: one each on the left and right sides of the engine bay, and a third stairway that crossed the radiator diagonally from the right side at the top to the left just above the ground. The front stairway and the left-side stairway met at the bottom at a small platform.

The Tesla pulled even with the platform. If he were Catholic, this was when Tyler would cross himself. Instead, he just muttered, "What am I doing?"

He leaped across the four-foot gap onto the platform and clanged onto the steel, grasping the railing so that he wouldn't slip off. Not only would a fall at 40 mph result in a spectacular case of road rash, but he'd most likely be flattened by one of the truck's tires.

He steadied himself and gave the thumbs-up to Grant. He pulled out the Glock again and crept up the front stairway, air whistling past him into the howling engine. As planned, Grant wheeled the Tesla away to draw attention away from Tyler.

It worked. The gunman sprayed another round of shots in Grant's direction. When Tyler reached the top, he saw the man leaning over the railing, looking toward the rear of the truck. He took aim to shoot the guy in the back. *Not very sporting,* Tyler thought, *but screw him. He made his choice when he killed those two deputies.*

Before Tyler could pull the trigger, the driver shot at him. The glass of the cab shattered, and bullets ricocheted off the metal around Tyler, sending him ducking down the stairway.

The second gunman appeared at the top of the staircase. Tyler got off a shot with his Glock, but the gunman knocked it out of his hand and over the side, using the rifle's muzzle. Tyler grabbed hold of the man's shirt, and they both tumbled down the stairs. In an effort to catch himself, the man let go of the AR-15, which fell over the railing.

As they rolled down the stairs, Tyler desperately tried to slow himself, the image of those massive tires in his mind. He came to rest at the ground-level landing and found himself on top of the gunman, who thrashed underneath him. Tyler held him down, trying to get leverage either to knock the man unconscious or toss him off the truck. He didn't care which.

Tyler heard the beep of a car horn tooting. He looked up and saw Grant in the Tesla next to him, yelling and pointing straight in front of him.

With his knees on the gunman's chest, Tyler twisted his head around and felt every muscle in his body tighten like guitar strings

when he saw what Grant was pointing at.
They were about to slam into a brick wall.

TWENTY-NINE

The suitcase sat on the floor next to Cutter as he drove. He couldn't destroy it back at the Gordian compound, which meant he'd had to steal it. The Liebherr had presented a unique possibility, and the plan had worked perfectly. He just needed to make sure he could get to his impromptu escape point before they could figure out a way to stop the truck. Once there, he could flee along with the crowds. If he was stopped before that, there would be no way off the truck without being spotted. He would be surrounded easily. He couldn't let that happen.

Then he'd seen Locke's face pop up. Simkins had rushed over without checking over the side and got surprised by Locke. Cutter had lost sight of them both, but he knew the stairs in front of the radiator went almost to the ground. If they were still on it, Cutter had an excellent way to take care of the problem.

Ahead was some kind of outdoor storage facility for a building supplier. Piles of bricks were stacked for shipping, each pile taller than the last and at least six feet thick.

All Cutter had to do was run into them. The truck would absorb the impact without slowing down. Even if the stairs weren't completely crushed, being hit by a ton of bricks would take care of Locke.

Too bad about Simkins, though. He was a good soldier, and he would die like one.

Grant, who kept the Tesla parallel to the dump truck, watched in horror as the Liebherr purposely approached the piles of bricks, spaced out at fifty-foot intervals to allow forklifts to carry the brick pallets out. The first was ten feet high, the one behind that fifteen feet, and the third one twenty feet. He was certain the driver knew Tyler was on the stairs.

He saw Tyler get his warning. Tyler kneed the man who had fallen down the stairs with him and scrambled up the front stairway. The gunman, still holding his midsection, was at the bottom of the stairs when the truck hit the first pile.

The hijacker was pulverized by the bricks, which also ripped apart the stairs just below

Tyler's feet. He lost his footing for a moment, and Grant held his breath. Tyler recovered and pulled himself up five more feet, out of the way of a second pile of bricks that exploded against the front of the truck, its hardened-steel radiator grill merely dented by the mass of bricks. Grant had seen him cheat death too many times to think Tyler would fail now, but he still couldn't believe his friend's luck.

Tyler leaped up to the top of the stairs just as the third pile wrenched the stairs loose from the top, and Grant was sure that Tyler was going to fall.

He blinked and saw that one bolt still held. Tyler dangled from a piece of railing that jutted out in front of the engine. He was too far from the right-side staircase to swing himself over. If he fell, it was twenty feet to the ground at 40 mph. Grant didn't care how lucky Tyler was, there would be no surviving that.

Grant had to help him somehow.

The Tesla started pinging. Grant looked at the instrument panel and saw the problem. The batteries of the all-electric car were almost out of juice. He could already feel it starting to slow down, which meant he had one chance to help Tyler.

The Liebherr driver, probably thinking

he'd killed Tyler, had swung back onto the main road, trailed by a gaggle of police cars, headed toward some unknown destination.

Grant would have to try something else, something even he thought was crazy.

He swung the Tesla so that it was alongside the foot of the right-side stairway. It had survived the battering by the brick piles. Grant hit the cruise control and took one final look ahead to make sure he had enough straight road. The adrenaline was flooding through him just like he was about to jump out of an airplane, except this was about a hundred times more dangerous. He shouted at the top of his lungs to pump himself up.

He stood on the seat, stabilizing the steering wheel. Then in one fluid motion, Grant jumped up and leaped onto the Liebherr stairway. He gave another shout for making it.

With the steering wheel uncontrolled, the Tesla swung left and disappeared under the truck's massive wheels. Grant heard the crunch of smashed metal. The Tesla was gone.

He turned and saw Tyler still hanging by two hands, but his grip seemed to be fading. Grant braced himself against the railing of the staircase and leaned out as far as he could stretch. Tyler let go with one hand.

They could just barely grab each other's hands.

"On three!" Grant yelled. "One! Two! Three!"

He yanked Tyler's hand as Tyler released his grip on the railing. He plunged down, and Grant reeled him in like a prize tuna. For a second, Tyler's feet bounced against the asphalt. Grant heaved and pulled him up.

When they were both secure, they fell on the stairs, panting for air.

Tyler wiped his brow with his sleeve, then pushed himself up slowly. He leaned forward with his elbows on his knees.

"And you think I'm nuts?" he said, his voice shakier than Grant had ever heard it before.

"Bat-shit cuckoo," Grant replied.

Tyler held out his hand, and Grant shook it.

"Thanks," Tyler said. "I owe you several for that maneuver."

"And we owe Tesla a new car."

"We've got bigger problems." Tyler pointed at an approaching sign. It said SPLASH WORLD PARKING LOT NEXT RIGHT. "That's how he's planning to get away."

Made sense, Grant thought, *in a sick sort*

of way. Splash World was the biggest and most popular water park in the city. Hot day like this, there'd be thousands of people there. The truck driver would just crash through the park and get out in the confusion.

"Let's get him then," Grant said, climbing toward the top of the staircase. He felt Tyler grab his ankle.

"Guy's got the AR-15 trained on us. He'll take us out before we get halfway to the cab." Tyler took out his Leatherman tool. "Here. You're the electrical engineer. Since you're on board now, you can do it."

The truck swerved around and into the Splash World parking lot. It began mowing through cars like Bigfoot's gigantic brother.

"And hurry," Tyler added.

Like most modern engines, the Liebherr's was computer controlled. If Grant could disable the computer, the truck's safeguards would kick in, cut off the fuel supply, and the brakes would automatically engage.

"If I had known you'd go to all this trouble to get me on the truck," Grant yelled as he climbed into the roaring engine bay, "I would have made you drive."

He could see a checkered view of the park fence through the front grill. It was swiftly approaching. He unfolded the Leatherman and opened the wire cutters carefully. If he dropped it, they'd be royally screwed.

Grant could make out screams in the distance, but he didn't see anyone getting run over by the truck. At least that was something. Up ahead, he saw what the driver was aiming for. A collection of water-slides. If the driver could demolish them, the panic in the park would be complete.

Grant found the wires leading to the on-board computer. He began snipping them one by one.

The truck burst through the outer fence.

Two wires to go.

Grant could see the huge wave pool pass to their left.

One wire left. With the last snip, the engine abruptly cut off. The sudden silence was deafening. The truck started to slow, but they were still rolling toward the water-slides. The screams of those who were stuck on the staircase waiting area got louder as the truck closed the distance.

Then the emergency brakes kicked in. The truck lurched, as if a giant had grabbed its rear. The truck crashed through two slides and ground to a halt just as it reached the teeming staircase, gently tapping it but nothing more. Grant whistled. Close call.

Now dripping with sweat from the heat,

Grant climbed out of the engine bay.

Tyler was above him, standing at the top of the staircase, looking at the cab. Since he wasn't being shot at, that meant only one thing.

"Don't tell me," Grant said. "He's gone."

Tyler nodded, his frustration apparent. "And he took whatever he had with him. Must have jumped into the wave pool when we passed it. Probably lost in the crowd by now."

"Lucky bastard," Grant said, mopping his brow. "At least he got to go for a swim."

THIRTY

The Tuesday evening news had been wall-to-wall coverage of the truck chase, and on Wednesday morning, the finger-pointing had begun. The damage done to the Deer Valley portion of Phoenix had been extensive, but not as catastrophic as it could have been. Except for the construction warehouse, most of the destruction was contained at Splash World. At least sixty-five cars in the parking lot were totally destroyed, and another fifty damaged. The total bill for the damage would undoubtedly run into the millions. It was a miracle that the only deaths had been the one hijacker and the two deputies. Several people at Splash World were injured, but none seriously. Still, Gordian would now have to brace for the inevitable lawsuits.

Miles Benson had made the flight down Wednesday morning to survey the destruction firsthand. Gordian was going to be blamed for not securing the Liebherr and allowing it to be used as a battering ram, and he had the ultimate responsibility. Using cranes, Gordian workers under Grant's supervision were already stabilizing the waterslide the truck was resting against and disassembling the truck for shipment back to the TEC.

"And you didn't even get the guy?" Miles said, watching the bed being lifted from the Liebherr. "How the hell did this happen?"

Tyler had returned to the TEC after the crash to assess the damage and investigate how someone had infiltrated the facility. Now that he was back at Splash World, he had an even tougher job: answering his boss's questions. The work was stirring up dust. Tyler coughed as if he was hacking up some of the dirt, but he was actually embarrassed by the slipup.

"Here's what we know so far," Tyler said. "We accounted for all of the people who entered the TEC yesterday except for two NTSB investigators. Maricopa County sheriff's department raided their hotel room. The real investigators were both dead. Shot and put on ice in the bathtub. Do not disturb sign on the door. A quick job that would have passed for a day or two at most."

"What did they get?"

"We matched the hangar's remaining contents to the G-Tag inventory. They got away with a hard-side suitcase, green, the size of a carry-on. It hadn't been opened yet by our team, so there's no way to know what was inside."

"Why bring so much attention to themselves?"

"I don't think that plane was meant to make it back to the U.S. That's the only reason I can guess as to why they made such a risky and hasty plan to get at something in that wreckage. They never thought we'd find it if it crashed in the ocean."

"Any leads?"

"The medical examiner is still pulling brick chunks out of one of the hijackers. Witnesses at the wave pool saw a man jump into the deep end as the truck passed, but he got away in the confusion. We're checking to see if any vehicle in the lot was stolen, but that will take awhile with all of the flattened cars out there. We've got the video from the camera at the TEC front gate. I'm having Aiden MacKenna run it to see if he can make an ID."

"They went to a lot of trouble to make sure we didn't open that suitcase," Miles said. "And now it's going to cost us a pretty penny."

"I'd worry more about their ultimate plans," Tyler said. "Miles, I know they built a bunker somewhere. They're planning to use it as an ark. This is all a prelude to something big, and the *Genesis Dawn* has some part in this."

"A field test for the bioweapon?"

Tyler nodded. "Could be. Maybe they were through with lab testing and wanted to see if it actually worked in an uncontrolled environment. The *Genesis Dawn* will either be another test or their endgame. Whoever *they* are."

"The end of the world is at hand," Miles said in an airy manner. "I just thought that was what crazies printed on pieces of cardboard."

"Nobody spends four hundred million dollars building a bunker unless they think they might need it someday. In this case, I think they *knew* they would need it."

"Has Dr. Kenner figured out the link with Noah's Ark yet?"

"She's back at the TEC working on it. She's convinced that her father found the actual Noah's Ark. That it's not just a metaphor for the Oasis bunker. She thinks that if we can find it, we might be able to tie all of this together. To say the least, I'm not confident."

"You don't believe." It was a statement, not a question.

"Come on, Miles. A four-hundred-foot-long wooden ship that survived six millennia and now is part of some madman's scheme to kill billions of people? You know me. I'm an empiricist. I'll believe it when I see it."

"I have to say that I'm skeptical as well, but something about Dilara Kenner's surety in her father . . . Well, I tend to listen to my gut. Her belief eases my doubts."

"And the big wooden ship that should have been rotted to dust by now?"

"Maybe your skeptical mind is latching on to the wrong thing. You should be asking yourself, how would Noah's Ark last six thousand years? If you answer that, you might actually find it. And find the perpetrators of this god-awful mess. Now I've got a real stake in solving this problem. Gordian's going to be on the hook for the damage from the Liebherr unless we find someone else to blame."

"What about the *Genesis Dawn*? It sails on its inaugural cruise in two days."

"From now on, that's your responsibility. I'm counting on you to make sure the world is still here next week. Grant will finish up here. I'll give you a lift back to the TEC.

I've got a dozen lawyers and insurance adjusters to meet with."

Following Miles back to the specially equipped van, which Miles could roll into with his iBOT and drive, Tyler for once wished his problems were as mundane as talking with attorneys about settling lawsuits. Instead, all he had to do in the next day was come up with a way to find Noah's Ark, an archaeological treasure that had been hidden since the beginning of recorded history, while preventing the deaths of virtually every person on earth.

No pressure.

THIRTY-ONE

Cutter started explaining to Ulric how, sopping wet, he had eluded the mass of police who had converged on the water park the day before and stole a car that he drove to Tucson. There, under an assumed name and using falsified documents, he boarded a plane that took him back to Seattle. As they walked back from the Orcas compound's helipad, Ulric held up his hand to say that was enough. The details of Cutter's escape were unimportant to him. The fact that he had the suitcase was all that mattered.

Although the test aboard Hayden's plane had potentially compromised the whole operation when it turned back to the mainland unexpectedly, he had to consider the mission a success. It proved that the Arkon-B could be administered in a nonlaboratory environment. Now he was assured that the delivery method for Arkon-C on the *Genesis Dawn* would be equally effective.

He had considered going ahead with the plan for the cruise ship without testing it first, but that course of action would have been risky. If it hadn't worked, and the device was discovered prematurely, it would have been difficult to mount a second attempt. Possible, because of his backup facility in Switzerland. The bunker under his castle near Bern was functional, but not nearly as comfortable as Oasis. Once Ulric had realized it would be more efficient to have all of his scientists and followers in one location, he had consolidated everything at Orcas Island and put the Swiss laboratory into hibernation. He could revive it at a later time, but only if necessary.

"Of course," Ulric said to Cutter, "this means you can't accompany me to the *Genesis Dawn* to activate the device."

Cutter protested. "I could wear a disguise."

Ulric understood. Cutter was as eager to be a part of the final operation as Ulric was. But Ulric couldn't allow anything to jeopardize their plans now.

"No, you'll stay. Take care of the preparations here. When I return, we should be ready to button up. Everyone is due to arrive in the next two days. It's just a matter of double-checking our stores and procedures."

"Yes, sir. But what about Locke? Our contact said that he went to Coleman's office."

"That avenue was thoroughly sealed off, both from Coleman's death and the subsequent scrubbing of his files. Without the device, he won't be able to make a connection to us. I thought Watson might have implicated me directly, which is why I wanted Tyler killed. Now it's obviously not necessary. Believe me, I know Tyler. If he knew anything remotely close to the truth, he would have come after me by now. He might have a few clues, but nothing that he'll put together before it's too late."

"And you completely trust our contact?"

Ulric nodded. "Absolutely. In fact, after I heard about your misadventures in Phoenix, I told him to meet me in Miami. He'll ensure that the device is activated after I leave."

When he had first heard about the *Genesis Dawn*'s inaugural sailing, Ulric knew it was the perfect way to launch the New World. The official maiden voyage of the world's largest and most luxurious cruise ship had been booked solid for years, but Ulric used the considerable clout that his billions gave him to rent the biggest suite on the ship. As part of the deal, he had promised to attend the inaugural gala. Going to the party was an annoyance, but the cabin was perfect for his needs, so he had readily agreed.

The ship would cruise to New York and then on to the major seaports of Europe, where thousands of dignitaries and passengers from around the globe would board to tour the immense vessel or even travel for a few days before disembarking, carrying their tales of the ship back to their home countries.

The entire itinerary was forty days exactly. The same forty days as Noah's Flood. When Ulric had seen the itinerary, he knew it was a sign.

When the passengers left the ship, they would travel through the busiest airports in the world. It was a perfect way to transmit the Arkon-C worldwide in a matter of weeks. By the time anyone realized the true source of the disease, it would be too late. It would have been unwittingly communicated around the world.

Ulric had been disappointed when he and his scientists had developed Arkon-B, the type he had used for the test on Hayden's plane. Although it produced the effect he wanted, it worked much too fast. The infected would be quarantined. A few thousand might have been killed. But that wasn't his plan. He needed a variant that would work more slowly.

It had taken another year to develop Arkon-C, but it finally allowed him to put his plan for the New World in motion. There was, of course, no cure, so once the Arkon-C was communicated worldwide, nothing would stop it. A few isolated groups might live through the outbreak, but it would be by sheer luck. Ulric's computer models estimated fewer than a million survivors worldwide. All he and his followers would have to do was wait it out and emerge as the leaders of the New World.

Which was why he had put so much of his fortune into building Oasis. His own underground ark. It would forever be known as Ulric's Ark.

How ironic, he thought, that finding Noah's Ark had made his own vision possible. For a brief moment, he had considered releasing news of his discovery to the world, his lifelong dream realized. But the discovery had enabled a new dream, one grander and even more profound. God had seen fit to make him the conduit for rebuilding the earth in his vision.

He would be the Noah of a new era. The father of all that would come in the New World. It was a heavy burden, but he knew that God saw something in him that generations would come to venerate.

The birth of the New World would be painful, as birth often is. Yet he was confident he would be seen as the hero he was, as God's representative who would usher in a golden era of mankind.

His companion for the New World, his beloved Svetlana, walked over to him, followed by a servant carrying her luggage. She would be there at the gala to toast the beginning of the New World with him.

"You look happy," she said. "Are you ready?"

"Do you realize," he said, "that we're about to embark on the greatest journey in history? One even greater than Noah's."

"I do," she replied. "I'm so excited. But this is the last time I'll be able to wear an Armani original, so let's hope it doesn't rain."

THIRTY-TWO

Tyler returned to the TEC Wednesday afternoon. Aiden hadn't found the identity of the hijackers in the FBI or military databases yet, so Tyler had been running the video of the car going through the TEC's front gate, trying to find some clue about their identities. Grant Westfield, having finished dismantling the Liebherr, joined him in the screening room, and a disturbing look crossed his face as soon as he saw the video.

"Son of a bitch," Grant said.

"What's wrong?"

"I know him."

"Which one?"

"The driver. The one that got away. His name is Dan Cutter."

"How do you know him?"

"I served with him in Iraq."

"Rangers?"

Grant sat heavily, the chair creaking under

the load. "For about four months. Just long enough to get to know how dirty he played it."

This was the first Tyler had heard any details about Grant's troubles in the army's Special Forces detachment. Tyler had served in the army before 9/11 and had returned to his unit as a reservist. In Afghanistan and then Iraq, where Tyler was a company commander, he had developed a close friendship and rapport with Grant, his first sergeant. Over Tyler's strenuous objections, Grant had been transferred to the Ranger Orientation Program because of his reputation as an electronics whiz, which they desperately needed for Special Forces. Combined with his combat skills, he was a formidable team member.

For all Tyler knew, everything in Grant's detachment was going well until two years later, near the time when Grant reached his in-service date. Tyler was already out at that point. He thought Grant was going to reenlist, but something happened that made Grant ask him about getting a job in the real world, so Tyler convinced him to become a partner at Gordian. Grant had never talked about his Ranger service except for vague references to an incident in Iraq.

"Is this about Ramadi?" Tyler asked.

Grant nodded slowly. It was one of the few times Tyler had seen him deadly serious. It made him nervous.

"This guy was the best," Grant said. "My superior NCO. Since I wasn't company top hat anymore, I was back to being a master sergeant then. Cutter was first sergeant, but he went by his nickname, Chainsaw, because of the way he cut the enemy to pieces. I refused to call him that, mostly to piss him off. He could sniff out insurgent hiding places no one else could find. He was a legend in the Rangers. Everyone knew him. Cutter had a better score than anyone else in the team." Score, Tyler knew, meant number of enemy kills.

"I could see that Cutter was on the edge of going too far," Grant continued. "He enjoyed the kills too much. Started notching his weapon. He had so many notches the damned thing looked like my mother's sofa after our cat got his claws on it. Then it all came to a head in Ramadi."

Grant paused for a moment. Tyler didn't interrupt. This obviously wasn't something Grant found pleasant to talk about.

"We were on an incursion looking for a suspected insurgent cell in a neighborhood in the north side of the city. We went in on foot for stealth, but we had chopper evac ready. Cutter had the cell zeroed in one of the few undamaged houses. We were approaching when a guy popped up out of nowhere with an RPG. Cutter got the rocket man in one shot, but not before the blast took out our lieutenant. That set Cutter off.

"We infiltrated the house, but we were only supposed to nab the suspects. Cutter wasn't having it. He ordered us to terminate them. So we did as ordered." Grant said it flatly, but Tyler could make out the underlying pain in his voice. "But it didn't stop there. Cutter went outside and herded all the families hiding in the nearby houses out into the street."

Tyler could sense what was coming.

"Said he wanted to question them," Grant said. "Then Cutter opened fire. Men, women, children. Maybe all of them innocent. Didn't matter to Cutter. As soon as I realized what was happening, I tackled him. The families scattered, or what was left of them. Cutter and I got into a fight right there in the street, and that's when a sniper opened up. He hit Cutter twice, in the shoulder and the groin.

"With Cutter down, I was the ranking sergeant. I called in our helo evac and got us out, including our dead. Cutter went to the hospital at Ramstein. Word was that his

329

shoulder was fine, but they had to lop off his private parts. I got out two months later. Never saw him again. But I know he remembers me."

"You think he saw you today?"

"If he did, it must have been killing him not to take me out right there. I'm sorry, Tyler. With so many people in the hangar, I didn't notice him. If I'd seen him, maybe those deputies would still be alive."

Tyler thought back to Grant jumping onto the truck to save him.

"It could have been a lot worse," he said.

"It's already pretty bad if Cutter's involved. Whoever hired him wanted the best nut he could find. And if they got Cutter, they probably got a bunch of other top-notch vets along with him. He'd know who to recruit, who'd be loyal to him, and who was willing to do the wet work. Maybe we should get the General involved."

Tyler rolled his eyes at the mention of his father. "Did Miles put you up to this?"

Grant put his hand on Tyler's shoulder. "Look, I know how you feel about your dad, but he's a pretty powerful guy, and he's got a lot of resources."

Tyler sighed. "Believe me, Grant, if I thought he could do something that we couldn't do on our own, I would go to him."

Grant looked doubtful. "Really?"

"I would be swallowing a bucketful of pride, but I'd do it."

"I'm sure he'd be willing to help."

"I'm sure he would, too. That's the problem. Then I'd owe him big." Tyler stood. "Now, I'd better call Agent Perez and let the FBI know what we're up against. Maybe they have more on the two who came at us in Seattle."

"Any more on the connection between Coleman and Whirlwind?" Grant asked.

"Not yet," Tyler said. "Things have been so busy I haven't had a chance to get back with Aiden. He's supposed to call me when he gets anything."

"I'm going back to the hangar to see if we have any other clues. Maybe Cutter left something behind, although I wouldn't bet on it."

Grant left the viewing room with Tyler, and they parted ways as Tyler turned to head toward the room he'd set up for Dilara in the main office building. He dialed Perez while he walked. The FBI agent answered on the second ring.

"Dr. Locke, you're just the person I wanted to talk to."

"You have the identities of the men in Seattle?"

"I do."

"Ex-army Special Forces?"

"How did you know that?"

Tyler told him about Chainsaw Dan Cutter and the stolen suitcase.

"I'll get him on our most wanted list right away. But he may have gone to ground."

"Have you had any threats to the *Genesis Dawn*?" Tyler asked.

"No, but I've beefed up security as much as I could. Without a direct terrorist threat, there's not much more I can do."

"Agent Perez, something is going down on the *Genesis Dawn*. It might be at the gala or it might be at sea. Either way, you're talking about eight thousand lives at risk. Don't you take Dr. Kenner's story seriously?"

"Of course we do. But we're also focused on the Hayden crash right now. Washington doesn't want to cause a nationwide panic that bioweapons might be loose on American soil. They are, however, giving me a lot of leeway and manpower just in case this leads to something."

"What about the suitcase that was taken from our TEC?" Tyler asked. "It was probably how the bioweapon was smuggled on board Hayden's airplane."

"We'll be examining every suitcase that goes on board the *Genesis Dawn,* but I don't even know what I'm supposed to find inside."

"You're going to be there yourself?"

"I told you. I'm taking you seriously. But all you've told me is that the *Genesis Dawn* is a possible target. How am I supposed to protect the world's largest cruise ship from an attack if I don't know what to look for?"

Tyler thought about that, lamenting that he'd let a possible link to hard evidence get away. If he had caught Cutter, he'd have a much better rationale for stopping the cruise.

Tyler hadn't yet told Perez about Whirlwind and the link to Project Oasis that he'd found at Coleman's. It was another unsubstantiated rumor, just a hunch that Coleman's death wasn't an accident. He didn't have any proof. But he needed to impress upon Perez the need for vigilance.

"Agent Perez, I have reason to believe this all may be connected with something called Project Oasis."

"What's that?"

"A bunker constructed underground to house hundreds of people for months at a time. I believe that whoever killed Hayden has a functional bunker ready to go."

"And how do you know that?"

"Because I worked on the project for two

months. It had a different name, but it was the same project."

"And that's why Coleman was killed," Perez said, catching on quickly. "They were covering their tracks."

"Exactly."

"Do you have evidence about Oasis?"

"No. Someone purged all of Coleman's files about the project. I was lucky to find the little I did."

Perez sighed and spoke mechanically. "I'll let my superiors know what you've found, but without evidence, it's going to be hard to convince them to do anything else. How big was the suitcase?"

"The size of a carry-on. The one on the *Genesis Dawn* may be bigger, but it would still be something portable."

"If there's anything suspicious, Dr. Locke," Perez said, "we'll find it. Don't worry." The tone was condescending, as if the FBI agent were soothing a doting mother sending her child off to kindergarten. Tyler didn't like being talked down to, and despite what Perez had said, Tyler didn't think he really was taking the threat seriously.

"That's good to hear, Agent Perez," Tyler said, "because if you don't find it, someone's

going to get on that ship with a device that
will kill every single person on board."

THIRTY-THREE

Tyler walked into the office he'd set aside
for Dilara to find her sitting at the desk,
which overflowed with books.

"A little light reading?" he asked.

"Your company was kind enough to retrieve my father's notes and research that
I'd put in storage. They arrived by FedEx
this morning. After I heard the news that he
was missing, I looked through them for
clues, but I didn't find anything useful, so
they've just moldered since then. I thought
this would be a good time to go back
through them."

"His research on Noah's Ark?"

Dilara nodded. "It was his obsession. He
believed in the historical relevance of the
Bible, that there was a basis in fact for the
Flood story. If he could find Noah's Ark, it
would show that the Flood had actually occurred."

"It might also piss off a lot of people if it

showed it didn't happen exactly as the Bible told."

"My father didn't care about that. He cared about truth. He was curious. He loved the thrill of discovery, no matter what the discovery contradicted. And he didn't believe that the Bible was an infallible document delivered directly from God's mouth. He thought that the Bible was fallible precisely because humans had manipulated it throughout the centuries."

"You mean the translations?"

"Exactly. The Bible has been translated from the original Hebrew to Greek to Latin to English. He knew it was possible that, along the way, errors were introduced in the text. The multiple English translations alone show that it can be interpreted in different ways."

She pulled out a sheaf of notes.

"These are his handwritten transcriptions from the Douay-Rheims version of the Bible, which most scholars view as the most accurate English translation. Specifically, Genesis seven through ten. Look at this line here."

Genesis 7:17: And the flood was forty days upon the earth: and the waters increased, and lifted up the ark on high from the earth.

The words "lifted up the ark on high from" were crossed out. In its place, Arvadi had written a new phrase. Now the line read:

And the flood was forty days upon the earth; and the waters increased, and the ark was high up above the earth.

"Doesn't seem that different to me," Tyler said. "Is there anything else?"
Dilara pointed to the next line.

Genesis 7:18: For they overflowed exceedingly: and filled all on the face of the earth; and the ark was carried upon the waters.

Arvadi had changed "was carried upon" to "hung above."

For they overflowed exceedingly: and filled all on the face of the earth; and the ark hung above the waters.

"Still seems like splitting hairs," Tyler said.
"I agree. But there's one more that's even stranger."

On the next page, he saw:

Genesis 8:4: And the ark rested in the seventh month, the seven and twentieth day of the month, upon the mountains of Armenia.

This time, he had replaced only one word. Instead of "upon" it said "within."

" 'And the ark rested in the seventh month,' " Tyler read, " 'the seven and twentieth day of the month, within the mountains of Armenia.' What's the significance?"

"Armenia is generally interpreted to mean Ararat. There are two peaks of Ararat: Mount Ararat and Little Ararat. Perhaps he thought the ark rested between the summits."

Tyler looked through the pages and found one more line underlined several times.

Genesis 9:15: And I will remember my covenant with you, and with every living soul that beareth flesh: and there shall no more be waters of a flood to destroy all flesh.

Destroy all flesh. Exactly what happened on Hayden's airplane. Tyler shuddered at the coincidence.

"God's covenant with Noah after the flood," Dilara said and then began reciting from memory. " 'And the bow shall be in the clouds, and I shall see it, and shall remember the everlasting covenant, that was made between God and every living soul of all flesh which is upon the earth.' "

"What do you think all these notes mean?" Tyler asked.

"He told me his pet theory a number of times, but he never had the historical data to back it up, so I dismissed it. Now I feel so stupid."

"Don't be too hard on yourself. For decades, the best scientists in the world discounted Wegener's theory of continental drift. Now any geologist who disputed it would be considered a crackpot. What was his pet theory?"

"That a mysterious scroll called the Book of the Cave of Treasures was the key to finding Noah's Ark. It contained a secret so explosive that no one would believe it unless the actual Ark was found."

"He never told you the secret?"

Dilara shook her head. "He said he was very close to finding it. In the days before he went missing, he had a breakthrough. The last time I spoke with him, he told me it was only a matter of weeks before he would stun the world with his pronouncement, and that I would be able to hold my head up and be proud of him. I thought it was another of his wild goose chases until Sam Watson came along and turned my world upside down."

Dilara leaned back and ran her fingers through her hair. The silver locket on her neck reflected the desk lamp and caught Tyler's eye. The locket that Dilara's father had sent her just before going missing . . .

"So you think the breakthrough was finding the Book of the Cave of Treasures?" he asked.

"That's as good a guess as any, but I've looked through all of these files. There's nothing like that here."

"He would have wanted you to find it, right? In case he couldn't complete his quest?"

"I suppose so. But he never told me where the scroll was."

"Maybe he couldn't. Maybe whoever killed him would have taken it if they had known about it."

"Then where is it?"

"You said that your father never took that locket off, that you were surprised to receive it. May I see it?"

She unclasped the necklace and handed it to Tyler. He opened it and saw the picture of her mother.

"Do you know why your father sent it to you?"

"He said it was a birthday present."

Tyler looked at the photo again. In the quick look he'd gotten at the oil platform after the helicopter crash, he hadn't noticed that it had suffered water damage from Dilara's time in the ocean. The photo was bowed out, as if something had expanded behind it. He took out his Leatherman and unfolded the knife.

"Do you mind? I won't harm the photo."

Dilara looked confused, but she nodded her assent. Tyler pried at the photo until the plastic covering came loose. The covering and photo fell to the table, along with a tiny piece of paper.

Dilara looked stunned.

"I think there was another reason he wanted you to have this," Tyler said. He carefully unfolded the paper until it was a flat square no more than an inch on each side. A fine pen had written precise lettering, but the ink had run.

"That's my father's handwriting," she said quietly. "Even with the smudges, I recognize it."

Tyler compared it to the notes and saw that she was right. He could make out three letters. *B C T.* Then a *1* followed by what looked like more numbers that had been rendered illegible by the smeared ink.

"*B C T,*" Tyler said. "The Book of the Cave of Treasures?"

Dilara leaped to her feet with excitement. "This note is telling me where it's stored! He must have hidden it before he died!"

"And if we can find it, it will lead us to Noah's Ark."

"But the note's ruined," she said. "We'll never find it now."

"Not necessarily. We've got some highly sensitive instruments here at the TEC. I'll have our lab see if they can pick up what it says. In the meantime —"

His cell rang. The display said it was Aiden MacKenna. Tyler answered it.

"Aiden, give me good news."

"Well, I might have something for you," Aiden said. "I finally had some time to delve into Sam Watson's background. He worked for a small drug company named PicoMed Pharmaceuticals. Some kind of think tank. They've never produced an FDA-approved drug. I tried to hack into their servers, but it's completely inaccessible. It smells like a military cover, but the odor is a little off."

"Why?"

"I backtracked through our military and government databases. No mention of them at all. If they were getting funding from the government, they've covered it up well."

"How does that help us?"

"Their CEO is someone named Cristian Bulesa. Ever heard of him?"

"No. Should I have?"

"Not really. Just a shot in the dark. Let's move on to Project Whirlwind. I thought I'd start with the shell company that funded Oasis, Juneau Earthworks. They folded three months ago."

"That's pretty convenient."

"I thought so, too, so I checked their business registration. They were a Delaware S Corporation. The CEO listed: Cristian Bulesa."

"Bingo!"

"Right. And Cristian Bulesa has one interesting thing in common with Rex Hayden's brother. They were both heavily involved with the Church of the Holy Waters."

"You're kidding!"

"I did a little digging and found that most of the church's funding comes from one source. A private corporation called Ulric Pharmaceuticals."

"As in Sebastian Ulric?"

"You've got it. He's the leader of the church. I thought Cristian Bulesa sounded funny, so I rearranged the letters and —"

Tyler saw where Aiden was going and couldn't believe it. "What an ego! He used an anagram of Sebastian Ulric for his shell companies?"

"A real comedian, that one. I saw that Gordian once worked on a contract for Ulric Pharmaceuticals. Have you ever met him?"

Tyler gritted his teeth. "Unfortunately."

Several years back, Ulric had hired Gordian on the development of a biological laboratory for his main campus in Seattle. The lab was to be state-of-the-art, and Ulric wanted Gordian's expertise to vet the containment facilities. It was an important project, so Ulric himself had been heavily involved, and Tyler had to work closely with him. The project went well, and Ulric seemed to be impressed with Tyler and Gordian.

After the design phase was complete, Gordian's involvement from that point on was simply to monitor progress during construction, so Tyler had moved on to the Whirlwind project. But he still did some work on Ulric's project, and that's when the problems started.

Ulric began to bring up the Church of the Holy Waters to Tyler in friendly conversation, talking about how he had conceived of the church while he was at Yale. At first, in the interest of maintaining the contract, Tyler politely rebuffed what he saw as recruitment efforts. Ulric invited Tyler out to Hawaii, ostensibly to talk about the lab project, but when he got there, Tyler was given the hard sell about the church. Ulric railed about how the condition of the environment was appalling and that humanity was a pockmark on the beauty of the earth. His church was the only answer, to bring in the brightest minds in the world who understood the need for a better tomorrow.

Ulric thought Tyler was just the type of man they were looking for, and even though he found Ulric charming, Tyler also thought the man was a certifiable loon. Ulric's disdain for those whom he considered beneath his intellectual capability, including Tyler, was apparent, and although Tyler agreed with much of what he lamented about the state of the world, Ulric's rants about the need for profound change bordered on the fanatical. Tyler made it very clear that he wanted nothing further to do with what he considered a wacky cult and flew back to Seattle on his own dime.

When he got back and reviewed Ulric's project, Tyler noticed that the construction process was flouting the environmental safeguards that Gordian had specified in the design. When Tyler brought it up to Ulric, he was immediately fired from the project and told in no uncertain terms that Ulric's team of lawyers would take Gordian apart if he pursued it further.

Two weeks later, the Whirlwind contract was abruptly canceled. The one-two punch had been a severe blow to Gordian, but at the time, Tyler hadn't seen any connection. Now it looked like Ulric was behind Whirlwind, which would explain why it was ripped out from under him.

"So Sebastian Ulric is involved in this?" Tyler said, dreading what that meant.

"He's certainly got the billions to pay for Project Whirlwind. And there's one more interesting tidbit." It sounded like Aiden was saving the best for last.

"Spill it, Aiden."

"Sebastian Ulric himself has reserved the biggest suite on the *Genesis Dawn* for the maiden voyage. He's supposed to make an appearance at the gala Thursday night."

"That's way too many coincidences for me."

"I thought so, too. And I think I know what you're going to say next. You want to go to the gala."

"Yes. Get me two tickets. I want to talk to Sebastian myself."

"And Aiden is right again! Gordian did some key work for the cruise line two years ago, so Miles was able to swing a cabin for you. The tickets are waiting for you at the ship in Miami. Bon voyage!"

Tyler hung up and looked at Dilara, who glanced up when she heard him finish.

"What?" she asked.

"I think we need to go shopping again. The only problem is, I have no idea where to find an evening gown for you."

"An evening gown?"

Tyler nodded. "Want to go to a party?"

■ ■ ■ ■

GENESIS DAWN

■ ■ ■ ■

THIRTY-FOUR

Through the open balcony door of the suite in the *Genesis Dawn,* Tyler could hear the faint burble of a cigarette boat cruising past the Dodge Island cruise ship terminal. In the distance, the high-rises of Miami were ablaze with lights now that the sun had set. He glanced at his watch. 7:30 P.M. The gala had already started a half hour ago. No sense arriving early. Not with the impression he wanted to make.

Tyler appraised his tuxedoed form in the mirror of the suite's living room. Not bad for a scruffy engineer who'd almost been crushed to a pulp by a pile of bricks just two days ago. Someone had recovered his Glock after he'd dropped it during the truck chase. It had been a little battered, but a quick cleaning had returned it to working condition, and since Florida allowed the carrying of concealed weapons, he'd gotten a tux jacket one size too big to allow him to carry the pistol without a bulge in the suit. After that chase in Phoenix, he had a feeling he'd be needing it again, as well as his trusty Leatherman, which he kept in a belt holster.

Once he had heard Sebastian Ulric's name, Tyler knew his previous client was involved with everything that had happened. There was no doubt in his mind. Now the problem was proving it. Tyler had spent the last twenty-four hours wondering how he was going to get the proof, with no success. It was a lot of coincidences that added up to a hunch. No one would question the word of one of the country's wealthiest men, even if he was the leader of a shady religious organization.

Tyler knew that Ulric's combination of wealth and self-righteousness made him a very dangerous enemy. The FBI was already searching the ship and the luggage, so Tyler decided to try a different approach. If he could surprise Ulric at the gala, he might be able to throw him off balance, goading him into making a mistake, or at the very least into postponing whatever he was planning for the *Genesis Dawn.*

For just a moment after he'd decided to come to Miami, Tyler had considered leaving Dilara behind. The thought of the two of them on a ship where a virulent bio-weapon was about to be deployed wasn't comforting to either of them. But when he'd seen her with that locket and realized how important it was to her to find out who was responsible for her father's death, he knew coming without her would be impossible. She needed to get to the bottom of this even more than he did.

"How's it going in there?" Tyler asked through the bedroom door.

"Almost ready," Dilara said. "Just a few snags getting it on. It's a little tight."

"Need any help?"

"I'll let you know if I do."

A moment later, she slid the doors apart. Tyler felt his mouth drop open, and he sucked in a sharp breath.

They had made a foray out of the TEC to an upscale Phoenix clothing store, where Dilara had picked out a simple black evening gown and matching high heels. Tyler hadn't seen her try it on, so he was surprised when she revealed herself. Up until this point, Tyler had seen her only in work clothes, her hair in a bun or ponytail and no makeup.

Now she was utterly transformed. Her raven hair fell past her shoulders and complemented the dress, which clung to her lithe torso before it draped to the floor. The front of the dress plunged into a V, showing off the sole piece of jewelry, her father's locket. Her soft makeup highlighted her high cheekbones and chocolate brown eyes.

She gave a slight curtsy and said, "Well?"

Tyler shook off his shock. "You look absolutely stunning."

She smiled, looking both embarrassed and flattered by the compliment. "In my line of work, I don't get to dress up often."

"Well, let's show everyone what they've been missing," he said. He held out his arm. "Shall we?"

With the heels, she stood almost as tall as Tyler. She took his arm and looked directly in his eyes, transfixing him. "I have to say that I never expected an engineer who looked so dashing in a tux."

"Maybe I should wear one more often."

"I think you should," she said appreciatively. Then her voice turned businesslike. "Now let's go see if we can get some answers."

They exited the cabin into a hallway that overlooked the center mall of the *Genesis Dawn*. The open atrium was the length of two football fields and nine decks high. The top seven decks held cabins that lined the balconies, while the bottom two decks were crowded with shops, restaurants, and bars. At one end, three glass elevators carried the passengers who didn't want to walk the spiral ramp that wrapped around them. The bottom level, fifty feet wide, had been transformed from a walkway into a grand ballroom for the gala. Thousands of guests jammed the atrium, while white-jacketed waiters carried trays of champagne and hors d'oeuvres.

Tyler was already scanning, looking for Ulric.

"Do you see him?" Dilara said as they walked down the hall to the elevator.

"Not yet," he said. "With this many people, it might take awhile."

But then Tyler spied a blond man animatedly holding forth with a group of couples intently focused on what he was saying. Tyler recognized the arm movements from his days in Hawaii when Ulric had talked his ear off about sin and retribution. The man looked around for just a second, and Tyler got a clear view of his face. He was a handsome man, his features not as soft as Tyler remembered, and his hair was as perfectly styled as his five-thousand-dollar tux.

It was Sebastian Ulric. He was accompanied by a slim young woman standing by his side.

"That's him," Tyler said, nodding at him.

He had told Dilara some of his history with Ulric on their flight over from Phoenix.

"That's the man who killed my father?" she said.

"I don't know. But I'm willing to bet that he's behind all this. He's certainly capable of it."

"He looks so charming. It's hard to believe he's a mass murderer."

"We need to be careful with him, Dilara. He's a dangerous man. Maybe even a sociopath. But he's extremely intelligent. If we're going to come away with anything, we're going to have to play it just right. Follow my lead."

He escorted her to the elevator, and when they got to the main floor, one of the ship's exceptionally perky cruise directors saw them entering the gala.

"Care to purchase additional tickets for the raffle?" she asked. "Because you're a guest, you're automatically entered to win one of the great prizes over there." She pointed to a platform in the middle of the floor. It was piled with shiny objects: a red Mustang convertible, two Suzuki motorcycles — one red, one black — plasma TVs, computers, and a myriad of other electronic equipment. The keys to the car and motorcycles, each with a fob matching the vehicle's color, were displayed in a locked glass case along with the electronics.

"You increase your chances of us handing you one of those keys at the end of the trip," the cruise director said, "if you buy additional tickets."

"No thanks," Tyler said and grabbed a couple of champagnes for him and Dilara from a passing waiter. It took several minutes for them to wind their way through the crowd to a position behind Ulric. Tyler felt Dilara's grip tighten on his arm.

"I think I've seen that woman before," she whispered in his ear.

"The one with Ulric?"

"Yes."

"Where?"

"In LAX. She's the businesswoman who tripped on her purse."

"The one who poisoned Sam Watson?"

She nodded. "Her hair was different, and I only glimpsed her for a moment, so I can't be sure. But her profile sent me back to that moment."

"Would you remember her voice?"

"Maybe. The woman at LAX had an accent."

"Let me know if you recognize it."

Tyler moved them closer so they could

hear the conversation. Ulric had just finished speaking, and one of the men gathered around him asked a question.

"I understand your point," the portly man said, "but don't you think it's important to balance the business perspective with protecting the environment?"

"What balance can there be?" Ulric said. He spoke in a baritone that to others probably sounded stately, but that Tyler found flat and chilling. "Humanity is the most rapacious, destructive creature ever to roam the earth, extinguishing more species than any other animal in the planet's history. I admit that many individuals care deeply for what we are doing to our world, but as a whole . . . well, I don't believe the devastation will stop until something drastic occurs."

"Something drastic? Like global warming?"

"I'm afraid climate change is simply a symptom of our efforts to wipe out other species, intentional or not. It might get our attention, but it will only shift our focus momentarily. Then we will go back to eradicating everything that isn't safeguarded in zoos. No, I imagine it would have to be more extreme."

"And God looked upon the earth," Tyler

interrupted, "and, behold, it was corrupt; for all flesh had corrupted his way upon the earth." Tyler had taken time on the flight to Miami to reread the Bible's story of Noah.

Ulric turned to see who had intruded on their conversation. Tyler made sure to keep his gaze on Ulric's eyes. For a split second, Tyler could see a combination of surprise and fear contort his face. Then like the consummate actor he was, Ulric immediately regained his composure. His face went neutral before erupting into a smile.

"Tyler Locke," he said. "I didn't know you were a biblical scholar." He didn't extend his hand, and neither did Tyler.

"I just dabble," Tyler said. "I'm surprised that a billionaire who can afford his own yachts would lower himself to ride on a ship with the rest of us peons."

The other passengers watched the exchange with curiosity.

"I happen to be a major stakeholder in this cruise line," Ulric said, "and I thought I'd lend my support for this historic occasion."

"What occasion would that be?"

Ulric paused for a moment, then widened his smile, as if acknowledging Tyler's meaning. "Why, the sailing of the world's largest passenger vessel, of course. On my left is

Svetlana Petrova. And who would your lovely companion be?" Ulric stole a glance at her locket. He knew very well who she was.

"I'm Dilara Kenner." With her eyes, she bored a hole into Petrova. "Are you originally from Russia?"

"From the outskirts of Moscow," Petrova said with a faint accent. "I moved here when I was thirteen."

Dilara nodded. A tightening of her grip told him it was the woman who had poisoned Sam Watson.

"Are you here for business or pleasure?" Ulric asked.

"A little of both," Tyler replied. "The cruise line asked me to consult on some engineering plans for their next ship, and they offered me a cabin on this one as part of the deal. I thought, why not?"

"Are you staying for the entire cruise?"

"Just to New York. Forty days is too much time on board for me. What about you? What do the next forty days hold for you?"

"Oh, I'm spending the night on board, but then I must depart. I have a busy agenda."

"What do you think about the Rex Hayden plane crash? I understand his brother was involved in your church."

"It's tragic for two brothers to die so young. The media has been somewhat cryptic up to this point as to the cause of the crash."

"I'm actually involved in the investigation."

Ulric's eyes glittered malevolently. "Is that so? What have you determined?"

"I can't talk about it. Still ongoing."

"Of course. I know you engineers are sticklers for process. And what is your profession, Ms. Kenner?"

"I'm an archaeologist. My father got me interested. Hasad Arvadi. Maybe you've heard of him?"

"As a matter of fact, I have. I'm something of a Noah's Ark buff, and I came across the work of your father. Intriguing ideas, if a bit misguided. I understand he's been missing for quite some time. A shame." He said it with exaggerated sympathy.

Ulric was having fun playing with them. Tyler could sense Dilara rising to take the bait, so he headed her off.

"So when you were talking about something drastic," he said, "you meant the Flood. Something to wipe out humanity and start over."

"If God were so inclined," Ulric said, "that would be His decision."

361

"But you know His covenant with Noah. God said He would never again send a Flood to destroy all flesh. The Bible is very specific."

"Yes, it is. But God could choose to eradicate only the human race — or at least most of it — by nuclear war, rogue asteroid, or some other means. Such a grim outcome, in His view, might be necessary to reset all of the damage we've done."

" 'To save the village, we had to destroy it,' as they said in Vietnam."

"Do you think humans will change their ways, Tyler? Do you really believe six billion people can make the right choice when it comes to protecting this planet?"

"If we don't, who will? A supreme being who believes he is the only one who knows what's right for everyone else?" Tyler made sure Ulric understood that the supreme being he was talking about was Sebastian Ulric.

"If that's what it takes, I have faith that God has chosen the best path for humanity. Now, my dear," Ulric said to Petrova, "I am worn out from this party. I think we should take advantage of our suite amenities. Good evening, everyone. It's been a wonderful celebration. And Tyler, if we don't see each

362

other again," he said pointedly, "enjoy your cruise."

He gave a last smile to Tyler, then turned. Before he could leave, Tyler leaned in and whispered in Ulric's ear.

"You'd better pray we don't see each other again, Sebastian. Because if we do, you'll know you've failed and I've won."

That finally got the smile to disappear from Ulric's face. The fear returned for a moment, then he dismissed Tyler with a sneer and walked away.

With a look of pure hatred, Dilara watched them leave.

"It took everything I had not to punch that woman in the face," she said.

"I know how you feel. But at least we know one thing."

"What? That Ulric is a psycho?"

"I already knew that," Tyler said, "and I could tell by his smug expression that he thinks we're too late. Whatever he has planned, he's here to kick it off."

"It won't happen with him on the ship."

"That's right. He said he's leaving before it sails. So we've got until the *Genesis Dawn* leaves port tomorrow morning. If we don't find out what he's planning before then, he's going to get his doomsday scenario."

THIRTY-FIVE

Tyler and Dilara took time to eat at the gala. Tyler kept one eye on his cabin door five decks up just to make sure that no one entered while they were gone. He had been quiet since the conversation with Ulric, considering his next move.

What was Ulric doing here? If the incident on Rex Hayden's airplane was related, they could be planning the same thing on this ship. With such an immense vessel, distributing the bioweapon would be much more difficult. He could use the food, which was how the norovirus that regularly sickened passengers was passed along, but the industry had gotten much better at maintaining a safe food supply. Tyler looked at the empty plate on his table and immediately discounted that method. Ulric wouldn't have infected people while he was still on board.

The water system might be vulnerable, but it would require accessing the central distribution point from the desalination plant. Someone would have to get access to secure areas of the ship. It was a possibility, but risky.

The easiest method, one that Tyler guessed had been used on the plane, was an airborne pathogen. That meant finding a central location for inserting it into the ship's air-handling system. But Ulric couldn't expect any device to be left alone for a significant period of time, not with the rigorous maintenance a new ship would be subject to. He'd need someplace that was guaranteed not to be disturbed . . .

The solution hit Tyler like a two-by-four. He shot out of his seat.

"That's it," he said.

"That's what?" Dilara asked.

"Ulric. He made a mistake when he told me he wasn't staying for the cruise. Come on. I need to call Aiden and have him send something to my computer."

The music had stopped, signaling that the gala was over, and they threaded their way through the thinned crowd toward the elevator.

On his way back to the room, he called Aiden to have him send a complete schematic for the ship, particularly the air-handling system.

Tyler made a quick sweep of the room to make sure it hadn't been disturbed, and when he was satisfied, he flipped open his computer. One of the ship's features was a wireless Internet connection throughout the vessel, so he immediately saw the e-mail from Aiden. In the body of the e-mail was the other piece of information he'd requested. Ulric's cabin number.

He called up the schematics. Ulric's cabin, a sprawling 2,500-square-foot suite, was on the highest residential deck at the bow of the ship, just above the bridge. The views from the balcony spanning from one side to the other would be marvelous.

Then he overlaid Ulric's cabin with the venting system and saw what he was expecting.

"I'll be damned."

"What is it?" Dilara asked. She bent over Tyler, and her perfume washed over him. He tried to ignore its exhilarating effect and pointed at the screen.

"His suite is the only one right next to the main air intake for the ship," he said. "Anything injected into the air stream there would be distributed throughout the ship."

"That's how he's going to infect everyone?"

"That's my guess. He could drill a hole

366

through his wall right into the air shaft, and no one would ever know. Even if he's not here, he could leave instructions not to have the room disturbed. There would be no chance that the device would be shut down."

"We should tell someone."

"The problem will be getting access to his cabin. It's probably guarded."

"What about the FBI?"

"I suppose that's an option, although they prefer to have warrants, and that'll be hard to get with the lack of evidence we have."

"Are you always so optimistic?"

He stood and found himself face-to-face with Dilara. His vision contracted to just her eyes, and he could feel her breath on his lips.

"I try to think through the alternatives. But believe me, I will get at whatever is in his cabin and stop it. Then we can find out what happened to your father."

"I appreciate you taking all of this on. You didn't have to."

"Yes, I did."

Before Tyler realized the impulse, he swept her into his arms. He kissed her deeply, with a passion he hadn't felt in a long time. Her body felt warm and firm against his own. She ran her fingers through his hair as they kissed. He ran his hands down her exquisite back . . .

A knock at the door interrupted them. They stepped apart, as though their parents had caught them making out on the living room couch.

Tyler smiled, and then he realized why that one simple kiss was different from any other in the last two years. For the first time, he hadn't compared the experience to Karen. He didn't know what that meant, but he didn't feel the guilt he thought he would.

The knock came again, harder.

Wiping the lipstick from his mouth with a handkerchief, Tyler went to the door and opened it to see Special Agent Perez, who walked in without waiting to be invited. He gave a lingering glance at Dilara, who was fixing her hair.

"I'm not interrupting anything, am I?"

"Not at all," Tyler said. "In fact, I was about to come find you."

"Now? You've been here all evening, and you didn't come tell me?"

"I didn't have anything when I arrived, so I didn't want to bother you. But now I do."

"Like what? Is this about our discussion yesterday?"

Tyler shook his head. "Sebastian Ulric. He's on board. He's behind Rex Hayden's crash. The same kind of thing is going to happen on this ship, and I know how."

"The billionaire?" Perez said in disbelief. "That's great. I suppose you have evidence?"

"I have a theory. I can show it to you on my computer."

Perez put up his hands. "That can wait. I need you to come with me. That's why I came here. When I saw your names on the guest list, I made sure to observe you during the gala. I didn't want to make contact there in case we were seen together, so I waited to get you until you returned to your room."

"Where are we going?"

"We have a cabin set up downstairs where we can talk about it."

"What's it about?"

"I'm afraid I can't talk about it here."

"Okay. Come on, Dilara."

Perez shook his head. "I'm afraid she doesn't have the proper clearance. She'll have to stay here."

"She stays with me," Tyler said firmly.

"No. Only you. Now." When Tyler hesitated, Perez said, "It's important."

Perez's secrecy was odd, but after a moment, Tyler grudgingly nodded.

"I have a key," he said to Dilara. "If someone knocks, don't let them in. Call me right away, and I can get back here in thirty seconds."

"You do look at all the alternatives, don't you?" she said with a smile. "I'll be fine."

Tyler liked her spirit. She was a lot like Karen in that way. But even with the similarities, she was her own person, and that's why his feelings were different this time.

He returned the smile and nodded.

Then Tyler left with Agent Perez to find out what was so important for him to see.

Dilara saw the door close and wondered what had just happened. The kiss certainly didn't come out of nowhere. She'd felt the attraction to Tyler for a few days now. But she had just dismissed it as a crush brought on by unusual circumstances. Now she didn't know what to make of it.

If they were going to find out what was in Ulric's cabin, she was damn well going to help. That meant getting out of her clingy dress and into something more appropriate. The first thing was to remove her makeup, so she went into the bathroom to wash it off.

She was about to turn on the sink when she heard the faint whine of the electronic lock on the cabin door. It had been less than a minute since Tyler and Perez had left. Her

370

first thought was that Tyler had come back for his computer.

"Forget something?" she yelled.

No one answered.

"It's okay. I'm in the bathroom."

Still no answer.

That was odd. Just a moment ago, he worried about her opening the door for strangers. Now he was creeping around the room? Dilara hadn't known Tyler long, but she knew that wasn't his style. He would have answered her. Something was wrong.

With a jolt, she realized the answer. Someone else was in the room.

The bathroom door was ajar, but she didn't want to take the chance that whoever was out there would see her peeking. She needed to keep the person off guard. Without a weapon, her one asset was surprise.

"I'm just changing," she said, attempting to maintain the same tone of voice. "I'll be out in a minute." She removed her high heels.

She took her compact, opened it to use the small mirror inside, and backed behind the open door, which hid her from the view of the bathroom mirror. She lowered the compact mirror out of eye level and used it to see the reflection in the bathroom mirror. If she timed it right, she could make the most of her surprise advantage.

The first thing she saw was an outstretched arm holding a gun slowly advancing toward the bathroom. Then the face came into view. It was Svetlana Petrova, the woman who had killed Sam Watson.

Dilara lowered the compact and waited until the hand with the gun protruded into the bathroom. With her full weight, she slammed the door shut.

Petrova's hand was crushed into the door frame, and she screamed. The gun clattered to the floor. Dilara rushed to pick it up, but Petrova was more resilient than she expected.

The door slammed inward, knocking Dilara backward into the shower. She bounced off the tile wall, using the momentum to launch herself at Petrova before she could reach the pistol.

She aimed her head like a battering ram and threw her shoulder into Petrova's stomach. She heard an "oof!" of air escape from Petrova's lungs, and she pile-drove Petrova onto the bedroom floor.

While Petrova lay on the floor, gasping for breath, Dilara scrambled back into the bathroom. She scooped up the pistol and pointed it at Petrova, who looked at her with an odd smile.

"Tell me why I shouldn't kill you right here," Dilara said.

"Because I wouldn't like it," said a voice to her left. She glanced in that direction and saw Sebastian Ulric aiming a gun at her. Like the one she held, it was equipped with a silencer.

"Put your gun down," Dilara said, "or I'll put a bullet in her brain." She hoped she sounded determined. She'd handled guns all her life, but she'd never shot anyone before.

"Then I would have to shoot you, and I don't think you'd like that."

"I'm serious. I'll do it." And it suddenly occurred to Dilara that she would.

"You might, but that counts on me caring about Svetlana more than I care about killing you. Are you willing to take that chance?"

Dilara saw the look in Ulric's eye and realized that he was a true sociopath. He didn't care.

"You hesitate because you think I'll kill you anyway," Ulric said. "I promise you, if I wanted to shoot you, we wouldn't be having this discussion. I am an excellent shot."

Dilara couldn't argue with that reasoning. Her best bet was to find out what they wanted. She dropped the gun.

Petrova took it and stood. Dilara expected a reprisal, maybe a smack in the head, but it didn't come.

"So what now?" Dilara asked.

"Our work here is done. We're leaving the ship, and you're coming with us."

That explained why they couldn't have her bruised and bleeding. Too many questions on their way out. Petrova retrieved Dilara's shoes from the bathroom.

"Where are we going?" Dilara said as she put on the heels.

"You'll find out when we get there," Ulric said. "But I guarantee it will be better than being on this ship."

She nodded. On her way out was her chance to alert someone to her predicament.

"And I know what you're thinking," Ulric said as he led her to the door. "If you try to tell anyone that you are being taken off the ship against your will, we won't shoot you. We'll shoot whoever you signal."

As they walked down the corridor, Petrova kept behind her with the gun hidden under a shawl wrapped around her arm.

"I saw how you hung on to Locke's arm during the party," Petrova said, her voice dripping with ridicule. "You can forget about him. You'll never see him again. He's as good as dead."

THIRTY-SIX

Tyler and Perez took the glass elevator down to a floor two decks above the central atrium. On the way down, Tyler could see crew members cleaning up after the gala, but passengers still wandered along the atrium and lingered at several of the bars along the sides.

They exited the elevator and started walking aft.

Tyler had no idea what was so important for Perez to show him, but he couldn't get the FBI agent to tell him.

"What are we going to do about Ulric?" he asked Perez. "We've only got a few hours before the *Genesis Dawn* sets sail."

"What do you want me to do?"

"Raid his room. If I'm right, he's got some kind of device hooked into the ship's ventilation system. I don't think he'll activate it until he's off the ship, but if we can catch him with it, it'll prove that he's behind this."

"You know, Dr. Locke, you lost a lot of credibility coming here without telling me. Why didn't you tell me your suspicions about Sebastian Ulric when I spoke to you yesterday?"

"At the time, I didn't know. Even after I got the information that he might be involved with building that bunker I told you about, I had no firm evidence. I wanted to talk to him myself, and I thought you might interfere if I told you I was coming."

"You're damned right I would have! Although Sebastian Ulric is involved with the Church of the Holy Waters — which the FBI has been investigating for some time without finding a single crime — to accuse one of the country's richest men of involvement in this Project Whirlwind is a serious charge."

A red light went off in Tyler's head, but he didn't know why. Something about what Perez said was off.

"Agent Perez, you checked all of the luggage, didn't you?"

"All of it. We found some contraband, but nothing that suggested a bioweapon."

"And Ulric's bags?"

"I'm telling you it was all searched."

They reached an outside cabin at the end of the hallway. Tyler wasn't satisfied by

377

Perez's answer. Ulric had to get the device on board somehow. His luggage would be the logical method, but how would he get anything through the bag search?

Something wasn't right. Tyler put his hand on his belt and fiddled with his Leatherman.

"Have you spoken to Aiden MacKenna or Grant Westfield?" he asked.

"Don't know them." Perez swiped his key at the door. He let Tyler walk in first.

Tyler was a step in when he finally understood why the red light went off. Project Whirlwind. That was the name it had during the short time that Tyler worked on it. But the name had been changed to Oasis when it was transferred to Coleman, and Project Oasis was what he called it when he talked to Perez the day before.

Only he, Dilara, Grant, and Aiden knew the connection between Whirlwind and Oasis. If Perez had never heard about it from them, there was only one way he could have known about Whirlwind.

Perez was in on it.

The cabin was a two-room suite like the one he and Dilara had. If it had been some kind of control room, Tyler would have expected to see agents sitting at high-tech equipment. But the living room area was empty.

All of those thoughts happened in one step. In one movement of his foot, Tyler had gone from utter safety to grave danger. He kept his gait unchanged, but he couldn't reach for his Glock, which was under his left arm. If he did, Perez would see the move before he had the gun out.

Instead, he slipped the Leatherman out of its holster and flipped open the folding knife.

"So what are we doing here?" he said. At the same time, he crouched down and whirled around. Perez had already unholstered his pistol, but instead of aiming it, he was bringing it down to pistol-whip Tyler.

Tyler ducked aside. The pistol slammed into his bicep, and pain shot up his arm. The knife in his other hand slung around and slashed Perez's wrist. Perez cried out, and the pistol went flying toward the door, where it landed on the carpet. Tyler brought his elbow around and sent a blow at Perez's face.

Perez lurched toward the door. He crashed against it, splintering the frame, but remained standing. He looked down and saw the gun at his feet. He bent over to pick it up. Tyler dropped the Leatherman and reached for his Glock. He had it aimed at Perez before the FBI agent could reach his service piece.

"Don't move!" Tyler yelled.

Perez froze, his hand inches from his weapon.

"You never said Whirlwind, did you?" Perez said. "That's what it was called when you worked on it, so my mind reverted to that code name. I knew it was wrong as soon as I said it. Funny how one little mistake can get you."

"Where's your partner?" Tyler demanded.

"She's in the next room. Alive. For now."

Tyler stole a quick glance at the bedroom. Out of the corner of his eye, he could see Melanie Harris's inert form on the bed. "You work for that wacko?"

"Sebastian Ulric is a great man. History will show it."

This guy was just as loony as Ulric was.

"Stand up," Tyler said.

Perez didn't move. "The world will soon be completely different."

"I will shoot you if you try to pick up that gun."

"Humanity is weak. We will make it strong again."

"I said, stand up," Tyler repeated.

"You can't stop it."

"Stop what?"

"The New World."

Like a striking cobra, Perez reached out and snatched the gun. He stood, bringing the weapon to bear. Tyler had no choice. He fired a three-shot burst at Perez's chest. Perez crashed through the weakened cabin door. The gun went flying out of his hand and over the railing. Perez slumped to the floor.

Tyler rushed over to Agent Harris. She was hog-tied, gagged, and moaning softly. She had a nasty bump on the side of her head.

He removed the gag and began to untie her. When he turned her to loosen the rope, her blouse came untucked, gathering up around her midsection. Beneath it was a gray material. Tyler touched it and felt the hard Kevlar. A bulletproof vest.

Dammit!

He ran back to the cabin door and saw what he dreaded.

Tyler saw nothing. Perez was gone.

THIRTY-SEVEN

Tyler ran out to the hallway balcony. It was already filling with passengers who had heard the gunshots. An elderly woman peeked her head out from the cabin nearest to him. She gasped when she saw the gun in his hand.

"Call 911," Tyler said to her. He pointed through the door. "There is an injured FBI agent in that cabin."

The woman slammed her door closed. Tyler had no doubt that the police were already on their way, if not the ship's own security team. But he had to make sure Perez did not escape, or worse, get to Ulric and warn him that Tyler had survived the assassination attempt. If he did, they might not be able to recover the device in Ulric's suite.

Tyler went to the railing, looking in both directions down the hallway. No sign of Perez. He must have made it to the stairs.

Tyler saw Perez stumble from the stairwell into the atrium two floors below, searching for his gun. Tyler quickly looked around and saw it almost directly below him. It wouldn't take Perez long to find it either.

Tyler's 9 mm rounds may have been unable to penetrate Perez's vest, but they sure as hell hurt him. He could see Perez wince from the effort of running. The shots would have left massive bruises on his chest, maybe even some broken ribs. If he could get his weapon back, Tyler would no longer have the advantage. Perez would never let Tyler leave the ship alive. He had to get down there first.

The stairs would take too long. A pizza joint had an awning spread out in front of the restaurant to give it the feel of an outdoor café. It was only about fifteen feet below Tyler.

Shoving to the back of his mind what a bad idea it was, he holstered his pistol and jumped over the railing. He thought the awning would cushion his fall, but the material was only designed to look like fabric, when it was actually metal. The jolt of the impact knocked the breath out of Tyler, and he artlessly tumbled over the side.

Gasping for breath, he crawled to the pistol and snagged it just before Perez reached it. He pointed the Sig Sauer at Perez, but Tyler didn't have enough air in his lungs to say anything. Perez ran past Tyler toward the far end of the atrium.

Tyler got to his knees. Perez continued to run down the atrium, zigzagging as he went. Partiers still lingered after the gala, and Perez used them to shield himself from Tyler.

"Stop!" Tyler yelled, pointing the pistol in Perez's direction. He hoped Perez would stop at the threat of being shot, but he kept going, and there was no way Tyler was going to take the shot, not with Perez in a bulletproof vest and so many bystanders around.

Tyler would have to run him down. He got to his feet and sprinted after Perez. Once he got his wind back, he was able to gain on Perez, who was still hurting from the bullets in his vest. Tyler would easily be able to stop him by the time they reached the opposite end of the atrium.

Perez looked behind him several times and saw Tyler closing fast. Apparently, he knew he wasn't going to outrun Tyler because he angled toward the raffle prize platform.

Perez jumped up onto the platform and kicked through the display case, unleashing a shower of glass. He plucked out the key with the black fob and inserted it into the ignition of the black motorcycle. The engine began to sputter, and Perez threw his leg over the seat. The Suzuki fired up. The sound of its high-revving four cylinders filled the atrium. He roared off the platform in the direction of the circular ramp surrounding the glass elevators.

Tyler leaped onto the platform and retrieved the other key. Crewmen who had rushed to find out what happened to the display case saw his gun and gave him a wide berth. Tyler tucked the pistol in his waistband and kick-started the Suzuki. A little different from his own Ducati, but almost as fast. It snarled in response, and he gunned the engine, laying a strip of rubber on the stand.

Perez started spiraling upward. Tyler aimed his own bike at the ramp. He could see startled passengers in the elevators watching a tuxedoed man on a Suzuki race toward them. He followed up the ramp, trying to keep an eye out to see what deck Perez exited.

They wound around the ramp at twenty miles per hour until they reached the top. Perez shot off the ramp and down the port balcony. Passengers, who by now lined the railings watching the spectacle of the chase, screamed and jumped back into their rooms as Perez roared past them toward the aft end of the ship. Tyler was only twenty feet behind him.

At the end of the balcony, Perez burst through an exterior door. He was looking for another way off the ship. Tyler knew from studying the *Genesis Dawn* deck plan that the aft gangplank was two decks down. Perez was trapped.

The trip through the door made Perez's bike wobble, and he slowed enough for Tyler to catch up. They were on the aft deck of the quarter-mile-long ship.

Perez regained his stability, and they raced side by side toward the back of the ship, Perez on Tyler's left, dodging sun chairs as they went. Perez tried to kick at Tyler's bike to knock it over, but he couldn't connect.

Tyler didn't take the time to look at his speedometer, but he guessed that they were now going at least forty miles per hour, and there wasn't much deck left. If he could get Perez to slow down and turn, he could take him down by ramming him.

They continued to charge forward, even with each other. The decking suddenly turned green, and Tyler saw that they had crossed onto a miniature golf course. At the end was the deck's aft railing and a ten-foot-tall balloon clown advertising the kid-friendly course.

Perez was concentrating on Tyler, so he didn't see the aft railing fast approaching. Tyler did. He hit his brakes with full force, skidding on the artificial turf, and realized that he wasn't going to stop in time.

He did the only thing he could. He laid the bike down, aiming for the clown, and crouched into the fetal position to protect his head.

By the time he laid the motorcycle on its side, he had slowed to less than 20 mph. The impact rattled Tyler when he hit the clown, but he bounced off. The balloon reduced his momentum enough so that when he hit the railing, all it did was crunch his side. Except for some rug burns and bruises, he came to rest unscathed.

Perez wasn't so lucky. Instead of laying his bike down, Perez tried to use the brakes. There wasn't enough room to slow down, so he crashed into the railing, vaulting over the handlebars and out of view.

Tyler heard screams from below. He rushed to the railing and looked over the side.

The aft end of this deck was not the aft end of the ship. Instead of falling to the water, Perez landed on the deck below. He lay next to the Suzuki, his neck cocked at a lethal angle.

It suddenly occurred to Tyler that Perez had insisted on leaving Dilara behind. In the heat of the chase, Tyler had forgotten about her. Why would Perez do that, unless . . .

Tyler sprinted back to his cabin. He launched himself into the room, his pistol drawn.

"Dilara!" he shouted. "Dilara!"

No answer. He checked both rooms, but there was no sign of her.

When he looked in the bathroom, he knew why. Someone had taken her.

There on the bathroom floor was her father's locket.

THIRTY-EIGHT

When Tyler couldn't find Dilara in the cabin, he went back out to search for her. Passengers recognized him as one of the people involved in the motorcycle chase, and he was detained by *Genesis Dawn* security. The police took him into custody, and he spent two hours in a station interrogation room frantically explaining what had happened. The police weren't convinced.

Tyler thought he was about to be brought up on charges for attacking and killing an FBI agent, not to mention making a mess of the ship, when the door opened and Agent Melanie Harris walked in. She still looked a little bleary.

"Leave us alone," she said. The detectives left the room.

"Are you all right?" Tyler said.

"Just a bad headache. Thanks for your help. You saved my life."

Tyler was surprised. "How did you know?"

"I just spoke to Washington. They didn't know that Perez and I came to Miami. He was my senior, so I was following his orders to come down here. Leaving me behind would have been too suspicious. I thought we were chasing your lead, but when we got to the cabin, he pulled his gun on me and tied me up. The only thing I could get out of him was that he was going to have a little fun with me before he dumped me overboard at sea."

"I'm guessing he was going to dump me overboard as well. He didn't shoot me because of the noise. Did you hear any of our conversation?"

"Just a little. I was pretty groggy. He pistol-whipped me once I was tied and gagged. I was coming out of it when you came in. What the hell is going on?"

Tyler told her about Ulric and the device he suspected was hidden in his suite.

"If Perez was staying on board," Harris said, "wouldn't he have been infected by the bioweapon, too?"

"I'm sure Ulric didn't tell him about that part. Just wanted him to get rid of you and me. Perez didn't know he was being sacrificed for Ulric's version of the greater good, and he probably didn't want to believe my theory when I told him."

"How could this happen? We do thorough background checks on every agent. If he was a member of the Church of the Holy Waters, we should have known."

"There's got to be a link to Ulric."

"We're checking that out now, but his FBI record seems clean." She began reading from his file on her laptop. "Perez grew up in Dallas, Texas. Mother died in childbirth. Father was a Dallas detective who was injured in the line of duty and left the force. Didn't do much after that except collect disability checks. Perez was valedictorian of his high school and was accepted to Yale on a scholarship. Majored in psychology . . ."

"That's got to be it!" He looked at Perez's graduation date. "Ulric bragged about going to Yale, and the two of them are about the same age. They must have been friends in college. We've only got a few more hours before the *Genesis Dawn* is supposed to sail. Whatever device is in Ulric's cabin might be on a timer. We need to get in there and find it before it activates."

"I've got ten agents from the Miami office on the ship."

Tyler brought up the subject that had been burning him up with worry ever since he found his cabin empty. "There's another problem," he said, his jaw clenched. "They've taken Karen."

Harris looked confused. "Karen? Who's Karen?"

Tyler flushed. *Karen? Where had that come from?* "I mean Dilara," he said quickly. "Dilara Kenner. I think she's been kidnapped by Ulric. We have to find her." The thought of her in Ulric's hands made his skin crawl.

"Then we have to get into his cabin as soon as possible."

"I need to be there." That was nonnegotiable.

Harris paused, then nodded. "All right. Let's go. I'll set it up on the way."

"No warrant this time?" Tyler asked.

"In an emergency like this, we don't need a warrant."

Thirty minutes later, they raided Ulric's suite. One of the FBI agents used a master key and walked in dressed like a steward. Two men inside confronted the fake steward and then were taken by surprise when the rest of the agents rushed in, capturing the guards without firing a shot. To Tyler's chagrin, neither Ulric nor Dilara was there.

He examined the room and found a metal case the size of a large valise sitting on a bureau, right where he was expecting it. A tube extended from the case into a hole that

392

had been drilled in the wall. Tyler flipped open a keypad and saw a display counting down. It would reach zero in another ten hours, three hours after the *Genesis Dawn* was scheduled to leave port. The case latch had a combination lock.

Tyler asked one of the two guards to open the case. The guard said that he'd been paid a lot of money to keep the room from being disturbed, especially the case, and that he didn't know what was inside or how to open it.

The suitcase might be booby-trapped. If Tyler tried to open it, a bomb might go off or the device might activate immediately, infecting everyone in the room. He requested a hazmat team to safely encase it in an impermeable enclosure.

They put the case, tube and all, into a plastic casing that was airtight. Now if it activated, the bioweapon would be contained.

"This needs to be analyzed right away," Tyler told Agent Harris. "We need to know what we're up against. And there are only a few labs in the country that are qualified to safely handle Level Four biohazards." Level 4 biohazards included the deadliest biological agents known to man, such as the Ebola and Marburg viruses. In addition to Ulric's high-tech lab, Tyler had worked on the containment facility at USAMRIID at Fort Detrick in Maryland when they had wanted to reinforce it against terrorist attacks.

"I know our facility in Miami can't do it," Harris said.

"The closest is the Centers for Disease Control in Atlanta," Tyler said. "I have a jet at Miami airport. I can get it there in two hours."

Agent Harris agreed, but only if she and one of the hazmat team members could accompany him, to which Tyler gladly agreed. While they were enroute, Harris would get the Bureau to begin the hunt for Ulric.

THIRTY-NINE

Dilara looked out the window of Ulric's private jet, trying to get a sense of where they were headed, but the cloud cover and darkness below made it impossible. It had been over five hours since they had taken off. All she could tell was that they were flying vaguely west. She rubbed her wrist, which was shackled to the armrest.

When Petrova had told her Tyler was dead, the pronouncement had been like a sledgehammer to Dilara's gut. She had become attracted to this amazing man, and now he might be gone. If he were really dead — a thought that she couldn't fully believe, not with what Tyler had already survived — then she was on her own. No one was coming to rescue her. If she was to get out of this, she had to do it herself.

Ulric emerged from the forward cabin, now changed into crisp slacks and a pressed shirt. He smiled and sat down across from her. He looked her up and down slowly, not bothering to hide his thorough scrutiny. She had not been allowed to change out of her dress, and his roving eye made her uncomfortable, but she wouldn't let him see it. Instead, she had to use the opportunity to assess her situation. Thinking clearly was the only thing that was going to save her life.

"Where are you taking me?" The question was an obvious cliché, but if Ulric thought she was dumber than she was, it might loosen his tongue.

"Our facility on Orcas Island," he responded without hesitation. "You have a beautiful voice. Of course, you're visually striking, but your alto register is just as attractive."

She was surprised at his candor, but she didn't know what to make of his compliment.

"Why are you taking me there?" she asked.

"I'd think that would be clear for someone as well educated as yourself. We need to find out what else you know."

"Wouldn't Agent Perez be able to tell you that?" She'd come to the conclusion that Perez had been working for Ulric. It was the only explanation for why Petrova was so confident about Tyler's death.

"Apparently, you and Tyler have not shared everything you know with Perez. There may be other items that you've been keeping secret. I need to know what they are."

"I won't —"

"And you can save your breath if you're about to say that you'll never talk."

Dilara felt a stab of fear. Ulric smiled.

"Oh, don't worry," he said. "I don't plan on torturing you. We have much more elegant and safe measures for getting information from you. You won't have a choice."

It had to be drugs. Maybe it would be better to start sharing now, possibly getting some information in return. Besides, she didn't know anything that would compromise anyone else.

"You had Tyler killed."

"Yes, that's a shame. He was a formidable opponent. I forgave him long ago for spurning my invitation to join us, but he got too close to exposing my plans. I expect to get confirmation at any moment that, yet again, he has lost and I have won. It seems to be a pattern between us."

"Maybe he got away from Perez," Dilara said defiantly. "He knew about the bioweapon you planned to inject into the ship's ventilation system. He's probably disabled it by now."

Ulric raised his eyebrows like he was impressed. "So Tyler figured it out? He certainly is clever. Was, I should say. Still, it doesn't really matter."

"What is Tyler's connection to all this?"

"My fault, actually. I thought Tyler was the person best suited to help me construct Oasis, or what he knew as Whirlwind. Through intermediaries that assumed the roles of top secret defense contractors, we convinced Gordian to take on the project, with Tyler to guide it. When he found out about the corners we were cutting on a project he was working on for me, I knew his curiosity would be a liability. Eventually, he might have discovered a link between me and Whirlwind. So we fired Gordian and went with Coleman instead."

"Look," Dilara said, "we discovered the existence of your bunker anyway. We know what you're planning to do. You want to wipe out the human race. And if Tyler got to your cabin, your plans are over."

Ulric chuckled. "You didn't really think that was the only part of my plan? I admit I liked the ceremonial aspect of starting our project using the *Genesis Dawn,* but it would be silly of me to put all my eggs in one basket like that, don't you think?"

"You mean there's another release point?"

"Several more, actually. You were in one of them just days ago. LAX. I also have plans for New York and London."

"When?"

"In two days, when the *Genesis Dawn* is en route to New York. Once all of our people are safely in the Oasis bunker, I'll order the devices to be activated. They're being prepped as we speak and will be shipped out tonight."

"Sam Watson said you're planning to kill billions."

"I mistakenly thought Watson would be an asset to our cause, and he betrayed me."

"That's because Sam was a great man. He would never work on something like that."

"Then you didn't know him as well as you thought you did. Before he joined my church, he was working for the U.S. government. I recruited him to a small subsidiary of mine, PicoMed Pharmaceuticals, where Watson thought he would be working on a germ warfare project for the Pentagon."

Dilara was stunned. Sam had never told her much about his work, but she had assumed it was vaccine research.

"After working with him for several years," Ulric said, "I thought he shared my goals,

399

so I recruited him into my church. Then he found out the details of my plan and stole that knowledge, endangering everything I'd put into place. He was a fool. He didn't see the bigger picture."

"What picture?" She spat the words at him. "Wiping out humanity?"

"No. Humanity will go on. But it will go on the right way. As it should. And yes, billions will die, but everyone currently alive, including me, will be dead in one hundred years anyway. I'm not wiping out the human race, I'm saving it."

"You're crazy!"

"And you're getting too emotional to see what I'm trying to accomplish. What if our leaders decide to start a nuclear war tomorrow? Then every single person on the planet will die, and the human race will cease to exist. Disease, environmental degradation, pollution, any one of these disasters could completely wipe us out. Even worse, humanity is on a path to destroy every other species, except the ones that are useful to it. It would repudiate Noah's work of saving animal life. I can't allow that to happen."

"So Noah's Ark is involved in this? My father really did find it?"

"Oh, yes. He discovered its location and a relic that has made my vision for the New

World possible. I was so disappointed when I couldn't reveal it to the world, but that would have interfered with my new vision."

Dilara couldn't help getting excited about the archaeological significance, even in her present situation.

"You actually saw it yourself?" she asked.

"I never went inside the Ark. It would have brought too much attention. But I know where it is, that it in fact exists, and that it holds an identical relic inside. All thanks to your father."

She exploded out of her seat, but the handcuff kept her out of reach of Ulric. "Where is my father?" she shouted.

"That I don't know." For the first time, she could see that he was lying.

"My father helped you plan all this?"

"His work was instrumental in setting all this in motion. In fact, it was your friend Sam Watson who introduced us. I had confided in Watson about my search for Noah's Ark, and he mentioned that your father was a leading authority. Hasad worked for me for two years, and then we had a breakthrough. Or he did. He wasn't as forthcoming as I would have liked. But without that discovery, none of this would have been possible. It was a sign from God that I was to be His messenger. His instrument."

This guy was nuts, but Tyler was right. He was an incredibly smart nut. Dilara had to calm herself and hold back her disgust. She sat back down and smoothed her dress.

"What could a flood six thousand years ago give you that would make all this possible?" she asked mildly. "So what if a river overflowed its banks or the Black Sea filled up when the Mediterranean burst through the Bosporus, or whatever the true origin of the story was?"

"Ah, we now get to the really interesting part. You assume the Deluge was a flood of water."

"What else could it be?"

"As much as I would like the Bible to be a literal, infallible document," he said, "it is truly useful for its metaphor. You are thinking literally." Ulric spoke as if he were talking to a child rather than a PhD archaeologist, but Dilara ignored the patronization.

She quoted from the Douay-Rheims Bible, Genesis chapter six. " 'Behold, I will bring the waters of a great flood upon the earth, to destroy all flesh, wherein is the breath of life under heaven. All things that are in the earth shall be consumed.' Seems pretty clear to me."

"The key phrase is 'to destroy all flesh,' " Ulric said. "The water was an agent of destruction, but it wasn't the cause of death. Think about it. What have you seen lately that fits that description?"

Dilara's mind immediately went to the wreckage of Rex Hayden's airplane. The gleaming white bone they'd found stripped of all flesh.

"The plane crash . . . ," she said, gasping in dawning recognition. "The passengers dissolved."

"Exactly," Ulric said. "Their flesh was literally consumed. That's because the Flood wasn't a deluge. The waters merely carried it. The Flood was a disease."

FORTY

"That's ridiculous," Dilara said, unable to control her amazement at Ulric's assertion that the Flood was a waterborne disease. "The Flood story is a central theme of many different ancient texts."

"And you believe that waters actually covered every mountain on earth to a depth of fifteen cubits?" Ulric asked, obviously enjoying the repartee. He seemed to have forgotten that Dilara was the enemy.

"That's just as ridiculous. There isn't enough water on the planet."

"Then you concede the story can't be taken literally. If you're ready to throw out one portion of the story, why do you adhere so vehemently to another part?"

"Floods were a common calamity in the ancient world. Most settlements were built at the water's edge. Tsunamis, hurricanes, rivers overflowing their banks. It happened all the time. It makes sense that stories of

God's retribution would encapsulate some of these events."

"Pestilence was also common in previous millennia," Ulric said. "Why is it so hard to believe that Noah survived a plague?"

"The Bible is very specific," Dilara said. "I'm quoting the King James version now. 'And it came to pass after seven days, that the waters of the flood were upon the earth.' It also talks about how the water covered the land. 'And the waters prevailed exceedingly upon the earth; and all the high hills, that were under the whole heaven, were covered.' "

Ulric held up a finger. "The Bible also says, 'And every living substance was destroyed which was upon the face of the ground, both man, and cattle, and the creeping things, and the fowl of the heaven; and they were destroyed from the earth; and Noah only remained alive, and they that were with him in the ark.' That description could easily describe the effects of a plague."

"Then why doesn't the Bible say 'plague' instead of 'flood'?"

"Who knows? Perhaps it was mistranslated long ago. Or maybe it's because the plague seemed to stem from the floodwater itself. Every beast that drank from the waters was destroyed. I know this for a fact."

"Because you found the Ark," Dilara said contemptuously. "That raises another question. If it was simply a plague, why did Noah build a huge ship to hold animals? It makes no sense."

"Ah, you're making assumptions again. And yes, I discovered where the Ark is."

"You mean, my father discovered where the Ark is."

"True enough. He was a brilliant man."

Dilara noticed his use of the past tense. She'd long ago given up believing her father was alive, but the certainty with which Ulric used the past tense was nonetheless heartbreaking.

"What was the relic?" Dilara asked.

"A remnant of the plague."

"One that remained intact for thousands of years?"

"As difficult as that is to believe, yes. Think, Dilara. Rex Hayden and his friends were reduced to skeletons. I know you saw the results. The relic from Noah's Ark gave me the seed to start with. I simply modified it."

"Why?"

"I didn't want to kill every animal on earth. I am a biochemist by training. My company has resources that most others can only dream of. The plague from Noah's Ark

406

was actually a prion. It was viciously lethal, attacking all animal matter and reducing any soft tissue to its base components. With years of research, we were able to reduce its effectiveness to one species. Humans."

"So you can be not only Noah, but God as well? You make the decision to wipe out humanity, and then you become the patriarch that repopulates it?"

"I didn't make the decision. God did. If He didn't, why did He allow me to find the Arkon-A? I'm simply his instrument."

"Arkon-A is the prion from the relic?"

"That's what I called it," Ulric said. "Arkon-A was the original disease. Arkon-B was our unfortunate first sample that worked on humans. Too virulent. It would never have worked for my vision. It simply killed too fast to spread among the general population. That's why I took my time and developed Arkon-C. That strain will be the one dispersed in the next day."

"Why are you telling me all this?"

"Let's face it, Dilara. You are not going anywhere, and being an archaeologist, you are one of the few people who can truly appreciate what I've done. Someday I even hope to go back and excavate Noah's Ark myself. I could use someone of your talents in my New World. Perhaps you will accompany me."

She choked back bile. "I'd rather die."

"You might change your mind after our new flood has wiped the earth clean. Being one of the last women on earth may be a headier experience than you can imagine."

She could see that he was actually attracted to her. Like most men who craved power, one woman wasn't enough for him, no matter how beautiful Svetlana Petrova was. And with a task like repopulating the earth, why wouldn't he want to build a harem? The thought disgusted her, but she might be able to use it to her advantage in order to escape and warn someone.

"You're right. I guess I'll have to see."

"Oh, I'm not delusional, Dilara. It will take time. You're not there yet and will probably betray me at your first chance. But with six months' time . . . well, a lot will have changed by then."

Ulric got up to leave. Dilara tried to stall him.

"Wait! This is fascinating. I want to hear more about the Ark."

"There will be plenty of time later. We're about to land."

"But I'd like to know everything. If I'm going to be a partner with you, I think I deserve it."

"I'm the only one who knows everything," Ulric said. Then he walked into the forward cabin and shut the door, leaving Dilara to ponder her next move.

FORTY-ONE

Three hours after leaving the *Genesis Dawn* with the device from Ulric's cabin, Tyler was in an observation room at the CDC. Space-suited technicians were visible on the closed-circuit cameras inside the Level 4 containment lab.

First, the tube was plugged to prevent material from being released. Then a hole was drilled in the case, and a tiny camera was snaked inside to make sure that there were no explosive materials. When they were satisfied it was safe, the case was opened. As Tyler suspected, the countdown timer immediately reset to zero, set off by circuitry inside the lid.

Inside the case was a complicated device. Three clear cylinders, each the size of a two-liter soda bottle, were connected to one another by metal tubing and were ringed with colors to distinguish them: red, blue, and white. The blue cylinder was connected to the external tubing.

Opening the case had started several mechanisms in the device. A clear liquid was being pumped from the white cylinder into the blue one. The red cylinder was disgorging its contents in a stream of air. The lab technicians stepped back, but whatever was being ejected didn't seem to be affecting their safety garments.

Within seconds, the pumping into the blue cylinder stopped, and the stream of air from the red cylinder slowed to a hiss. They capped each cylinder and drew samples from all of them.

Tyler had already briefed the technicians that whatever was inside was probably related to the bioweapon that had been used on Rex Hayden's plane, so it was exceedingly lethal. He noticed that the technicians had heeded his warnings and were proceeding cautiously, although not as fast as Tyler would have liked.

Now that the danger of explosion was over, Tyler's expertise was no longer needed. He was escorted to a waiting area while the technicians analyzed the samples. The adrenaline drain of the day's events finally caught up with him, and Tyler dozed off on a break room couch.

He felt a hand on his shoulder, and his

411

eyes popped open. He glanced at his watch. It was after nine A.M. Friday morning. Tyler saw a slim, balding Indian man in a white lab coat hovering over him. Next to him was Special Agent Harris.

"Dr. Gavde has the test results," Harris said. "Since you're involved with the Hayden crash, I thought you should hear them. Remember, this is all classified, but you're cleared for it."

"Did you find out what the bioweapon is?" Tyler asked as he stood. Harris seemed edgy. She must have heard some of this already.

"I'm afraid so," Gavde said in a slight accent that sounded like a combination of Hindi and BBC British. "Of course, we have only done preliminary tests, but the findings are quite disturbing. This is very scary stuff we are dealing with here."

"So is it a bacteria or virus?"

"Neither. The active agent inside those cylinders are prions. Do you know what they are?"

"Vaguely. They're what cause mad cow disease."

"Bovine spongiform encephalopathy is the best known disease, yes, but there are many others. Prions are not well understood. They're infectious agents that are composed

412

entirely of proteins. One thing that prion diseases all have in common is that they are fatal, and this one is no different. But in other ways, it's like no prion disease I've ever seen."

"Why is that?" Tyler asked.

Gavde sounded like he was in awe of it. "The way this one works is quite insidious. It attacks human cadherins, the proteins that hold together your body's cells. However, it does nothing to animal cadherins. We tested samples of mouse, rat, and monkey cells. They remained unharmed. But human cells were attacked with vigor."

"What happens when the cadherins are attacked?"

"All the cells in your body are bound together with these cadherins. If they break down, the cells no longer hold together, and the cells themselves burst open. The only part of the human body that wouldn't be affected would be the skeletal system because the osseous tissue in bones is mineralized."

Tyler thought back to the pilot of Hayden's airplane. In the transcript of his communication with LA Control, he had screamed that they were melting. But just like the Wicked Witch of the West, he had used the wrong word. They hadn't melted.

They had dissolved. Only in this case, their bones were left.

"Is there any way to stop it once you're infected?" Tyler asked.

"I asked the same thing," Harris said.

Gavde shook his head. "Other than being fatal, the other thing this prion has in common with others is that it's untreatable. As a by-product of its attack on the cadherins, more prions are produced, so it's self-sustaining."

"How fast would this stuff work?" Tyler asked.

"That's an interesting question," Gavde said, clearly fascinated by the prion. "As you saw, there were three cylinders inside the case. When the case was opened, a valve was switched on, so that the red cylinder was emitting prions, and the blue cylinder was injected with saline from the white cylinder."

"Salt water?"

Gavde nodded. "At first, we couldn't figure out why. When we tried to obtain a sample from the blue and white cylinders, we could only find a few active prions. The rest had been destroyed by the saline. Under the microscope, the prions from the blue cylinder looked virtually identical to the ones in the red cylinder. But they weren't.

When we tested them, one type of prion was much faster acting than the other. A more thorough examination of the device showed why."

The booby trap, thought Tyler.

"I'm guessing the red cylinder had the prions that were faster acting," he said.

Gavde looked surprised. "How did you know?"

"That's how I would have designed it. If it was left alone, it would operate as intended, infecting the entire ship. If it was disturbed, whoever did it would be killed in minutes with all those prions blowing at them and infecting them."

Gavde nodded again. "That makes sense. Whoever designed these prions was very clever. I would say that the longer-lasting prions would take days before any symptoms would manifest, allowing the disease to spread beyond any possible quarantine."

"Designed?" Harris asked. "So you're confirming this is man-made?"

"Because of small but specific differences in the two types of prions, I have to assume they were engineered. However, it's very unlikely that they were produced from scratch. I would guess that they started with a prion source that was similar in some ways and then biochemically altered. But I've never heard of a prion disease that's even close to this. Where they found it, I don't know."

"Anything else, Dr. Gavde?" Harris said.

"One more interesting point. We detected trace amounts of argon, so we believe the cylinders containing the prions were sealed with the inert gas."

"Why is that important?" Tyler asked. He found the entire conversation both intriguing because of the science and nauseating because of its implications.

"The fast-acting version begins to break down within minutes if it isn't acting on a cell. It's life span — if a prion can be said to have life — is very short. They act quickly but must replace themselves just as quickly. Once all the human cells are robbed of their cadherins, the prions themselves dissolve. I would bet that the longer-acting ones do the same, only over a longer time period. Unfortunately, we didn't discover this fact until all of our prion samples had destroyed themselves."

Another answer to why they hadn't found any prions at the crash site. They had broken down long before the plane crashed. Their inherent self-destructive nature also made sense if Ulric was going to unleash these prions on an unsuspecting world and had a bunker to hide in. All he had to do was wait out the end of civilization, and eventually the prions would self-destruct, leaving Earth wiped clean of humanity. He could then emerge and claim the planet for himself.

"Can anything kill these prions before they're released?" Tyler asked.

"We did some quick tests of their durability. They don't break down unless they are subjected to a temperature above five hundred degrees Fahrenheit. The other way, of course, is with saline. The salt is highly corrosive to them."

"I've got to make some calls," Harris said abruptly, opening her cell phone and striding down the hall.

"You were lucky to get to that device before it was used to infect that ship," Gavde said. "I hate to think there might be more of this stuff out there."

Tyler was sure there was. The only question was where.

FORTY-TWO

Tyler was on the Gordian jet flying back from the CDC to the TEC in Phoenix, but he wasn't piloting this time. It was already 11 A.M. Eastern time, and he had too much work to do.

His first order of business was to arrange with the FBI a ruse to put Ulric off guard. He had the FBI release that, along with one of its agents, Dr. Tyler Locke had been killed during a melee on board the *Genesis Dawn.* Ulric wouldn't be concerned when Perez didn't check in with him. He'd think that both of them were killed.

The next job was to find out where Ulric was taking Dilara. Tyler suspected that they kidnapped her as some kind of potential bargaining chip or maybe to question her. If they wanted her dead, too, they would have killed them both instead of having Perez separate them. She was still alive, but Tyler didn't know for how long.

"Where's Ulric's plane?" Tyler asked Aiden MacKenna, using the jet's satellite phone. Aiden had been working with the FBI trying to track down Ulric.

"According to the Bureau," Aiden said, "they landed in Seattle more than five hours ago. We know they didn't get on another plane, but we've lost their trail. They must be somewhere in the Puget Sound vicinity."

"Do you have a list of Ulric's facilities in the area?"

"I do. We found ties between Ulric's company and PicoMed Pharmaceuticals, where Sam Watson worked. It's in Seattle along with most of Ulric's other real estate, including his company headquarters."

"What I'm looking for is the place where the bunker was built. Ulric's getting ready to release this prion. That means he should be holing up in Oasis. He wouldn't have built it in the middle of Seattle. It would be on some piece of land that's out of the way. Does he have a ranch somewhere?"

"Not that I've found, either under his own name or his company names."

Tyler thought about the possibilities. If Ulric were really trying to re-create the effects of the Flood, and he thought he was Noah . . .

"Aiden, what about the Church of the

419

Holy Waters?"

"Let me tap into the FBI database and cross-check with a little illicitly obtained financial data." He paused. Tyler heard typing. "I think we may have a winner. The church headquarters is in downtown Seattle, which wouldn't fit your parameters, but they have a large property on Orcas Island."

"What kind of buildings?"

"According to the latest DoD satellite imagery, it looks like five. Another mansion. What looks like an enormous hotel. And then three warehouses the size of airplane hangars. They've also got helipads and a huge dock."

That was it. The perfect place to build a bunker that wouldn't draw much attention.

"Do you see any earthworks?" Coleman would have had to move thousands of tons of earth to dig out the tunnels and rooms of the underground bunker.

"None visible on the satellite image."

That was odd. Tyler was sure the Church of the Holy Waters facility was the only option, especially since Ulric had landed at Seattle, only sixty miles from Orcas Island. Still, there should be ample evidence of earthmoving.

"Check to see if the coastline has

changed."

More typing. "As far as I can tell, except for the addition of the buildings, it looks exactly the same over the last three years."

"You said they were the size of airplane hangars?"

"Big enough to hold a couple of 747s each. I can't imagine what they're for."

"I can." That was it. The hangars. Tyler knew why they were there.

A beep came on the cell phone, indicating an incoming call. Tyler looked at the caller ID and grimaced. It was the call he had been dreading.

"Aiden," Tyler said, "I have to take this. See if you can get anything that proves Ulric is on Orcas Island. Check all the boats and helicopters."

"Okay, Tyler. I'll call you back."

Tyler took a breath and switched over to the other line.

"General. Thanks for returning my call."

"I heard about that mess on the *Genesis Dawn*," came the blunt response. "What the hell have you gotten yourself into?"

Tyler could already feel his hackles rising. Even after two years of virtually no contact, the man knew how to push his buttons. "It wasn't really my choice, Dad. They've tried to kill me three times."

421

"Three times! And you're just coming to me now?"

This conversation was going just as badly as Tyler thought it would. *Not if my life depended on it* was what he had thought when Miles had first suggested calling Sherman Locke. But it wasn't his life that was now in danger. It was Dilara's.

Given the results from the CDC testing, Tyler figured it was only a matter of time before the military got involved. The discovery of a new bioweapon was a matter of national security, and the FBI would have to coordinate with them. With Dilara taken hostage, Tyler didn't want to be left out of the loop, so he'd reluctantly placed the call to his father's office and provided some details about Oasis.

"I didn't have any evidence until now that you would be able to do anything about," Tyler said. "But the situation has become critical, and I think the military has the capability to handle it."

The General made a clicking sound with his tongue. Disapproval. "Sounds like you're in over your head."

"What do you want me to say, Dad? That I need your help?"

"There's nothing wrong with that, son."

His father's voice was harsh, but Tyler also

detected a concern behind it he hadn't often heard. The hackles lowered slightly.

"Fine," he said. "I need your help."

"That's what we're here for. The CDC tells me we've got a Level Four bioterrorism agent on our hands."

"It's bad stuff."

"It looks like none of it survived, so we don't have any way to develop a response."

His father used the typical military code for a cure, but Tyler suspected that the General really wanted the weapon for the military's use.

"I spoke to the president," the General said. "When he heard how nasty these prions were, he decided, on my recommendation, that this was a clear and present danger to the country's security. He directed the military to do anything in its power to secure them."

"And the FBI?"

"When I briefed him about Oasis, the president decided that the FBI counterterrorism unit doesn't have the specialization to take on a hardened facility like that. He's authorized an army assault team to attack it. He just needs to know where."

"I know where. The Church of the Holy Waters compound on Orcas Island."

"Are you sure?"

"Ninety percent sure," Tyler said, then winced when he realized how wishy-washy that sounded.

To Tyler's surprise, his father said, "That's good enough for me."

"I've got an idea about how to verify it. Where are you now?"

"I'm on my way to White Sands," the General said. "I want you there by noon. You're attending a demonstration." It was a command, not an invitation. Tyler knew better than to argue.

"Of what?"

"I can't say. But it's relevant to our current problem."

"Okay. I should be there by 11:30 A.M. local time." White Sands was on the way to Phoenix from Atlanta. "I'm going to have Grant Westfield meet me there."

"This is on a need-to-know basis."

"You've met Grant. Former Ranger and combat engineer. He's got the same clearance I do, and he's a top-notch electrical engineer. He also knows more about the Hayden crash than anyone else."

"Fine. Don't be late." He hung up.

Tyler looked at the phone, puzzled. The conversation hadn't gone as he'd expected. For a moment, it actually seemed like his father wanted his advice. Whatever the

General wanted to show him at White Sands must be pretty important if he himself was making an appearance.

Tyler went to the cockpit and poked his head in.

"Change of plans, guys. We're going to New Mexico."

FORTY-THREE

At 3,200 square miles, three times the size of Rhode Island, White Sands Missile Range is the largest U.S. military installation. It has been used as a test facility for some of the military's most powerful weapons ever since the first atomic bomb was detonated at the Trinity site on the base's eastern portion in 1945. Tyler's pilot landed on the runway used as an emergency landing site for the space shuttle.

The jet was guided to a ramp not far from a helicopter. Grant was standing next to it. Before the plane's engines were silent, Tyler opened the door to a blast of heat. He put on a cap and sunglasses and walked over to Grant, whose bald head was already beaded with sweat.

Grant gave Tyler a serious look. "Man, I'm sorry about Dilara," he said. "I'm sure she's okay."

"We'll get her back," Tyler said confidently, even though he was burning up with concern.

"Damn right we will."

"We going for a ride?"

"Your father sent instructions when I arrived. The test site is fifty miles from here, and he wants us there in a hurry."

"Any idea why?"

Grant shook his head. "Apparently, he likes his secrets. Said he'd tell us when we got there." They climbed in and were airborne one minute later.

In another twenty minutes, the helicopter landed next to a collection of trailers hooked to a massive generator and satellite dishes.

Tyler led Grant to the biggest trailer, a double-wide. Inside, they found rows of computer monitors manned by technicians, some in civilian clothing, others in air force and army uniforms. The AC cooled the room to a chilly sixty-five degrees. Tyler could hear a countdown and saw a red timer centered above a huge window that had a great view of a mountain ten miles away. A plasma screen next to the window showed a closer view of the mountain. Fifteen minutes were left on the clock.

Major General Sherman Locke was conferring with two other generals at the other end of the trailer. When he saw his son and

Grant enter, he cut off his discussion and approached them. He wore a grim expression.

Even in his late fifties, the General was a physically imposing man, fitter and taller than most of the younger soldiers in the room. Anyone who knew Tyler Locke could immediately see the resemblance between father and son. It was in their demeanor that they differed. Tyler had a relaxed way of dealing with others, preferring to lead by example and a soft touch. The General, on the other hand, commanded with an iron fist, demanding to be in charge in every situation he encountered, and this was no exception.

"Captain," the General said, holding out his hand to Tyler, "glad you could make it. Your sister told me to say hello."

The General was the only person who insisted on using Tyler's military rank after he resigned his commission. It probably was also a message to the others in the room that his son was an officer.

"General," Tyler said, taking the General's granite grip and returning it hard, "please return the favor for me."

The General nodded at Grant and shook his hand perfunctorily. Tyler and his father silently appraised each other, neither revealing anything beyond a blank stare.

"I bet it took a lot for you to call me," the General said to his son.

Tyler ignored the dig. "You saw the report from the CDC?"

"I've warned Fort Detrick and the FBI for years that computers and private labs would eventually put dangerous bioweapons in the hands of nongovernmental actors. They were concerned about anthrax and smallpox, but I knew it was a matter of time before we saw something worse, and now it looks like we have."

General Locke was in charge of the military's Defense Threat Reduction Agency, which was responsible for countering weapons of mass destruction. His thirty-five years in the air force had made him one of the best-connected and most respected officers. His position allowed him to be involved in practically any operation he wanted, especially when units were testing out new weaponry in the battlefield.

A full bird colonel approached and quietly asked the General a question. The General answered and the colonel responded with a smart, "Yes, sir!"

Tyler had been around his father during parties with other officers, but he'd never seen the General in a command situation before. Despite everything, he felt a certain amount of pride seeing his father in charge.

"General," Tyler said, "the people who deployed the bioagent on Hayden's airplane tried the same thing on the *Genesis Dawn*. I'm sure they'll make another attempt soon."

"And you claim that Sebastian Ulric is behind this?"

"Yes, sir," Tyler said, marveling at how quickly he felt himself becoming an army officer again in his father's presence. "We have evidence that Sebastian Ulric is responsible. He owns one of the biggest pharmaceutical companies in the country, and he's an expert in biochemistry. He also has the financial resources to build Oasis."

"This bunker you think he has."

Tyler told the General about Project Oasis's connection to John Coleman and how Tyler had briefly worked on the project when it was called Whirlwind.

"If they didn't substantially change the design specs from the ones I saw," Tyler said, "we're talking about a bunker that would rival Mount Weather. It could easily keep three hundred people alive and comfortable during the time it took for this prion agent to kill the rest of the world's population and then disperse."

The General paused, as if he were deciding what to say to them next. He took Grant and Tyler aside out of earshot of the nearest technician and lowered his voice.

"What I'm about to tell you is highly classified," he said. "I believe you. I believe you because we've had Ulric under investigation for two years."

Tyler and Grant looked at each other in surprise.

"What?" Grant said a little too loudly. He quieted his voice and went on. "Why? Ulric not pay his taxes?"

"Someone's been hiring away some of the best bioweapon designers in the country from various subcontractors that were working with USAMRIID at Fort Detrick. At first, we thought they were being lured by more money at private pharma firms. But when the numbers got larger, we started to investigate. We speculate that they were promised work on other defense projects in biowarfare by entities claiming to represent secret government projects. Of course, these companies weren't under contract to the Defense Department, but the people they recruited didn't know that."

"Sounds like the trick used on me with Project Whirlwind," Tyler said.

"When we dug deeper, we found some

tenuous links to Sebastian Ulric, but we could never prove it."

"Was one of these scientists named Sam Watson?"

"Yes. He died of a heart attack last week."

"No," Tyler said. "He was poisoned." Finally something his father didn't already know.

The General narrowed his eyes. "How can you be sure?"

"Because the person who was with him at the time, an archaeologist named Dilara Kenner, came to see me two days later and told me he was poisoned."

"Where is she now?"

"Sebastian Ulric has her," Tyler said, disgusted at the thought of her at Ulric's mercy. "She was abducted while I was chasing that rogue FBI agent. We need to get her back."

The General gave a dismissive wave. "She can't tell him anything. Don't worry about it."

"I will worry about it," Tyler snapped. "She's my responsibility."

The General put his index finger on Tyler's chest. "What you should be worried about is that Ulric will be on alert now, which puts our plans in jeopardy. We're at-

tempting an assault on their compound tonight."

"You mean on Orcas Island?"

The General nodded. "We did some
checking on your guess that his facility on
Orcas is where the bunker is located. The
FBI found a record of earthmoving equipment leased for use by one of his shell
companies. The only problem is, if a bunker
is there, there should have been a substantial
amount of earth removed. We still haven't
figured out what happened to the dirt."

"It's still there," Tyler said.

"Where?"

"Inside those hangars. I did some calcula-
tions. Based on the size of the bunker, those
hangars could easily hold the dirt and rock
that was excavated."

"You're sure?"

"It's the only thing that fits."

"Well, we're going to make sure tonight,"
the General said.

"How?"

"We're going to infiltrate the compound.
Once our ground-penetrating radar is on-
site, we can verify that there are underground chambers there. We've already
checked his other labs. This prion agent
wasn't found in any of them. It must be
underground."

"How are you assaulting the lab?"

"With a full platoon of Delta Force. The compound is heavily guarded. It might be impossible to get in, so we have a backup plan. We either have to secure the agent for ourselves, or we need to destroy it before it's released."

"What about Dilara?"

"She's not a mission priority."

"Then I'm going with the team," Tyler said.

The General glowered at him. "The hell you are."

"What's your intel on the internal bunker schematics?"

"We don't have any," the General said grudgingly.

"You're going in blind?"

"We don't have any other choice."

"Yes, you do. I saw the original specs. I know how they designed and built the bunker."

The General looked up at the ceiling, as if searching for some other alternative. Tyler knew there was none.

"Dad, you know that for this mission to have any chance, I need to be on the ground with them."

"And if he's going," Grant said, "I'm going."

"You don't have to do that," Tyler said.

"Have I ever volunteered for something I didn't want to do?"

"Only if you thought you'd get laid as a result."

Grant smiled. "No chance of that here."

"Okay, enough!" the General growled. "Against my better judgment, you're both going. Tyler's got the expertise we need, which is the reason I invited you here in the first place."

"For what?" Tyler asked.

Someone in the trailer called out, "One minute to release."

"Have you heard of MOP?"

"The Massive Ordnance Penetrator?" Tyler recalled it from an article in the international journal *Propellants, Explosives, and Pyrotechnics.*

"That's right. Boeing has been developing it for us specifically to target underground bunkers holding weapons of mass destruction. I never thought we'd use it on our own soil. We're doing final testing today. If it succeeds, I've been authorized to use it to take out Oasis."

"You mean, that's your backup plan, sir?" Grant said.

"If we can't get in and neutralize it by conventional means, yes." The General turned back to Tyler. "So my question for you, Captain, is will it work?"

Tyler recalled the specs on the bomb. At twenty feet long and thirty thousand pounds, it was heavier than the infamous MOAB, the Massive Ordnance Air Burst bomb, and could destroy bunkers that were up to two hundred feet below ground.

Tyler was aghast. "There are three hundred men and women in that bunker," he said. *Including Dilara.*

"That should make you understand the lengths the president is willing to go to keep this prion agent from being released. So I repeat, will it work? Will it completely destroy Oasis?"

Tyler nodded solemnly. "If they built it according to the original specs, it'll wipe out the entire facility."

The timer was counting down from ten, and a voice accompanied it. One of the screens showed a view from a chase plane of the B-52 that was carrying the MOP. When the count reached zero, a huge bullet-shaped bomb fell from the B-52, which banked away once the bomb was clear.

"Thirty seconds to impact," the countdown voice said.

"Dad," Tyler said, "you're making a mistake. We aren't even sure that this agent would be destroyed by the bomb."

"There are fifty-three hundred pounds of explosive in that bomb. Whatever isn't incinerated will be buried in the rubble."

"But we're talking about three hundred lives."

"The president agrees with our assessment. Those lives are expendable to make sure this threat is neutralized. If you want to save those people, make sure you secure that compound before 2100."

The airman reached the end of the countdown. "Three . . . two . . . one . . ."

For a fraction of a second, Tyler could see the enormous bomb that plunged into the earth. The side of the mountain rose then collapsed, creating a depression three hundred feet across and forty feet deep. Dust cascaded into the air, but the explosion was too far underground to blast outward. The trailer erupted in cheers and applause, but Tyler was chilled by the fearsome sight.

"The cave that MOP just destroyed was buried in one hundred twenty-five feet of granite," the General said.

"The rock at Orcas Island isn't as strong," Tyler said.

"You still want to go?"

Even more now, Tyler thought as he nodded.

"You're a stubborn bastard," the General said with a hint of a smile. "Just like your father. All right. You'll have until 2100 hours tonight to give us the all clear. After that, I'll have no choice but to turn Ulric's compound into a crater."

"When does the assault begin?"

"We can't give them any time to prepare. It's set for 2000 hours, Pacific time, enough time for complete darkness to set in. We estimate that if Oasis can't be breached in one hour, it won't happen and the team's been eliminated. That puts us in serious danger of losing containment of the bio-weapon."

"We'll make it," Tyler said.

"I'm heading up the joint operation," the General said with a steely gaze directly at Tyler. "And I *will* order that bomb dropped at exactly 2100 hours if I don't hear from you. Don't be late. That's an order, son." Then the General turned away to speak with the colonel again. They were dismissed.

Tyler could hear the helicopter outside spooling up its engine. He and Grant would have to move fast if they were going to coordinate with the strike team.

He looked at his watch. Just nine hours until the assault.

OASIS

FORTY-FOUR

When Ulric's private jet had flown over the Seattle metro area, Dilara had finally known where they were, but it didn't make a difference. On the helicopter ride from the airport to Orcas Island, there had been no chance for her to make an escape.

They arrived at some kind of compound with a mansion that lorded over the estate. She had been hustled through a security pass-through, and then onto an elevator that went down, taking her underground. The panel had seven buttons on it. When the doors opened at level three to reveal a hallway bustling with people, she understood the purpose of the warren. It was Oasis.

A bear of a man with a shaved head met them at the elevator. He was flanked by two other men armed with submachine guns.

"Status?" Ulric demanded.

"All our members are accounted for and

441

inside Oasis."

"Good. We're going on lockdown tonight. Dr. Kenner, this is Dan Cutter. He'll take you to your quarters." Ulric turned back to Cutter. "I have some business to take care of. Then we'll begin the interrogation." With Petrova at his side, he got back in the elevator.

Cutter took Dilara by the arm and led her to a room that was more lavishly appointed than she expected. It was the size of a cruise ship cabin, with a small bathroom to the side. The bed, nightstand, and dresser were antiques. A change of clothes lay on the bed, and a pair of shoes were on the floor.

"You can wear that, or you can stay in your dress and high heels," Cutter said. "Doesn't matter to me."

He slammed the door behind her and locked it. She heard him tell one of the two men to stay behind and guard the door. Footsteps retreated down the hall. Dilara had never felt so alone.

She wasn't going to wear the dress. Though the odds of her overpowering a trained soldier were slim to none, she needed to be in more practical clothes to make her move when the time came. There were probably cameras in the room, but there was no use trying to find them. If she covered them up, guards would be in here immediately.

She'd been in the field too many times, where privacy was not always the greatest concern, to let voyeurs embarrass her, but she didn't want to give them more of a show than she had to. She changed into the new outfit, covering herself with the shirt before taking off her dress. The clothes fit surprisingly well, even the tennis shoes. Going to the bathroom was more uncomfortable, but she had no choice, again keeping herself covered from prying eyes.

Then all she could do was wait, so she sat on the bed and meditated. She was brought some food, but she didn't eat it and only drank water from the faucet in the bathroom. She was used to going all day without eating when she had to. If they wanted to drug her, she wasn't going to make it easy for them.

She was so deep in her meditation that when the door opened, she only vaguely noticed it. Cutter grabbed her arm and pulled her to her feet.

"Come on," he said.

"Where are we going?"

"The lab. We have some questions."

He heaved her to her feet and pushed her in front of him out the door.

They made a turn into a longer hallway and entered a laboratory. Ulric stood to the side with a rail-thin forty-year-old man whose white hair matched his lab coat.

The lab held three pieces of furniture: a chair that wouldn't be out of place in a dentist's office, an examination table, and a seat for the doctor. The counter along one wall held a sink and various pieces of electronic equipment. It looked like one of the rooms that would serve as a medical infirmary during their stay underground.

Cutter guided her to the dental chair.

"Sit." It wasn't a choice. Once she was in the chair, she nervously watched as Cutter strapped her wrists to the armrests. The calm reprieve of her meditation was already distant.

"Listen, Sebastian," Dilara said, "I'm willing to tell you anything you want to know."

"That may be true," Ulric said, "but I can't take your word for it. I don't have time. My men will be activating the devices tomorrow, and I have to be sure that they won't be intercepted."

"How would I know that?"

"You seemed to know a lot before. I've received news that both FBI Special Agent Perez and Dr. Tyler Locke were killed in a shoot-out on board the *Genesis Dawn*.

Therefore, you are now my only link to what Tyler knew."

Dilara's heart sank at the news of Tyler's death. Ulric didn't seem to be lying.

"I know this is a shocking confirmation for you," he said. "You must realize that no one knows where you are now. You're alone. All you have is us."

She strained at the wrist straps, but they wouldn't budge. "You're going to drug me anyway?"

"Dr. Green will do the injection. It's a new serum that my company developed for the CIA. A more reliable variant of sodium amytal. It won't hurt, but there is a risk to its use because it depresses nervous system functions. That's why a medical professional will administer it."

"I swear I don't know anything!"

Ulric ignored her. "Dr. Green, let's begin."

Green walked to the counter and stuck the needle of a large syringe into the cap of a bottle and withdrew 20 ccs of a clear fluid. He swabbed the vein on her left arm with rubbing alcohol.

"You're a doctor," Dilara said to Green. "Please don't do this."

Green smiled. "You'll feel a small poke." Then he jabbed the needle into her arm.

She felt the cool fluid flow into her vein.

When the plunger was all the way down, Green removed the needle.

"It should reach its full efficacy in five minutes. Dilara, I want you to count backward from a hundred."

She was already feeling woozy. She shook her head.

"I'm not doing anything!" She pulled at the restraints until her veins bulged.

"This will be easier for you if you don't struggle."

"Let me go!"

Then as if someone turned off a light switch, the room went black and her head seemed like it was plunged into a bucket of ice water. Green's voice became indistinct and faded until she sensed nothing at all.

"What happened?" Ulric asked. She wasn't supposed to pass out. She was supposed to be awake to answer his questions.

"She dropped her blood pressure and lost consciousness," Green said as he pointed a penlight into her eye. "As I said before, it happens in five percent of cases. Let's get her on the table."

Green had told Ulric about the potential risks. He could tell Green wanted to say I told you so, but the doctor didn't dare.

"Help him," Ulric said to Cutter. "Five

percent! Idiot!"

Cutter unstrapped her and lifted her dead weight from the chair and laid her on the table.

Green propped her feet up with a pillow. He checked her blood pressure.

"Her pressure is low, but stable."

"What now? Can you wake her up?"

"I can give her a shot of adrenaline. It would wake her up, but it would also offset the effects of the serum. Then we'd have to start all over. A second injection so quickly might be fatal."

"If we wait for her to wake up, will she still be under the effects of the serum?"

"We won't know until she's conscious. That may take a few hours."

"Dammit! All right. You'll stay here with one of Cutter's men. When she wakes up, let me know immediately."

"Yes, sir."

"Come on," he said to Cutter and stormed out of the room.

FORTY-FIVE

Once Tyler and Grant touched down at Mc-Chord Air Force Base south of Seattle, it was a short drive to Fort Lewis, where the assault team was making its final preparations inside one of the barracks. A map of Orcas Island was tacked to the wall, and thirty hardened commandos were busy checking weapons and loading their packs with ammo. Most of them were in their early twenties. Tyler and Grant were older than every one of them by a good five years.

They introduced themselves to the team's commander, Captain Michael Ramsey, a pale, lean thirty-year-old with a brush of close-cropped red hair. Ramsey, whose neck tendons looked strained to the breaking point, eyed them warily, apparently checking to make sure they measured up to his team's standards. He shook their hands, but he didn't look pleased to see them.

"Sorry to barge in on your mission, Captain," Tyler said, "but we have some tactical information that will be useful when we're on-site."

"If General Locke says you need to be here, then you're on the team," Ramsey said like a soldier who knew he had no choice but to follow orders. "As long as we're clear that I am in command."

"Absolutely. I'm sure you've seen our service records."

"Yes. I had the base quartermaster get some BDUs for you. Get changed, and we'll do the mission briefing." Ramsey looked at his watch. "I have 1743 hours. We're wheels up at 1900."

Tyler tossed the larger set of battle dress uniforms to Grant and put his own on. He hadn't worn fatigues since he'd left the service five years before, but donning them put him right back into military mode.

"Seems like old times," Grant said. "Except I feel like an old man compared to these young whippersnappers."

"You need your walker for this mission?" Tyler asked with a chuckle.

"Just my cane. You have your hearing aid in?"

Tyler shook his head and spoke louder. "Can't hear you without my hearing aid in. Got my reading glasses, though, in case I

449

need to read the instructions on my pills."

Ramsey broke into their fun. "You two ready?" he said curtly.

Tyler finished tying his boot laces and stood. "Grant was born ready, but I'm a late bloomer."

Ramsey rolled his eyes. He obviously didn't share their sense of humor.

"Listen up," he said, and the room grew still instantly. The soldiers' eyes were riveted on Ramsey. These guys were all-business.

"The intel on this op is sketchy at best," Ramsey continued. "Our mission is to infiltrate this complex here, and secure the bioweapon inside before 2100 hours." He pointed at a satellite photograph of the Church of the Holy Waters compound on Orcas. The island was shaped like a drooping, upside-down W, with three peninsulas pointing south. The compound was located on the east coast of the westernmost peninsula, bordered by a finger-shaped bay.

"We considered coming in by boat to Massacre Bay."

Tyler and Grant looked at each other when they heard the name. Not a bright omen.

"But that angle is well lit," Ramsey continued, "and we would be exposed trying to breach the shore fencing. They have a dock,

450

but it is heavily guarded. We estimate at least thirty guards on the premises. No knowledge about their disposition."

Tyler spoke up. "I believe I can answer that, Captain. Sergeant Westfield has served with one of the hostiles. He's ex-army Special Forces. His name is Dan Cutter, and it's logical to assume that he has stocked his guard crew with others like him. These won't be typical rent-a-guards. They'll be well trained and alert."

"I got the briefing on Cutter," Ramsey said, the distaste evident. "Our best chance for a successful mission is to take them by surprise. Because of time pressure, we can't wait to ferry in our Humvees. And if we try to land with Blackhawks within two miles, they'll hear us coming. Therefore, we're landing here." Ramsey pointed at the easternmost peninsula of the upside-down W, about ten miles due east of Ulric's bunker. "We've arranged for one of the island's school buses to be left at the LZ. We drive the rest of the way and dismount here."

Ramsey pointed at a spot less than a mile from the northern edge of the massive compound.

"When we're within one click, we'll do on-site recon with the UAV." To his left sat an unmanned aerial vehicle, a battery-powered helicopter not much bigger than a toy kids play with. When it was flown fifty feet above the observed area, it couldn't be heard by ground forces. The camera on board, which included infrared and light amplification for night ops, was powerful enough to beam back real-time battlefield images.

"Once we have their positions, we'll breach the outer fence and eliminate each hostile as we reach them. When the perimeter is secure, we'll enter the bunker here." The hangar-size building closest to the mansion.

"How silently can we do this?" Tyler asked.

"We'll try to take out as many of them as we can before the alarm is sounded. By that time, we should have overwhelming numbers."

Tyler shook his head. "That would jeopardize the mission."

"Why?"

"Because any alarm will cause an immediate lockdown. Concrete doors will slide over all the entrances to the bunker. Game over."

"How do you know that?"

"Because it was in the specifications. I constructed a preliminary blueprint for the facility three years ago, and although there will be changes, the basic elements are likely the same. The elevators are powered by electric motors in the cabs themselves, so there are no cables to cut. Concrete slabs three feet thick will block the shafts, and we don't have the firepower to blast through them. It'll be impossible to get in after that unless it's opened from inside."

"How about air shafts?"

Tyler shook his head again. "Only in the movies are ventilation shafts big enough for people to crawl through. I know for a fact these will be designed to prevent that."

"We could smoke them out. Drop smoke grenades down the shafts."

"No good. Even if we find some of the shafts, their filters would absorb any smoke."

"Do you have an alternate plan?" Ramsey said in exasperation.

Tyler shrugged. "All I know is, we have to get through that entrance and down into the bunker before the alarm sounds."

"Then we'll be really, really quiet. Anything else?"

"Yes. Once we're inside, we need to be very careful not to release any of the bio-agent. If any of us is exposed to it for even a second, we're dead and we might as well let the MOP do its job."

453

"I'm so glad you're here to give us good news, Captain Locke," Ramsey said flatly.

"Believe me, Captain, I want to get out of this mission in one piece. Speaking of that, how do we signal when we're successful?"

"When I'm satisfied that the bioagent and the facility are secure, I'll give the okay to radio the all-clear signal, which is 'The well is dry.' The B-52 that is on station will be told to return to base."

"I'll be glad when I hear that phrase," Grant said.

"One more thing, Captain Ramsey," Tyler said. "There will be unarmed civilians inside, as well as one friendly, a woman named Dilara Kenner. Make sure we only fire at the bad guys."

"My orders are to shoot anyone who poses a threat. If they aren't armed, they're not a threat."

"That's all I ask."

"All right, people!" Ramsey shouted, trying to pump up his troops. "Check your gear and lock and load! We need to move!"

"And let's synchronize our watches," Tyler said. "Because my father is nothing if not punctual. If we radio even one second after 2100 hours, we've got about thirty more seconds on this earth. Then there won't be enough left of any of us to fill a shot glass."

FORTY-SIX

It seemed a little silly to be riding to an attack in a yellow school bus, but Tyler and Grant were the only ones who were amused. The rest of the team looked uncomfortable and embarrassed crammed into the vehicle's tiny seats. With no military bases on the island, the bus with the letters ORCAS ISLAND SCHOOL DISTRICT on the side was their best choice.

While they drove into the fading light of sunset, Tyler rechecked his bag of tricks that he had outfitted from the Fort Lewis armory. He was armed with the Glock on his hip and an H & K MP5 submachine gun. Some of the soldiers were equipped with longer, more powerful M4 assault rifles, and Grant had one lying against his arm as he dozed.

It took twenty minutes on winding roads to get from the landing zone on the east side of the island to the point where they crossed the remaining terrain on foot. The Church of the Holy Waters compound was surrounded by ten-foot-high razor-wire fencing, but it was unlikely to be electrified. Too many potential lawsuits that would bring unwanted attention to the site.

They did, however, suspect sensors hidden in the ground and trees for motion detection. Although the island was crawling with wildlife, any animals that were large enough to trip the sensors, like deer, wouldn't be able to jump over the fence. Tyler agreed with Ramsey's assessment that once they crossed the fence, they would be detected if they didn't disable the sensors somehow.

All the trees fifty feet on either side of the fence had been chopped down so that using the branches to drop over it would be impossible. The only way through would be to cut the fence.

The team, which was now spread out in the trees a hundred yards from the fence, was signaled to halt by Ramsey, and everyone dropped to the ground. Tyler lay down next to him. The soil was soaked by rain that had pounded Puget Sound since he and Dilara left on Tuesday morning, letting up just in time for this operation. He and Ramsey both pulled out binoculars. They saw no guards patrolling the fence line, which confirmed the suspicion about motion sensors. Anyone patrolling would continuously set them off, rendering them useless.

The guards must be patrolling the central compound, ready to rush to any sensor that detected movement.

"What do you think?" Tyler asked.

"We'll have to cut through the fence."

"Then what? It's about five hundred yards to the central compound from the fence. Lots of opportunities to set off the sensors if we miss one."

"We'll have to risk it. My men are trained to spot and disable them."

"Then we just barge in the front door of the hangar building, guns blazing?"

"You got any other options?" Ramsey asked.

Tyler thought about it, but he didn't have any. "Maybe we'll see something with the UAV." It would be another ten minutes before the full dark would allow them to use the UAV without it being seen.

Grant, who was using Tyler's binoculars, nudged him and handed them back.

"Take a look at the fence. Two o'clock, at the base of the post."

Tyler focused on the spot with the binoculars. It took him a second, and then he saw what Grant was talking about.

"Crap."

"What is it?" Ramsey asked.

"The fence is wired."

"But with high voltage —"

"Not high voltage. Just a sensor wire." One of the wires had become exposed, just slightly, but enough for Grant's eagle eyes to see it. "If we cut the fence, they'll know immediately."

"Can we bypass it?"

"Maybe, but it would be tricky," Tyler said. "These guys are good."

"So the concrete doors would close instantly as soon as the fence was breached?"

"Unlikely. They'd want confirmation of an intrusion before they did something that drastic. But as soon as they saw the hole in the fence, or us crawling through it, they'd sound the alarm. Then we're toast."

"Maybe we should try a full assault through the front gate," Ramsey said. "Catch them by surprise."

"Same problem. When they suspect their guards are taken out, the alarm goes off and they shut themselves in."

"You're not being very helpful, Locke."

Tyler knew he sounded pessimistic, but when you eliminated all of the obvious

458

choices, less obvious choices suddenly made themselves known.

He concentrated on the fence again. He had laid the binoculars down while he was talking to Ramsey, and the lens was covered in water from the high grass. He paused to wipe it off, then stopped. He dug his gloved finger into the soil, which was soaking wet. His finger plunged through up to his top knuckle as easily as if he'd pushed it into pudding.

Tyler looked up at the tree next to him, a giant evergreen over 150 feet tall.

"Captain Ramsey," Tyler said, a big smile spreading across his face, "I'm about to be helpful. I have a way to get us through."

Sebastian Ulric checked his laptop to make sure that the inventory for Oasis was up-to-date and then radioed Cutter. The device on the *Genesis Dawn* should be in full operation by now. He'd wanted an immediate lockdown, but not everyone had completed the move from the main house into the bunker. Once the bunker was sealed, it would open up only once more: the next morning, when the three prion-emitting devices were ready and their bearers were sent off to LAX, Kennedy Airport, and Heathrow in London. When they were gone,

Oasis would be closed off from the rest of the world for three months, the time he expected it would take the Arkon-C to run its course worldwide. The men delivering the devices would have to be sacrificed, but they didn't know that. They were told that they would be let back in, but Ulric couldn't take the chance that they would be infected.

"How are we coming?" Ulric asked Cutter.

"Another twenty minutes, sir."

"What? Why is it taking so long?"

"We've still got equipment to move down that is crucial to our operations."

Oasis was equipped with positive-pressure air locks and hazmat suits for external forays in emergencies, but Ulric didn't want to use them if he didn't have to. The bunker was powered by two generators, and an enormous fuel tank buried next to it, with enough diesel stored for the entire three-month stay. Water from the desalination plant ensured a sterile supply, and the food stockpile contained twice what they should need.

"All right," Ulric said. "But when the equipment is inside, close it up. Tell everyone so there are no stragglers."

"Yes, sir."

He put the radio back on his desk. A knock came at his door.

"Come!"

A head peeked in his door. It was his replacement pharmacologist, David Deal.

"What is it, Deal?"

The man came in, stopping at the threshold. He looked nervous.

"I'm sorry to bother you, sir, but . . ." He hesitated.

"Come on, Deal. We're busy trying to close up."

"I know that, sir. That's why I'm here. They told me I would need your permission."

"To do what?"

"Well, with all the rush, you know, with my new Level Ten status just the last few days, and then the quick move down here, well, I left some things at the Lodge that I need for my work."

"What?"

"They're some critical notebooks. In the rush, I left them behind. I was told that to go back and get them, I would need your approval."

"How long will it take?"

"Just a few minutes. I think I know where they are."

"You think?"

"They're quite important."

Ulric considered it. To keep his people

happy, he needed to make sure they were engaged, and Deal was a last-minute addition.

"Very well. But be quick about it."

"Yes, sir."

Ulric radioed the guard at the entrance chamber to let Deal out.

FORTY-SEVEN

Night had fallen, giving the assault team the cover of complete darkness. A corporal opened what looked like an elaborate laptop computer. The main difference was the pair of joystick controls at the base of the panel. He would pilot the UAV from this terminal.

Captain Ramsey nodded, and the soldier who had prepared the UAV backed away. The corporal tapped a button, and the helicopter whirred to life. The sound was no louder than a hair dryer set on low.

The UAV rose into the air neatly, and it was soon out of earshot. The pilot kept it ascending until the UAV was higher than any of the trees. The only reason Tyler could see it was because it occasionally blotted out a star. As long as it remained high up, no one would notice it.

Tyler, Ramsey, and Grant focused on the video feed coming back from the onboard camera. The Starlight scope showed the helicopter flying past the fence and then over more trees. In two minutes, it passed over the first lights at the outskirts of the compound's main area.

The UAV flew over the hangar farthest from the main house and then circled it. No activity. Same for the second hangar. Arc lamps like the ones that lined city streets lit up the compound.

At the last hangar, the one closest to the main house and a large hotel-type structure, a dozen men could be seen hauling equipment from a truck through a large delivery door. The UAV maneuvered to get a better look inside, but the angle was too high.

"Should I take it lower?" the pilot asked.

"No," Ramsey said. "With all those people, we'd never get in unobserved that way. Let's keep looking."

Next to the truck, two armed guards, both in black caps and clothes, stood by a Ford SUV, their rifles slung at their sides. Another SUV pulled alongside, and one of the guards went over and spoke to the driver.

The UAV circled the compound to find more guards. Three more SUVs were spotted, as well as five guards on foot. Fifteen so far. There were probably more inside one of the buildings. All of the lights were out at the main house. A few were still on in the bigger building. Other than the guards and the men working by the truck, the compound seemed deserted. Tyler could only guess that most of the rest of the residents were already in the bunker. They didn't have much time.

The UAV came back over the central part of the compound, and a lone man could be seen walking out of a different door in the hangar.

"Another guard?" Ramsey asked.

"I don't see a weapon," Grant said. "Or a black cap."

"And he's wearing khaki slacks," Tyler said. "It's one of their civilians."

"What's he doing?"

"Heading to the building that looks like a hotel. This may be what we've been waiting for."

"What do you mean?"

"If we try to take any of these guards alive, they're not going to help us, no matter how much we threaten them. I've already had two of them kill themselves right in front of me. But a civilian might be another matter. If we can get to him fast enough, he could be our ticket inside the bunker."

"Then I guess it's time to try your idea. You really think this will work?"

"Depends who we get out here. If it's Cutter, we're screwed. Someone else, we might catch a break."

"Very well," Ramsey said. "Let's see that bag of tricks of yours do some magic."

Justin Harding, an ex-Ranger who had been recruited by Dan Cutter, was leaning against the passenger side of the SUV when he heard a loud crack come from the north end of the compound. It was quickly followed by a crash that reverberated through the woods.

He looked at the driver, Burns, and was about to report it in when he got a radio call from Cutter.

"Echo Patrol, this is Base. We just detected a breach in the north fence. Get out and find out what's going on. Bravo Patrol will meet you there. Report back. If there are hostiles, engage."

Cutter gave them the exact location of the breach.

"Affirmative. Echo Patrol out."

Burns fired up the SUV and screeched out of the central compound. The SUV bounced up and down as Burns weaved through the trees.

When they were within a hundred yards, they came to a stop and dismounted. If there were hostiles, Harding didn't want to barrel right into an ambush.

He and Burns, another ex-Ranger, advanced with classic covering positions. When they reached the tree line, he scanned the fence with his infrared. No bodies, human or animal in the vicinity. He switched on his flashlight and immediately saw the problem. He stood up and lowered his weapon.

"Not another one," he said to Burns. "And right on the fence this time."

He radioed to Jones, who was driving the second SUV.

"Bravo Patrol, pull up to the fence and shine your headlights on it."

The SUV pulled forward, and the fence was brightly illuminated.

"Damn!" Jones said as he got out. "Smashed right through it."

A huge pine tree had fallen from the tree line outside of the fence and rammed a twenty-foot-wide section of the fence into the ground.

"Just what we need tonight." During the storm two days ago, a tree had fallen in the windstorm, setting off the alarms, but that one had been in the woods and merely caused some noise. This one was a much bigger problem.

"Base," he radioed, "we've got another tree down."

"Where?"

"Right on the fence. That's what set off the sensors."

"Can you fix it?"

"No chance. It's crushed."

"We can't attempt large-scale repairs until tomorrow. You and Burns stay there to keep guard. Send Bravo Patrol back to the central compound. They'll relieve you in a couple of hours. I want status checks every fifteen minutes."

"Roger that."

Harding replaced the radio.

"You heard the man," he said to the three other guards, who were all standing in front of the SUV, staring at the massive tree. "Looks like we're pulling shit duty tonight."

Harding heard a faint pop from the opposite tree line. Burns's head flew back, and Harding smelled the blood shooting from Burns's mortal wound for only a moment before his own world went black.

The driver in Echo Patrol was the first to be taken out by the assault team's snipers. Tyler saw them adjust their silenced PSG-1s and take aim at the other three guards. It was all over in less than two seconds, far too quickly for the guards to react.

The assault team had been monitoring the radio calls, so they knew when it was time to take the shots. The plan had worked just like Tyler envisioned.

The ground was so wet that the trees' roots were grasping at the soil to stay upright. He had remembered the windstorm that hit Seattle while he was gone had damaged trees all over the Puget Sound. With the ground still soaked, it wouldn't take much to topple another tree.

He had selected one that was already tipping in the direction of the fence, enough to make sure he could control the direction of the fall. Then it was a simple matter of burying explosives from his bag of tricks in strategic locations around the base of the tree. He picked several with small charges so that they would sound like the crack of a rotten tree trunk when they went off. Using the ground-penetrating radar, they found the biggest roots. The shape-charges were placed so that they focused down on the largest of them.

The pine had fallen right across the fence. Literally in one fell swoop they had already cut a way through the fence, taken out four guards, had two vehicles at their disposal, and circumvented the motion detectors.

The team quickly crossed the fifty feet to the fence and went through the opening.

Tyler saw the four bodies of the guards lying at the front of the SUV. The headlights were still blazing, showing the gory detail of the takedown. Tyler felt no remorse for the surprise attack, not after all he'd been through in the last week.

"You heard the man on the radio," Tyler said to Ramsey. "We've got fifteen minutes before they have to check in."

"Right," Ramsey said. "Let's go."

FORTY-EIGHT

The Lodge, as everyone called the Church of the Holy Waters' hotel building, was lit only sparingly. Once the main power to the Lodge was cut off, it would be completely dark. Given how many times he'd been in the Lodge before, David Deal thought he would be comforted by the building, but now the emptiness of it seemed disturbing. He had an eerie feeling that any minute the visions he'd had before would come back with a vengeance, and this time they wouldn't be so benevolent.

He crossed the lobby and took the stairs to his room on the third floor. He'd told the Faithful Leader that he'd left some papers important to his work, but in truth what he'd left behind was something more valuable to him. He wouldn't dare tell Sebastian Ulric that what he wanted special permission to retrieve was a letter that his daughter had written him long ago. A letter he had hidden under the mattress so it wouldn't be discovered.

His wife had left him with their only daughter so that she could shack up with another man, a drug dealer who lured her into a life of debauchery and sin. Deal bid her good riddance. He could raise their daughter on his own. But two years later, his daughter succumbed to leukemia.

The loss devastated him, and he turned to religion to find answers. When his old church couldn't satisfy him, he found his way to the Church of the Holy Waters, which promised a utopian New World in the near future, something he would see in his lifetime. In the church, he found others like him, intellectuals who needed faith in something bigger than themselves, in which science wasn't a boogeyman to be shunned but the answer he'd been seeking.

When he began having the visions during the Leveling, he became convinced Diluvianism was the way he could find meaning in the world.

Then the Faithful Leader, Sebastian Ulric, revealed that the New World would be upon them soon and that David Deal was selected to be part of it. Deal didn't know what it was, but Ulric promised them that after ninety days in seclusion in the underground waiting area, they would emerge to the New World, an earthly Eden that Deal would help shape.

Only a few in Ulric's inner circle knew exactly what the New World meant, and though Deal was curious, he accepted the fact that he was not one of them. Ulric had told them that others might try to take away their Oasis, which was the reason for the extraordinary security measures — the guards, the fences, the guns, the passwords to get in and out of Oasis. This week, the safe word was *Searchlight,* and the warning word was *Heaven.* Deal was excited by the intrigue and the world yet to come.

Because he was taken into Oasis so hastily, he'd forgotten about the letter under the mattress. Normally, he kept it in a hidden pocket in his suitcase, but he read it every night before he went to sleep, so the mattress was a more convenient place for it. Only when he got to his quarters in Oasis did he realize that he'd left the letter behind. If the Lodge were burned or ransacked, he might lose the last communication from his daughter forever, and even Utopia would be meaningless without that.

He found his room, and it took only a moment to locate the letter where he'd hidden it. He pocketed the letter, closed the door behind him, and retraced his path down the stairs.

He got three-fourths of the way across the lobby when the exterior door opened. Two guards in their black pants, sweaters, and caps walked in. He didn't recognize them, one a tall Caucasian man with the hint of a smile and the other a powerfully built African-American, but then he was so new that he didn't know most of the guards.

Deal guessed he had taken too long and they were sent to bring him back, which was fine with him. He'd retrieved what he wanted and was ready to await the New World.

"What's your name?" the taller man said.

"David Deal. I'm sorry I took so long. Dr. Ulric gave me permission to get something from the Lodge."

"Well, he wants you back now, and we're supposed to take you there."

Deal shrugged. He was already heading back, so this just seemed like overkill.

Tyler had learned from experience that the best way to get through any security was to act like you belonged there. This Deal just assumed he was one of the guards, so Tyler ran with it.

They walked out the lobby door of the

Lodge and escorted Deal to the SUV they had appropriated back at the fence. Ramsey sat in the driver's seat, and Private Knoll from the assault team sat in the back. Grant got in the passenger seat and Tyler got in the back with Deal, who squeezed into the middle. Ramsey drove toward the door where they'd first seen Deal emerge.

Once the dead guards had been dragged out of the way at the outer fence, Ramsey had ordered the rest of his team to stay behind with one of the vehicles and shoot anyone else who might come out to investigate. With two SUVs out there, no one would pay any attention to one of them driving back. No motion sensors would be tripped. In fact, they'd probably all been turned off in this area to eliminate false alarms.

If more than four of them drove back in the SUV and they were seen by other guards from a distance, the number of men in the vehicle would have raised questions. Of course, if anyone who knew the guards saw them up close, the jig would be up anyway.

The ground-penetrating radar confirmed that a large bunker lay below them. This was Oasis. When Tyler had seen the original specs, it had called for a Level 4 containment lab like the one at the CDC, ostensibly for analyzing any WMDs that had made the bunker necessary. Now Tyler realized it was actually for *creating* the bioweapons.

Ramsey left a burly sergeant in charge at the fence breach with the order to monitor the radio. If they encountered trouble in the compound or if the main alarm was sounded, the team would begin an all-out assault. Since Tyler knew the basic layout of Oasis and it was his idea how to get in, he was going along, and he insisted on Grant being the fourth.

They had changed into the guards' clothes. From the four who were killed, they were able to scrounge up three outfits that weren't too bloody. Three of the kills had been head shots, and two of those caps were destroyed. The other kill had been to the neck. Ramsey and Knoll went capless, and Ramsey wore one of the bloodied sweaters. It would stand up to scrutiny from a distance.

The drive to the hangar with Deal took almost no time, but Tyler's watch said they only had eight minutes before the expected check-in from Harding. They'd have to make this quick.

Tyler suspected that getting into Oasis wouldn't be as simple as walking through a door, but he couldn't question Deal without tipping him off that he wasn't who he said he was. Tyler would have to improvise. He told Grant, Ramsey, and Knoll to wait in the car. They'd be able to hear him over their headsets. They'd know when to move in.

The light from the arc lamp was strong over the entrance. Tyler got out, followed by Deal. He turned as Tyler closed the door behind him. Deal stopped, peering past Tyler at Ramsey. Then he leaned in closer, and his eyes went wide.

"My God! What happened to you?"

In the light of the arc lamp, the residual blood on Ramsey's sweater was still bright.

Tyler grabbed Deal and pushed him into the hood of the car. He jammed his hand over the man's mouth.

"Pay attention. Do exactly what I say and I won't have to shoot you. No sudden movements and no shouting. Nod if you understand."

Deal nodded quickly. Tyler removed his hand, ready to replace it if he thought Deal would yell.

"What do you want?" Deal asked, trembling.

"I want you to take me into Oasis. How do we get in?"

Deal swallowed nervously. "There's . . .

There's a guard inside behind bulletproof glass. He opens the door after you do a handprint scan and say the password."

"What's the password?"

"It won't do you any good without the handprint."

"I'm not going to say it. You are. What's the password?"

Deal looked like he might not say it for a second. Then he spoke. *"Heaven."*

Something about how Deal said it made Tyler doubt him.

"You sure? Because if that guard doesn't open that door, I'm going to shoot you right there and walk out." Tyler was bluffing. He wouldn't shoot an unarmed noncombatant, but he thought he sounded pretty convincing.

"The door will open," Deal said, whimpering. "I swear."

"Good. Now get it together. Just play along, and you'll be fine."

Deal nodded again, regaining his composure, and Tyler followed him through the door.

He walked into a small antechamber that faced a metal sliding door, and there was the guard, sitting behind the bulletproof glass. The guard looked at the two of them while Deal pressed his hand on a biometric pad.

"Who are you?" the guard asked Tyler, who ignored the hand scanner.

"Tyler. James Tyler." Use something close to the truth, and it's easier to cover a lie. James was his middle name.

"I haven't seen you before, Tyler."

"I'm new. Cutter hired me two days ago to replace Howard Olsen."

"Scan your hand."

"I can't. With all that's going on lately, they haven't put me in the system yet. But Dr. Ulric wants me to escort Mr. Deal here back down."

Tyler had remembered the name of the man who fell from the Space Needle elevator, Howard Olsen, and assumed he was on the guard staff. It seemed to do the trick. So many names being dropped so quickly must have convinced the guard that Tyler was legit.

"Password," the guard said.

Tyler kept his eyes on the guard. Either Deal would say it or he wouldn't, but Tyler wanted to know immediately whether the guard would open the door.

"Heaven."

The guard nodded. Tyler had been focused on his eyes, and for just a split second, the guard's eyes had opened slightly and the eyebrows had lifted in the middle. The guard covered well, and if Tyler hadn't been looking directly at him at that moment, he would have missed it. But the guard was surprised. It wasn't the password he was expecting.

Nevertheless, he lazily tapped a button on the panel in front of him and the door slid open. Then his hand fell back to his side, and he waved them through with his other hand. Classic misdirection. Something was about to go down.

So Tyler did the same thing. He waved his hand at Deal to walk through ahead of him, drawing attention away from his other hand, which reached into the pack hanging at his side. He had to time this right, or he'd be dead the second he walked through that door.

FORTY-NINE

The guard manning the Oasis entrance that night was George Henderson. The job wasn't his favorite, but he was a professional, so he paid attention, particularly to anything that didn't fit standard procedure. This guy who called himself Tyler was definitely in that category.

Normally, Henderson would be one of the first to know if a new member of the security team had been hired. But given how fast the last few days had gone, it was conceivable that he wouldn't have been notified. The guard duty rotated among the security team, and this was the first time he'd pulled the duty in a week. When Tyler had mentioned Cutter and Olsen and Ulric, he assumed that the guy was valid.

Until Deal said *"Heaven."* That was the warning password. Whoever Tyler was, he wasn't welcome.

Henderson briefly considered calling

Cutter and reporting the incident without opening the access door, but he decided that this was a perfect opportunity to take care of the matter himself. His standing orders were to use his judgment in handling these matters, including taking the subject down himself. Which was exactly what he chose to do. He could eliminate this intruder on his own, and with that kind of heroic deed, he'd never be asked to perform desk duty again.

So he pressed the button to open the door and simultaneously dropped his other hand to his sidearm. He'd be able to draw it as the intruder rounded the corner. Henderson would get three shots into Tyler before he knew what hit him.

The intruder waved Deal to the door. Deal came through, and at the same time Henderson heard a clatter on the floor. Instinctively, his eyes dropped from Tyler to the floor. He saw a metal cylinder bounce against the wall and come to rest near his feet.

His peripheral vision registered that Tyler threw himself to the ground behind the glass, but Henderson realized too late that the cylinder at his feet was a flash-bang grenade. He was looking directly at it when it exploded in his face.

Tyler crouched against the wall, pressed his fingers into his ears, and shut his eyes tightly. He'd pulled the pin on the flash-bang and counted to two before flicking it with his wrist in the direction of the open door.

The grenade went off with a loud thump. The grenade disabled with a bright light and concussive force of the explosion. In most cases, the explosion wasn't injurious, but stunned its targets by rendering them deaf, blind, and dizzy.

Tyler leaped to his feet and dashed through the doorway. Both Deal and the guard were lying on the floor, clawing at their eyes. Before the guard could recover, Tyler slammed him in the back of his head with the butt of the rifle he'd appropriated from one of the guard's dead colleagues. The guard dropped to the deck unconscious, but breathing. The smoke lingered as the ventilation system struggled to dissipate it.

Tyler took advantage of the smoke cover and smashed the sentry room's camera, but he knew that it wouldn't take Cutter's security team long to notice it wasn't working. When that happened, they'd first think it was a technical glitch. Then they would call the guard to confirm there wasn't a security breach. When they got no response, they'd send a guard to check. Tyler guessed that they had two minutes at most.

Grant and Ramsey, who'd heard the blast through the earpiece, rushed through the outer door. Tyler hadn't been able to tell them about his improvisation, so they came through the door with their guns at the ready. When they saw Tyler was the only one standing, they lowered their weapons.

"Looks like you've got things under control," Grant said.

"He tried to take me down by himself," Tyler said.

"Big mistake."

"Where's Knoll?"

"He's keeping watch outside."

"We'd better hurry."

Ramsey removed a packet of plastic restraining ties from his pocket. He threw a couple to Tyler, who used them to bind the guard's hands and feet. Grant did the same with the groaning Deal while Ramsey radioed his sergeant.

"Ares Leader to Ares One," he said.

"Ares One here."

"We're through the front door. We've still

got five minutes before those guards are supposed to check in. Maintain your position. I'll alert you when we've secured the barriers. Make no move before then unless you get confirmation from me."

"Roger that."

Tyler checked the hallway leading from the guard station, where it reached an intersection. To the right and left were long corridors that ended in doors. Tyler turned and saw two elevators with only one call button. Down. Across from the elevators was another door, a triple-thick heavy-duty metal slab that could probably take a direct hit by an RPG. Tyler eased it open.

It was the interior of the hangar, a huge chamber. About fifty feet away, Tyler could see the open hangar door and next to it, a large service elevator. Two guards stood at the elevator, observing the movement of equipment. Apparently, the thick door had muffled the flash-bang well enough for it to go unnoticed amid the noise the guards were making.

The hangar contained only one thing, but there was a hell of a lot of it. Dirt. Massive piles of it stretching to the ceiling and filling every corner of the hangar, leaving only a wide path to reach the service elevator. The other hangars must have been filled to the brim as well.

Tyler closed the door without the guards seeing him. They were too focused on the other side of the hangar. He walked down one end of the long corridor past the elevator and opened the door to see a wide stairway leading down.

At the first landing, there was the horizontal concrete barrier, which was recessed into the wall. At the press of a button at the central security station, the barrier would come out of the wall over the landing and nestle into the opposite wall, covering the entire stairwell. It would take far more explosives than Tyler had in his bag of tricks to blast through it.

He couldn't hear anyone in the stairwell and closed the door. Tyler jogged back to the guard station and saw the computer monitor sitting on the guard's desk. If they could log into the system, they might be able to get a schematic for the underground facility.

"I'm going to check —"

Those were the only words Tyler got out. He heard a shot outside the building. The outer door crashed open, and Knoll's lifeless body tumbled inside. A guard rushed in and jumped over Knoll. He stopped in his tracks when he saw the residual smoke and the three men standing in the guard's chamber.

The guard raised his weapon to fire, and Tyler lunged for the button controlling the security door. He slammed his hand down on it as bullets from the guard's machine gun thudded into the wall behind the open door. Grant ducked under them, and the security door slammed shut. The guard put another round into the glass, but it was, indeed, bulletproof, and the rounds simply smacked into it.

The guard whipped the radio to his lips, and Tyler realized that he, Grant, and Ramsey had only seconds to get down the stairs because the guard was radioing that security had been breached. Oasis was going to be locked down.

"Come on!" Tyler yelled and ran toward the east stairs.

Grant was behind him, and Ramsey followed, yelling into his radio.

"Ares One! This is Ares Leader! We've been made! Start your attack!"

"Roger, Ares Leader!"

Tyler plunged through the door and took the stairs down two at a time. A klaxon sounded. He was just past the landing when the barrier began to emerge from the wall and slide across the stairwell. The concrete slab must have weighed tons, but it was closing quickly. It was already halfway to the opposite wall as Grant hopped over it and down the stairs.

Ramsey dove over the railing and into the opposite wall. He tucked himself in and rolled down the stairs, just squeezing through before the barrier slammed with a clunk into the wall.

The klaxon reduced to a quarter volume, and a female voice said, "Intruder alert. Stay in your rooms." The message repeated ten seconds later. Tyler assumed the message was aimed at the facility's civilian occupants.

He helped Ramsey up. "You all right?"

"I'll be fine," Ramsey said, massaging his shoulder.

"Try your radio."

Ramsey called for the sergeant three times. No answer except static.

"The barrier's too thick," Ramsey said.

"And if we can't raise them, we can't radio the bomber."

"Then our first objective after we find the bioweapon is to get the barrier open again."

Tyler simply nodded. They all knew what they were up against. There were seven levels to explore, at least twenty guards still inside, hundreds of unarmed civilians, including Dilara Kenner, to worry about, and if they didn't secure the bioweapon and reconnect with their team in the next thirty minutes, the most powerful non-nuclear bomb in the military's arsenal would turn the entire complex into a sinkhole.

Grant cleared his throat.

"Well," he said, "this should be a challenge."

FIFTY

Dilara Kenner was vaguely aware of a banging noise, and it sounded like a voice was yelling at her. Her eyes fluttered open. Her head lolled to the side and felt like it was mired in quicksand. For a moment, she had no idea where she was. Then she saw two men at the other end of a room. One man, dressed all in black, was talking into a radio. The other man, who was in a white lab coat, was looking at him intently. Then she recognized them and the chair she had been strapped into, and her adrenaline kicked in.

She didn't know how she had gotten to the table. Whatever they had drugged her with made her light-headed, but the horn that still blared in the background had awakened her.

The words coming from the speakers became clear.

"Intruder alert. Stay in your rooms."

Someone was assaulting the complex. And

if rescuers were inside, her best chance was to find them herself.

The fuzziness in her brain was clearing. She closed her eyes and willed herself to concentrate. If they knew she was awake again, they'd strap her back down or put her back in the bedroom.

The guard's deeper voice said, "Stay here and watch her. I'm going to find out what's going on. Lock this door and don't open it. I'll come back and unlock it when we have the all clear."

The door opened and closed. She was alone with the doctor.

She silently flexed her hands and legs. They were working, but she couldn't tell how much strength she still had. She'd have to chance it.

She let out a soft moan and rocked her head back and forth slightly as if she were just coming out of her stupor.

The doctor came to the side of the bed, as she thought he would. She fluttered her eyes open and closed. He was standing next to her, probably figuring out what he should do. His crotch was level with the top of the table. Perfect.

She turned over on her side, facing the doctor, and moaned even louder. The doctor reached out with his hand to steady her, never seeing her knee lash out at him.

She hit him squarely in the groin, and the skinny man doubled over with a squeak. He fell to his knees, sucking in air.

Dilara jumped off the table too quickly. She got a severe head rush and leaned against the table to steady herself.

The doctor wobbled, trying to get to his feet. Dilara fell back on her defensive training. When she knew she'd be spending a lot of time excavating digs in dangerous locations, she'd taken hand-to-hand defense and weapons training, just in case. Now she was glad she had. And the first thing she had learned was that the elbow was one of the strongest points on the body. You could use it for maximum damage with the least amount of danger of injuring yourself.

The doctor's head was now even with her elbow.

With what strength she had, she threw her elbow backward, slamming the doctor in the side of the head. His opposite ear smacked into the countertop. Dilara's arm rang with pain from the impact, but she'd accomplished what she wanted. The doctor fell to the floor, out cold.

She wasn't strong enough to heave him into the chair and strap him down. Besides, there wasn't enough time. They'd find out she was gone soon anyway. She had to try to rendezvous with the intruders. All she was sure of was that whoever was attacking the facility was her friend.

She looked around the room for anything that could be used as a weapon. She had no intention of leaving unarmed.

Ulric and Cutter had been in the fifth level's scientific laboratories when Cutter got the call from the guard that the entranceway had been breached. They had been supervising the last stage of readying the prion devices for shipment. As soon as the call came in, Cutter had ordered the entire facility locked down.

Soon after that, he got reports from his team still outside that they were being attacked by hostile forces, probably army special ops. Cutter went to a monitor and called up the sentry camera's digital playback. It showed a guard with David Deal coming through the security door, and then a flash and smoke. After that, the camera went dead. Cutter played it back again and recognized the man dressed as a guard.

"Tyler!" Ulric shouted. "That news story was a fake! Did we get the barriers closed in time?"

"My guard can't get to the stairs," Cutter

said, "but he thinks they might have made it in. Only three of them. He saw them go toward the east stairwell."

"Dilara Kenner. We can use her as a hostage. Have the guard bring her here. I don't care if she's awake or not."

Cutter called the guard he'd left with the doctor.

"Is the woman conscious yet?" Cutter asked.

"I don't know," the guard replied.

"What do you mean you don't know?"

"I'm on my way down to the control room," the guard said.

"What? Get back to the exam room now and get Kenner. Bring her to the lab level. Carry her if you have to. Use the west stairwell."

"Yes, sir."

"If Tyler has only two other people with him," Ulric said, "what could they do?"

"It sounds like they have army reinforcements outside, so they'll try to open the barriers. If they succeed, the soldiers outside may be able to launch a full-scale assault of Oasis and wipe us out."

"The control room then. Go. And shut off that damned klaxon, but tell everyone to stay in their rooms. I'll finish up here. When we have Kenner, patch me into the loudspeakers. I don't think Tyler will let her die a slow death. When the devices are ready, I'll destroy the remaining samples. We can't let our research get into the army's hands."

The control room, located deep down on level seven, was the central nervous system of the Oasis complex. Guards posted there could watch any room in the facility via the cameras mounted throughout the structure. The control room was the only place from which the barriers could be opened.

"Where's Locke now?" Cutter said into his mouthpiece as he drew his pistol and sprinted for the north stairwell. If he could circle around and sneak up on them from behind, he might be able to end it quickly.

"They're still at the top of the east stairwell. Shit!"

"What happened?"

"They just took out the camera."

The internal cameras were meant for observing the inhabitants in order to control them, not to track intruders, so they weren't secured. A good smack from a rifle butt could take one out.

"Tell no one to use the east stairs. Use the north or west stairs. We'll lure them down and then get them from above. Prepare for an assault. I'm on my way."

Cutter eased the north stairwell door

open. No shots. No one there. He ran down the stairs.

The klaxon shut off, followed by a message to the inhabitants to stay where they were until further notice.

Tyler opened the door to the first level. He saw a long hallway that was bisected by a T intersection at its halfway point before it got to what looked like another stairwell door at the other end. No guards. The civilian occupants were heeding the warning to stay in their rooms. Finding Dilara would be a tedious task, Tyler realized with dismay, that they didn't have time for.

Ramsey kept an eye on the stairwell. Grant had busted the camera, but that didn't give them much protection. They'd have to destroy cameras as they went.

"How do we get those barriers open?" Ramsey asked.

"There's a control room on the bottom level," Tyler said. "It'll be a hardened facility."

"And the hazmat lab?"

"Fourth or fifth level. It'll be the only other one that's secure. They won't want nonessential personnel wandering in there."

"So what's our plan?"

"Lab first?" Grant said.

Tyler nodded. "If we don't find the bio-weapon, we might as well just wait there for the bomb to fall and sterilize the facility."

"Then let's go," Ramsey said. "Keep an eye on the doors as we go. I'll be ready with grenades if we hear someone below."

"But first, a little surprise." Tyler dug around in his pack.

"Something else in your bag of tricks?"

"We don't want someone coming from behind us unannounced," Grant said, knowing what Tyler was planning. "Makes his back prickly."

About four inches from the door, Tyler placed an updated version of a claymore mine. If the door opened, it would hit the striker, and anyone standing within twenty feet of the door would become "nonoperational," as the army liked to put it.

Tyler finished placing the striker and stood. "Now that the itch in my back is scratched," he said, "let's find the lab."

Fifty-One

The exam room seemed like any other Dilara had visited in her life. She rummaged through the drawers and cabinets looking for something that she could take with her for protection, but the only thing sharp was the hypodermic that had been used on her.

Without a weapon, she was defenseless. The guards were much tougher than the doctor and would take her down in a second. Still, she couldn't just wait for someone to rescue her. Better to be proactive and go down fighting.

Her best option was to head for the stairs and try to make an escape while their attention was focused on whoever had invaded the facility. Once she was aboveground, she could make contact with the invaders.

Dilara's heart was pounding as she inched the door open to see if anyone was in the hall. If she just popped out, her escape might be over before it began. She peered through the slit.

No one in that direction. She opened the door wider until she could see the "315" on it and looked the other way. Clear. She made a motion to leave and then heard a man talking. Coming this way, but down a hall she couldn't see. He paused while he spoke, as if he were talking on a phone. One set of footsteps. He was alone.

She recognized the voice. It was the guard who'd just left.

"I'll be down there with her in a minute," he said.

He was coming for her.

Dilara slid the door closed quietly. She only had a few seconds. The guard would need to open the door fully before he saw the doctor on the floor. That might give her a second of surprise.

She grabbed the hypodermic and stuck the needle into the same vial she had seen the doctor use. She drew five times the amount used on her. Then she crouched behind the door, which opened inward.

She held the syringe with one hand and placed her other palm over the plunger. The footsteps outside approached the door. No hesitation in them. The guard expected to see Dilara still lying on the table.

The door swung open, and the guard

walked in, stopping even with her when he saw the doctor on the floor. Dilara lunged out from behind the door and thrust the needle into the guard's thigh up to the plastic and at the same time shoved the plunger down hard. The clear liquid surged into his leg before he could move.

The guard yelped and pulled his leg back. Dilara still gripped the syringe as the needle withdrew, and she held it like a switchblade.

"You bitch!" the guard shouted and rushed her. The muscular guard knocked the syringe out of her hand and picked her up by the shoulders.

Even though the drug went into muscle, Dilara hoped the high dose would have the same effect as it had on her. She had started silently counting the moment she had injected him.

At the count of six, the guard shoved her against the wall, knocking the wind out of her. She doubled over, gasping for air.

"Stay there!" the guard shouted. All she could do was count.

At the count of eight, he raised the radio to his lips.

At the count of nine, his eyes rolled back in his head.

At the count of ten, he hit the floor.

The guard wasn't unconscious, but he was

out of it. He moaned softly and babbled something Dilara couldn't make out. She sucked in a breath and finally stood straight.

She kicked at the guard's arm, but it was limp, so she was easily able to take his submachine gun. She also relieved him of his spare magazines.

She examined the gun. Heckler & Koch MP5. She'd fired one once during her training. Nice, light weapon. Just what she needed.

She stuffed his Sig Sauer pistol into her waistband and went in search of the stairs.

At the second level, Tyler repeated the precautions he'd taken on the first level. They disabled each camera and then placed a claymore against the door. With the cameras out, whoever came through first would have no idea how unhappy he was going to be for the thirty milliseconds he had to live.

Grant broke the third-level camera, and Tyler knelt near the door. He placed the mine and was about to set the striker when he heard footsteps squeak lightly on the tile in the hallway beyond the door. Someone was coming.

Tyler hadn't finished setting up the claymore, so he shoved the mine and striker aside and backed away on the landing, aiming his gun at the door. Grant and Ramsey were on the stairs below him, their weapons trained. It opened, and when Tyler saw the face peer through, he eased up on the trigger.

"Hold your fire!" he yelled.

It was Dilara, and she was armed to the teeth.

"Tyler!" she said. "You're alive!" She threw herself into his arms, and Tyler hugged her tightly. After a few seconds, he let her go and gave a sheepish grin to a surprised Ramsey while Grant explained who she was.

"Are you okay?" Tyler said to Dilara.

"Ulric drugged me, but I'll be all right." Her voice was a little thick, as if she were eating sticky peanut butter.

Tyler pointed to the MP5 she was carrying. "You sure you're up to handling that right now?"

"When I came through that door, I almost shot you."

"I'll take that as a yes."

"They said you were dead."

"Good. That's what I wanted them to think."

"We have to stop them," Dilara said. "They're planning to release some kind of prion in New York, LA, and London. They're shipping the stuff out tonight."

"That's why we're here. And we've got about twenty minutes to find it."

"Why twenty minutes?"

He told her about the bomber circling overhead.

"Is it just the three of you?"

Tyler nodded. "The rest of our team is locked out on the surface. We've lost communications with them."

"Then what do we do?"

"After we secure the prions, we have to figure out a way to get into their control room."

"Maybe a guard would be able to give us a way in," Dilara said.

"Even if we find one," Tyler said, "these guys aren't the talkative types. It would take too long to get anything out of them."

"I know one who might talk."

"Why would he do that?"

"Because I just pumped him full of truth serum."

FIFTY-TWO

Sebastian Ulric watched his scientists load the last of the Arkon-C into the dispersion devices. In a few minutes, they would be ready for deployment. The assault had been a great inconvenience, but nothing more than that if he could get these scientists finished.

"Hurry up," he said into the microphone. "This is taking too long."

The transfer of the Arkon-C was taking place, as it always did, inside the chamber he'd used only a few days ago to make his point about traitors. All of the Arkon that existed in the world, except the one sample still on Noah's Ark, was in that chamber. And once the transfer was complete, he would destroy the surplus.

The computer files had already been erased. He kept the only remaining copy of the files in a USB drive in his pocket. It held all of the plans for modifying Arkon-A, the raw form on Noah's Ark, into Arkon-C. He didn't want to take the one-in-a-million chance that the government would get their hands on the process and engineer some kind of antidote.

The men inside the closed chamber were wearing biohazard suits, just in case containment was compromised during the job. The other labs had already been sterilized with salt water, a process that took longer than using heat but was just as effective. It was the reason Noah had been able eventually to emerge from the Ark and repopulate the world, the Arkon having been destroyed after it wiped out the animals and flowed into the salty seas.

In the observation room were the three men who would deliver the devices. Each of them assumed they would come back to Oasis once their jobs were complete, but there was a slight risk that they'd be infected during their missions. When they returned, they would get as far as the entranceway and be terminated there by guards waiting in hazmat suits. Ulric regretted losing believers, but it was necessary to ensure the safety of Oasis.

The only other people in the observation room with Ulric were the chamber operator and Petrova. Dilara Kenner should have been here by now.

He spoke into his radio.

"Cutter, where is Dilara Kenner? I can't bargain with somebody I don't have. He'll want to hear her voice."

"She got away, sir," Cutter said.

Ulric's hand clenched on the walkie-talkie. "What? How?"

"I don't know. But we just saw her run into the third-level stairwell, right about where Locke should be."

"So they're together now?"

"I don't know. The stairwell camera is out at that level."

"Well then, what *do* you know?"

"None of the hallway cameras has picked them up, which means they're all in the stairwell, and we're about to start our attack."

"Fine, then. I obviously don't need Dr. Kenner anymore. Kill them all."

Cutter watched the camera on level four. It was still intact and didn't show any movement, which meant that Locke and the others must still be at the third-level landing.

Perfect.

Cutter planned a three-pronged attack. Team One would come up the stairwell below them and serve as the decoy. Team

Two was stationed halfway down the third-level corridor, ready to ambush Locke when he came out the door. They would remain hidden until Cutter signaled that Locke and his companions had entered the range of the third-level hallway cameras. Then his men would pop out and mow them down.

Once the attack had started below, Team Three, who had used a different stairwell to get up to the first level, would close in a pincer movement from above. Locke would be driven right into the ambush in the third-level hallway.

Cutter wanted to be leading the battle himself, especially because he had seen Grant Westfield with them, but he could help the team best by directing the attack from the control room. At least he'd get to watch Westfield die on his monitor.

"Teams Two and Three, wait for my signal. Team One, go."

Team One burst through the seventh-level door and charged up the stairs, firing their weapons.

"Team Three go!"

Cutter saw the Team Three leader in the hallway of level one kick the door open.

The door exploded.

The two men who were right in front of the door were blown to pieces. The other two men, who had been covering them, went down holding their faces. Cutter gritted his teeth. The door had been booby-trapped.

Cutter called for Team One to pull back. Too late.

He heard an explosion before the Team One leader could respond.

"Team One leader is gone!" Cutter heard from another man. "They're dropping grenades down the stairs!"

Cutter was losing his men fast. "Team One, get out now! Use the closest door! Team Two, hold position and wait for my command." Maybe Locke would still come out through the third-level door, and he could salvage this debacle.

He waited and saw nothing from the third-level hallway camera. Thirty seconds passed. Nothing.

"Switch to the level-two hallway camera," he said.

The monitor showed Dilara Kenner behind Locke, and another soldier holding Grant Westfield up to the camera. All looked uninjured. Westfield's face took up almost the whole image. His arms were extended past the camera behind it. Why didn't he just break it? What was he . . .

Dammit!

"Shut down power to that camera!" Cutter yelled. "Hurry!"

The operator wasn't fast enough. With a flash, all of the video feeds blinked out.

FIFTY-THREE

After backtracking up to level two, Grant had seen the remains of the camera on the landing and told Tyler he had a way to take out the cameras, which were becoming a real nuisance. Even if they shut down each camera as they went, doing so would eat into time they didn't have.

The unshielded cameras were all on the same circuit. If Grant could find a high-voltage wire and tie it directly into a powered camera's video feed, he could overload the whole system. The sparks leaping from the camera told Grant that's exactly what had happened.

"We should be good to go," he said. "That'll teach them for giving the construction contract to someone without my amazing skills."

Tyler led them to the stairway at the west end of the hallway. Ramsey followed without a word. Since Tyler knew the basic layout better than anyone else, Ramsey had deferred the point position to him.

Only fifteen minutes were left, and they all felt the pressure to move quickly, but they couldn't risk attacking head-on a fortified position they had little intel about. Anything the guard doped up on truth serum might be able to tell them would be worth the time.

They went cautiously into the stairwell and saw no one. They were halfway down when the door from the third level opened. Ramsey had the angle and fired two quick bursts, taking down two guards before they could react. The bodies kept the door from closing, and Tyler could see another two guards retreat down the hallway.

He ran into the hall, firing shots at the retreating guards, who were going for the east stairwell. Just like Tyler wanted.

He could see one of the guards halt before opening the door, as if the man were listening to someone in his earpiece. But the other soldier barreled past him and launched himself at the door. The first guard tried to hold him back, but the door was already swinging open and hit the striker of the claymore that Tyler had reset there.

The blast threw them backward, and the

guards came to rest facedown, their bodies a mess of blood and dust.

"Which room?" Tyler asked Dilara.

She led them to 315. They found the doctor and the drugged guard still on the floor.

Grant and Ramsey picked up the guard and put him in the chair, clasping the restraints over his wrists.

"What's your name?" Tyler asked the guard while Ramsey wrapped the doctor's wrists and ankles with plastic cuffs.

The guard's eyes were completely dilated, unable to fix on who was speaking to him.

"Connelly." He voice was slurred, like he'd chugged a twelve-pack.

"How many guards are there, Connelly?"

"Guards?"

"Your men. How many?"

"Thirty-two total security forces."

"Looks like this stuff is working," Grant said.

"How many inside?" Tyler asked.

"Fifteen."

If Tyler was lucky, Cutter had fewer than half of them left now. Cutter would pull his men back to the control room and make a stand there. He would make it a battle of attrition, but Tyler had to worry about the time. Ten minutes until the bomb dropped.

"What about the civilians, Connelly?" Tyler asked. "Are they armed?"

Connelly shook his head lazily. "Ulric doesn't want them to have weapons. Only us."

That would feed into Ulric's plan for dominating the group once he had wiped out everyone outside Oasis. He wanted a bunch of sheep he could command in his New World. Cutter wouldn't be getting help from anyone else, just his security forces.

"Where is the bio lab?"

"Fifth level," Connelly said.

"How do we get in?"

"Palm scanner."

"What about the control room? Where is it?"

"Seventh level."

"How do we get in?"

"Can't. Locked from the inside. Have to wait until they come out."

How do you get the men inside to come out? Only one way Tyler could think of. Panic.

"Connelly," Tyler said, "does your palm print give you access to the bio lab?"

Connelly nodded.

Tyler turned to Grant. "Help me pick him up. We're taking him with us."

They had their way in.

FIFTY-FOUR

On the fifth-level landing, Ramsey and Grant watched up and down the stairs while Tyler pressed Connelly's hand against the palm scanner leading into the bio lab. The screen changed into a keypad and said, "Enter pass code."

"What's the pass code?" Tyler asked.

"Seven-eight-nine-two-four," Connelly responded robotically.

Tyler entered the number. The door buzzed, and the bolt disengaged. Now that the klaxon had been shut off, the buzz sounded like an air horn in the empty stairwell.

Tyler opened the door and shoved Connelly through it. No gunfire. Tyler went in and saw another white hallway. Ramsey, Grant, and Dilara followed him in, their weapons held high.

"Where are they?" Tyler said as he wrapped plastic ties around Connelly's wrists. He didn't need the guard anymore. "Where's Ulric?"

"Observation chamber."

"Where's that?"

"Right at the elevator. Halfway down."

"What are they doing there?"

"Preparing the dispersion cases. Burning everything else."

"Dispersion cases?" Tyler stood and faced the others. "Must be like the one I found on the *Genesis Dawn.* That's why my father wanted the bomber as backup."

"So what's the plan?" Ramsey said.

"Not much time left," Tyler said. His watch showed 8:53. Seven minutes. "We need to go in full throttle."

Leaving Connelly on the floor, Tyler jogged down to the elevator and peeked around the corner toward the north stair-well. Empty.

Tyler waved at the others. They crept down the hall toward the observation room door. They were a quarter of the way down the hall when a door opened at the other end seventy feet away. A woman in a bio-hazard suit walked out and stopped in her tracks when she saw the four of them.

She shrieked and ran back into the room. That was all it took.

A guard with a weapon stepped out of the

observation room, and Ramsey took him down with a three-shot burst. Tyler ran down the hall and slid on his back past the door on the slick tile. For a moment, he caught a glimpse of Ulric and Petrova going out a door on the opposite side of the room as he sailed past. A hail of bullets dotted the wall above Tyler. He took a shot in that direction and thought he hit someone.

Ramsey leaped over the fallen guard and into the room. He took a hit in the shoulder and fell to the ground, but it was enough of a distraction for Grant, who followed him in and shot the last guard. Tyler went in next.

A man in a white lab coat was crouched under a control panel in terror. Through a large window, Tyler could see three others in biohazard suits inside a steel-lined chamber. On the chamber floor were three cases identical to the one Tyler had taken from Ulric's stateroom to the CDC. The men inside the chamber stopped what they were doing and watched the gun battle inside the observation room.

Tyler noted all of this in a second, including that Ulric wasn't there. Tyler plunged through the opposite door and rolled onto his knees, ready to dodge gunfire. He saw Petrova throw open the stairwell door, and

516

Ulric turned and looked straight at him. Even from this far away, Tyler could see the hate on Ulric's face. Tyler saw that Ulric wasn't carrying a case.

Tyler raised his gun to fire, but Petrova pulled Ulric into the stairwell with her, and he missed the shot. Tyler went back into the observation room.

Grant was pressing his hand to Ramsey's left shoulder.

"How is he?" Tyler asked.

"I'll be fine," Ramsey said with a grimace. "We're running out of time. Let's finish this."

Tyler turned to the man at the control panel.

"Tell those people to get out now. Don't bring anything out and lock it up."

The men in the biohazard suits complied quickly, locking the chamber.

"Is that all of it?" Tyler said, pointing his weapon at the cowering operator, who nodded furiously.

"That's all the Arkon we have left."

"Arkon? That's the prion agent?"

"Yes."

"And you can burn it all in there?"

Another nod.

"Then fire it up."

"Wait a minute, Locke," Ramsey said.

"We're supposed to secure it, not destroy it."

"Sorry, Captain. Nobody's getting their hands on this stuff. Especially my father." To the operator, Tyler said, "Do it."

Ramsey made a move to stop him, but Grant put his hand on the captain's gun.

"Uh-uh," Grant said. "I didn't go through all this just to let the army get hold of a new weapon."

"Captain Ramsey," Tyler said, "you didn't see what Arkon can do. Do you have a family?"

"A wife and two sons," Ramsey said.

"Ulric was planning to use the Arkon to kill them and everyone else you've ever known. I'll sleep a lot better knowing we've destroyed it. Won't you?"

Ramsey paused, then said, "My official order to you is to secure that bioagent. In my current condition, it might be difficult for me to stop you if you disobey my order." He gave Tyler a weak smile.

"Well," Grant said, "that takes care of the technicalities."

"Now," Tyler said to the operator, who pressed a red button marked STERILIZE.

Flames shot up inside the chamber. Tyler watched the temperature gauge. Within seconds, the chamber was more than a thousand degrees Fahrenheit. The cylinders of Arkon in the open cases began to burst open, spewing their contents into the fire. Anything not metal melted and burned.

Tyler breathed a sigh of relief. The threat was gone, and the military was not going to have a new bioweapon to play with. Now they could focus on opening the barriers and saving their own butts. Tyler looked at his watch.

"Five minutes left," he said. "Dilara, can you handle this guy?" Tyler pointed at the chamber operator.

Even though a round was already chambered, she racked the bolt on the submachine gun and ejected a bullet for effect, which frightened the operator even further. "I'm ready." Her voice sounded much clearer.

Tyler gave her Grant's radio. They'd have only one chance, and the timing would have to be perfect.

"And you, Captain? Are you up to it?"

"I've still got one good arm. I can do my part."

"Good. We're only going to get one shot at this. We need them to be convinced they're going to be infected by the Arkon. Captain Ramsey, when you're in place, blow the seventh-level door. Dilara, that will be your signal to press this button."

Tyler pointed to a button next to the one marked STERILIZE. Inside a flip-up lid that was in place to prevent accidental activation was a black-and-yellow-striped button boldly labeled CONTAINMENT BREACH.

FIFTY-FIVE

The B-52 from Fairchild AFB turned to begin its final pass over the Olympic peninsula. Even with the 30,000-pound MOP in its bomb bay, the immense bomber made the turn easily. It would take exactly four minutes and thirty-nine seconds to reach the drop point.

Major Tom Williams listened to the command come in from General Locke.

"Drillbit Flight, you are go for release."

"Acknowledged, Drillbit Command. Go for release at 2100 hours."

"Drillbit Flight, be prepared to receive the abort code at any point before that."

"Roger that." On the internal comm, he said, "OK, boys, keep sharp. Let's get this thing right on target." Williams was the only officer on board who knew the true nature of the mission. He understood the importance of containing a deadly bioweapon, but he sure didn't want to drop a bunker buster on American soil. He had his orders, but he kept hoping for that abort transmission to come in.

The bomb bay doors opened.

Tyler and Grant were in position at the seventh-level landing. Ramsey was stationed in the stairwell on the opposite side of the facility. Dilara was still in the bio lab observation room.

Tyler hadn't run into more guards, so Cutter had to be holed up with his men in the control room.

"Everybody ready?" Tyler said. Even though their scrambled radio transmissions couldn't reach outside, the radios worked within the confines of Oasis.

"In position," Ramsey said.

"I'm ready," Dilara said.

Tyler looked at his watch. Four minutes left. The only objective was to communicate the abort code to the bomber.

"Okay, Ramsey. Execute."

Ramsey's reply came over the radio. "Fire in the hole!"

The explosion was more than 150 feet away, but it rattled the complex like it happened in the next room. Ramsey had set up the rest of the explosives from Tyler's bag of tricks just outside his stairwell door. The dust and smoke would provide an effective barrier to anyone thinking of going out that way.

"Dilara," Tyler said. "Now."

A siren blared throughout the complex, different from the intruder klaxon heard earlier.

"Warning!" the amplified voice now echoed. "Containment breach on level five!"

As the warning repeated, Tyler threw his stairwell door open. If Connelly's information was correct, the control room would be at the midpoint of the seventh-level hallway. Between the explosion and the containment breach alarm, Tyler was hoping to cause a panic with the remaining guards. Surely they knew what the Arkon could do.

As he predicted, two men burst through the door of the control room. Tyler and Grant had to get there before the door closed on them.

Tyler shot the guard on the left, and Grant took the man on the right, neither of whom had time to raise their weapons. Ramsey, his left arm slack at his side, came from the opposite direction, but he wouldn't make it to the control room door in time to keep it from closing.

Tyler raced down and grabbed the door handle just before it clicked shut. He pulled it back as bullets pounded into it. Grant tossed the last flash-bang grenade into the room. They couldn't risk disabling the barrier controls with a fragmentation grenade.

The flash-bang blew, and Grant charged in, followed by Ramsey and Tyler. The control room sprawled across fifty feet. Two guards sat at a control station on the left, blinking their eyes. Grant took them down with two blows from his rifle stock.

Shots came from the right, and Tyler saw Cutter and two more guards herding Ulric and his girlfriend into a hallway that had no outlet. It looked like Ulric had his very own panic room. Cutter fired as they retreated.

The panic room's door began to slide closed. Just before the door shut, Tyler saw Ulric smile and mouth the words, "You lose." Then Ulric, Cutter, and Petrova were gone.

Tyler didn't have time to worry about them. They'd be as dead as him if he didn't get the barriers open.

The only people still upright in the control room were Tyler, Grant, and Ramsey, and they were faced with a control panel that stretched almost the length of the room.

The clock on the wall said 8:58. Half the monitors were black screens for the blown video cameras. The other half of the screens showed the status of different systems for operating the facility.

"Quick!" Tyler said. "Everyone look for the barrier control!"

"Hard switch?" Grant said.

"Yes. They wouldn't use a software control. They'd have something dedicated."

They started running their eyes over every switch and LCD panel.

"I think I found it!" Ramsey cried out. "It's called Lockdown!"

"Try it!"

Ramsey flicked the switch. The monitor above it changed from red to green. The barriers were opening.

Sixty seconds.

Ramsey spoke the abort code into his radio. "Ares Leader to Drillbit Command. Come in Drillbit Command. The well is dry. I repeat, the well is dry."

Nothing but static came back.

"We're too deep," Ramsey said. "Too much interference. We need to get to the surface." Ramsey was beginning to go white from blood loss. He wasn't going anywhere fast. And Grant was stronger, but Tyler was faster.

"I'll go," Tyler said. He dropped his weapon and his pack and ran for the stairs.

As he leaped up the stairs two at a time,

he kept repeating, "Drillbit Command. The well is dry. Drillbit Command come in."

By the time he got to the second level, he was out of breath. The last hour of nonstop action had sapped him, and his adrenaline was gone. But as he reached the landing, Tyler heard a voice drop in and out. He willed himself up higher.

"Ares . . . come . . . can't . . . you . . ."

"I repeat, the well is dry. The well is dry!"

"This is Drillbit Command." It was his father's voice. "Say again."

"Dad, it's me! The well is dry! Don't drop the damned bomb!"

His father yelled in the background, "Abort! Abort! Abort!" Tyler's new favorite word. He fell to his hands and knees, panting like he'd just run a marathon.

"Abort! Abort! Abort!" came the radio call. The pilot, Major Williams, relayed the command to the bombardier, who had been about to release the weapon.

Williams realized only then how tightly he had been clenching the yoke. Now that he no longer had the specter of bombing his own country hanging over him, he eased up on the grip and relaxed.

"Drillbit Flight returning to base," Williams said into the radio and turned the

B-52 on an eastern course, back toward Spokane.

The bomb bay doors closed.

FIFTY-SIX

Tyler emerged from Oasis to find that the Special Forces team outside had already taken care of the rest of the guards, capturing a few, killing most, with three casualties of their own, including Private Knoll. As soon as the abort code had been given, Blackhawk helicopters that had been on standby flew in with two platoons of military police from Fort Lewis. Scores of soldiers patrolled the grounds, looking for any stragglers who might be trying to make an escape through hidden exits. It took the MPs nearly an hour to roust the inhabitants of Oasis and gather them outside. Hundreds of dazed people sat under the arc lamps, wondering what had happened.

When the containment breach button had been pressed, the entire fifth level locked down, so it took awhile to extract Dilara. When she was free, Tyler took her topside, where they both took a moment to enjoy the cool night air before heading for the staging area where the wounded were being treated.

Tyler had already told Dilara about how Ulric had holed himself up in the panic room.

"We still don't know how all this was tied to Noah's Ark," she said. "Ulric said that a relic in the Ark was the source of the prion. I don't know whether to believe him."

"The CDC scientist told me that the prion must have been engineered from some raw material," Tyler said. "The relic would fit that description."

"So you think Ulric was telling the truth?"

"We'll know soon enough. When they finally pry Ulric out of that room, he's going to use every bargaining chip he has to save his skin, including the location of Noah's Ark. Ulric has a talent for self-preservation."

"The only thing I want to know is what happened to my father," she said.

"I've told them to call me as soon as they capture Ulric. I promise you'll get an answer."

They reached a clearing where six men lay on stretchers. Medics hovered around them, inserting IVs and bandaging wounds. Grant was standing next to Ramsey, whose shoulder wound was being dressed before he was transferred to Madigan Army Medical Center at Fort Lewis. The redheaded captain looked even paler than normal, which Tyler hadn't thought possible.

"How are you feeling?" Tyler asked him.

"It isn't the hardest Purple Heart I've earned," Ramsey said weakly.

"Your men did a great job."

"I trained them well. You didn't do so bad yourself. I'm glad we brought you along."

"Now the hard work begins. Sorting this mess out."

"These people look like they don't know what hit them," Grant said as another helicopter landed.

"I don't think most of them do," Tyler said. "From what I gather, the majority seemed to think this was some kind of test of their faith."

"You mean, they had no idea about what Ulric was planning?"

"I'm sure some of them did. It'll take Homeland Security some time to find out which ones."

"But you burned all of the evidence," Ramsey said. "Ulric's going to get away with it, and we'll have a hell of a political mess on our hands. These religious nuts are going to make the government miserable."

"I don't think so," Tyler said. "I only burned the dangerous stuff. The man who operated the sterilization chamber was so frightened about being blamed for everything that he led us to a trove of documents detailing the plan inside the lab level."

"And a good thing," said Miles Benson, who rode toward Tyler from the helicopter on his iBOT wheelchair. "Ulric's company can take the heat for that road race you had with the dump truck in Phoenix. I've already contacted our lawyers and the insurance company. Now I won't have to take it out of your next partnership share." He smiled. "Strong work."

"Thanks."

"You look exhausted."

"I could use a nap."

A sergeant yelled, "Ten hut!" and the soldiers who were standing came to attention before an immediate "At ease!" followed. Tyler's father, now in a forest camouflage BDU instead of his Class A service uniform, marched up and came to a halt next to Miles. Other than Miles's disability, the two men had the same appearance. Military stature, crew cuts, hard faces. They could have been brothers.

The General held Tyler's eyes as he addressed the soldiers. "Excellent job, men. I

531

couldn't be prouder."

"General Locke tells me you insisted on coming on the mission," Miles said.

"He's always volunteering for some damn fool thing," the General said. "Someday it's going to get him killed. Where's the prion weapon?"

"Your prion weapon is clogging the filters somewhere in this facility," Tyler said with satisfaction.

"My orders were to secure the weapon. What happened?"

"Sir," Ramsey said, still prone, "the weapon posed a serious threat to our mission. The only way to accomplish our objective was to burn it."

The General's eyes narrowed at Tyler. "Is that right?"

"It was my call whether you like it or not."

General Locke took off his cap and ran his fingers through his hair. "I'd like a word with my son. Alone."

As the General strode away, Tyler leaned down to Ramsey.

"You didn't have to do that," he said.

"We take care of our own. And now you're one of us. Unofficially."

"Let's get you on the next chopper out of here," Grant said, helping Ramsey up. Tyler left them hobbling toward the Blackhawk.

Tyler approached where the General stood ramrod straight and stopped with his nose just a foot from his father's. His face was a rigid mask, ready to take whatever punishment his father wanted to dish out.

"You disobeyed orders," the General said.

"I wasn't going to let you get your hands on that prion weapon."

"I don't give a damn about that weapon. In fact, I'm glad you destroyed it."

Tyler's face relaxed. Now he was confused. "What?"

"I told you that there's no place in the world for these kinds of things."

"But you ordered Ramsey —"

"Tyler, I'm a soldier, and my first duty is to follow orders. I was ordered to secure that bioweapon, so I passed that order on to Ramsey. Officially, that part of the mission failed, and I will have to take Ramsey's report for what it is. Unofficially, I think you did the right thing. That took guts."

"Surprised?"

"Not really. I've read your service record. Impressive enough, but back at White Sands was the first time you've really stood up to me. Not avoiding me, not like in college when you went behind my back and joined ROTC. To my face. Now seeing you in action for the first time only reinforces that impression."

This was nothing like what Tyler was expecting. *The General was actually giving him a compliment.* Other than the condolences he gave Tyler when Karen died, it was the first positive thing he'd said in years.

"Why didn't you want me to come on this mission?" Tyler asked.

The General sighed. "You don't have kids. I'm sorry you don't. Then you might understand the position you put me in." He paused. "I was going to order that B-52 to drop its bomb."

The gruffness in his father's voice was still there, but it had softened just slightly. Tyler realized that his respect for the General had just ratcheted up a few notches. He thought about what his father had said about him destroying the bioweapon and Dilara's revelation that a relic on Noah's Ark held the last remaining specimen of it.

"If there were another sample of this prion somewhere," Tyler said pointedly, "and *somebody* knew where this small remnant was, what would you say to that person?"

"I'd say that I don't want to know anything that I'd have to officially act on," the General said, "but I'd hope that person had the fortitude to do the right thing and destroy it."

Tyler held the General's eyes, then nodded. "I'll keep that in mind."

They started walking back toward Miles and Dilara, who were still at the medic station.

The General gave him one last look. "And Tyler, stop being so pigheaded and stay in touch. Maybe next time I'll need *your* help." Then he headed to the command post.

Miles looked at Tyler in amazement. "You finally on good terms with him?" he asked.

Tyler just shook his head, still stunned by his conversation. "I don't know. For now, I guess."

"So that means he's a legitimate business contact now?"

Miles knew how to strike while the iron was sizzling.

"If you can get the contract, go for it," Tyler said. He held up a finger. "Just make sure I'm not the principal on the project. I don't think we're ready for that yet."

"Excellent," Miles said, practically rubbing his hands together at the thought of the money rolling in. "Oh, before I go, Aiden contacted me on the flight out. He wanted you to call him. Said he's got some interesting news for you." He handed Tyler his cell phone. "While you do that, I'm going to talk to General Locke about all the

535

capabilities Gordian can bring to the Defense Threat Reduction Agency." He motored away toward the command post and left Tyler standing with Dilara.

"Just one call," he said to Dilara, "and then we head back to Seattle."

"Good," she said. "I could use a shower."

He dialed Aiden, who answered on the first ring.

"Tyler! I heard you had a wee bit of excitement out there. I'm jealous."

"No, you're not, I promise you. Listen, I'm beat, Aiden. Miles said you had something for me."

"Absolutely. Remember that slip of paper from Dilara's locket that you had us analyze? The one that said *B C T*?"

The Book of the Cave of Treasures. "To be honest," Tyler said, "I had forgotten about it. You found something?"

"Two sets of numbers and letters. We were able to read the pen indentations with the TEC's scanning microscope. I think it's a latitude and longitude." Tyler wrote them down — 122.bggyuW, 48.hutzsN — and studied the odd coordinates.

"Why do these look familiar?" he said.

"Because you're standing right at one twenty-two west and forty-eight north," Aiden said.

Tyler realized that he had seen the coordinates when they had been planning the raid on Oasis.

"Without the decimal digits, this could be anywhere on the island. What's with the letters?"

"You tell me. That's what the paper in the locket said."

Tyler turned to Dilara. "Did your father use a code for his notes?"

"Why?" Dilara said.

"He left you a message." He showed her the coordinates. "And I think it leads to something else. Do you know how to read this?"

"I think so. For notes he didn't want anyone else to read, he had a cipher. He taught it to me when I was young, and I use it in my notes sometimes. He and I are the only ones who know it."

She looked at the coordinates and took Tyler's pen. She quickly crossed out each letter and substituted a number.

"Thanks, Aiden," Tyler said. "We'll take it from here."

"Let me know what you find." Aiden hung up.

"What do you think it is?" Dilara asked.

"Only one way to find out." He flagged down a passing soldier. "Sergeant, I need your GPS locator."

"Yes, sir," the surprised sergeant said and handed him the unit.

The coordinates were so precise, Dilara's father must have used a GPS unit to record them. Tyler entered them into the unit. He wasn't surprised by the answer.

"It's in this compound," he said. Dilara looked completely reenergized.

The location was about three hundred yards north of their position, back in the direction of the woods that Tyler had driven through from the fence.

Using his flashlight, he and Dilara walked until they reached the coordinates. In the exact center was a pine tree that had to have been five hundred years old. A black hollow in the tree showed where it had survived past forest fires.

"He must have buried it," Dilara said. "He's an archaeologist, after all. We'll have to come back with a couple of shovels."

Tyler looked at the ground, which was covered with pine needles. If her father had buried something here three years ago, all traces had been washed away. Maybe the ground-penetrating radar could help them.

He was about to go back with Dilara, and then he stopped.

"Why would your father hide something

out here?" Tyler asked.

"I don't know. It must have been something he didn't want Ulric to find."

"If he was a visitor, don't you think it would have been odd for him to walk out here with a shovel? Someone would have noticed."

"Maybe he used his hands."

"With just his hands, he wouldn't have been able to dig too deep. If he had, he would have come back all dirty and bloody. Ulric would have known something was up."

"Then how else could he . . ."

She paused. They were both looking at the tree. The one with the hollowed trunk.

Tyler shined the flashlight down inside the hollow. Nothing but wood chips and water. Then he bent over and looked up. A circular reflection. It was the end of a tube two inches in diameter, pushed up into a part of the trunk further hollowed by insects. He tried to reach it, but his hand was too big.

Dilara snaked her hand in and grasped the tube. It took her three tugs because the tube was wedged in so tightly, but on the last one, she yanked it free.

The tube was white, opaque, two feet long. The top was sealed shut and seemed watertight. Dilara wiped the gunk off the tube with her shirt. She took a deep breath, then opened it.

In the dim light, Tyler could see a roll of yellowed parchment, ancient-looking. In the center of the rolled parchment was a slip of modern white notepaper. Dilara carefully tugged the note free.

As she ran her eyes over the paper, her eyes welled with tears. When she got to the end, she looked up at Tyler.

"Your father?" he said.

Dilara nodded. "He wanted me to find this. This is the Book of the Cave of Treasures. It's the way to find Noah's Ark."

FIFTY-SEVEN

When he stepped out of the Blackhawk at Boeing Field, it seemed to Tyler like months had passed since he and Dilara had first arrived here from Las Vegas just five days ago. All Grant would talk about on the flight was Tiffany and his long-delayed return to Seattle, and Tyler couldn't be happier for him. Grant lived in an apartment downtown, so he hitched a ride in Miles Benson's van back to Gordian headquarters. Tyler took Dilara with him in the Porsche. Since she had already stayed at his house once before, he offered again. The big difference this time was that they didn't have trained killers looking for them.

Her father had been smart about coding the message in her locket. The leading numbers showed that they were latitude and longitude, but the coded lettering made the coordinates too imprecise to be of use in finding the hidden documents. No one who found the note, other than Dilara, would be able to decipher it.

As Tyler drove, she read the note from the sealed container to him. As she spoke, she became so choked with emotion several times that she had to stop and compose herself.

My dearest Dilara,

I am sorry that you have come to find this note because it means that my suspicions have proven correct, and in all likelihood I am dead. I am sorry I was not able to share my greatest professional achievement with you, the greatest achievement of my life. To satisfy my curiosity and ambition, I am afraid I have taken league with someone who does not seek the knowledge I do for the same reasons. I have begun to suspect that Sebastian Ulric is disturbed, power mad, that he will betray me somehow. Therefore, I have hidden this document for you to find. The scroll is the only known copy of The Book of the Cave of Treasures.

I unearthed the scroll during a dig in northern Iraq. I chose not to release the contents to the media in the hopes that I could find the Ark myself. However, I ran short of funds, and through my old friend

Sam Watson I fell in with a new benefactor, Ulric. He has seen the Book, but I am the only one who can decipher it. I felt the need to hide it when I found out he was searching for other translators.

You can be one of those translators. If you read it carefully, it will lead you to Noah's famed vessel and the scourge that it still holds within its bowels. Ulric has come to suspect that I am withholding information from him. His trust is shallow and limited. The locket was the only way I could spirit my message out to you. I hoped that sending it to you as a birthday present would free it from suspicion.

If you are reading this, you must have already outwitted Ulric to some degree. But be careful. I fear he may take extreme measures if he knows you have these documents.

I hope you elect to complete the work that I could not finish and unveil Noah's Ark to the world. If you take on the quest, I wish you good hunting. Whatever you decide, know that your mother and I love you always.

Hasad Arvadi

"He's dead, isn't he?" Dilara asked. Her pain was palpable.

"We don't know that," Tyler said, but he didn't really believe it.

"No, he is. I know it."

He put his hand on hers. "I'm so sorry, Dilara. I promise you we will find out what happened to your father."

She squeezed his hand. "Thanks. That means a lot to me."

He let her weep quietly. After a few minutes, she took her hand away to use a tissue and said, "My father wanted me to find the Ark, and that's what I'm going to do."

"Your father's note says that the 'scourge' is still in the Ark's bowels," he said. "That confirms what Ulric told you. That a relic with the prion disease — Arkon — is still in Noah's Ark."

"But Ulric told me that he never got to the Ark. If he didn't get *into* the Ark, how did he find a relic *from* the Ark?"

"We'll have to ask him. Maybe use his own truth serum. In the meantime, what's our next step?"

"*Our* next step?"

His father's words echoed in Tyler's ears. "I need to make sure the last of the Arkon is destroyed."

"I'll take the scroll back to my laboratory at UCLA and analyze it there. We have a controlled environment for examining ancient documents, and this one looks at least three thousand years old. It'll be extremely fragile."

"Who else will be involved?"

"No one. If it looks like the scroll really leads to Noah's Ark, then I don't want there to be a stampede to the site. I know you're worried about the Arkon getting loose again, but I'm worried about the potential historical loss as well. Priceless artifacts could be looted, trampled, or destroyed."

"It'll be quite a find for you. It'll change your life."

"And yours, too."

"No, I'm an engineer, not an archaeologist. I'll leave the glamour stuff up to you."

The rest of the ride passed in silence, each of them mulling the implications of such a find.

When they reached Tyler's house and went inside, Dilara carefully replaced the curled note back into the tube with the scroll and sealed it. She sighed heavily.

"He'd be very proud of you." His words brought on the opposite effect from the one he intended. Dilara burst into tears.

"I'm such an idiot," she sobbed. "All those years, I thought he was crazy, and he was right all along. Now he's dead, and I'll never be able to tell him how proud I am of him."

Tyler pulled her to him and cradled her head in his shoulder. "He knows. He knows."

She looked up at him, tears streaming down her face. She had never looked more beautiful or more vulnerable, nestled in his arms. He leaned forward and kissed her cheek, tasting the salty skin.

Dilara exhaled a breathier sigh and turned her face to him. Their eyes met. The pent-up tension flooded out of them, and they kissed deeply, as if they had fit together this way forever. Tyler felt her entire body press against him, and he responded in kind.

"Shower?" she breathed into his ear.

Only then did he notice that they were both sticky with sweat and dirt.

He nodded and kissed her again. His need for her was almost unbearable. He felt like a randy teenager again.

They shuffled toward the bathroom, locked in an embrace as they maneuvered down the hall. They took turns unbuttoning and unlacing each other, tossing clothes and shoes as they went until there was nothing left to toss.

They staggered into the bathroom, their bodies still entwined, and Tyler blindly fumbled with the shower control. Dilara pulled his hand away from it with an urgency that he completely understood.

"Later," she said, and dragged him to the carpet.

The shower would have to wait.

The next morning, Tyler woke before he was ready. The light was streaming through the window because, in his hurry to get into bed, he had neglected to close the blinds. He had the unfamiliar feeling of warmth next to him. Dilara was curled up beside him, her smooth naked body snug against his, her face resting on his chest, her breath puffing lightly on his skin. The smell of shampoo wafted from her hair draped over the pillow. The effect was intoxicating, and Tyler smiled to himself at the memory of the bathroom floor, the long lazy shower that followed, and then the epic lovemaking session on the sheets that now swaddled them.

Intruding into all of these pleasant sensations was the shrill sound of his phone ringing. He grudgingly extricated himself from Dilara and picked it up.

"Whoever this is," Tyler said groggily, "your next words better be, 'Congratulations, Powerball winner.' "

"Prepare to be disappointed," Grant said.

"Okay. What time is it?"

"Eight A.M. I'd rather not be up either, but we have a big problem."

Grant's tone of voice got Tyler's attention, and he sat up.

"What happened?"

"The army finally got into that chamber that Ulric, Cutter, and the others retreated into."

"You caught him?"

"I wish. It wasn't a panic room like we thought. It had a hidden corridor. It led to a subterranean submarine pen, big enough to dock a small sub like the one from Ulric's yacht."

"You've got to be kidding me," Tyler said.

"It kills me to say it," Grant replied, "but Ulric and Cutter got away."

NOAH'S ARK

FIFTY-EIGHT

As he boarded his refueled Learjet at Heathrow Airport in London, Sebastian Ulric had new appreciation for Cutter's insistence on backup plans. The original specifications for Oasis had nothing about a submarine docking facility, but Cutter hadn't liked the idea of being trapped within Oasis by the concrete barriers. When they had switched the contract from Gordian to Coleman, Cutter had convinced Ulric to add the new requirement for the submarine escape dock, and now he was glad he had. Without it, Ulric would be in the custody of the U.S. Army.

Ulric had piloted the submarine to a marina in Orcas Island's Deer Harbor. There, they stole a sailboat and scuttled the submarine so it wouldn't be discovered. Then it was an easy sail to Vancouver, British Columbia, where Ulric's funds in the Cayman Islands secured a chartered Lear, no questions asked. Cutter knew where to procure perfect fake passports.

Tyler would eventually find out he had escaped, but Ulric had an eight-hour head start, maybe more. He would be in and out of Noah's Ark before Tyler could determine where he'd gone. By that time, Ulric would have the only other sample of Arkon in the world.

He twirled the USB drive in his fingers and smiled at Petrova, who sulked at their predicament. She and Cutter had taken the setback harder than he had. Ulric's serenity came from the knowledge that, like Cutter, he always had a backup plan. The U.S. government would freeze his assets, but they didn't know about all of his money. With hundreds of millions of dollars still at his disposal, even a disaster of the previous night's magnitude could be overcome.

Switzerland would become his new haven. The Swiss lab, built under a medieval castle purchased under an untraceable pseudonym, would be able to perform the same function as Oasis. It was not as comfortable, but it would do the job. Once he had the sample of Arkon in his possession, it would take only a matter of weeks to synthesize the new Arkon-C. By the time the authorities figured out where he was, it would be too late.

The only task now was getting access to Mount Ararat and Noah's Ark. He knew its location, thanks to Hasad Arvadi, but like Arvadi, Ulric had never actually been there. He had not tried reaching it before now because the Turkish government protected the mountain with zeal. An expedition to the area three years before would have been watched carefully and would have brought unwanted attention to his plans. Now that his plans were exposed, he would have to risk going directly to it. With enough money for bribes, and Cutter and the two guards at his disposal, Ulric felt sure that he would be inside Noah's Ark in less than twenty-four hours. Then he would take the second Arkon sample and disappear.

Ulric entertained himself by thinking about how he would get retribution for the invasion of Oasis and the delay of his plans. He was a patient man and had a vision for the long term, but that didn't mean he was beyond exacting revenge. During the weeks it would take to complete his goal to make a New World, he would hire the best assassins money could buy, and Tyler Locke would find out how painful his curiosity could be.

Tyler convinced Dilara that Gordian's

Seattle laboratory had everything she would need so they wouldn't have to waste precious hours flying to UCLA. In the lab, she carefully pulled the delicate scrolls from the tube with rubber-tipped tongs. A huge examination table had been set up so she could lay it flat, and the humidity of the room was dropped to 25 percent to protect the document. To Tyler, the cool, dry air felt like a January evening in Phoenix. Grant and Miles stood to the side, watching as Dilara spread the document out with her white-gloved hands.

Although time was quickly slipping away, Dilara moved slowly and deliberately. She was firm about protecting the ancient scroll. Since all they needed was the translation, Tyler suggested she unfurl the scroll and photograph it. That way, they could take the photographs with them and keep the original scroll safe. While she prepared the scroll, Tyler was busy setting up the high-definition camera in its articulated frame.

The key would be how long it would take Dilara to decipher the language printed in faint script. It seemed to be a primitive variant of Hebrew.

"How old is this paper?" Tyler asked.

The hint of a smile continually played at the corners of Dilara's mouth. She was excited about the archaeological significance of this find, even if it meant the possible end of the world.

"It isn't paper. It's papyrus. Same as what was used in Egypt. Without carbon dating, there's no way to tell for sure how old it is, but I'd guess at least three thousand years, predating the Dead Sea Scrolls."

Grant whistled.

"The scroll itself is a huge archaeological discovery," she said. "Only Noah's Ark could outdo it."

"Let's hope something in there actually leads us to it," Tyler said. "I'm ready when you are."

"Just a few more minutes. I have to handle this like you handle explosives. The slightest miscue, and I could reduce it to dust."

After she was through unrolling it, Tyler shot a photo of each section. In turn the pictures, enlarged to five times their original size, appeared on the screen at the end of the room.

"Can you translate?" Tyler asked.

Dilara peered at the first segment. "I think so. It's proto-Tannaitic Hebrew, the language used in the Copper Scroll of the Dead Sea Scrolls. It's unusual and not seen often, and it's very difficult to translate. Only a few people in the world can sight-read it. My father was one of them."

"And lucky for us, you're another." Tyler pressed a button on the room's phone. "Did you get these photos uploaded, Aiden?"

Aiden's voice came back over the speakerphone. "Absolutely. I'm transferring them to your laptop. I've also begun to parse them. If I can get a translation matrix from Dr. Kenner, we might be able to automate some of it."

"Good. The goal is to find out anything the scroll says about Noah's Ark."

"Oh my God!" Dilara said, still reading.

When she didn't elaborate, Tyler said, "What?"

"There's a lot more here than just Noah's Ark," Dilara said. "It's a version of the entire book of Genesis. This would be the earliest version ever found of a biblical document. It describes God making the heavens and the earth, the Garden of Eden, Adam and Eve, but enhanced, in more detail than I've ever seen. Remarkable!"

"I hate to interrupt," Tyler said, "but we do have a time crunch. When we come back, you can take all the time in the world to read this. Can we skip ahead to Noah?"

"Yes, I know. I'm sorry. Next section. Next section. Next section. Stop!"

She stepped closer. Her eyes were so wide

as she read that Tyler thought they would fall out.

"This is it!" she said.

"Does it say where the Ark is?"

"Not exactly, but now I can see why my father was retranslating the Bible. Remember how he had crossed out words and replaced them in certain chapters? For example, this line here could be interpreted as the Ark being within the mountains of Ararat."

"How does that help us?"

"I don't know." She kept reading, then stopped, and a puzzled look crossed her face. "Huh? That's new." She paused.

"Will you stop that?" Grant said with a laugh when she didn't explain. "You're driving us nuts."

"Sorry. There's a section here that's not in the Bible. It talks about a map."

"A map to Noah's Ark?" Tyler said.

Dilara nodded. "It also describes two amulets of such power that they can destroy the world."

"That fits. At least now we know we're looking for an amulet, although how an amulet can hold a prion disease is still a mystery. Where's the map?"

"It tells of a city. I can only guess the pronunciation. Something like Ortixisita. In this city, there is a temple called Cur Ferap."

"Have you heard of them?"

"They sound familiar, but I can't quite remember. If I had my books here . . ."

"Aiden, you hearing this?" Tyler said toward the speakerphone.

"I'm already looking it up," came Aiden's reply. "I'll try all possible vowel substitutions and narrow my focus to the area around Mount Ararat."

After a few seconds, Aiden said, "Got it. There's a city in western Armenia called Artashat. Originally built in 180 B.C. as Artaxiasata. It's well known for a monastery on its outskirts."

Dilara snapped her fingers. "Now I remember! Khor Virap! The prison for St. Gregory the Illuminator!"

"You're good, doctor," Aiden said. "I've got a great picture of it. I'm sending it through to your screen."

As soon as Tyler saw the photo of Khor Virap, he was sure that's where they needed to go.

"Aiden," he said, "have them get the jet ready for us. We're going to Armenia."

Tyler continued to stare at the picture and started to believe that they might actually find Noah's Ark after all. On a hill overlooking a green field was a stone structure with thick walls and a central tower, a fortification that must have been the monastery of Khor Virap. And dominating the horizon in the background, framed against a bright blue sky, was the towering white outline of Mount Ararat.

FIFTY-NINE

With all of the flying she'd done to digs throughout the world, Dilara Kenner was an experienced traveler, but the toll of the last week, including the latest twenty hours to Armenia's capital, Yerevan, was too much. She could go without getting on another plane for a year.

She had spent all of her waking time on the Gordian private jet poring over the scroll photographs, trying to decipher anything else she could about finding the map at Khor Virap. Tyler and Grant had left her alone to work, and before they had landed, Dilara reported back to them on what she had discovered. Unfortunately, even with Aiden's help, it wasn't much.

"You think the map is still there?" Tyler asked. "Why wouldn't Ulric have taken it with him?"

"Because it's not portable. The scrolls talk of a map of stone. I think that means the map is written on a wall."

"Aiden did a thorough search in both public and private databases, and he said no one has ever heard of a map like this."

"Right here," Dilara said, pointing to a photo of the scroll on her laptop, "it says that the descendents of Japheth, one of Noah's sons, built the temple as a shrine to God's forgiveness. One of the amulets and the map were kept in a secret chamber that was known only to the worthy. The other amulet was sequestered inside the Ark itself."

"So the priests at Khor Virap don't know about the chamber?"

"The temple was razed in a Persian invasion, and the keepers fled without revealing the chamber, which must have been well hidden. They preserved its location in this document, but they must have perished before they could return and secure its contents."

"There must be some clue in the scroll to finding the chamber," Tyler said.

"Whoever wrote this feared it would fall into their enemies' hands, so they used a cipher."

"You mean the scroll is coded?"

Dilara highlighted a section of the scroll that talked about Khor Virap, then a Jewish temple and now a Christian monastery.

"Notice anything different about this section?" Dilara asked them.

"The spacing and indentation are slightly different," Grant said. "It's subtle, but since you pointed it out, I noticed it."

"Exactly." She pulled up the photo of the note her father had written to her. "Something about the way my father wrote the note to me seemed odd, which is why I wanted Tyler to photograph it as well. He was sending me another message." She overlaid the handwritten note over the Khor Virap section. The lines aligned perfectly.

Tyler pointed at her father's note. "The first word in each line . . ."

". . . is written in slightly more bold print," Dilara said. "Anyone looking at the note would think he was using a simple transposition cipher where the first word of each line would form a sentence. But whoever tried to decode it that way would go crazy trying to figure it out because the resulting phrase would be gibberish. My father was trying to tell me that the scroll itself used a transposition cipher, and only in this section."

"So don't keep us in suspense," Grant said. "What does it say?"

"It translates to 'The fifth and eighth

stones from the cove reveal. The fourth and seventh stones from the cove conceal.' "

Grant looked doubtful. "They rhymed it in Hebrew?"

"No, that's me. It sounded better than, 'The fifth and eighth stones from the cove open. The fourth and seventh stones from the cove hide.' "

"You're right," Grant said, smiling. "More cryptic."

"Any idea what that means?" Tyler asked.

Dilara shook her head. She'd been puzzling about it, which was why she had taken so long to discuss it with them, but she still couldn't decipher its meaning.

"My guess is, we'll know it when we see it."

Tyler shrugged. "Then let's find out what's at Khor Virap."

Dilara was amazed by him. He always seemed to roll with the punches. No matter what happened, he knew he'd be able to figure a way through it. She supposed that's what made him a good engineer, his ability to solve whatever problems arose, and he carried that confidence into every part of his life. It was why she found him so attractive. She didn't know where the night they'd spent together would lead, but she savored the memory.

The jet landed in Yerevan, and Tyler had arranged for an interpreter to meet them with a car at the airport. When they got to the car, Tyler gave a wad of American dollars to the interpreter, who gaped at more money than he normally made in six months.

"I hope that will keep our expedition confidential," Tyler said.

"Certainly, Dr. Locke," the man sputtered in outstanding English. "My name is Barsam Chirnian. I will be happy to help in any way I can."

"How long will it take to get to Khor Virap from here?"

"It's only thirty kilometers to the southwest. We should be there within the hour."

That would put them there around 5 P.M. local time.

"Good," Tyler said. "On the way, you can tell us about Khor Virap."

The four of them climbed into a well-used Toyota Land Cruiser and wound through city streets before getting on a major road south. To their right, Mount Ararat and its little brother to the south loomed over the plains. Even though Armenians considered the 16,854-foot-tall mountain their own, making it their national symbol, it actually sat across the border in Turkey.

As they drove, Chirnian gave them what sounded like a tour guide spiel about the monastery. Artashat, the town where the monastery was located, was the first capital city of Armenia and remained so until it fell in the fifth century. No one knew the exact date Khor Virap had been built, but it was one of the first Christian monasteries in existence. It sat on the only major hill for miles and had served as an early fortification against invaders because of its strategic position on the Araks River. The site was revered as Armenia's holiest shrine because of St. Gregory the Illuminator.

Grigor Lusavorich had returned from Israel to his native Armenia in the third century to proselytize the new religion of Christianity. The father of King Trdat III had been murdered by Grigor's father, so Trdat imprisoned Grigor in a pit at Khor Virap for thirteen years, where he miraculously survived untold torture and suffering. When Trdat fell ill, he received a vision that Grigor would be the only one who could heal him. Grigor cured Trdat's disease, and the king converted to Christianity. In 301, Armenia became the first Christian nation. Grigor was beatified as the country's patron saint.

In the time it took Chirnian to relate the

story of St. Gregory, they had arrived in Artashat. The October afternoon sun bathed the flat plain with a golden hue. Vast rows of vineyards and farms stretched toward the foothills of Mount Ararat, which climbed into the few wisps of clouds that decorated the blue sky.

The ancient monastery of Khor Virap was perched on the southern end of a crusty mound that lacked any vegetation. The Land Cruiser wound up the monastery's hillside road until it passed through the main gates. The site's reputation as one of Armenia's biggest tourist attractions was well founded. Even though it was close to closing time, a dozen cars were parked in the lot. They got out and walked through an arch formed in the thick stone exterior walls and up a set of stairs.

They emerged into a central courtyard that held a full-size church, which Chirnian said was often used for weddings. There were no nuptials going on, but men and women, some in Western clothes, others in the native Armenian garb, snapped photos of the church and the mountain that was so famous as the Ark's resting place. Even though it was a monastery, the monks had left long ago, and it was now administered by priests of the Armenian Orthodox

Church.

"We need to see the priest in charge," Tyler told the interpreter.

Chirnian nodded and went to find him. A few minutes later, a priest with a friendly face emerged from the church. He didn't speak English, but through Chirnian, he introduced himself, shaking Tyler's hand.

"I am Father Yezik Tatilian. How can I help you?"

"Father Tatilian," Tyler said, "my name is Tyler Locke. I'm an engineer from America. Thank you for meeting with us."

"Are you interested in the architectural history of our monastery?"

"In a way. Have you ever met an archaeologist named Hasad Arvadi?"

Dilara didn't realize she was holding her breath, hoping that this was the final key to finding her father, until the priest shook his head.

"We have many scientists and historians who come to study the monastery," he said, "so it's not surprising I don't remember him."

Tyler pointed at Dilara, who couldn't hide her disappointment. "Dr. Kenner is his daughter. We have reason to believe he was here."

"I'm sorry," the priest said. "His name

567

isn't familiar."

Tyler took Dilara's digital camera and, using the LCD screen, showed the priest the most recent photo Dilara had of her father.

Father Tatilian shrugged. Tyler showed him two more photos, one of Ulric from *Forbes* magazine and the other of Cutter from the TEC security camera.

The priest didn't recognize either of them. "Perhaps if you tell me why you are looking for them, it may help my memory."

Tyler looked at Dilara, who nodded. They had to tell him at some point if they were going to get his cooperation.

"We have reason to believe that your monastery holds a secret chamber, one that even you may not be aware of."

The priest laughed. "This monastery has been here for thousands of years. I'm sure I would know if there were such a chamber. And I assure you there isn't."

Tyler showed him a picture of the scroll. "This is an ancient document Hasad Arvadi found in northern Iraq. Dr. Kenner has translated it, and it tells of a map to Noah's Ark located somewhere in Khor Virap."

The interpreter, Chirnian, paused, not sure if he had heard correctly. When he saw that Tyler was serious, he translated. Father Tatilian smiled.

"We often have treasure hunters come through here, searching for the blessed remains of Noah's Ark, but no one has asked for a map before."

"Dr. Kenner's father went missing three years ago. We think he was murdered."

That wiped the smile from the priest's face. "I'm sorry for your loss."

"Father Tatilian," Tyler said, "did anything unusual happen here three years ago?"

"Yes," the priest said warily. "Very unusual. Two novitiates had made a pilgrimage at that time and were staying at the monastery. One of them was killed, and the other went missing. He was never found."

"How was the novitiate killed?"

"Shot. The police investigated, but no one was ever arrested. The case remains unsolved."

"Any motives?"

"Robbery, most likely. I entered Khor Virap one morning and found the body."

"It had to be Ulric," Grant said.

"You know who might be behind this?" the priest said.

"Possibly," Tyler said. "Can you tell me exactly what happened?"

"There isn't much to tell. It occurred at night when the monastery was closed. Brother Dipigian was found with two shots to the head. We never saw Brother Kalanian again. We assumed he had been kidnapped. For what reason, we couldn't fathom, and we never received a ransom demand. Not that we could pay much. We take honoraria for weddings and other parties held here, but most of it goes to the monastery's up-keep."

"Where was the body found?"

"That was the oddest thing. It was in the pit."

"The one that held St. Gregory captive?" Dilara asked.

"Yes. But if it was a robbery, it was a strange place to take him. As a holy shrine, the pit of St. Gregory is unsurpassed, but there is nothing of value in there. A few candles in an alcove, that's all."

Dilara gasped. "An alcove?" The scroll mentioned a cove. The Hebrew could be translated many different ways, including *alcove.*

"It's where pilgrims can pay tribute."

"The fifth and eighth stones from the cove reveal," Dilara said to Tyler, who immediately saw what she meant.

"Father," he said, "please show us to the pit of St. Gregory."

At the top of the hill overlooking the courtyard of Khor Virap, Ulric focused binoculars on the figures two hundred yards away. He saw Locke, Westfield, and Kenner with someone who appeared to be an interpreter talking to a priest. Ulric lay next to Svetlana Petrova and Dan Cutter, who cradled a Russian VAL silenced sniper rifle, which fired subsonic 9 mm rounds. Cutter had acquired the hard-to-get rifle in Armenia along with their other weapons.

"Do you want me to take them out?" Cutter asked.

Ulric had already been to the Ark's location, and if he'd been able to get inside it, he'd already be long gone with the second amulet. But when he had arrived at the site of the Ark, he realized Hasad Arvadi had tricked him. The old man had been crafty, leaving out key information that would have made the Ark accessible.

When Ulric couldn't get into the Ark, the next step had been to return to Khor Virap. There must have been additional information about how to get into the Ark that Arvadi had concealed from Ulric. The plan was to photograph every square inch of the map to make sure they had missed nothing, and Ulric would find another translator to tell him what the map really said. Finding a qualified translator might take time, so to ensure no one followed in his footsteps, he would obliterate the map.

Ulric and Cutter had been lying in wait to make their move on the monastery, just like they'd done three years before. Then to Ulric's surprise, Locke and the others had appeared.

Although their arrival had jolted him, he quickly reassessed the situation and realized it might be to his advantage.

"Hold your fire," Ulric said to Cutter. "Maybe we can get Tyler Locke and Dilara Kenner to do our work for us."

If Kenner was as skilled an archaeologist as her father, she would be able to decipher the map's text and uncover what her father had not divulged to Ulric. Ulric would know as soon as they emerged from the pit if they had seen the map and determined the Ark's location. Then it would just be a matter of following them to the Ark and killing them all once they had shown him the way inside.

SIXTY

The priest led them away from the church in the central courtyard to the small St. Gevorg chapel. It was after five-thirty at this point, and the monastery was closed, so the tourists had been escorted out. They had the chapel to themselves.

To the right of the altar, Tyler saw a hole with steep aluminum stairs leading down. Father Tatilian climbed down backward, and the rest followed.

The pit was a cistern, vaguely round, with rough gray stone walls. Even with five of them, there was plenty of room, although it would get stuffy quickly with just the hole above to circulate air. The space was larger than what Tyler had imagined when he had heard it was a prison cell, but then again, he couldn't imagine being confined within it for thirteen years. It was a miracle that Grigor hadn't gone insane during that time. Maybe that was one of the miracles that qualified him for sainthood.

A standing candelabra had been set up across from the bottom of the stairs. On the right was the alcove Father Tatilian had mentioned. It was six feet tall, with an arched roof, two feet wide and three feet deep. It seemed to have a stone seat inside it, and a stone shelf set back about four feet high.

Tyler stepped up on the semicircular dais in front of the alcove and examined it. The stones were crudely mortared, and he couldn't see any noticeable seams where mortar had been removed. To all appearances, the entire cistern was as solid as the rock it was made from.

"Where was the murder victim found?" Tyler asked.

The priest pointed to the floor on the other side of the cistern.

"And you didn't notice anything else unusual down here?"

"Not that I could tell," the priest said, "although it was hard to concentrate on anything but the pool of blood that we cleaned up."

Tyler didn't bother asking about forensic evidence. Even if the killers were sloppy enough to leave fibers or prints, which he seriously doubted, he didn't think the local police would have had the resources to do any sophisticated analyses.

The novitiate was brought down for a reason, and the reference in the scroll to a cove had to be meaningful.

He counted out the stones from the left of the alcove, starting with the corner stone. *The fifth and eighth stones from the cove reveal.* The stones that made up the wall ranged from a few inches to a foot across. They had cut the stones to fit what was needed for each space.

He assumed that the key stones would be at eye level, which to people at that time was about five feet. Tyler saw that the fifth and eighth stones from the alcove were both about the same size, large enough to press his palm against. When he examined them more closely, he found a half-inch notch carved into each one in exactly the same place. These had to be the ones.

If the builders had constructed a secret passage, the key to unlocking it would be fairly simple because the engineering and construction methods of that age were rudimentary. On the other hand, the mechanism couldn't be activated by accident, or it would be discovered too easily.

Two stones. There was a reason for two of them, and Tyler thought he knew what it was. He tried to position himself to push both stones simultaneously, but they were so far apart that he couldn't get leverage with either one.

"Grant, give me a hand here. On my count of three, I want you to push hard on the eighth stone. At the same time, I'll push the fifth stone."

Grant got himself in position.

"What are you doing?" the priest asked.

"I think I'm going to show you something about your monastery that you didn't even know existed," Tyler said.

"I'm ready," Grant said.

"One. Two. Three."

They pushed with all their strength. At first, nothing happened. Then Tyler sensed the slightest movement of his stone.

"Did you feel that?" Grant said.

"Yes. I think we need to push with equal force. Let up on your side a little. Again. One. Two. Three."

This time, he could feel the stone begin to move immediately. It slid slowly backward, and so did Grant's. At the same time, the fourth and seventh stones slid slowly forward. The stones stopped moving when they were pressed into the wall six inches.

Tyler glanced at Dilara and saw the same excitement that he felt at their discovery.

Father Tatilian, on the other hand, was apoplectic and blurted something in Armenian.

"What's the matter?" Tyler asked the interpreter.

"The priest is very upset," Chirnian said. "He asks what you have done."

"I think we've just unlocked a door."

Tyler inspected the stones projecting from the wall. Except for the small notches, they were carved to be extremely smooth on all sides and fit into the spaces precisely. The edges on the outside were filed down and covered with a half inch of mortar to give the illusion that the stones were unmovable parts of the structure.

Tyler went to the alcove and saw that the side wall had moved, but just barely. He put his shoulder into it, and the corner of the alcove swung stiffly on a central pivot, revealing an opening on the left. Tyler shined his flashlight into the darkness. Stairs led down. A musty smell of decay filled his nose. To the left, he could see the mechanism that sealed the door.

As he thought, it was a simple stone pivot. A wooden one would have disintegrated long ago. The two stones they had pushed were connected to each other, and because of the leverage, pushing either one of them alone would merely cause stress on the pivot, not allowing them to move. But together, the stress was balanced, and the pivot not only pushed the other stones out, but also moved another piece of stone from the door that normally kept it from opening.

To reseal the entry, you would just push the door closed and then push the fourth and seventh stones back into place. *The fourth and seventh stones from the cove conceal.* Tyler marveled at the primitive cleverness of it.

"What do you see?" Dilara asked.

Tyler remembered why they were there.

"It's a stairway. We've found the chamber."

Grant and Dilara broke out their flashlights as well, and Chirnian and Father Tatilian took candles from the cistern.

Tyler went down ten steps, and then turned to the right to see twenty more steps. It must have taken a year to dig this out of the sandstone.

He got to the bottom and found himself in another round room, twice the size of the pit. He stopped when he saw what was on the wall opposite him. A map. He played the flashlight over it and could see a carefully drawn outline of Mount Ararat. Several points of black dotted the map. Next to the map were lines of text similar to those on the scrolls Dilara's father had discovered.

The flashlight beam came to the end of the text at the bottom of the wall, and Tyler saw a foot still encased in a shoe. He ran the light along the body until he reached a desiccated yawning face. The gruesome image was the result of years of slow decay in the dry climate. The brown robes of the mummified remains identified him. The missing novitiate.

The priest and translator gasped at the sight, and Tyler heard a yelp from Dilara. Her response to the corpse was unusual for someone who unearthed them for a living. He turned and saw that she wasn't looking at the novitiate's body. Instead, she was looking at a second one, in much the same condition.

This body was dressed in jeans, a collared shirt, and a khaki jacket. The graying hair suggested that the man was older, at least in his fifties. A notebook and pen were on the floor next to him. Then Tyler realized who he must be.

In the dim light reflected on Dilara's face, he could see the horrified recognition as she spoke softly, lovingly.

"Daddy?"

SIXTY-ONE

Dilara knelt on the floor next to her father, and Tyler joined her, putting his hand on her shoulder. He knew the feeling of arriving too late to tell your loved one everything you wanted to say before they were gone. The one solace was that she finally had closure. She put her hand on Tyler's and silently wept, her body shuddering with sobs.

"I'm so sorry, Dilara," he said. She nodded but said nothing.

They rest of them withdrew as much as the small space allowed to let Dilara grieve for a few moments. Bloodstains caked the floor, and Tyler saw the source. A bullet hole perforated each of Arvadi's legs, and another was in his midsection. His death hadn't been an easy one. Tyler picked up the notebook that had fallen out of Arvadi's hand. It looked as though he had been writing in it when he died. The printing was jagged and forced, not the smooth cursive from the rest of the notebook.

The note had only three lines, which were scrawled haphazardly across the page, like they were written in the dark, and they probably were. The last line trailed off. Arvadi must have died in the middle of writing it.

Sebastian Ulric killed me. Shot me to reveal Ark.
Didn't tell him real entrance. He took Amulet of Japheth.
Don't tell

Tyler peered at the second line.
Didn't tell him real entrance.
Her father had misled Ulric. But what did that mean? The real entrance? On a six-thousand-year-old wooden boat, it wouldn't matter if you didn't find the right entrance. You'd simply chop a hole in the side and go in that way. It didn't make sense.

With the pain and blood loss, Arvadi might have been delusional. The last line was useless, but the first two seemed lucid enough. If Ulric had been tricked somehow, they might still have a chance to beat him to Noah's Ark and find the second amulet before he did.

As much as Tyler wanted to let her mourn a little longer, he knew he couldn't. Even though finding her father was traumatic, Dilara still needed to help them decipher the map.

"I'm sorry, Dilara," Tyler repeated. "Are you going to be okay?"

She took off her jacket and covered her father's face with it. Then she stood and nodded solemnly. "I knew he was dead a long time ago. But it's different confirming it. Especially like this."

"I know."

"He was so close to achieving his goal. His life's dream. And Ulric killed him just when he was in reach of it." She wiped away the tears and looked at Tyler. "We're going to get him, aren't we? We're going to kill that son of a bitch."

Tyler wouldn't be upset if Ulric ended up pushing up daisies, but feeding Dilara's revenge would be a distraction they didn't need.

"We'll do what we have to do. But first, we need you to finish your father's work if we're going to stop Ulric. Do you think you can focus?"

The heat in Dilara's eyes smoldered for another moment and then faded. She nodded, but the grief was still there.

"Tyler, look at this," Grant said. He shined his flashlight on a small offering table. In the dust, there was the shape of a round object that used to rest on the table. The amulet. The source of the prion disease.

Dilara took several photos of the map, then focused her light on the text. Several times, her eyes flicked back to her father's body and the tears would return. Each time, Tyler would hold her gently then turn her attention back to the map. The words were written in the same language used in the scroll.

"It's like Ulric said." Her voice wavered, and her words were punctuated by an occasional sniffle, but her astonishment was apparent. "He told me that the flood was a plague. I didn't believe him. I thought, why would he tell me the truth? But this says the Amulet of Japheth rests here and contains a horror that almost destroyed man. It was hidden in this chamber in remembrance of God's wrath, His justice, and His love for mankind, that it was a testament to God for giving humanity a second chance to change our ways."

"But how could an amulet cause the deaths of everyone on earth?" Tyler asked. "How could it be the source of a disease?"

"I don't know. It says that the flood is

captured for eternity inside the amulet. It says to find the true story, you must find the Ark, where the Amulet of Shem is kept."

"Great," Grant said. "We're finally getting to the good part. Where is it? There are dots all over this map. The Ark could be any one of them."

"The Ark's resting place is in the eastern face of Mount Ararat," Dilara said. "The other marks are false Arks, decoys to throw off anyone who found the chamber but could not read the text. The majority of people in ancient times were illiterate."

"Got it," Grant said, pointing at the location on the east side of the mountain.

"Wait a minute," Tyler said, looking at the map, "if the Ark was where this dot says it is, people would have found it years ago. That elevation is lower than the year-round snow cover."

"The text says, quote, 'The great vessel in which Noah took refuge from the flood is found in the east flank of Ararat.' "

"You mean, *on* the east flank of Ararat," Grant said.

"No, I mean *in,*" Dilara said.

"This makes no sense," Tyler said.

"The text describes two entrances into the Ark. One that is sealed, and one that is passable."

"Your father's last note mentions a real entrance, as if he could deceive Ulric into choosing the wrong one. But how could that possibly keep Ulric from retrieving something from a rotting wooden ship thousands of years old?"

Dilara read further. When she got to the bottom, she staggered backward, as if she had been shoved in the face.

"Oh my God!" she said. "They hid it deliberately. They lied about Noah's Ark to keep it from being discovered."

"What are you talking about? Lied about what?"

"Everything."

"Hold on," Tyler said. "Are you saying Noah's Ark isn't on Ararat?"

"In a way, that's exactly what I'm saying," Dilara replied. "It isn't *on* Ararat. It's *in* Ararat. That's why no one has ever found the Ark. It's a vessel, but not the kind that floats. For the past six thousand years, everyone has been searching for a giant boat. Noah's Ark is a cave."

SIXTY-TWO

Now Arvadi's entrance reference made sense. Dilara had even called Oasis a new Ark. Tyler could have kicked himself for not making the connection sooner, but he had been so focused on Noah's Ark as a ship that he had never entertained the idea it could be a cave. "But the Bible says it's a ship, doesn't it? That it was made of wood?"

"It does," Dilara said. " 'Make thee an ark of timber planks: thou shalt make little rooms in the ark, and thou shalt pitch it within and without.' "

"That sounds like a ship to me."

"We're using the English translation of something that's been passed down through thousands of years. It all comes down to translation and interpretation. Think of the telephone game. Little errors in the process can end up as huge errors down the line. I think that's what happened here. What if Noah's Ark was the structure inside a cave?

A vessel can also mean a container." She looked back to her father. "I'm so stupid. Why didn't I listen to him?"

"You couldn't have known," Tyler said. He considered the language. "The cave must have been the refuge. The words would fit. But we're talking about a huge cavern. Three hundred cubits long, fifty cubits wide, thirty cubits high. That's four hundred and fifty feet long, seventy-five feet wide, and forty-five feet high."

"You were saying a few days ago that a ship that big in ancient times would have collapsed as soon as it was floated onto water. This explains why it could be so big."

Tyler saw the irony of arguing for the case of Noah's Ark being a boat, when before he had been the one arguing against it.

"And the window and door?"

"I don't know," Dilara said. "Openings in the cave? What I do know is that this text clearly states that Noah's Ark is a cave inside Mount Ararat."

"It does explain why no one has ever found it. New caves are still being discovered all the time. The problem is that Mount Ararat is a shield volcano, which don't typically contain caverns."

"Why not?"

"Caves are usually carved out by water

over millions of years, and Mount Ararat is too young for that to happen. Most large caves in the world are found in limestone, which is soluble and can be dissolved by slightly acidic water." Tyler had learned that little tidbit when consulting on a sinkhole collapse in Florida that destroyed an entire mall.

"But remember those big lava tubes that we explored in Hawaii?" Grant said.

"I didn't say it was impossible. How does the Flood fit into all of this?"

"The Flood was the disease," Dilara said. "Ulric told me that he had to modify the prion from its original form. Waterborne diseases were virulent and common in the ancient world. Still are. Typhoid contaminates drinking water in many countries. But when the original translators misinterpreted the Ark as a ship instead of a container, they must have assumed the references to the waters meant a flood, not a plague."

" 'A flood of waters upon the earth,' " Tyler said, " 'to destroy all flesh.' "

"What if the prion disease in the amulet attacked any animal matter, not just humans?" Dilara said. "If this prion disease was released into rivers and lakes, it would have wiped out every living thing in that watershed. The only trace would be bones.

No flesh. To people who rarely ventured thirty miles from where they were born, it would seem like God had cleansed the earth."

"And Noah would have had to take all the animals he wanted to save with him. Once the disease destroyed everything, the remaining prions would die out or reach the ocean, where the salt water would kill them."

"If Noah didn't know how long it would take for the disease to subside, he might have built a huge Ark, with enough food to feed him, his family, and his animals for months."

"So when the Bible talks about the waters of the Flood," Tyler said, "it means that the waters *carried* the Flood, which was a plague."

"And if it was a particularly rainy season," Dilara said, "it would look to Noah like the rains were the harbinger of doom. It even fits sending out the raven and the dove to see if the waters had abated. The raven never returned because it was killed by the prions. With some reinterpretation of dates and wording, everything seems to fit."

"But it doesn't explain how the prions were related to the amulets. Everything we've found implies that the prions are *in-*

side the amulets."

"We'll have to find the last amulet to know for sure, and to do that, we have to find the Ark."

Chirnian had been interpreting the conversation as it proceeded, and Father Tatilian had listened attentively without comment. But at this point, he exclaimed through the interpreter, "No, it would be best if you did not find the Ark."

"Why not?" Tyler asked.

"Because if true, this information will cause much distress and confusion. We consider the Bible to be the inspired word of God, carefully compiled over hundreds of years, so a fundamental challenge to something as important as the story of the Flood is very serious. It would undermine our confidence in our understanding of much of the Old Testament."

"We have to find it," Tyler said. "If we don't, there will be no one left to debate the point."

"God will not let the earth be destroyed again. His covenant with Noah was clear. 'Neither shall all flesh be cut off any more by the waters of the flood.' He would not let this happen."

"But we're not dismissing that promise," Dilara said. "Sebastian Ulric just wants to wipe out the human race, not all flesh. That's why he spent so long modifying the disease in his lab. He specifically designed it so that it wouldn't affect animals. And what if we're the ones who have to stop him from wiping out all flesh? We could be God's soldiers who will prevent it and preserve God's covenant."

"God helps those who help themselves," Tyler said.

"The Bible doesn't say that," Father Tatilian said.

"I know. Benjamin Franklin's words, not mine."

"The Bible is infallible. This story about the cave cannot be true!"

"If we find the Ark," Dilara said, "it will support the Bible, not hurt it. It will finally provide physical proof that the book of Genesis has an historical basis, that it's not just a book of faith or literature. And the people who want to believe that it is literally correct can continue to do so. It's the human translators who were fallible, not the words themselves. With just a few changes to the text, the story is still accurate. So the King James version needs a little tweaking? So what?"

The priest scowled, but he didn't object. "I will have to pray for guidance on this."

"It's up to you how you want to reveal this chamber," Tyler said, "but you're going to have to bring the local police down here to retrieve these remains."

Father Tatilian nodded. "This discovery will change everything about Khor Virap."

Dilara stared at her father's prone body, but her eyes held no more tears.

"They'll take care of him, Dilara," Tyler said.

"I know. At least he died knowing he was right."

"He would want you to finish his work."

"And I will," she said with conviction. "Let's go find Noah's Ark."

SIXTY-THREE

Tyler had to assume Sebastian Ulric was on his way to the Ark, and he had to move fast to get to the site first.

Tyler returned to Yerevan with Grant and Dilara, where they reboarded the Gordian jet to fly the short distance to an airport in Van, Turkey. Using the plane's satellite phone, Tyler updated Miles Benson on their progress.

Tyler kept his father out of the loop, knowing the military would take over the search and try to secure the prion for itself. Not only that, but if the Turkish government got any hint that they had discovered Noah's Ark, their access to Mount Ararat would be denied. They had to keep their expedition quiet if they wanted any chance of stopping Ulric without creating a major international incident and without handing over the prions to another party.

By the time they arrived in Van, it was

already dark, too late to attempt to find the Ark cave. They would have to wait until morning, which gave Tyler time to gather some of the supplies he needed for the expedition. He had some mining contacts in western Turkey who could provide him with what he required. While he did that, Dilara, who spoke fluent Turkish, chartered a helicopter for the hundred-mile flight to Mount Ararat.

The final job was to acquire some muscle to add to their ranks. Ulric had at least Petrova, Cutter, and the two guards who had been with him when he escaped. Tyler didn't like the idea of being outnumbered five to three. Grant, using his military contacts, found three mercenaries who could make it to Van from Istanbul before dawn. Tyler had outfitted the jet with enough weapons to arm himself, Grant, and Dilara for the trip. The mercenaries would supply their own weapons.

Then it was a matter of waiting for daylight. Tyler told the pilots to find a hotel in town, but he, Grant, and Dilara stayed with the plane, sleeping in the cabin. Even with the comfortable furniture, they slept fitfully.

By early morning, the equipment that Tyler requisitioned had arrived, followed soon after by the three mercenaries, who reported for duty straight off their plane. Tyler briefed them about the mission, leaving out any mention of Noah's Ark. The helicopter would drop them on the eastern flank of Mount Ararat and fly off to a staging area to the south. When they were ready to be picked up, Tyler would radio the helicopter. He didn't want the helicopter around to tip off Ulric in case Tyler arrived first.

The helicopter charter was a surprisingly new Bell 222, roomy enough for all six of them and their gear. During the flight out, the pilot told them that oil and mineral exploration had jumped dramatically in the last five years. For a fifteen-year stretch starting in the mid-1980s, Mount Ararat had been off-limits to nonmilitary personnel because of attacks by the Workers Party of Kurdistan, or PKK. The Kurdish rebels had taken tourists hostage and set off bombs in the southeastern cities of Turkey. But when the PKK leader was arrested in 2000, the attacks had become rare. The mountain was reopened to tourism, and business interests in the area had grown.

The flight to the mountain took less than an hour. The rugged slopes were lined with rock-strewn valleys and overhangs that could have hidden hundreds of caves. The helicopter was above the tree line, but some plants survived at this altitude because it was below the permanent snow line. The helicopter flew over the approximate location shown on the map in Khor Virap, and they began searching for the distinctive rock outcropping described in the text.

It was depicted on the map as the prow of a boat jutting from a cliff face and topped by a sail mast. That's the way it would look from the southern view. The Ark door would be found a hundred paces south of it, and the window would be another hundred paces beyond the door. The biggest problem would be if the outcropping no longer existed.

Mount Ararat was a dormant volcano, and in the previous six thousand years, minor eruptions and earthquakes could have easily destroyed it. Tyler remembered New Hampshire's famed Old Man of the Mountain formation, which resembled a bearded man peering from the side of Cannon Mountain. It was so well known and loved that it adorned the state's quarter. Ironically and tragically, the rock formation collapsed soon after the quarter was circulated, showing just how suddenly the topography of a mountain could change. The odds that the prow formation had survived were not good.

They made six passes from the south

before he heard Dilara shout and point out the left window. Sure enough, the profile of the bow end of a sailing ship extended from a rocky cliff face. They were directly over Noah's Ark. Dilara grinned at Tyler, her excitement obvious. His own enthusiasm was tempered by caution.

They circled to see if they could spot any signs of others. The mountainside appeared empty of any human presence, but the terrain was so harsh, a company of soldiers could be hiding down there without being noticed. Tyler instructed the pilot to set down on the nearest flat spot, which ended up being almost a mile away.

Tyler, Grant, Dilara, and the three mercenaries jumped out and quickly pulled out their weapons and equipment. The mercenaries were armed with heavy automatic rifles, while the rest of them carried pistols and submachine guns. Because of how Dilara had handled the MP5 inside Oasis, Tyler had offered one to her as well, and she accepted without hesitation.

The helicopter dusted off, and the six of them began the hike to the entrance of Noah's Ark.

"What's our altitude?" Grant asked.

"Only about eight thousand feet," Tyler said, looking at the peak that reached another mile and a half above them. Previous searchers had expected the Ark to be higher in the mountain, but the lower altitude made sense. To get building materials and animals into the Ark, it had to be accessible enough to walk to. The climbing wasn't easy, but the grade was wide and flat enough to allow pack animals to climb.

The summer hadn't fully abandoned the mountain. Even though it was October, the sky was clear, and the air was a brisk fifty degrees. As they walked, one of the mercenaries ran his hand over some leafy plants with fading purple blooms, just the idle move of a bored hiker.

"I wouldn't do that," Dilara said, nodding at the mercenary. The man gave her a look that said *give me a break* and kept doing it.

"Why not?" Tyler said.

"Because that's monkshood. The leaves and flowers contain a deadly poison that can be absorbed through the skin. It's been used throughout history to poison the tips of arrows."

The mercenary ripped his hand away, as if the bush were on fire, and wiped it on his pant leg.

"If your hand goes numb for a little while," Dilara said, "don't worry. It'll go away. Just don't lick your fingers after lunch."

In thirty minutes, they reached the rock formation, and Tyler began counting his footsteps. When he got to ninety-three, he saw a dark hole in the mountain face. A cave.

The cave opening was a twenty-foot-radius semicircle, and from this angle, Tyler couldn't see the back of it. If Ulric were already here, the cave would be a perfect place to stage an ambush. Using hand signals, he instructed the mercenaries to circle below the view of the cave entrance and approach from the opposite side. When they were in place, Tyler popped a flare and threw it into the opening.

No shots rang out, but he didn't expect them to. Cutter and his men were too disciplined for such a simple ruse. From his pack, Tyler removed one of the pieces of equipment shipped to him: a remote-control vehicle with large knobby tires. It was the size of a loaf of bread and had a camera mounted on top.

Tyler set the vehicle on the ground and took out the controller, which had a pistol grip with a trigger for the accelerator. A small wheel allowed him to control the steering with his other hand. He gently pulled the trigger, and with a muted whine, the vehicle leaped forward and darted into the cave. A color LCD screen above the controller's wheel showed the view from the camera.

Lit by the flare, the cave had a uniform shape all the way back to a wall at the rear fifty feet beyond. He could make out a few objects, but nothing large enough to hide behind. No one was inside.

Tyler gave the all clear. He replaced the vehicle and controller in his pack. He picked up the flare and walked farther into the cave, followed by Grant and Dilara, who used their flashlights. The mercenaries stayed outside on guard duty.

Halfway in, Tyler saw a pile of boxes, some broken, some still intact, lying against the cave wall. He bent down to look at them. They obviously didn't date from Noah's time, but they weren't new. They must have decomposed in the cave for twenty years. There was crude writing on the nearest box. It looked Turkish.

"What does that say?" Tyler asked Dilara. He saw another box that was partly open and peered into it, pushing the flare in close to light it better.

"I can't read it," Dilara said. "It not Turkish. It's Kurdish."

The flare lit the box contents. When he saw what was inside, Tyler jumped back before a spark from the flare could fall into it.

"What?" Grant said.

"Remember the PKK?" Tyler said. "The Kurdish separatists the pilot told us about? This must have been one of their hideouts. If Dilara spoke Kurdish, she'd be seeing the word DYNAMITE on the side."

Dilara froze when she heard the word *dynamite.*

"Get up slowly and ease away from the explosives," Tyler said. "Be careful not to touch the boxes."

"Sweating?" Grant said as Dilara moved backward.

"Like a fat man in a sauna."

If dynamite is left in an uncontrolled environment, the nitroglycerine inside will weep from the sticks, leaving behind crystals on the sticks and pooling in its liquid form. From Tyler's short glimpse, he could see the sparkle of thousands of crystals on the dynamite, which were cheaply made, not the newer sticks that resisted sweating. The boxes must have been there for years, subject to the extreme weather that blew into the cave.

"Is it going to blow up?" Dilara asked quietly.

"Not if we leave it alone. But nitro is touchy stuff. The bottom of the crate is full of it. A good nudge could set it off. The explosion could bring the entire roof down."

"Let's walk on the other side," Grant said.

Skirting to the opposite side, they moved to the back of the cave, where it ended at a crack-covered wall that spanned the entire width. Tyler examined it closely and noticed that one of the cracks was contiguous and framed a rough square eight feet on each side. He knelt and ran his hands over the floor. His fingers dug into a soft spot of sand that had been used to fill in a groove in the floor. He excavated the groove and found that it formed an arc away from the right side of the crack border.

"This is a door," he said. "That border is man-made. This channel must be used to guide it. I'd love to know how they built it."

"I'd love to know how we open it," Dilara said.

"We can't. At least, not from here."

"Why not? Is there another secret button?"

"No. My guess is that it can only be opened from the inside. That's what your father meant when he said Ulric can't get

602

in. He only gave Ulric this entrance, but he knew it was a one-way door, probably as a security feature for the Ark. Once the construction was completed and the animals were inside, they could push this closed from out here and use the window to get in. It would be smaller and more easily defended. To open something this big, you'd have to push it from the inside." Tyler couldn't hide his admiration for the accomplishment. "Noah must have been a hell of an engineer."

"Then the Ark is behind this rock?" Dilara's voice was suffused with hushed awe.

Tyler ran his hand over the door to Noah's Ark.

"Let's hope Ulric isn't waiting for us on the other side."

SIXTY-FOUR

Sebastian Ulric looked through his binoculars at the three men huddled near the cave entrance four hundred yards below him. The morning sun was directly in front of him, so he had to be careful not to shine a reflection in their direction. The men at the cave were scattered in what cover they could find around the entrance, and Ulric could see the heads of only two of them.

Locke had come, just as Ulric knew he would. When Ulric saw Locke and the others emerge from the church at Khor Virap, the priest gesticulating wildly, it was obvious they had found the chamber. Destroying the chamber after that would only alert Tyler to Ulric's presence.

As soon as he saw them leave, Ulric had taken his group back across the border into Turkey, lavishly bribing the border guards to get across. Then, using the GPS coordinates Cutter had established from their previous visit to the Ark's location, Ulric led them up the mountain in the darkness. All of them were equipped with generation-three night-vision goggles that amplified the faintest starlight to make the terrain look as detailed as it was in the day, making the hike relatively easy when they could drive no more because of the terrain. With the help of stimulants, they remained awake and arrived just in time to watch Locke's helicopter swoop in.

Petrova and the two guards were concealed behind a rock. Cutter crouched at Ulric's side, holding the VAL sniper rifle to his shoulder.

"How close do you need to get to take out those men?" Ulric asked.

"I could hit one of them from here," Cutter replied, "but the others are spread out. They'd be able to find cover before I could take them down."

"We need a diversion." Ulric lowered his voice so the others couldn't hear. "Your men are expendable."

Cutter nodded his agreement and whispered, "I'll have them circle around from the south. I'll tell them to surrender, and when Locke's men come out to get them, I can take all three of them down before they can react."

"Excellent. What about their communications gear?"

"I'll activate our broadband radio jammer right before we attack. Should we get into place now?"

"Not yet. We examined that cave from top to bottom. There's no switch like the one in Khor Virap. I don't think it's the real entrance, but if Tyler doesn't emerge in the next few minutes we'll have to assume he made it in somehow."

"It's risky to try to infiltrate through a choke point like that. I still think it's better to wait until they come out with the amulet and kill them all then."

"No," Ulric said firmly. "We have to follow them in. I don't want to take the chance that Tyler will destroy the amulet inside the cave. Once we know where the real entrance is, we make our move."

Cutter pointed. "There they are."

Locke, Westfield, and Kenner stepped into the sunlight.

"See," Ulric said. "That cave isn't the way in."

He watched as Locke waved to his three men and began walking south.

"Keep your eyes out for an opening a lot smaller than that one," Tyler said. "Probably just big enough for a man to get through."

He began counting paces again. When he reached ninety-seven, he was even with a crevice that fit the bill. It was narrow, no more than two feet across and seven feet high, and filled with dirt and rocks, as if the roof had caved in hundreds of years ago.

"You think that's it?" Dilara said.

"If it is, it means we got here first. No way did Ulric get here and plug it up after he was gone. Why would he go to that trouble?"

"I feel some manual labor coming on," Grant said. He handed out two folding shovels and took a third for himself, shoving the blade into the crevice.

There was no telling how far back the cave-in went. They might have to dig for hours or days before getting through. Still, they didn't have much choice. They had to be the first to get into the Ark, and this was the entrance. Tyler was sure of it.

It turned out that they only had to dig for two hours before Grant's shovel plunged through into air. They swept out the remaining dirt and shined flashlights down a passageway that ended farther than the light could reach.

Everyone was wearing radio earpieces. Tyler told the mercenaries that at least five hostiles might make an attempt for the cave. The mercenaries were to stay outside and radio if anything out of the ordinary occurred. Tyler would check in every fifteen minutes.

The mercenaries took covered positions. Tyler made sure the packs he and Grant carried fit through the opening. The three of them put on hard hats, and Tyler looked at Dilara.

"Ladies first?" she said.

"Given that you're the one who started all this, I thought you deserved to be the first one to see the Ark."

She smiled. "Thank you. I'll remember this day for the rest of my life."

Dilara took a deep breath and entered the crevice. She was immediately swallowed by the darkness. Tyler went in behind her, dragging his pack, and Grant took up the rear.

The going was slow. At several points, the passageway was so narrow that Tyler wasn't sure Grant would be able to squeeze his bulging pecs through.

"You going to make it?" he said to Grant.

"It's a tad tight," Grant said between gasps. "If I get stuck, we'll radio the guys outside to send in a bucketful of warm butter."

Tyler grinned at that. Grant was doing fine.

"You see anything ahead?" Tyler said after they had gone about fifty feet.

"Yes," Dilara said. "I think I see it widen in thirty feet."

In another minute, the crevice opened and Tyler was standing next to Dilara. The cave didn't have the dank odor of a limestone cavern. Instead, it had a dry, dusty aroma that reminded him of the time he had visited Tut's tomb in Egypt's Valley of the Kings. The air had the same feeling of history, of ageless wonder.

Tyler focused his flashlight on the wall to his left. He played the light up the wall to the fifty-foot-high ceiling and then followed the wall away from him until the surface ended at a right angle to another wall. Judging by the dimness of the spot, he guessed the far wall was at least seventy feet away. To his right, the flashlight beam was soaked up by the gloom.

Grant emerged next to him and took a huge breath.

"Thank God we're out of there. I'm not claustrophobic, but I might convert after that."

Grant's low voice echoed off distant surfaces, as if they were in a box canyon.

"This place sounds huge," he said.

"Let's find out how huge," Tyler said. He removed a strobe light from his pack. The battery wouldn't last long, but its high-intensity power would give them a feel for the size of the cavern.

"Don't look directly at the strobe when I turn it on." He placed his hand on the switch. "Is everyone ready?"

"Let's do it," Grant said.

Dilara nodded eagerly. "Show us."

"Lady and gentleman, I give you Noah's Ark."

He flicked the switch and stepped back. He could hear the capacitor storing energy for its first flash, and then the strobe blasted its wide beam outward every half second. The persistence of the human visual system allowed the eye to view the scene almost as if it were a continuous light.

Dilara gasped. No one spoke. The image was too breathtaking. Stretching as far as the eye could see, a huge wooden structure three stories high ran down the left side of a cavern so vast that the other end was lost in the darkness. The building hadn't been just slapped together but showed a degree of sophistication Tyler wouldn't have believed an ancient civilization capable of. The pieces fit together as well as if he had designed it himself.

He couldn't imagine the amount of effort it would have taken to build such a thing miles from the sources of wood needed to assemble it. Even with modern equipment, building such a structure inside a cave, without sufficient lighting, would have been an enormous undertaking. Constructed thousands of years ago, with only human hands and beasts of burden to do the labor, it was truly astounding. Tyler could barely grasp what he was witness to. He was looking at the oldest wooden building still in existence, a construction that rivaled the great pyramids for sheer majesty. A magnificent structure that Noah himself had designed and built.

"My God," Dilara finally said. "It's still intact. After all this time, it's still standing."

"The dry air," Tyler said. "No water, no termites, no rot."

"Looks like we won't need all the spelunking gear we dragged along," Grant said. "Judging by the size of this, Noah and his family planned to settle in for the long haul."

"So are you still a skeptic?" Dilara asked Tyler.

He shook his head slowly. "I'm proud to say I was wrong."

"This has to be the most incredible archaeological find in history."

"I'd go further than that. I'd say it's a miracle."

SIXTY-FIVE

After a few minutes, the strobe's battery was drained. Except for the flashlights and the faint light visible through the crevice, the cave was plunged back into darkness.

Using a laser range finder, Tyler confirmed that the Ark cavern had the dimensions described in the Bible: 450 feet long by 75 feet wide by 45 feet high. Tyler, Grant, and Dilara stood at the southern end of the 450-foot chamber, with the structure on the left and the bare cave wall on the right. The cave was surprisingly uniform, and Tyler could only guess as to how it was formed. Maybe some kind of fantastically huge lava tube. It was an unlikely formation for this type of volcano; some might say miraculous. Except for the lack of water, it provided the perfect refuge.

The Ark itself was a three-level stepped construction like the bench seats at a high school football stadium, with each higher tier set back from the one below. All three levels abutted the left cave wall, which also served as the back wall of the structure, with rooms separated by interior walls along its 450-foot length. There were no doors or walls on the front side of each tier.

Tyler examined the wood used to build the Ark. It was a strong hardwood, treated with pitch to prevent rot. He rapped on the wood in several places. Still solid after six thousand years. Over Dilara's objection, he dug the knife from his Leatherman into a beam. It didn't give. The construction should be stable enough to walk on and under.

The trappings of ancient life abounded, as if the inhabitants had left only minutes before. No effort had been made to take the wooden furniture or pottery that littered the cavern.

Every fifty feet, a ramp ran parallel to the structure and angled up to the next level like a switchback trail. At the front of each of the upper two levels, there was an open fifteen-foot-wide promenade that ran the length of the structure and would allow anyone walking along it to peer down to the level below. The cave floor served as the promenade for the lowest level.

The largest rooms were on the bottom

tier, and with the stepped-back construction, the rooms were not as deep on the second and third levels because they had to make room for the promenades. The rooms on the bottom level were 45 feet deep, 30 feet deep on the second level, and on the top level the rooms were just 15 feet deep. From the few rooms Tyler could see with his flashlight, they ranged in width from 10 to 50 feet.

He made a quick mental calculation and guessed that there were more than fifty rooms to search. It could take days unless they got a head start. Tyler turned to Dilara.

"Any ideas for where to begin the search for the amulet?" he asked.

Dilara shook her head. "No one has ever seen anything like this. I'm just guessing, but the bottom rooms were probably used for storage, animal pens, and refuse collection. The second level might have been used for common rooms. The top level could be individual quarters. But this is all speculation. The amulet could be anywhere. I suggest we split up."

"I agree. Since we're alone in here for now, the danger should be minimal. But first, I have something that might help us in our search."

Tyler unzipped his bag and removed the remote-controlled vehicle again. He also unfolded a laptop computer.

"How will that help?" Dilara asked. "It'll take longer using the camera on that thing."

"The camera is just one tool on the vehicle," Tyler said. "This time we're going to use its laser mapping system."

"What will that do?"

"As I drive the RCV all the way down the cave on each level, the laser will measure the distance to every surface it passes and beam the dimensions back to the laptop. In real time, the laptop will construct a three-dimensional image of the structure that I can then send to the memory chips in each of these."

Tyler took his hard hat off to show it to Dilara. It looked like a standard miner's helmet, with a powerful light on the top. But on each side, it had articulated view-finders that could be folded down to fit over the eye. It also had an infrared camera that could pick up the heat signature of a warm body from a huge distance. Since they were alone, the infrared wouldn't be necessary.

"Gordian developed these to assist in underground mining disasters when visibility is poor. I had them shipped here from a Gordian job in Greece."

"You mean, this helmet will show me what the cave looks like?"

"Wherever you turn your head, it'll show you a graphical representation of what you're looking at. When you shine your flashlight at anything, you'll see the visible image superimposed over the computer-generated image. It communicates with this emitter, which serves as the reference point." Tyler placed the small transceiver out of the way at the base of the wall.

"How long will it take before we can use it?" Dilara asked.

"Just a few minutes to get the data. The RCV's top speed is forty miles per hour. All I have to do is drive it straight to the end, and the laser and computer will do the rest. When it's at the other end, I'll drive it up to the second level and we'll do the same thing. Of course, it won't be able to see behind anything, but it'll give us a quick look at everything in here."

Tyler plopped the RCV on the floor, tapped on the computer's mouse pad, and when he confirmed that the data collection had begun, he pressed the trigger. The RCV zoomed away, its own flashlight guiding the way. Within seconds, all they could see was the pale spot of light in front of it. Tyler concentrated on the controller's LCD screen. In ten minutes, Tyler had run the RCV down all three levels of the Ark and back to their current position.

"Nice driving, Andretti," Grant said.

"All those video games finally paid off," Tyler said as he downloaded the data to the helmets. He put one on, turned down the eyepieces, and looked around.

He could see Dilara and Grant clearly through the lens, but the background was no longer black and formless. As Tyler moved his head, the computer calculated its position and the distance to each hard surface. Then using wire-frames and texture-shading, it built a crude representation of everything in his field of view. Graded textures were assigned to different depths so that items against a wall would stand out.

He took a few steps to the side, and the view shifted instantaneously. Anything that wasn't a wall, floor, or ceiling would now quickly grab their attention.

"Try it," he said to Dilara, handing her a helmet.

She put it on and rotated her head side to side, up and down.

"This is incredible! I can see everything so clearly!" She wobbled and lost her footing. Tyler caught her.

"It may take a few minutes to get your balance wearing these," he said. "If you feel unsteady, just close your eyes for a few seconds."

"Right."

"We'll leave the equipment here. No sense toting it everywhere. Let's divide up the place by level. I'll take the bottom. Grant, you take the second level. Dilara, take the top."

"This goes against everything I've ever learned or preached about archaeological discovery. We should be doing a methodical, inch-by-inch study, not rifling through it like treasure hunters."

"No need to get fancy. Nobody touch anything unless you absolutely have to. We'll leave the scientific analysis for later. Our goal is to find the amulet."

"Which looks like what?" Grant asked. "A brooch?"

"It's probably some kind of jewel," Dilara said. "It will be displayed on the same kind of dais we saw in the map room of Khor Virap. If you find the amulet, don't touch it until I can see it in situ." She waved her digital camera at him. "I want to get a photo to document it before we remove it."

"And watch your step," Tyler said. "The Ark seems sturdy enough, but even without water in here, there might be parts of the floor that have rotted through. Test before each step."

Even with the mercenaries on guard outside, Grant and Tyler kept their submachine guns with them out of caution, but Dilara decided to shed the excess weight and dumped hers with the packs. Speed at this point was more important than anything else. If Ulric did eventually come, Tyler wanted to be long gone.

They split up as Tyler suggested. Grant and Dilara carefully crept up the nearest ramp, and they were soon just two bobbing lights.

Ceramic pots, thousands of them, ranging from the size of a coffeepot to five feet in height, were stacked along the wall of the cavern opposite the Ark. A few were broken, but most were in pristine condition. Tyler peered into a few of them, but they were all empty or contained the dried remains of food. The amulet wouldn't be found in any of them.

Tyler entered the first room and quickly surveyed the contents. More ceramic pots. Nothing stood out. He had a feeling that the amulet would be stored in a more exalted place, but he did a thorough scan anyway.

He repeated the same for the next two rooms. Empty. Tyler guessed these were storage rooms. Food, water, supplies. Everything needed to sustain a family and a herd of animals for months at a time. More than enough space. Tyler did the math. Almost seventy thousand square feet of floor area. The equivalent of thirty-five average American homes. The size of the Ark was staggering. Noah must have had hundreds of animals to justify building something so huge.

In the fourth room Tyler entered, a wooden fence stretched the width of the room, with a six-foot-wide gate in the center. An animal pen. A few desiccated piles of hay were piled in the corners, but the animals had been removed. There were no bones.

The next four rooms were all animal pens. Tyler was now almost halfway down the Ark and had found nothing of significance. He radioed the others, but they had similar luck. Grant and Dilara had found more artifacts — pottery, clothing, tools — but no amulet.

Tyler inspected one more animal pen, then came to a room three times as wide as the rooms he had seen up until now. The room was ninety feet wide, the ceiling supported at regular intervals by stone pillars. The three-dimensional rendering showed a variety of texture gradients, meaning the room was filled to the brim with something. Tyler cast his flashlight around, and reflections sparkled back at him from all directions.

It was as if Tyler had stepped into a pirate cave. In every direction, gold ornaments and vessels, ivory statuettes, and jewel-encrusted objects covered the floor. Chests brimmed with bronze, silver, and gold pieces. Jade carvings adorned gleaming masks of gold. Marble busts lined the walls. Sapphires, rubies, diamonds, and amethysts were scattered like pebbles. The cache was so vast, Tyler wouldn't have been surprised to see a dragon resting on top of it.

For a minute, he forgot all about the reason he was there. The effect of the glittering treasure was mesmerizing. Then he snapped out of it and remembered what he was looking for. If there was an amulet in Noah's Ark, it would be in this room.

He radioed Dilara and Grant to get down there as fast as they could without telling them why. They had to see this for themselves.

SIXTY-SIX

While he waited for the others, Tyler walked among the hoard. The statuettes and urns were a mishmash of different styles and shapes, adorned with a wide variety of languages, all piled carelessly, as if they were just dumped in the first place that was available. Some of the treasure was stored in stone boxes or pottery, but most spilled out onto the floor.

Grant was the first to arrive and stopped dead in his tracks, his mouth agape. He said nothing. It was the first time Tyler could remember him rendered speechless.

Dilara walked in behind him, but she was focused on her camera's LCD screen.

"I found an amazing storehouse of weaponry . . ." She looked up and froze in place. "My God!"

"Apparently," Tyler said, "King Midas used to live here."

"I'm retiring early," Grant said.

"Unfortunately, the Turkish government might have something to say about that."

"Or the Armenians," Dilara said as she scanned the room in awe. "I can't believe this! It's incredible! Once word of this gets out, there's going to be a massive international fight over who owns it. This room alone has to be worth billions."

"What about a finder's fee?" Grant said hopefully.

"We'll see," Tyler said. "First things first. The amulet has got to be in here somewhere. And Grant, no souvenirs."

"Spoilsport."

"We can come back later when we've got better equipment and supplies. Then you can help Dilara pick through this piece by piece. Right now, I want to find that amulet."

"The amulet was of tremendous significance," Dilara said. "It wouldn't be tossed on the floor. Let's try the back wall of the room."

They snaked their way through the maze of wealth around them and came to a row of seven stone boxes six feet in length lying with their ends against the back wall. Each was perched on a pedestal. Extensive writing covered the wall behind them, the same writing found in the Khor Virap map chamber.

"These look like coffins," Grant said.

"Sarcophagi," Dilara said. She snapped pictures of each of them and ran her hands over the surface of one, casting centuries of dust into the air. "The text will tell us who is entombed in them."

"Hold on," Tyler said. "Look." He shined his light on a pillar that stood in the center, with four sarcophagi on one side, three on the other. The pillar was four feet high, and on its flat top sat a translucent orb the size of a softball and the color of maple syrup. It was surrounded by other orbs, slightly smaller.

Dilara read the text on the pillar. "Here resides the Amulet of Shem. Here it remains as a symbol of mankind's wickedness and a reminder of God's love and a warning to those who would tempt His wrath."

Tyler knelt beside the pillar and shined the light through the orbs. He recognized what they were immediately. Enormous pieces of amber, sap from a tree that had fossilized millions of years ago. Often insects would be trapped in the amber, preserved virtually intact, protected from the effects of air and water.

The orbs around the edge of the pillar

were completely transparent, flawless, but the Amulet of Shem contained the skeleton of a frog two inches long. It seemed to be floating in a pocket of viscous fluid the shape of a living frog.

After Dilara took a picture, Tyler picked up the orb. The fluid circulated, causing the bones to slowly float around.

"This is the source of the disease," Tyler said. "Ulric's raw material. The frog was caught in the amber and then dissolved from the disease, leaving the frog-shaped cavity behind. The prion must still be viable, protected in the amber. When he found the Amulet of Japheth, he realized the fluid inside held some kind of lethal plague."

"He got the Arkon from a frog?" Grant said. "Like in *Jurassic Park,* only gooier?"

Tyler nodded. "The text at Khor Virap said that the amulet held the horror. Ulric rightly assumed that inside the amulet was a plague that wiped out every person and animal in Noah's time. He knew he had the resources to analyze it and potentially develop a deadly weapon from it. Back in the lab, when he found out what he had on his hands, he devised the plan for Oasis."

Grant took the amulet from Tyler and gazed at the suspended bones. "Just like

626

what happened on Hayden's plane."

"If that dissolved frog is a carrier of the Arkon," Tyler said, "then the disease must date from the time the frog was alive. At this point, we have no idea when that was. For all we know, that thing might have been hopping away from a T-rex when it got trapped in the amber."

"You think this stuff could have killed off the dinosaurs?" Grant said.

"We'll never know. But Arkon would certainly be virulent enough to do the job."

Dilara had been reading the text on the wall.

"Hey, guys," she said, snapping a photo. "This is the story of what happened." She laboriously read the text. "It says that Noah found these pieces of amber in an exposed riverbed. The discovery was his first sign from God that he should build the Ark." She turned to Tyler and Grant. "Amber has always been prized as a gem for its color and luster. Finding these must have seemed like a fortune."

"How did the prion get released?" Tyler asked.

Dilara ran her finger along the writing. "I hope I'm getting this right. It says that Noah saw a vision that these pieces of amber were special, given by God to him alone. Three of the biggest ones contained the frog bones. A traveling trader saw them and claimed that the fluid inside could be sold for medicinal purposes. Noah suspected that such use would be an affront to God and tried to hide them, but the trader stole one of the orbs and disappeared."

She told the story haltingly, pausing when she had trouble translating.

"Noah had another vision that the thief was an example of mankind's wickedness, that even God's servant was not free from tyranny by his fellow man. Then Noah heard of a strange sickness spreading from the foreign land the trader was from. He took this as a sign that God was exacting his wrath, and he had another vision with instructions for how to construct the Ark. He and his sons built it, trying to persuade others that death was coming and they should join him, but they wouldn't listen."

"Then the rains came," Tyler said.

Dilara nodded. "And brought the Flood, as the pestilence had become known throughout the land. Noah closed the entrance to the Ark, for fear that the infected would seek refuge with him."

"This place is as dry as a bone," Grant said. "Where did they get water?"

"It doesn't say, but probably from a

stream of uncontaminated glacier melt just outside the crevice entrance. Then they waited it out."

"And the treasure?"

Dilara read on. "When the Flood passed, no living thing existed anywhere. No animals, no birds, no people."

"It killed everyone on earth?" Grant said.

"Probably not," Tyler said. "But I'm sure Noah didn't travel beyond the Mount Ararat watershed. To him, it would have seemed like the whole world had been cleansed."

"Outside the cave, all they found were bones and the remnants of humanity's material greediness," Dilara said. "They collected everything they could find, from kings' palace hoards to merchants' possessions and brought them here, as an offering for God's deliverance." She stopped.

"What?"

"Now I understand," she said. "The Book of the Cave of Treasures. Noah's Ark *is* the Cave of Treasures."

"And let me guess who is buried with the treasures," Tyler said. "Noah and his sons."

She took a deep breath and laid her hand on the sarcophagus to the right of the pillar the amulet sat on. "We are standing beside Noah. Physical proof that an event in the first book of the Bible actually took place. Buried with him are two of his sons, as well as the four wives."

"Why'd they leave out one son?" Grant asked.

"Ham was the one who wrote this," Dilara said. "He sealed the bodies of his family in the Ark as each of them died. He was the only one who could be trusted not to loot the treasure and bring down God's wrath again."

Tyler carefully took the Amulet of Shem back from Grant. He also removed one of the clear amber orbs from the pedestal. He put them both in his pocket.

"Hey!" Grant said. "I thought we couldn't take anything besides the amulet!"

"The amulet itself is too dangerous to test. But if the other orb was found at the same time, it might be able to tell us when the frog dates from. Wouldn't it be amazing if it came from sixty-five million years ago?"

"Fascinating," Grant said dryly.

Tyler looked at his watch. Time for the radio check-in.

"This is Tyler," he said into his walkie-talkie. "Come in."

No answer. All he got was static. He tried again with the same results.

"Maybe we're too far from the entrance,"

Grant said.

"Since we have what we came for, I suggest we all leave."

"Just let me stay for a few more minutes," Dilara said. "I want to get a few more photos."

Tyler paused. The loss of contact was troubling, but the mercenaries would have radioed if they were under attack.

"I'll stay here with her," Grant said. "If she doesn't leave when you say the word, I'll carry her out."

"Don't worry," she said. "Just a few minutes, and I'll be done."

"Okay," Tyler said. "You've got five minutes. I'll go back and contact our guys to call for the helicopter. If I still can't reach them, we'll have to assume something has happened outside the cave, and I'll want you there on the double."

Dilara was already snapping away with the camera, ignoring Tyler.

He wound back out of the treasure room and walked toward their packs, trying to raise the mercenaries as he went. If anything, the static seemed to get stronger the closer he got to the cave entrance.

Tyler reached the spot twenty feet from the crevice through which they'd entered the cave. It was where they had left their

631

packs, but all he saw was empty floor. He knew that was the spot. The only explanation was that somebody had taken their packs.

The radios had been jammed deliberately. Someone was in here with them. Then the static abruptly cleared.

"Hello, Tyler," said a smooth voice from behind him. "Hands on your head, please. Slowly."

Tyler complied.

"Now turn around."

As Tyler turned, his miner's light fell on the image of Sebastian Ulric walking toward him, aiming a pistol at Tyler. Ulric pushed a pair of night-vision goggles onto his forehead. He stopped walking when he was twenty feet away, and his face broke into a satisfied smile.

"Thanks for showing us the way in."

SIXTY-SEVEN

"That helmet light is in my eyes," Ulric said. "Turn it off. And no sudden movements. I'm not the only one here."

Someone clicked a flashlight on behind Tyler. One of Ulric's guards by the crevice. Tyler flipped the switch on the helmet light. The guard's light focused on Tyler was now the only illumination. Any other lights still on in the massive Ark were too dim and too far away to be useful.

"Our men outside?" Tyler said, already knowing the answer.

"They were good. Not great, but good. They even got one of my men before Cutter was able to take them out. Now drop your weapons. Slowly. The radio, too."

Tyler put the submachine gun, pistol, and radio with its earpiece on the ground.

"Turn and kick them to Brett."

Tyler turned and saw a lean man armed with an automatic weapon and grenades strapped to his chest and a set of night-vision goggles perched on his forehead.

"Where are your other bootlickers? Waiting outside?" Tyler needed to goad Ulric into giving him some info.

"No, they're in here with us. Cutter and Petrova are similarly equipped with night-vision goggles and are searching for Kenner and Westfield right now."

"Ulric's here!" Tyler shouted into the darkness.

"Crude, but effective. It won't matter. You don't have starlight scopes like we do. Otherwise, you would have seen me when you came back here. Besides, I have an offer to make."

"I'm not going to tell you where the amulet is."

"I already know where it is. I can see it's in your pocket. What I can't have is Kenner and Westfield roaming about like this, maybe finding yet another way out after I've gone. That wouldn't do. Ergo, my offer."

Just like Ulric. Pretentious enough to use the word *ergo* when he's making a threat.

"You're just going to kill us anyway," Tyler said.

"Yes, I can't let any of you live. And I will find all three of you eventually. I just don't want to wait." He gestured at Brett. "The radio."

Brett tossed Tyler's radio to Ulric, who caught it easily. He keyed the mike.

"Dilara Kenner and Grant Westfield. I know that you can hear this. If you come forward in the next two minutes, I will promise each of you a quick and painless death. If you don't, I will begin shooting Tyler Locke. First the feet. Then the hands. Knees. And so on. Nothing vital. Nothing that would kill him immediately. But it will be an agonizing way to die. You have two minutes starting now."

"They won't do it," Tyler said.

"You'd better hope they do."

"You were waiting for us all along, weren't you?"

"You're a resourceful man. As soon as I saw that you had made it to Khor Virap, I knew you'd be able to find the Ark and show me the way in."

"And you're always good at thinking about all the angles, Ulric. That's why you got away with cutting all those corners building your lab and firing me."

Ulric smirked. "I win yet again. By invading Oasis, you may have changed my plans, but the outcome will be the same." He spoke into the radio. "You now have sixty seconds left."

Grant had made a mistake not keeping Dilara with him.

If he was going to save Tyler, he had to move fast, and Dilara would have slowed him down. He told her to go back up to the third level and hide. That she should use only her 3-D mapping system to guide herself, not her flashlight or helmet light.

They'd separated, and Grant doused his own flashlight. He flicked the infrared scope on. Any heat source — particularly a human body — in his field of view would flare like a campfire on a moonless night. He knew Cutter was around somewhere, and he wouldn't be content to wait for the full two minutes. He'd come find Grant.

Grant ran low and fast toward the crevice, but when he got to a ramp, he decided height would be an advantage, so he ran up to the second floor, keeping his footsteps as light as possible.

That's when he realized leaving Dilara had been a mistake.

As he was running, he peered up to the third-level promenade to see where Dilara had gone to hide so he could find her later. With the infrared, he saw her go into a room. To his surprise, he saw another figure on the third level carrying a weapon. Then a second unfamiliar person caught his eye on the first level. Neither of the hostiles were looking in his direction, so he ducked into one of the rooms. They both seemed to be quietly and methodically searching each room. He flipped up his eyepiece and crept out to look up to the third-level promenade and down to the first-level cavern floor. No lights, which meant they had night scopes.

He flipped the infrared eyepiece back down. The images weren't distinctive enough to let him identify the hostiles, but the one above him looked smaller. A woman. Svetlana Petrova, Ulric's girlfriend. He was sure the other one was Cutter.

Petrova would make a perfect hostage. He could exchange her for Tyler. Or at least buy enough time for him to figure out the next move and keep Tyler alive and free of bullet holes. If Grant could sneak up on Petrova from behind, he could grab and disarm her.

Grant crabbed up the ramp to the third level as fast as he could. In his earpiece, he heard Ulric say, "You now have sixty seconds left." He was running out of time.

He peeked over the edge of the third-level walkway. There was Petrova, just forty feet in front of him. She was almost to the room he'd seen Dilara go into. If Petrova saw her first, Dilara was dead. These people weren't looking for hostages.

He got to his feet and crept toward Petrova, ready to take her in a headlock.

"You've thought of everything," Tyler said. "Even those night-vision goggles. Generation-three?"

"The newest we could get on short notice," Ulric said. "Amazing devices. All we need is the light coming through that crevice to see this entire cavern as visible as if it were in daylight."

"You've thought of everything. Except one. What if the amulet isn't really in my pocket? What if I've hidden it somewhere in the Ark?"

"You didn't have time. And if one of your colleagues has it, they will realize that my offer includes bringing me the amulet."

"But if they've hidden it, it could take you a long time to find it. Noah's Ark is a big place."

"You're bluffing."

"Just trying to get you to think about all the angles."

Ulric kept his pistol trained on Tyler and looked at his watch. "We still have thirty seconds left. All right. We'll make sure." Ulric spoke to Brett. "Search him, starting with his left front pocket."

As Tyler had hoped, Ulric took the bait. And as he knew, Ulric wouldn't do the dirty work himself. He'd leave that to his minion.

Brett approached Tyler. Tyler had noticed the guard carrying the flashlight in his left hand, the pistol in his right. To search Tyler's pocket, he'd need to holster his pistol.

Brett removed the Amulet of Shem, and when he tossed it to Ulric, Tyler seized his chance. As Ulric caught the amulet, Tyler whipped his hands down and grabbed Brett's vest. Brett's flashlight clattered to the floor, leaving them unlit. Brett sent body blows into Tyler's midsection, but Tyler wouldn't let go and drove Brett backward.

Ulric started shooting. In the darkness, Tyler felt bullets zinging past him. One hit his thigh, causing him to stagger, but with the adrenaline dulling the pain, he couldn't tell how bad it was. His only chance was to keep hold of Brett until he could get to the crevice. In another two steps, Tyler gave a final shove, and Brett tumbled into it.

Tyler scrambled away from the opening. He only had two more seconds, because as he let go of Brett, he'd grabbed the pin from one of the grenades on Brett's vest.

Tyler rolled ten more feet and covered his head, hoping his plan didn't bring the whole cavern down around their heads.

The shock of the explosion pummeled him. The grenade went off before Brett had a chance to get up, setting off the others. A thunderous clap echoed through the cavern, and when it was over, Tyler heard the walls of the crevice collapse. It was completely sealed.

It was exactly what he was hoping for. Not only was that way out closed, but light was no longer coming from it. Without a light source, caves aren't just dark, they're pitch-black, like swimming in a barrel of ink. The type of night-vision goggles that Ulric wore work well in the night sky, even without a moon, because although it's dark outside, the stars still provide some light. In a cave, with no external light source, the night-vision goggles have absolutely no light to amplify. They would be useless. Ulric, Cutter, and Petrova no longer had the advantage. They would have to use flash-lights.

The odds were even.

SIXTY-EIGHT

Cutter had been hoping that he'd find Grant Westfield crouched in the corner of a room so that he could shoot him like a dog, but no such luck. He got his break when he looked up to check on Petrova's progress. They were in comm silence to mask their positions. On a ramp above him, he saw a huge figure not forty feet behind her get up and move toward her. That slab of meat could only be Westfield. Cutter finally had him in his sights, but the angle wasn't good. He wanted to make sure he got that bastard dead center.

Westfield didn't see him. Just like in the army, Westfield was too focused on his target, not paying attention to his flank. Now he'd pay for it.

Cutter found a ramp and tiptoed up. He'd ditched his sniper rifle in favor of a submachine gun.

Westfield was close to Petrova, his weapon

at his side. He was only twenty-five feet above Cutter, that big chest centered in his sights. There was no way Cutter would miss. He couldn't resist seeing the expression on Westfield's face when he realized he was about to be shot by Cutter, so he called out.

"It's Chainsaw," he taunted.

Westfield's head turned, and even with the night-vision goggles, Cutter could see the flash of recognition.

A huge explosion from Ulric's direction blasted like a cannonade through the cavern. At the same time, the viewfinder on his goggles went out. Nothing. Black.

Cutter fired, but he knew it was too late. He heard the bullets chew into wood, but no screams of pain.

He had missed. And now he was blind.

Dilara hated the idea of hiding, and the explosion, followed by a splat of bullets nearby, spurred her to action. She couldn't stay there, waiting to be hunted down. She drew her pistol.

Dilara had taken refuge in the weapons-filled room she had found earlier. She'd been awed by the knives, swords, and spears that lined the room. She recalled that an array of bows leaned against a wall, and next to it was an urn painted with a purple

642

symbol that looked like a cloaked figure praying. The urn held a bolt of arrows, points down. The symbol had looked familiar to her, but she didn't know why.

She made her way to the open part of the room, and peeked around, hoping there would be some light to supplement the 3-D mapping system.

The blackness was total, then a beacon lit. At least, it seemed like a beacon to her, but it was just Grant's helmet light. It was sliding on the floor out of a room fifteen feet in front of her.

That's when she saw the figure of Petrova close enough to touch. Petrova fired at the helmet and backed up at the same time, right into Dilara's gun hand. Dilara was so unprepared, the pistol was knocked from her grip. Her hands free, Dilara did the only thing she could think of. She tackled Petrova and wrestled her to the ground.

The impact sent Petrova's machine gun flying. Petrova elbowed Dilara, and Dilara responded with a punch of her own. But she could tell she wouldn't win a hand-to-hand fight with this woman, not without the element of surprise that she'd had on the *Genesis Dawn.*

She twisted around and saw Grant rushing toward her in the helmet light. Then he abruptly changed his direction and bull rushed Cutter, who was standing at the edge of the walkway, training a gun on her and Petrova. The two men disappeared over the side and crashed into the walkway below.

She looked back down at Petrova, whose face was a mask of fury in the dim light, and Dilara knew this was a fight to the death. Nobody was coming to save her. If she was going to live, she would have to finish the fight on her own.

SIXTY-NINE

Tyler knew it was too much to hope for that the explosion had killed Ulric. He pushed himself up, suppressing a cough so that he wouldn't give away his position. His helmet had fallen off, and he felt around for it. His hand brushed against it. He put it on, relieved that the 3-D modeling system still worked. He could see the Ark, but the infrared sensor had been damaged. He wouldn't be able to see Ulric unless he turned on the helmet's light. And if he did that, Ulric would have the perfect target to shoot at.

He heard the click of a pistol magazine being ejected, then another inserted and the slide racking. Then the ratcheting of a machine gun bolt. Ulric was heavily armed, and Tyler wasn't.

"You idiot, Locke!" Ulric yelled. "Do you realize what you've done? The entrance is gone! A thousand tons of rock is blocking it."

Ulric was hysterical. Good. That meant he didn't know that the slab door to the outer cave could be opened from the inside.

Tyler stood, and the gunshot wound in his leg announced its presence with a jab of pain. He could walk, but with each step, it felt like an ice pick stabbed his thigh.

"Are you satisfied, Tyler? You've doomed humanity! I wanted to preserve the human race. Don't you understand that? We're destroying ourselves. My plan was the only way. We had to start over. And now you've ruined that!"

Now Ulric was baiting him. He wanted Tyler to respond so that he could empty his magazine in Tyler's direction. Tyler wasn't biting.

He heard Ulric call into his own radio. "Cutter! Svetlana! Come in!" Ulric repeated the names several times. They weren't answering.

Tyler tiptoed forward as gracefully as his leg would let him and almost fell when his foot hit something that wasn't on the 3-D image scan. He bent over and felt his pack. Tyler ran his hands through it. The RCV, the controller, and the laptop were all inside, but no weapons.

Gunshots rang out farther along the Ark, but he couldn't make out anything else. His hearing was still muffled because of his proximity to the explosion. Tyler looked in the direction of the shots and thought he could make out a faint light. Tyler felt a pang of fear for Dilara and Grant, knowing they were being hunted by trained killers.

Tyler couldn't fight it out with Ulric, not with a bum leg and no gun. He desperately needed to come up with a plan. He thought about his only asset, the RCV, and sketched out a plan in his mind. Risky, but it might work. He picked up the pack and slung it over his shoulder.

Tyler needed to buy himself some time and distance. He took out the laptop, careful not to make a sound. He held it like a Frisbee and tossed it as far as he could toward the direction of the crevice.

The laptop smashed into a wall. Ulric unloaded a burst of machine gun fire at it.

Tyler took that cue to limp in the opposite direction toward the exit door. The explosive clatter of the gun masked his movement. He used the clusters of urns lined against the cave wall for cover.

"I'm going to find you, Locke!" Using his flashlight, Ulric began a search pattern down the cave, pausing to check in each room as he went.

Tyler moved faster, trying to stay ahead of the sweeping beam. He had to get to the exit before he was discovered.

But to make his plan work, Tyler needed Dilara and Grant with him. He wasn't going to leave without them. He couldn't yell out, so he had to hope Grant still had his own infrared eyepiece working.

Tyler raised his arm over his head as he walked and started signaling to Grant in the darkness.

Grant couldn't let go of Cutter, not if he wanted to win this battle.

Cutter was the best shot Grant had ever seen and could throw a knife with precision. But Grant was his equal in hand-to-hand combat, and even though Cutter was a big man, Grant had the size advantage.

During their tumble onto the second-level walkway, Grant had landed on Cutter. They had rolled over, and for a moment Grant lost his grip. Cutter turned his flashlight on and tossed it aside, out of Grant's range, but close enough so that they could see each other in the dim light.

During the motion, Grant was able to get his arm around Cutter's chest, but he couldn't maneuver himself for a headlock.

The position reminded him of his wrestling days, but he wasn't play-acting this time, and he wasn't going to follow any rules. He was going to play dirty, and so was Cutter.

Grant punched Cutter in the left kidney, and Cutter responded by stomping on his foot. Pain shot up his leg, and he fell backward. Cutter flipped over Grant and sprang to his feet. In the distance, Grant heard gunfire, and he hoped it was Tyler taking Ulric out.

Cutter reached for his pistol. Grant lunged at Cutter and got to him before Cutter could raise the pistol to fire. The gun flew into the air, and the impact took them to the ground. Grant was behind him again, still without a good hold, and when they rolled to a stop, he spoke into Cutter's ear.

"I'd knee you in the groin, Cutter, but I know it wouldn't do any good. One advantage of missing your Johnson."

Cutter roared with rage and twisted free. He whipped a knife from behind his back. Grant reached for his own but found the sheath empty.

"This is your knife, asshole!" Cutter yelled with triumph. "I always was the better soldier."

He slashed at Grant, who leaped back toward the walkway edge. With every sweep of the knife, Cutter punctuated it with a growled word.

"You . . . are . . . dead."

If Grant jumped to the first level and ran, Cutter would simply find his gun and hunt Grant down. He had to finish this now.

"Come on!" he shouted. He purposely left himself unguarded on the left side.

The knife sliced forward, plunging into Grant's shoulder. The pain was intense, but it was what he wanted Cutter to do.

Using a variation of his signature pro wrestling move, the Detonator, Grant twirled around and wrapped his arm around Cutter's neck. Making sure he had a firm grip on Cutter, Grant tossed himself off the side of the walkway.

They fell as one, but with the years of experience coming back in an instant, Grant rotated his body. When they landed, Grant's right shoulder smashed into the ground. The force of the impact amplified the strength in his arm and crushed Cutter's windpipe and spine.

Grant pulled his arm out from under Cutter, then removed the knife embedded in his left shoulder. He felt some blood spill out, but it didn't come in a torrent. No arteries had been hit.

He heard Cutter's wheezing in the darkness and knew the man had only seconds to live.

"Feel The Burn, asshole," Grant said.

A hiss escaped Cutter's throat, and then he was silent.

Cradling his left arm, Grant stood, picked up the flashlight, and staggered to the nearest ramp to see if he could get to Dilara in time.

Petrova threw Dilara off her, and Dilara sprang to her feet, not sure what to do next. The defensive techniques she had learned were enough to hold off a mugger, but this woman seemed like a trained fighter.

Petrova clicked her flashlight and focused it right in Dilara's face, blinding her. Dilara moved backward into the weapons room and grabbed one of the swords piled on the floor. She thrust it at the flashlight, knocking it aside still lit.

With a nimble move, Petrova somersaulted to grab a sword for herself. She stood and waved it back and forth gracefully, assuming a practiced stance.

"So swords are your choice," she said. "Fine. It's one of my favorites."

Dilara had never used a sword before, so this fight would be over quick if she didn't think of something else. Petrova raced at her, swinging the sword down. Reflexively, Dilara raised hers above her head to block the blow. Petrova's sword glanced off to the side, but Dilara's grip wasn't in the right place, and her sword went flying, knocking over the urn with the purple symbol, scattering arrows on the floor.

"I should have stayed and poisoned you at LAX when I had the chance," Petrova said.

Poison! That's why Dilara recognized the symbol on the urn. It wasn't a praying figure. It was a flower, the blossom of the monkshood plant. The arrows must have been dipped in a poison extracted from the monkshood flower, and the urn was marked to make the lethal arrows distinctive.

Dilara grabbed a handful of the arrows and began flinging them at Petrova, who was able to knock them aside. Dilara took the last arrow and charged. She stabbed the point into Petrova's leg before Petrova was able to react. Petrova slashed with her sword, slicing a gash into Dilara's arm and sending her reeling against the wall.

With a smile, Petrova pulled out the arrow. "Is that all you can do? Amateur."

Dilara pulled a spear from the wall and held it in front of her. She made a few thrusts, but Petrova neatly sidestepped them.

"Pathetic," Petrova said and swung her sword at the spear.

Dilara was able to hold on to the spear, but the sword cut it to pieces. When the spear was down to three feet long, Petrova swung her leg in a roundhouse kick, connecting with Dilara's torso. She dropped to the floor, gasping for breath, and her helmet rolled away.

Petrova swaggered over and put a knee on Dilara's chest. She raised the sword, pointing at Dilara's neck for a killing blow, but she froze. Her hand moved jerkily to her throat, and the sword started quivering. Petrova's hand went limp, and the sword fell. Dilara wrenched her head to the side. The sword landed so close to her neck, she felt it nick her skin. It clanged to the floor.

With a violent spasm, Petrova tipped over. She lay on the floor, twitching. Her mouth moved, but no words came out.

Dilara rose and put her hand to her neck. She pulled it away to find some blood on her palm, but not much.

Footsteps pounded behind her, and Dilara plucked the sword off the floor. She turned to see Grant coming toward her. In the dimness, she could see liquid shining on his left arm. Blood.

"My God!" she said. "Are you all right?"

"I was about to ask you the same thing." He looked at Petrova, wracked with tremors on the floor. "What happened to her?"

"Poisoned-tipped arrow. Remember the monkshood plant outside? Amazingly potent. Even after six thousand years, it's still one of the deadliest poisons known to man. No antidote."

She looked dispassionately at Petrova, whose eyes shined with the fear of death. "Now you know what Sam Watson went through."

As if in response, Petrova's body arched up. She crashed back to the floor and went limp.

"Cutter?" Dilara asked.

"He arrived in Hell a few minutes before this one." Grant grabbed Dilara's helmet and put it on. "Come on. This isn't over. Ulric is still out there."

"And Tyler, too," she said, but she realized her tone wasn't as sure as she wanted it to be.

"Let's hope," Grant said.

SEVENTY

Grant found Dilara's pistol and retrieved his own helmet, which had been blasted by Petrova. He turned off the helmet light and put it on Dilara's head, then guided himself and Dilara to the edge of the third-floor walkway. He switched on the infrared sensor of Dilara's helmet, which he now wore. Their position gave him an expansive view of the Ark.

Immediately, he saw two figures on the cavern floor. One had a flashlight and was moving it back and forth, searching for the other man, who was seventy-five feet ahead of the flashlight, almost directly below Grant. He had his arm raised above him and walked with a limp.

One of them was Tyler, but which one? The infrared goggles didn't have the resolution to identify them, and Tyler and Ulric were about the same size. If Grant yelled out, he'd give away their position.

He looked back at the figure who had his arm still above his head. Then he understood why. It was Tyler. He was signing, careful to exaggerate the motions. If his arm were in front of his body, Grant would never have seen his hand motion, but against the cool cave wall, he could see what Tyler was spelling out.

Grant. Go to exit.

The stone door in the cave. That's how they were getting out.

Grant signed back, but Tyler just kept blindly repeating the same message.

Grant whispered into Dilara's ear. "We're leaving."

"What about Tyler?" she whispered back.

"I see him. He's in trouble. Let's get him."

Grant took her hand and led her down the ramp, the 3-D mapping system showing the way.

Tyler felt a change in the air. Subtle, but it was there. Someone was coming. He tensed, ready for an attack.

He sniffed and caught a familiar scent. It was Dilara's shampoo. The aroma was still in his nose from their shower and night together.

Tyler felt a vise grip his arm. He reached out and touched Grant's massive shoulder, which flinched backward. The stickiness on Tyler's hand told him why. Blood. Grant was injured. But they'd gotten his message.

His faulty helmet was removed, and a different helmet was placed on his head. The infrared system worked on this helmet. Tyler saw the fiery images of Grant and Dilara in front of him.

Grant pressed a pistol into Tyler's hand. He signed, *Cutter and Petrova are dead. Lead us to the exit.*

Tyler holstered the pistol, then took Dilara's hand and Grant's good arm.

Now that he didn't have to sign as he walked, he could move faster, but he was still limited by the leg and the need to be quiet. He estimated the exit was another hundred feet on their right.

They were moving along at a good clip and got fifty feet father along when Grant tripped on some unseen rock.

Grant went down on his bad shoulder, dragging Dilara with him. Her helmet went skittering along the cave floor. Grant restrained a scream, but the resulting grunt was still loud enough.

"Gotcha!" Tyler heard from behind him. The flashlight beam swung toward them and locked on. Ulric's machine gun opened up, and bullets pinged on the floor and wall,

657

but at this distance, in the darkness, his accuracy was terrible.

"Go!" Tyler yelled. "I'll cover!"

Grant got up, turned on his flashlight, and dragged Dilara after him.

Tyler dove to the ground and started firing in Ulric's direction.

Ulric knew he had them. It looked like Locke, Westfield, and Kenner had all survived, which meant that Cutter and Petrova were dead. He didn't feel anything for them. They were dead to him as soon as Locke had blasted their only way out. His grand plans were over, his vision for a New World ruined. The realization tore at him, and he silently raged at God's unfairness. But he could still gain one more small satisfaction.

Ulric had the amulet in his vest pocket, but it didn't matter. None of them were getting out of here. Still, Ulric wanted the pleasure of seeing Locke suffer.

Ulric shined his flashlight from the cover of a wall. Nine millimeter rounds whizzed by him. Locke's shots were close, but not close enough. All he had was a pistol, no match for Ulric's machine gun.

He crouched and crabbed away from the wall, unloading the rest of the magazine in the direction of Locke's prone form. He couldn't see if any of the shots hit.

Ulric went back to the safety of the wall to reload. He peeked out and saw that the spot where Locke had been lying was empty except for a backpack. Locke had taken the few seconds when Ulric was reloading to get up and move, but to where?

Ulric heard grinding stone. It sounded like the motion of a huge rock from the other end of the Ark. He also heard groans of people straining. Then he saw something that astonished him.

It was faint, but it was there. A light from outside. Another exit. Of course! The wall at the back of the cave where Hasad Arvadi had directed him to three years ago wasn't just a wall. There was a door!

He had a way out. And now he could see in the darkness again. He pushed the Star-light night-vision goggles back down and flipped them on. Just as Cutter had told him, the faint light from outside was enough to make it look like the cavern was bathed in green sunlight.

His vision for a New World was still possible! God had answered his prayers.

He could see Westfield and Kenner struggling to push the door open, but Locke wasn't with them. Ulric leaned out to finish them, but three more shots from Locke's pistol kept him pinned down. Westfield and Kenner disappeared through the opening.

Locke was somewhere among the vast number of ceramic urns at the opposite cave wall.

There! Behind three shoulder-height pots. Ulric could barely see the top of Locke's helmet behind the middle urn. He stepped out from behind the wall and aimed the submachine gun at Locke's head.

SEVENTY-ONE

Tyler was down to his final two bullets, so he had to make them count. Dilara's helmet was perched on top of the pot, and he was crouched on the ground with just enough room to see between the urns. The infrared viewfinder in his helmet made it difficult for him to aim precisely. He would only get one chance.

Ulric's glowing red form emerged from the wall with the weapon leveled at the top of the urns. Tyler targeted Ulric's head. He fired at the same time Ulric did.

The sound of his two shots was drowned out by the crack of Ulric's submachine gun. Shards of pottery showered down around Tyler as he watched Ulric's head snap backward. His body crumpled to the ground.

Tyler dropped the pistol and limped over to Ulric. With the infrared goggles, he could see Ulric's prone red form and the hot yellow gun lying between him and the wall.

He saw the bulb of Ulric's flashlight still faintly glowing. He picked it up, clicked it on, and shined it on Ulric's torso. While Tyler fished the amulet out of his vest pocket, he pointed the light at Ulric's face. Instead of a bullet hole in Ulric's forehead, he saw the smashed Starlight goggles askew on his scalp.

Ulric's eyes flew open, and Tyler could see the rage in them. Before he could react, Ulric kicked him in the leg with the bullet wound. Tyler screamed in agony. He dropped the flashlight but kept hold of the amulet in his right hand. He was determined not to let it go again. Ulric jumped to his feet, threw the goggles aside, and crouched into a fighter's stance.

Tyler was just trying to keep from passing out from the pain. He focused on getting past Ulric to the submachine gun lying next to the wall.

"I want that amulet back," Ulric said. He lunged, striking Tyler in the chest and knocking the wind out of him, but Tyler was able to swing his right hand around and smash the rock-hard amulet into Ulric's head. Tyler never heard a more satisfying sound than the smack of the orb against Ulric's skull.

While Tyler caught his breath, Ulric reeled backward, shook it off, then charged again. This time, Tyler fell to his good knee and struck with an uppercut straight into Ulric's solar plexus. Ulric doubled over, and Tyler elbowed Ulric in the kidney, sending him to the ground.

Tyler stood and began hobbling toward the submachine gun. Ulric lashed out with his leg, tripping Tyler onto his back. Ulric jumped onto Tyler's prone form, punching him with fury.

Tyler reached up, grabbed Ulric by the back of the head with his left hand, and rammed his helmet into Ulric's face. Blood gushed from Ulric's ruined teeth and nose. Then with all his strength, Tyler used his good leg to flip Ulric up and over his head. Only too late did he realize that Ulric was rolling toward the wall and the submachine gun.

Despite the pain of his splintered face, Ulric sensed the weapon lying under him, the barrel still warm. He spit blood from his mouth and grabbed the submachine gun. He sat up and fired wildly in the direction where Locke had just been.

The bullets hit only the cave floor and pottery pieces. Ulric found Locke's silhouette against the light streaming through the cave door. He was stumbling toward the exit, a backpack on his shoulder.

Ulric took off in pursuit, shooting as he ran. He wasn't able to hit Locke before he went through the opening. At the rate Locke was going, he wouldn't get far.

It was sad, really, how close Locke had been to escaping. But it would make Ulric's satisfaction all the sweeter. He'd follow Locke outside and gun him down just as he reached freedom.

Ulric reached the exit and peered through, ready for an ambush, but Locke was staggering toward the cave entrance. Ulric fired again, and Locke fell to his knees.

Tyler turned and tossed something in Ulric's direction. It rolled toward him like a grenade.

"Take it!" Locke said. "Just let us go!"

As it rolled closer, Ulric saw the amber hue, dazzling in the backdrop of sunlight. He knelt to pick up the amulet and stuffed it in his pocket.

Locke left his pack behind and got up, desperately trying to make it outside.

Ulric shook his head and reloaded a fresh magazine. Unarmed and injured, Locke must have thought that giving him the amulet was a worthy last resort. Ulric casually walked toward him, the machine gun trained on Locke, who was limping wretchedly. Ulric's head throbbed, but he felt elated.

"You can never defeat me, Locke," Ulric gloated.

Locke stopped just outside the cave entrance and turned. He was now bathed in the midday sun. And for some reason, he had a smile on his face. Ulric shook his head again.

Locke was delusional.

Ulric's finger tightened on the trigger.

Tyler knew he might die right here, but at least he got to see that Sebastian Ulric's golden-boy face was now a mess of blood and broken bones.

Ulric was still in the middle of the cave, his machine gun aimed at Tyler, his smug grin telling Tyler everything he needed to know. Ulric hadn't seen what Tyler had left inside the cave.

"I tried to get you to think about all the angles," Tyler said.

"I did," Ulric said. "You lose. Again."

Tyler shook his head. "I win," Tyler said and pulled the trigger on the RCV controller.

The RCV he had placed when he pretended to fall was pointed straight at the crusty box of sweating dynamite. It whirred to life, and Ulric glanced down as the vehicle accelerated past his feet. Then his head turned, and he saw the corroded boxes. Tyler was sure that Cutter had told Ulric how delicate the explosives inside them were. So sensitive that getting hit by a five-pound toy traveling forty miles an hour would detonate them.

Tyler saw the revelation dawning on Ulric's face a fraction too late to stop the RCV. Tyler propelled himself to the side with his good leg just as Ulric squeezed the trigger on the submachine gun. Bullets coursed through the air where Tyler's head had just been.

As he hit the ground, the RCV hit the box of dynamite and the cave exploded. Tyler used his momentum to roll against the cliff face. He covered his head and felt the fireball fly by him, singeing his clothes.

The roof of the cave collapsed, snuffing the explosion and sending out huge volumes of dust. He looked up at Mount Ararat, expecting an avalanche. A few rocks bounced down, but that was it.

Tyler sat up and put his back against the cliff.

Grant and Dilara emerged from their

refuge behind a rock. Both of them hobbled over and sank to the ground next to him. Their clothes were battered and ripped, they were covered in dust and grime, and spots of blood were everywhere. Tyler was sure he looked even worse. He felt as bad as each of them looked. They were going to get that nice clean helicopter very dirty, and Tyler couldn't care less.

"If this is your idea of archaeology," Dilara said, "you are never going on a dig with me again."

"I promise," Tyler said. "Right now, I'm thinking more about finding a hotel with room service."

"All I want," Grant said, "is a warm, comfy bed and about twenty milligrams of morphine."

"Ulric's dead?" Dilara asked.

Tyler nodded. "He's in that cave. Blown to bits and buried with the Ark."

"The Ark will be excavated someday. I guarantee that." She took her camera out. "The archaeological community can't ignore this."

"What about the amulet?" Grant said.

"Incinerated in the blast. It's gone."

"We're lucky Ulric didn't cut us off from the exit," Grant said. "Otherwise he'd be long gone with it."

"Why didn't he?" Dilara asked.

"He didn't know about the exit door," Tyler said.

"How do you know?"

"Just a guess. Even though Sebastian Ulric was extremely intelligent, he had one big flaw."

"What's that?"

Tyler smiled. "He wasn't an engineer."

SEVENTY-TWO

Tyler stood on the balcony of his room in the Istanbul Four Seasons and drained the last of his morning coffee. Rain clouds loomed over the minarets of the Hagia Sophia, but he could see blue sky in the distance. The sun should come out just in time for his walk with Dilara.

He set the cup down and walked back inside, his leg protesting each step. The doctor said it would ache for another few weeks, but he didn't need a cane. The bullet wound had been painful, but not serious.

Tyler didn't bother to turn on the television. He knew what would be on the news. It had been three days since they escaped from Noah's Ark, and the world was just starting to become aware of the discovery of the map in Khor Virap. The implication that it could lead to unearthing Noah's Ark had the media in a frenzy. Tyler had been able to keep out of the limelight and let Dilara and her father take all of the credit.

Still, his role gave them some perks. After they'd found the mercenaries' radios, they had the helicopter take them back to Van, where they were all treated for their injuries. Of course, the three dead bodies had raised lots of questions with the Turkish authorities, but Sherman Locke's pull with his political allies in Washington combined with the evidence on Dilara's camera convinced the Turks that the questions could be answered later, as long as they all stayed in the country for a few days.

The blood loss from Grant's knife injury required a few nights' stay in Istanbul's finest hospital, where he underwent surgery on his torn shoulder muscle. His recuperation would take longer than Tyler's, but he was expected to make a full recovery. Tyler and Dilara would check him out of the hospital later that morning, but they had one thing to do first.

"Ready?" Tyler said.

Dilara sat at a table, gazing at a small urn. It held Hasad Arvadi's cremated remains. After the autopsy in Yerevan, the police in Armenia had expedited the paperwork and shipped his body to Turkey. Dilara elected not to have a memorial service. Most of Arvadi's friends and colleagues were in

America, and it had been Arvadi's wish for his native Turkey to be his final resting place.

"Dilara?"

She nodded and wiped her face. She lovingly cradled the urn in her arm. "Yes. Let's go."

They exited the hotel and began the short walk to the Kennedy Caddesi. They strolled slowly. Tyler sensed that Dilara wanted to take her time. She finally broke the silence.

"I wish he could have seen it. He was so close."

"I think he'd be glad you found it," Tyler said. "And he'd like that you're dropping Kenner and going back to Arvadi."

"It's something I should have done a long time ago."

"Dilara and Hasad Arvadi are going to be famous names."

"Are you sure you don't want to share the credit?"

"Not my style," Tyler said. "Besides, Miles Benson is already milking our exploits for future contracts. No, you and your father deserve it."

"You saved the world, you know."

"Makes me think the Bible needs to be reinterpreted again. God's covenant with Noah said He'd never wipe out humanity again."

"He didn't."

"Only because we stopped Ulric from using the Arkon weapon."

"How do you know you're not God's envoy? God works in mysterious ways. You yourself said that the Ark was a miracle."

"I'll give you that. It was pretty amazing to find it intact after all these centuries. But that was a factor of its location and isolation. All of it could be explained scientifically. Nothing supernatural about it."

"That's the beauty and complexity of God's work. There are lots of ways to interpret it."

"I have to admit," Tyler said, "I was too quick to shoot down your theories about the Ark."

"What about your reputation as an inveterate skeptic?"

"There's no harm in keeping an open mind." He took Dilara's hand. "So a few more days here and then back to Mount Ararat for you?"

"I've already contacted the Turkish government about excavating the site. Since it's my discovery, and I have the only photos of the interior, they've been willing to involve me. But the process could take months, then digging through those tunnels will take awhile, not to mention surveying the interior. Properly, this time."

"Sounds like you'll be there a long time. I have to go back to Seattle soon."

She nodded. "Who knows? Maybe someday we'll both be ready to settle down."

"Maybe someday," he said and squeezed her hand.

They reached the avenue of Kennedy Caddesi and crossed it to the seawall along the Sea of Marmara. The Asian side of Istanbul was on the opposite shore, and ships crowded the link between the Black Sea and the Mediterranean.

Tyler let Dilara go, and she walked to the water. He saw her lips moving, then she knelt and poured the ashes of her father into the sea.

She stood, fingering the locket at her neck. Tyler went over and wrapped his arms around her.

They stayed that way for a while. Finally, Dilara turned.

"Shall we go get Grant?"

"You go on ahead. I'll meet you there, and we'll take him out for a big lunch. I'm sure he's starving after eating hospital food for three days."

"Where are you going?"

"I've got an errand to run. Gordian business."

He kissed her, then enjoyed the view as she strode off toward the hospital. Now there went a woman who had purpose. Tyler found it incredibly sexy.

She looked back once and waved. He waved back and lost sight of her as she rounded the corner.

Tyler hailed a cab.

"Araco Steelworks," he said to the driver.

Fifteen minutes later, the taxi drove through an industrial sector of the city. Smokestacks cleaved the sky. The cab pulled to a stop in front of the gate of a massive iron foundry. Through the building's large open door, Tyler could see sparks flying where molten steel was being poured.

"Wait here," Tyler said. "I'll only be a few minutes." The driver nodded and slipped the cab into idle.

At the gate, he showed his passport. "Miles Benson arranged for me to go in."

The bored guard looked at his log sheet, gave him a hard hat, and waved him through.

Gordian had consulted on one of Araco's mills in Bulgaria, so Miles knew the owner. It seemed like Miles's reserve of contacts was bottomless, but Tyler didn't question or complain. It was Miles's schmoozing skills that had built Gordian into an engineering powerhouse.

It also made Tyler's current plan much easier.

He wasn't sure why he didn't tell Dilara what he was doing. He told himself it was because she didn't need to know, but deep down he supposed it could be because he didn't want to put her in any more danger. He'd already lost one person he loved. He didn't know if he loved Dilara, but he cared about her, and the events of the past two weeks made him realize that he wasn't ready to risk losing someone else he cared about.

The foundry building was stifling. The heat from the blast furnace washed over him like a summer afternoon in Phoenix. He scaled a ladder to the second-level catwalk. When he was over one of the hoppers containing molten iron, he reached into his pocket and extracted the Amulet of Shem.

The amber gleamed in the firelight, revealing the outline of the amphibian that could have caused countless deaths. When Tyler tossed the solid amber orb to Ulric, he didn't think Ulric would take the time to inspect it closely, not with so much going on. And Tyler didn't want to take the chance of the amulet being recovered when Noah's Ark was eventually excavated. Somebody would have used it to redevelop the prion

675

weapon. Tyler was sure of it. Then all of his efforts would have been for nothing.

No one knew Tyler had the real amulet. Not Dilara. Not Grant. If the U.S. military found out he had it, soldiers would have swooped in before Tyler got off the plane in Istanbul.

Tyler looked at it one last time, marveling at how something so simple and beautiful could be so deadly. Then with a flick of his wrist, he tossed it into the molten iron. The orb caught fire and settled into the three-thousand-degree liquid. The prions were destroyed at last.

He climbed back down and gave back the hard hat at the front gate. His cell phone rang. It was Miles Benson.

"Thanks for setting us up in the Four Seasons, Miles."

"Not at all, Tyler. You rate it. We're settling all of the lawsuits on the truck case, thanks to you. Won't use a cent of Gordian's money. All of it comes courtesy of Ulric's estate. Did you get into the foundry?"

"I'm just leaving."

"I don't suppose you want to tell me why you needed to get in there."

"I'll tell you when I see you in a week."

"I may have to cut short your vacation.

676

Your recent escapades have gotten us a lot of attention in military and law enforcement circles. I have a few new projects brewing, and you're just the man for the job. Is Grant out of the hospital yet?"

"I'm about to pick him up."

"Well, tell him to get his butt out of bed. I need you both."

Tyler suppressed a laugh. Miles knew how to milk a business opportunity. "Sorry, Miles, you're breaking up. Bad reception. I'll give you a call in a few days."

"Tyler, do you know how much money —" Tyler ended the connection and turned off the phone's ringer. Gordian and the rest of the world would survive without him for a week. He needed a little time to relax.

As he opened the back door of the cab, he felt a mist on his face, the last of the rain before the clouds disappeared. He looked up and wondered what Dilara would make of the phenomenon arcing across the sky. It had a perfectly rational scientific reason for existing, but she might think it had greater significance, given their recent experience.

I do set my bow in the cloud, and it shall be for a token of a covenant between me and the earth.

Whatever the explanation, he stayed there for a moment and appreciated the sight, a reminder that life was short and that you might as well stop to revel in nature's beauty once in a while. And Tyler had to admit, no matter who or what was responsible for creating it, he'd never seen a more beautiful rainbow.

AFTERWORD

In a contemporary thriller, sometimes it's difficult to tell which of the technologies and locations are real and which are made up. If that's the case in *The Ark,* I take that as a compliment because it means I've done my job and made them believable, at least in the context of the story. For those who are curious, I spend a little time below talking about what's real and what's not real (yet).

Prions do, in fact, cause mad cow disease, among other illnesses. What makes prions so fascinating is that they are not alive. They are infectious agents formed by complex proteins that have misfolded. The diseases caused by them are especially scary because they are untreatable and always fatal. So far, no prions have been discovered that affect the body's cell integrity. The Arkon disease is obviously made up, but prions are still not well understood. Let's hope Arkon stays a fantasy.

Some of the technologies used by Tyler and Gordian do not exist. The G-Tag system for tagging airplane crash debris, the speech-to-text translator that projects onto Aiden MacKenna's glasses, and the 3-D mapping tool used in the Ark are fictitious, but there is nothing scientifically impossible about them. Something similar to these tools may even exist, but I haven't found them. The iBOT wheelchair used by Miles Benson, however, is an impressive real product developed by Dean Kamen, the inventor of the Segway.

USS *Dunderberg* was a Union ironclad warship with a wooden hull and, at 377 feet long, is considered the longest wooden vessel ever built, much shorter than the 450-foot length of Noah's Ark. While some say that the schooner *Wyoming* was the longest wooden ship at 450 feet long, its length was measured from jib-boom tip to spanker-boom tip. The deck was only 350 feet long, and so its hull was shorter than *Dunderberg*'s.

Several real tragedies are referenced in *The Ark*. Payne Stewart's private jet did crash as described, and an unemployed plumber did go on a rampage in San Diego using a stolen tank. In one true incident where tragedy was averted, a British Airways 747 flamed out after flying through volcanic ash. The crew restarted the engines and landed the plane safely.

Most of the vehicles in *The Ark* are real. The Liebherr dump truck is the largest in the world, and the Tesla electric roadster is an actual car, though a Tesla has never been crushed by a Liebherr to my knowledge. Although the *Genesis Dawn* cruise ship is fictitious, new megaships such as Royal Caribbean's 220,000-ton *Oasis of the Seas* are rolling off the slips every year.

Polycarbonate panels do become brittle when treated with acetone, a discovery I made when reading Mark Eberhart's excellent book, *Why Things Break.* I leave it to *Mythbusters* to verify that.

The Massive Ordnance Penetrator, or MOP, has already been tested, and the bomb is scheduled to join the Air Force's arsenal soon.

Khor Virap is as described in the book, a beautiful monastery and revered Armenian shrine situated in the shadow of Mount Ararat.

Noah's Ark may indeed be a cavern filled with a vast treasure, but until it is found, it remains only a theory.

ACKNOWLEDGMENTS

Writing and publishing can be a long and arduous journey, but when you have great people around you like I do, the voyage is a whole lot easier, not to mention more fun.

I'm so lucky that my superb agent, Irene Goodman, saw potential in my writing and stuck with me through the lean times. She's better than the best agent I could have asked for.

My foreign rights agents, Danny Baror and his daughter and coagent, Heather Baror, are not only great agents but wonderful people, and I'm proud to have them represent me to the world.

I'm grateful to Sulay Hernandez, my fantastic editor at Touchstone, for giving me a chance when no one else would and for helping me mold the raw material of my story into a finished novel.

Thanks to Stacy Creamer, David Falk, Marcia Burch, Kelly Bowen, Josh Karpf,

Cherlynne Li, Ervin Serrano, and the entire team at Touchstone for shepherding this newbie through the publication process.

Many people provided crucial input to the content of this book, and they deserve special mention. However, any errors in fact or detail, whether intentional or not, are mine alone.

I'd like to thank Dr. Mark Eberhart, professor of chemistry and geochemistry at the Colorado School of Mines, for his help with material science.

Thanks to Gary Brugger for his advice on the engineering consulting business.

My good friend, trauma surgeon Dr. Erik Van Eaton, was generous with his medical expertise.

My brother, retired Lt. Col. Martin Westerfield, is a former Air Force pilot and provided important information about aircraft and flight procedures.

My sister, Dr. Elizabeth Morrison, curator of medieval manuscripts at the J. Paul Getty Museum, gave me invaluable guidance about ancient manuscripts, document translations, and religious sites.

My father-in-law, geologist Dr. Frank Moretti, provided much needed information about geological processes as well as early editorial insight.

Susan Tunis, a friend since the very first ThrillerFest conference, gave me critical feedback on the manuscript at an early stage.

When I originally self-published the electronic version of this novel, many enthusiastic readers took a chance on an unknown writer and championed my work. Without that passionate response, my life would be quite different, so I'd like to recognize some of my very earliest readers: T. J. Zecca, Catherine Weatbrook, Leo Bricker, Charlie Roth, Gayla Timmerman, Gwyn Evans, and S. J. Dunham. I wish I could list everyone who wrote to me and generously recommended my e-books to others.

Finally, I couldn't have done this without the unwavering support of my wife, Randi. She has been my rock, my cheerleader, my sounding board, and my best audience. We had no clue where our path would lead us, but we knew that, as long as we traveled together, it would be an awesome and memorable experience. And we were right. My life with her is a better adventure than any I could write.

ABOUT THE AUTHOR

Boyd Morrison has a Ph.D. in industrial engineering and was formerly employed at NASA, Microsoft's Xbox Games Group, and Thomson-RCA. In 2003, he fulfilled a lifelong dream and became a *Jeopardy!* champion. He is also a professional actor who has appeared in commercials, stageplays, and films.

He lives with his wife in Seattle. Visit his website at www.boydmorrison.com.

The employees of Thorndike Press hope you have enjoyed this Large Print book. All our Thorndike, Wheeler, and Kennebec Large Print titles are designed for easy reading, and all our books are made to last. Other Thorndike Press Large Print books are available at your library, through selected bookstores, or directly from us.

For information about titles, please call:
    (800) 223-1244

or visit our Web site at:
    http://gale.cengage.com/thorndike

To share your comments, please write:
    Publisher
    Thorndike Press
    295 Kennedy Memorial Drive
    Waterville, ME 04901